D1588673

THE ENGLISH DAUGHTER

Recent Titles by Lindsay Townsend

THE ENGLISH DAUGHTER

Lindsay Townsend

This first world edition published in Great Britain 2004 by
SEVERN HOUSE PUBLISHERS LTD of
9–15 High Street, Sutton, Surrey SM1 1DF.
This first world edition published in the USA 2005 by
SEVERN HOUSE PUBLISHERS INC of
595 Madison Avenue, New York, N.Y. 10022.

British Library Cataloguing in Publication Data

Townsend, Lindsay
    The English daughter
    1.   Corfu Island (Greece) - Fiction
    2.   Suspense fiction
    I.   Title
    823.9'14 [F]

    ISBN 0-7278-6176-X

Except where actual historical events and characters are being
described for the storyline of this novel, all situations in this
publication are fictitious and any resemblance to living persons
is purely coincidental.

Typeset by Palimpsest Book Production Ltd.,
Polmont, Stirlingshire, Scotland.
Printed and bound in Great Britain by
MPG Books Ltd., Bodmin, Cornwall.

To my family and friends

AB		MM	
MA		MN	
MB		MO	
MC	11/04	MR	
MD	4/06	MT	
ME		MW	4/05
MG			
MH			

In Corfu town, the tourist police and traffic police are now in the new town. For the novel, I have placed the tourist and traffic police offices back in their former locations in the Palace of St Michael and St George.

The Demeter Hotel, Zeus bar, Cypress House and Val's old family home are fictional, but based on real Corfiot hotels, bars and houses.

Prologue

*S**he was dreaming a murder and her dream was true.*
A park at night. A park in Fenfield, the Pennine town where she lived, or a formal garden in Corfu, close to her old home? *Where am I?* Marble staircases, palm and cypress trees, grandiose statues. A massive villa, striving to be heroic but achieving instead a bombastic sadness. The Achillion: that classical folly built on Corfu island a century earlier, a shrine to the mythical hero Achilles. *When am I?* Her feet touched sun-scorched grass and she was rushing under the wisteria pergola, the scent of white lilies catching in her throat as she ran past the rose beds and hibiscus, fleeing into the pine forest below the palace grounds. Sprinting for her life, terrified under summer stars. *Who am I?* Starting awake, she reached for the bedside light and lay panting in its pencil beam. 'You're Val,' she whispered.

Still the dream persisted, stirring memories which she had tried for so long to suppress. After-images danced in her mind. Blood. Lips. Razors.

She knew too much about this murder, a killing which had disillusioned her father. He should not have lifted and copied the murder file from the police station in Corfu town and she should not have looked at it. Hilary had been an acquaintance and Val had been curious and horrified.

'Stop it,' Val muttered. She hated to dream of Hilary's murder, but she had been free of nightmares only when Nick was with her. Now he, too, was gone and their double bed was bleak, cold at the edges.

Val stared at the night light, aware of some difference in

1

tonight's dream. Was the difference a warning? Her grand-mother would have been in no doubt. 'You dream true.' She had told Val that often enough.

'But not with *this* nightmare,' Val whispered. It was ten years since Hilary's murder and still the dream kept returning. She had dismissed the idea of therapy: the thought of admitting weakness to a stranger made her cringe. She forced her mouth into a mocking smile. 'I make my own way.'

Mouth. *Lips.* She had made the wrong association – the words flooded back. She was gawping at the pathologist's report, reading it over in her mind's eye as she had done at seventeen. A memory, perfectly recalled.

> The victim, a young woman in her late teens, was found naked under an olive tree in the grounds of the Achillion. Her body had been posed as if to show the artistry of the murderer. See attached photographs.

Her father had found Hilary's body, Val remembered. Stripping off the bedclothes, she hurried to the bathroom. Hanging over the sink, she sucked water from the cold tap. She had done what she could for Hilary. She hadn't lied to the police, or to her father. Sins of omission are different.

> A lack of lacerations to the victim's forearms and of foreign skin or other tissue under the fingernails would suggest that the victim was rendered passive by other means. Those means I shall go into later. Cause of death is a broken neck. There were substantial bruises around both wrists, indicating possible use of handcuffs. A single post-mortem injury to the face, inflicted by a sharp object, possibly a razor blade, is the removal of the woman's lips.

Val had never seen the photographs but the words were enough. She dry-heaved, just as her daughter's light snapped on and a piping voice called, 'I want to watch cartoons! Can I get up and go downstairs? Can I watch TV?'

'Go on, love,' said Val from behind the bathroom door,

2

glad that Judith couldn't see her as she cleaned her face with trembling fingers.

One

'Why are people bad?'

Val had been thinking of Nick. A mouthful of coffee went down the wrong way. 'I beg your pardon?' she gasped.

Sitting opposite Val at the kitchen table, Judith speared a chicken nugget and ate it like a toffee apple. 'Helen Flower called me foxy-locks today.'

'And what had you called her first?'

'Rabbit teeth. She has, Mummy!' Judith vigorously nodded her head.

'But no one likes to be picked on, do they? You don't like it when you're called "Carrots". Perhaps that's why Helen taunted you back.'

'Perhaps.' Judith gnawed a chip. 'Can I play with my Thunderbird?'

'Have you finished your tea?'

'Yes, thank you.' Judith's knife and fork clattered on to the plate. A May sun, striking through the sash window, flared on her red curls as she charged into the cramped sitting room, a bundle of auburn energy as Nick had been.

The phone rang. Glad of the distraction, Val took the call. 'Val Baker.'

'You got Steve there? Sorry, you can't have – nobody's screaming. Sure you want him with you tomorrow?'

'If it's still okay with you, Penny.' Val was very careful with Nick's ex-wife.

'You know he's only coming for a free ride? A month of sun, sex, raves . . .'

'We don't get many raves where we're staying.' Clearing

3

away Judy's plate, Val hunted under the sink for the washing-up liquid. 'Last time we talked, Steve said he was looking forward to windsurfing.'

'Oh, he's full of it. But he'll have to come back here tonight.' Penny laughed. 'I've got his passport.'

When the musical doorbell rang moments later, she wondered if she would find Steve on her doorstep. Instead it was another six footer, altogether more disconcerting.

'Harry.' Blushing at finding the new bottle of Fairy Liquid still in her hand, she stood back in the hall.

'How are you?' he asked quietly. 'Are you all right?'

She stared up at him without answering, seeing the new harsh lines round his mouth, the new bruise on the side of his neck. She could smell the whisky on him, for her an unseen badge of office for the plainclothes force Nick had been part of, before he had died in his sleep of a heart attack at the impossibly young age of thirty-three.

'Val?' Harry ducked under the lintel, a big blond fellow in a trim grey suit, his tie stuffed into a pocket. 'May I come in?'

Resigned, Val stalked back into the kitchen, letting Judith and Uncle Harry complete their frenzied hellos in the living room. She was uneasy with his calling in tonight. Every year for five years, on the day Nick had died, he visited, offering support. She was wary of breaking down.

Making fresh coffee, Val heard Judith begin another count-down to *Thunderbirds*. She guessed that Harry had left the sunny sitting room, strewn with books and toys, and would soon be joining her.

A cleared throat indicated he was close behind her. Val twisted round and stepped sideways so that the table was between them.

'Coffee. Black, three sugars.' She thrust the blue mug handle-first at him.

He took it. 'You always remember.'

'Sit down,' Val said. 'Please.' She felt easier when Judith's chair creaked under more weight than it was designed for and the shadow was lifted from her head. Harry was taller and bulkier than Nick had been.

4

Joining him at the table, she watched as Harry glanced about her home with wary blue eyes. His blond hair was still more gold than grey, but his squarely handsome features had refined with age, while in her memory Nick was always youthful and sharp, younger looking than his years.

'How are you?' They spoke together and both replied, 'Fine.'

'Off to Corfu again tomorrow.' Harry sipped his coffee.

'Yes.' Watching his mouth, Val was reminded of her recurring dream.

'How is the piano restoration business?'

'Fine.'

'Judith tells me she's started French at playschool.'

'Nick would tease me in French . . .' Val thought of Corfu, as blue and bright to her as anywhere in France.

'Val?'

She blinked. 'Sorry, I was miles away.'

Harry flicked her a look from under thick pale lashes, his voice indulgent. 'Anywhere special? You and Nick?' he added softly.

'I don't want to burden—'

Harry reached across and caught her hand in his. 'Never that, Val.'

'You'll have heard it before.' Newly widowed, she had told Harry the whole run of hers and Nick's courtship, a holiday romance that had stuck.

He smiled. 'I like to hear you,' he said.

Faintly embarrassed, Val heard the floating notes of an ice-cream van weaving through the Fenfield streets. The tune, 'Greensleeves', reminded her of the first time Harry had sat with her at this kitchen table, telling her how he had met Gilda. An ice-cream van had been passing then, playing 'Greensleeves'. He and Gilda had been married for four years. This wasn't bad for a police marriage, especially as Gilda was also on shift-work as a nurse. Their divorce was quick and both had moved on.

Val waited for 'Greensleeves' to fade away, and Harry said, 'The first time you and Nick met.' He brushed her fingers. 'Where was it again, Corfu town?'

'Yes, it was,' she admitted slowly. 'I was tending my

5

mother's grave in the British cemetery. Nick came up and asked me something in Greek and when I answered in English I think he was so grateful for someone to talk to that he invited me for tea at the Liston. We were married next spring.' Val blushed again. Harry knew this: he had been their best man.

'There was some opposition to your marriage: Nick told me at the time. Your Greek relatives liked him, but not as a future son-in-law.' Harry smiled, unrepentant. 'Later, you told me more about them.'

'Yes,' Val said faintly, remembering.

'You and Nick looked right, as a couple,' Harry said. 'Gilda and I never managed that. I look at Judy and see Nick in her—'

'No.' Listening for Judith's patter heading their way, Val cut across him. 'Don't worry about Judy or me. We're going to Corfu.'

The square planes of Harry's face changed subtly to a look Val knew well: cop curiosity. 'You're going earlier this summer. Why is that?'

Val gently disengaged her fingers, wrapping both hands round her cup. 'I'm going to work. A restoration job for an old friend. A girlfriend,' she added, wondering why she felt it necessary to justify herself.

Harry grunted and relaxed, draining his drink and glancing round the small, spare kitchen, so different from the cheerful clutter of her music workshop in Corfu. 'Want me to cruise past here, now and then?'

'If it's no trouble.'

'None whatsoever. What kind of job will you be going to?'

Val's dark-blue eyes twinkled. 'Repairing a giraffe piano.'

'A what?' Harry was laughing too.

'A giraffe piano. Looks like a cross between a piano and a harp. Alexia – the school friend I always stay with when I go back to Corfu – she wants me to restore one that's been in her family for years. We're hoping it'll get Chloe interested in playing her modern piano again.'

'Chloe. Your god-daughter.'

Val nodded, mentally cursing Harry's prodigious memory

6

for names and relationships. He was recalling more, snippets of conversation.

'Tipped for a big career in music, wasn't she? When you came back from Corfu last summer, brown as a tea bag, I remember you said she played like an angel.' Harry frowned, embarrassed by his tea bag simile.

Val found it endearing. 'Yes, she did,' she agreed quickly, to cover his embarrassment. 'She was wonderful.' Her smile faded. 'But this year it's all stopped. Chloe won't play a note.'

'Why?'

'I'll find out when I get there.'

On his way home, Harry stopped the car on a grass verge in sight of the spire of Fenfield Church, where his best friend was buried close to the ancient yew. Nick had loved that tree, Val said.

He couldn't blame Val if she was a bit spiky with him. With her he became a fourteen-year-old trapped in a thirty-seven-year-old's body. After the night Nick died, he rarely touched whisky – except when he called on her, a touch of grisly Dutch courage.

Harry thought of tiny prickly Val, with her short black hair, aquiline nose, dark-blue eyes and coral-red, expressive mouth, a Celtic style of beauty that would not be so out of place in Corfu. When she spoke of the first time she had met Nick, Harry had shamelessly put himself in the dead man's place. Leaning back on the head-rest, he imagined strolling through that hot foreign cemetery, imagined walking up to Val, speaking to her.

He remembered how he had once trapped his hand in a door. She had bathed and bound his wounds, her touch comforting and sure. She had not spoken much, except to ask if the bandage was too tight.

'It's perfect,' Harry had said and she'd blushed, the colour of paprika.

In her workshop, engrossed, Val showed another side: deft and endlessly patient, the corners of her mouth turned slightly upwards as she laboured at the thing she loved.

Harry wanted to buy jewels for her ears and chocolate for

her mouth. He wanted to take her to concerts on his arm, have her with him every day, have her in his bed at night. But how could he make a play for the love of his best mate, a young woman made a widow when she was seven months pregnant? To Val he might always be nothing more than a friend.

Opening the car window, Harry studied the churchyard where Nick was buried. 'Christ, I'm tired.' He hadn't had a proper holiday away in fifteen years.

But he was between cases now. A day or so would see him caught up on paperwork and he'd some leave due. He loved ancient ruins, culture, art.

Corfu would be perfect.

Two

Alexia had a house near Komméno on the north-east coast. Surrounded by woodland, the pantiled white and pink villa had its own jetty, gardens and an orange grove where guests could pick fruit from the trees. It was even more peaceful than Val remembered, a place to recharge.

From a stone bench on the patio, she looked down the terraced garden to three swimsuited figures playing on the white jetty and a strip of shingle – a 'beachlet', Val thought with a smile. Judith and Steve were enjoying the first morning of their vacation and since both could swim like dolphins the bracing May water held no fears for them. To Val's relief, Judy had also taken to Jessica, the young English nanny hired so that she could devote more time to the giraffe piano. It was a joy to hear their voices drifting into the cloudless sky as they dashed about, leaping off the jetty into the sparkling blue sea.

'Why not join them?' Alexia emerged from the darkness of the house with a tray of iced coffee. 'You could easily have a day off.'

'Thanks, but I ought to look at the piano.' Thinking she had heard Chloe, Val paused but it was the gardener humming as he weeded amongst the cineraria under the balcony. 'Where is Chloe? I've not seen her yet.'

'She's at a wedding in Peritheia – the bride's the grand-daughter of my cleaning-lady.' Sitting in the shade of a bougainvillaea, Alexia poured two glasses of coffee. 'There you go.'

'How is she? Any change?'

Alexia stared at the wooden tray. 'She hasn't set foot in the music room for the last six weeks. Nobody says anything, there's no pressure. You know we never had to persuade her to practise.' She frowned, placing her glass precariously on the marble balustrade. 'I wish I knew what was wrong.'

She rose to pace the length of the patio. Alexia was a woman who would never be described as anything less than elegant, with fine auburn colouring and a sensitive mobile face: a Corfiot version of one of the Redgraves, Val often thought. She was a head taller than Val, slim and graceful, perfectly turned out in her taupe and tangerine Italian sundress.

Val joined her in her pacing. 'What is it, Alex?'

'I spotted Chloe last week, in the garden. She was standing under that olive tree, looking into the music room, staring at her piano with such an expression of . . . of longing.'

Val clasped her friend's hand. 'Tell me,' she said softly.

'It was more than longing.' Alexia spoke without looking at Val. 'Chloe was scared. Something was holding her back. Only she won't say what it is. Chloe won't talk to me.' Alexia was trembling.

Val hugged her. 'Chloe *will* play again. It'll be all right.'

Alexia shuddered. 'No it won't. I'm pregnant.'

Val caught her breath, her grip tightening protectively around the taller woman. This close, Alexia's skin had a pallor to it. Val could feel her shoulderblades and ribs. 'How do you feel?'

'I don't know. I've only just found out myself. This morning.'

'You've gone very warm, shall we go in?'

Alexia allowed herself to be guided towards the villa. 'What will Chloe say? She's already not talking to me, not playing.

How can I explain? This wasn't planned. The poor girl will be so embarrassed.'

'I think she'll be interested, and very protective. It's early days yet. You don't have to rush.' Aware that she had no experience of dealing with a teenager, much less a musical prodigy, Val hoped she was saying the right things. 'You can pick your moment. You and Theo will be fine, believe me.'

Alexia sagged on the marble step. 'Theo will blame me.'

'This is a Greek husband! Theo will peacock for weeks.'

Smiling, Alexia laid a hand across her stomach but then she shook her head. 'I shouldn't be burdening you with this.'

'You've already given me a glorious welcome, Alex. You do every year.' Val opened the patio doors. 'Now come inside before you faint.'

Retrieving the tray and their untouched coffees, Val followed Alexia and closed the patio doors on the tumbling swifts and finches.

Pregnancy had not altered Alexia's deceptively languid stride. As she sped after her friend through the cool, shuttered villa, Val had little time to absorb the changes since her last visit. Six of Theo's bonsai in the tiled, unfurnished anteroom had been replaced by orchids, his latest passion. Three strides ahead, Alexia shrugged her shoulders. 'This is all Theo's project. He'll give you the five-euro tour after dinner this evening.'

Recalling how queasy she'd been when expecting, Val said, 'It doesn't have to be formal for us. Steve loves bread and Judy will eat anything.'

'Lucky you – Chloe was incredibly fussy when she was small.' A welcome flicker of humour warmed Alexia's voice. 'You don't have to worry about me. Six months ago Theo insisted I hire a cook. He said I was doing too much: running the house, running the music festival every summer, escorting Chloe everywhere.' She went quiet, then added, 'Leave the tray on that low table. One of us can collect it later.'

Skirting a faded family crest, the two women moved along a corridor, squeezed past a grandfather clock and entered a mirrored receiving room leading from the formal main entrance. From there, Alexia turned on to the cypress-wood staircase rising from the receiving room. Val was vividly aware that, even with hired help, this house required a lot of work.

Her closest friend was connected by a complex family tree to the Sardinas, former Venetian counts of Corfu. Experienced in restoring antique pianos in old rural seats, Val knew the classically designed Cypress House was not large as palaces go, but every one of the fourteen rooms had some feature needing care. The spine of the house, the wide cypress staircase which gave the house its name, had to be checked: one year she had treated nineteen treads for woodworm. The 'public' areas of the first-floor dining and music rooms were panelled in expensive inlays, with fluted wall candle holders of Venetian glass and delicately carved marble fireplaces, fashioned in the icing-cake style of a Venetian palazzo. The oak banqueting table, large enough to accommodate a party of thirty, had to be washed down with vinegar and anointed with olive oil, as did the walnut carver chairs.

If there ever had been any old master paintings they had long gone to cover the upkeep of the villa. Still, money would never be one of Alexia's concerns. Her teaching brought a steady income and Theo, a thirty-nine-year-old slender, bespectacled man bounding with enthusiasms, was a successful accountant and the heir of a banker who owned acres of olive trees.

Nevertheless, Val tried to repay her friend's hospitality. After Nick's sudden death, only a few people had broken through her black walls of grief: Harry, her grandfather Carlo, Alexia and Judith – Judy most decisively by being born. Harry had visited Val daily through her first winter of loss, Carlo had written to her every week, and Alexia had phoned, enticing her to Corfu: 'Come when you like, when you can. Come this summer.'

Although Alexia did not yet know it, Val would restore the giraffe piano free. Alexia welcomed her, kept a room for her, and she remained in her debt.

Val's room was where it had always been, in the attic. She, Judith and Steve were in former servants' rooms, cool and

11

plain, with comfortable brass beds from town. Val usually slept well in Cypress House: no bad dreams.

She had slept soundly last night, but it was clear that Alexia had not. Alex paused on the first-floor landing, glanced in the direction of the silent music room and sighed.

Stopping beside her, Val asked tentatively, 'Is Chloe still with Mr Agostini? I'd like to have a chat with him.'

Alexia sighed again. 'I thought I'd emailed you, months ago. Chloe's with a new piano tutor now, Mr Zeno.' She looked at Val, her bony, fragile face looking old before her time. 'We were told he's very good.'

'I'm sure he is, and you probably did tell me about him. I forgot.'

Alexia wagged a finger at her. 'I don't think so, not with your memory. Anyway, I know I didn't tell you this. Stefan Gregory has agreed to play at our music festival this year. *And* he's giving two recitals this month at the Achillion; that's several months ahead of the festival. I'm going to his second recital – none of the other music committee members can make it to that one and I prefer the pieces he'll be playing then.'

'Why isn't your head twice the size it is?' Val leaned against the staircase and peered in mock intensity at her friend. 'It's such a coup, Alex.'

'I suppose it is.' Alexia ran her tongue over dry lips.

'I'll go down to the kitchen for some mineral water.'

'No, thanks, I'm going for a lie down. The giraffe piano is next door, in the study. Do whatever is needed. If it inspires Chloe . . .'

'I'll do everything I can,' said Val.

Val made a beeline for the pine desk with its red phone and fax. Behind the desk was a print of *The Bower Meadow*, by Dante Rossetti, with the dark and auburn beauties pouting over musical instruments. Alongside it was a signed and framed programme for a madrigal group. Smiling at Theo's support of local music, Val did not allow the Prospero Singers to distract her. From the corner of her eye she spotted the giraffe piano, registering it with a flicker of pleasure. She turned to lean against the desk, studying her prize.

It was old: a handsome, dark-wood affair with the vertical strings encased in an elegant sounding board. Val knew from her emails that Alexia had only recently inherited the giraffe piano and had no idea of its age. The keyboard had been snapped off its bracket at the upper end of its register and sloped down at a wild angle. The keyboard cover was missing, as were several keys and the maker's porcelain plaque. At its base was a gaping hole where there should have been a pedal.

Lifting paper and pencil from her pocket, Val began to make notes.

Later, clambering off her hands and knees, she heard a delicate snoring coming from the master bedroom and slipped out of the study.

Now she had a few moments alone, she decided to look at the latest letter from the lawyer dealing with her Italian grandfather's estate. Carlo Cavadini had died last year, leaving her his workshop here on Corfu. Her family were contesting the will. Probate had dragged on for months.

Reluctantly, Val climbed up to her attic bedroom and plucked the smooth white envelope from the top of a chest of drawers. When this had arrived at Cypress House this morning she had put it aside. She had guessed what it was about: the family had raised more objections.

'Let's get this over.' Val tore open the envelope. Another envelope fluttered on to her pillow. Sitting on the bed, she read the enclosed letter.

> Dear Mrs Baker,
>   This unopened envelope came to light last month, when I at last received permission from the Corfu town authorities to have your grandfather's safe deposit box opened . . .

Val touched the undated brown envelope lying on her pillow. Her full name, in her grandfather's sprawling hand, invited her to open it and read.

My dearest granddaughter, Carlo began in Italian.

I intend to post this on, but if for any reason I cannot, I have left a copy amongst my most personal papers so that you, and only you, will see it. I am sorry, child, that my passing will give you so much trouble with our family, but I know you will win through. The workshop is yours; a legacy I am proud to hand on to you.

I wish I had more time to speak with you, but time is always short. Our times together, at peace in the workshop, or, more lately, on the telephone, were so precious to me that I never wanted to introduce anything distasteful.

Now I know I must. You must be warned. As we have always known, Markos, your half-brother, the hero of our family, is your most dangerous opponent. But I believe he is more than the bully you knew too well at home. I now have to wonder if Markos had some connection with that poor girl Hilary Moffat, the music student whom we met at Corfu town hall the evening before she was raped and killed.

Do you remember, child, how Hilary was wearing a jade ring? It was unusual and I noticed it particularly as, I am sure, did you.

Val nodded and read on.

Last month, I happened to pass Markos's room in our family's house. The door was ajar and through it I saw Markos, sitting on his bed, holding up a small clear plastic pouch. He had opened the shutters to his room and was squinting into the light, peering intently at what was inside.

It was Hilary's jade ring. Although my memory is not as good as yours, I have an eye for these things. I would swear that Markos had Hilary's ring.

Markos sensed my staring, rose from his bed and kicked the door shut. Later, at dinner, when I asked after the ring, he first claimed it was not a ring, then that it was a present for a girl. I let the matter rest there, because your grandmother and father were also present, and Yiannis,

14

I know, has always been affected by the case, but when I was able to speak to Markos alone I asked him, 'What is that jade ring? May I see it?'

And Markos claimed that he had lost it!

So there it is. I cannot prove anything, but I am convinced he has Hilary Moffat's ring. How has he acquired such a token?

It is too late for anyone to help that poor girl, but I knew that I must warn you. I cannot believe that Markos is capable of murder, but I do wonder if he knew her, had met her, before she was killed. You must be careful.

Yours, with much sadness and great love, Carlo Cavadini.

'My God.' Val stared at the letter, trying to think. This revelation, following on from her most recent dream, was terrible. 'Markos? My own family?' The death of Carlo, her beloved grandfather, had broken her last close tie with the family, but this was surely impossible?

Val tucked the letter into her handbag, feeling a crazy relief when it was out of sight. She had to move; she had things to do at Cypress House for Chloe and Alexia. They were alive, they needed her. She needed to check on Judy and Steve, to give Jessica a break. She wasn't going to be long, though. There were more tests to do on the giraffe piano.

Outside, the dazzling sun made her sneeze. Val gloried in the dappled light, soaking up its heat as a sponge absorbs water. Please let Theo and Chloe support Alex, she found herself thinking as she ran down the terraces, while the rest of her mind remained determinedly preoccupied with the giraffe piano and with Alexia's startling news concerning Stefan Gregory.

She had seen and heard Stefan Gregory ten years ago, when he was a wiry twenty-year-old soloist with several recital seasons already under his belt. On her seventeenth birthday she had watched him perform breathtakingly on a concert grand in the open air outside Corfu town hall.

Hilary had been sitting next to her at the recital. In an eerie

15

coincidence, Stefan Gregory was going to perform at the Achillion, where Hilary's body had been found.

Trying not to think about Hilary – *when had Carlo written his final letter to her? Like the envelope which contained it, the letter had been undated* – Val told herself that she was at Komméno now. Shading her eyes from the sun, she stepped out of the garden. The scent of bruised thyme rose around her as she waved and called to the three swimmers bobbing about the jetty.

Three

S teve boosted himself out of the water and on to the jetty to greet her. 'Hi, is it lunch-time yet?'

'Not quite.' Val found herself struck afresh by the likeness between Steve and his father. Torn between loss and an odd pride, she nudged Steve's forgotten heap of clothes with a foot. Wet from the sea, the fine red hairs on his body looked dark against his pale, lanky frame. 'You're going to get burned.'

'The two Js slapped some sunblock on me.' Steve sat on the jetty, dangling his feet in the sea. 'Actually, I think Judy wants you.'

Turning, Val saw Judith and Jessica out of the water at the end of the narrow strip of shingle, close to the wooded point. Judy was almost dancing with excitement. 'Look at this, Mummy!'

Val ran to her child by the seashore. She knelt on the gritty shingle and lowered her head to admire, holding back her dark hair.

'It's lovely, poppet.' Dazzled by the razor shell's reflected light, Val squinted at Judith. 'Have you been good? Not driving Jessica wild?'

16

'Oh, no,' Jessica said quickly. 'She's been absolutely no trouble.'

Further explanations were curtailed by a yell from Steve. 'Jessica! Your sail-board's floating away!' Even as he shouted, Steve was belly-flopping into the water to retrieve it. Part of his actions was showing off, but he was good-hearted. With only ten years between them, Val was at times aware of a speculative gaze in her stepson's lively hazel eyes, but in her present floppy top and baggy shorts she was safely 'Mum'.

'Mummy.' Judith tugged on Val's shirt as the blonde, slim Jessica dived almost straight off the shingle into the sea, a move she executed with far more grace than Steve had managed.

'Thank you, love.' Val dropped the razor shell into a pocket. 'Here, have my hat.' She brought her battered sun hat out of her waistband and dropped it on to Judith's prolific curls. 'There! You look like an explorer.'

'I do?' Judith preened for a second before dropping on to her mother's lap. Val kissed her neck, tasting the sunblock that she'd smothered on Judith's body. 'Do you like it here?' she asked.

'Yes. I can say "good morning" in Greek.' Judith twisted her head to look up at her mother. 'Steve says Auntie Alexia is older than you. All my friends are the same age as me. Did you meet Auntie Alexia at school?'

'We went to the same senior school.'

'How old were you then?'

'I was thirteen. Cousin Chloe's age.'

To Val's relief, Judith asked no more questions, but while she gathered her brood together and shepherded them up the terraced garden and into the villa for lunch, Val remembered being thirteen. With the stark warning of her grandfather's letter, she could not stop remembering the day when Markos had shown that he was not only a bully but an actual danger. A threat to her and perhaps to other young women, including and especially Hilary, who had looked rather like her.

June 10th, 1988: she had never forgotten the date. She and her friend Tassia had been going through a religious phase

17

and had arranged to go to the Orthodox cathedral to pray. She had sneaked out of the family home. Had Yiannis, her father, or her grandmother Irene known of it, the excursion would have been forbidden. Her grandfather Carlo – *Nonno* to Val – would have stood up for her, Val knew, but she didn't want to cause him trouble. Besides, no one was going to miss her, not during the afternoon siesta.

It was in the cathedral itself, while Tassia was lighting a candle in the small side chapel before the silver coffin of Saint Theodora, that Val came face to face with her older half-brother Markos, her father's son from his first marriage.

'Valerie.' Markos wrapped his arms around her waist. 'Valerie,' he repeated, drawing out the syllables as if chewing on a toffee. 'Sweet Lips.'

He kissed her then, in church, a far from brotherly kiss, knowing that not even the priests would reprove a uniformed officer of the Greek police.

Val was shocked. Conscious of a hiss of disapproval from a black-garbed widow, and Tassia's glazed stare, she stiffened and endured.

Markos chuckled. He relaxed his grip, grinning as Val broke free. On the raised area beside the altar they faced each other across a sequence of floor tiles, Val horribly aware of the stares from tourists and worshippers.

'What have you to say for yourself?' her half-brother demanded. 'Does Grandmother know you're here?'

'I have to go.' Val nodded to Tassia, a signal for them to leave, and began walking away, weaving round a knot of German tourists.

'Not so fast.' Markos caught up and marched her into the outside glare. He jerked a thumb at Tassia. 'You – go home.'

After a furtive appraisal of this good-looking young policeman, Tassia slipped down the steps leading away from the cathedral.

'And now you, Valerie-Chloe.'

'Why did you do that?'

They were standing in the shade of the cathedral. Flowing round them on the broad white steps, the crowds took no

18

notice. Val knew she would have to deal with Markos by herself.

Markos tightened his grip on her upper arm, watching her face as she tried not to flinch. It was always this way between them. Markos had been taught to despise her as the daughter of the woman who had seduced their father away from his mother, Lefkosia. For the past year, since he had come to live at their father's house following his mother's remarriage, Markos had caused Val trouble. He was a spy for their grandmother. Yesterday, in the face of Irene's complaints, Val had protested, 'I'm not my mother! Why can't you see me for a change?' and Markos had slapped her for disrespect.

Bad as the slap was, this was worse. He had not kissed her in that lingering fashion before. Val was frightened. She felt out of her depth.

'The kiss?' He laughed as a scarlet tide rushed up Val's face. 'We were in church – I knew you wouldn't dare fight me in front of the high altar. And I like that dress.' His free hand brushed the simple peter-pan collar of her blue gingham school dress. 'I've liked it for some time.'

Unsure what to make of Markos's confession, Val wet her lips with her tongue. A peal of bells warned her that the siesta was over. She must return home before she was missed. She looked up at him. 'Aren't you on duty?'

Markos smoothed his new black beard between thumb and finger. He was amused by her seemingly artless question, his dark eyes darting over her. 'I have just come off duty. After a brute of a shift.' His face clouded. He drew her closer. 'We can walk home together, Valerie-Chloe.'

Val hated the way he used her full name. 'I've errands to run.'

'You're lying.' Markos let her go with a spiteful backward shove. 'You are out. Wandering alone, like some cheap foreign tourist. Just like your mother. It's no wonder our father worries that you'll turn out just like her – bring more shame on our family.'

He was speaking in English, a language Val had always considered to be uniquely hers within the family, because of her English mother.

19

Holy Mother of God, help me, Val prayed in English, then Greek. Feigning defeat, she hung her head, then tried to step back when she sensed Markos relax, but he had too long a reach. He stopped her, draping an arm about her middle, holding her fast as he pointed down the cathedral steps.

'Do you think any of these people in the square will intervene?'

'Don't.' Val squirmed to escape. Where were the priests? Surely she could appeal to them. She bunched both hands into fists, ready to fight.

'You take a reckoning with me, or Grandmother,' Markos was saying.

'Then let's go home!' Val answered, in a voice that had people in the café lifting their heads from their newspapers.

Out of the shadow of an awning strolled a tall, graceful figure. Elegantly turned out in an Athenian trouser suit, the young woman's heels were audible on the stone sets as she made straight for the young Greek policeman and girl. As she closed on them, she nodded to Val, then winked with her left eye, an impudent gesture Markos would not see.

'Excuse me, Officer, I'm having problems with my Vespa.' Straight faced, she addressed Markos. 'It's double-parked outside my father's office.'

The stranger smiled for the first time and Val was able to wrest herself easily from Markos's grasp as the power of that attractive grin and the knowledge of who this slender young socialite was hit him.

'Shall we go?' the young woman continued. 'It's only a few streets from here, by the town hall.'

No need for her to add that her father was the mayor. Both Val and Markos knew that, and Val knew something else: she and the mayor's daughter attended the same senior school.

Markos had no choice but to obey. And Val had been able to escape, shooed away by her rescuer: 'You don't have to tag along. We'll be a while.'

Later, the stranger had made herself known to Val at school. Alexia admitted then that she had recognized Val because of her uniform. 'I didn't think a fellow student should be manhandled in that manner. What had you done to annoy him?' And, before

Val could stammer a reply, 'You must come to tea on Saturday.'

From such a small beginning their friendship had grown, but even when they became close Val had never told Alexia what happened when Markos returned to the family home.

Back at Alexia's with Judith and Steve, she did tell Harry.

Four

It was her own fault, Val conceded later; the result of a bungled email. Slipping up to the attic before lunch to check if she'd had any messages on her laptop, Val found one from Harry. He had sent her a scanned photograph with the question: *Is this Cavadini your relative? I notice he's a Markos, too.*

Opening the attachment, Val stared at her half-brother, one of five uniformed Greek policemen, taken that April outside the New York Police Department HQ.

Still online, she emailed back.

> Yes, it's our Markos. The uniform looks tighter on him now than when he first pounded the streets here and thought he was God's gift to everyone, including me.

The glowing words were there on the screen, to send or delete. About to edit her reply, remove the inflammatory statements, Val pressed 'send'.

'No!' she said, realizing what she had done. Scowling after her message, Val saw an answer come in.

> You never did tell me much about Markos. Don't you think it's time?

As Val considered the message her mobile began ringing.

She answered, still distracted by her action. Had it been an accident?

'What happened, Val? Between Markos and yourself?'

Val started to laugh. 'You don't give up! But I can't talk – there's lunch.'

'They'll call you when it's ready.'

'I ought to help.'

'You're on holiday, Val. And I'm about to go to work, so make it quick.'

Perhaps it was his indulgent tone. Perhaps it was because she couldn't see him, like a confessional. Perhaps it was the added urgency she felt because of Nonno's letter. To her own surprise, Val began to talk.

She told Harry about being thirteen and meeting Markos in the cathedral. She told of the kiss which had so disturbed her and her return home, where she had tried to explain to Irene and Yiannis.

'They thought I must be exaggerating what Markos had done. My father said he would wait until Markos came in before he passed judgement.'

'Your father actually used those words: "passed judgement"?'

Val realized she was nodding and said quickly, 'He did. He wouldn't hear another word on the subject. Nonno wasn't home, so we sat in silence in the best room, the three of us, until Markos stalked in.'

Markos had been plausible. He hadn't denied kissing Val, he merely said she was overwrought – a teenage girl, overplaying. 'He said he'd had a terrible day, that he'd seen his first dead body and that he didn't know what he'd been doing since he came off shift. That he'd seen his innocent little sister in church and rushed to embrace the normality she – I – represented.'

'What a convenient corpse,' Harry remarked.

'He may have seen one.' Val thought of Hilary, murdered, and Hilary's jade ring, now in Markos's hands, and suppressed both thoughts.

'And come from there to sexually assault his younger sister? I don't think so.'

'It wasn't an assault.'

'Wasn't it?' Harry asked quietly. 'Your instincts tell you it was. I'd go with them, if I were you, Val.'

'But father and grandmother were sorry for Markos. They said he must have been under stress—'

'I imagine your grandfather wasn't impressed by that excuse.'

'No, Nonno wasn't. He called Markos a pig – worse things, too, in Italian. I'd never seen him so angry. But Yiannis and Irene . . .' Val faltered.

'You wanted them to berate Markos, and they didn't.'

'Oh, they believed me by then,' Val began.

'They just didn't believe you enough. They didn't want to accept that their precious boy had feet of clay.'

'I stayed with friends whenever I could after that,' Val whispered into the receiver. 'Maybe I did make too much of one kiss, but it showed me, then, how my father would always make excuses for his son.' The incident between her and Markos had also been the moment when she'd realized that she should leave the family home as soon as possible.

'I agree,' said Harry. 'You did the right thing.'

'Lunch!' bawled Steve up the cypress staircase.

'It's okay, Val, I heard him. You take care of yourself now, and have a great holiday. Just keep in mind you did the right thing. Bye, love.'

'Bye, Harry.' The mobile died, stranding Val between regret that she had spoken and relief that Harry had understood.

Five

'You're quiet,' Alexia remarked. She and Val were clearing up after a simple lunch laid out in the kitchen. Jessica, Judith and Steve had returned to the jetty for the afternoon. Alexia was making coffee.

'Sorry.' Val was distracted by memories of Markos and by flashbacks to Hilary's murder. But Hilary had never come to Komméno.

She made an effort. 'You're looking much brighter, Alex. The sleep's done you good. Did you say you were going into town this afternoon?'

'Yes – a reception to welcome Stefan Gregory. Chloe won't be back until tomorrow.' Alexia poured their coffees into tiny cups. 'Want to come?'

'Thanks, I will, but not to your reception, if you don't mind. I've some tools to collect from my workshop.'

'That's fine.' Alexia blew on her coffee. 'What will you do if you run into your father?' she asked, careful not to look at Val.

'He won't be looking for me.'

'Of course. But does he know you're here now?'

'I imagine so. He knows I stay with you every summer.'

Val could not enjoy her coffee. Her stomach was in a knot. She knew that Nonno would have wanted her to call on Yiannis, but could she?

'Would talking to him alone about Carlo's will help?'

'Maybe.' Val saw the sense of Alexia's suggestion. Away from Irene and Markos, Yiannis was less abrasive with her. 'I suppose it's worth a try.'

Val asked Alexia to drop her near the Café Musetti, on the corner close to the start of the Spianada, Corfu town's wide green park. She parked her hire car here whenever she first returned to the town, because her mother had stayed at the nearby Demeter hotel, in one of the side streets.

She had never really known her mother, Elizabeth, the English tourist whom her father had met and fallen in love with. Yiannis had divorced his Corfiot wife to marry her, but Val remembered her mother crying: their marriage had not been happy. And when she was just seven years old, Elizabeth had died.

Now it gave Val a sad pleasure to walk into town along Kapodistriou Street beside the open space of the Spianada, retracing Elizabeth's steps when she had been a carefree tourist.

24

Just as she tended her mother's grave on her return to Corfu, Val always took her first stroll into town this way.

There were really two towns, an old sea town and port built between two beetling fortresses, and the modern new town spreading away from the sea. Val's Corfiot family and her workshop were in the old town, but her mother's grave was in the British cemetery, in the new town.

Sometimes, when Val returned to Corfu town, she would stroll around the Spianada, imagining that Elizabeth had done the same. Walk down Kapodistriou Street, passing the former mansions of the old Venetian nobility on the one side and the park and bandstand on the other. Stroll along the Liston, with its broad pavement and cafés. Wander up to the Palace of St Michael and St George, a building of classical design, delightfully in scale with the rest of the friendly, intimate architecture of Corfu's old town.

Today, although grateful for the shade of the park and conscious of the sweet scent of the lime trees, Val made straight for the Palace of St Michael and St George. The tourist police had an office within the palace and that was where she would find her father.

Passing one of the palace's triumphal arches, Val stepped under the building's neo-classical facade, counting the off-white limestone columns as she made her way towards the central entrance. Her feet almost soundless on the grey marble flooring, she ignored the doors leading to the state rooms and the museum of Asiatic art, stopping at a room next to the main entrance.

This room was shuttered and its door closed, but Val heard the whirr of a fan. This was the office of the tourist police, now closed for the siesta. She knew that her father would be inside, stooped over his computer, drinking a glass of kumquat liqueur – he had a sweet tooth – while playing Tomb Raider.

As soon as she put her head round his office door, Yiannis motioned her in, showing no surprise or pleasure at her appearance. He flicked a finger across his moustache, an act of perfunctory grooming.

'Come in, girl, and sit. Lift those files off that chair.'

Yiannis Cavadini, half Greek, half Italian, resolutely himself, looked Val up and down without smiling. He now spoke Greek – to test her, Val supposed.

'Close that door, before more tourists start pestering me.'

'Good afternoon, Father,' Val answered in Greek. She closed the door and peered at Yiannis in the dim light. Her father had the same wavy black hair and blue eyes, but there the similarities between them ended. The habitual expression of his bronzed, hawkish face was penetrating; he was an interrogator by nature. In height and build she and her father were very different: Yiannis was tall, strapping, while she was puny.

Val was aware that she was a disappointment to her father. If her mother had lived, if Elizabeth had not been an orphan without any family of her own, she thought, stepping into the high-ceilinged, dim office, she would have been less desperate for his affection.

'How are you, Father? And Grandmother?' Always when she saw him there was a small hope that this time they would connect.

'My mother is well enough,' Yiannis growled.

Val approached him warily, her sandals flopping on the tiles. When he had found her in his study with Hilary's murder file, Yiannis had silently taken the folder from her, pointing to the door. Afterwards she had endured days of waiting, anticipating punishment which never came.

Yiannis now endured her kiss against his tanned cheek.

'Good flight? You have settled in at your friend's?' He barked the questions, answering them himself as he keyed commands into his computer. '*Kyria* Alexia is always the gracious hostess, *neh*? It is a pity that she and her husband have only your god-daughter and no son.'

Val said nothing. That might have been a dig at her, for producing Judith rather than a grandson. Her father's face was hard to read.

'Are you busy?' She tried to find a safe topic before broaching Carlo Cavadini's will. She had always seen Nonno whenever she returned to Corfu. Her grandfather was the one reason she ever saw the rest of her family, since she knew that he would have liked her to have a reconciliation with her father and grandmother. But then Nonno had left her his work-shop, which the family resented, and also his mother's wedding ring and twenty gold sovereigns, which Irene claimed were lost. Like Hilary's jade ring, which Markos appeared to have acquired, Val knew that these were not missing.

The dispute depressed her. She wanted to say to Yiannis, 'Forget the wedding ring and sovereigns; you accept that the workshop is mine and let's leave each other in peace.' She drew in a breath. 'Father, can't we forget—'

'Let's get rid of that.' Yiannis lifted his cap off the front of the desk. 'Are you going to sit, or must I develop a crick in my neck from staring up?'

'No, of course . . .' Val could hear herself being flustered. It was so unfair; her father was being absurd. She would have teased someone like Harry, but with Yiannis she was caught between anger and a desire to please.

She cleared the chair he had offered, stripping it of manila folders and laying them on the tiles. Sitting at the opposite side of the wide walnut table, the largest of the three tables in the room and a relic of Corfu's colonial past, she leaned forward to try again.

Yiannis spoke first. 'Is it not time that you grew your hair? You look like a boy!' He laughed, displaying large, gold-filled teeth.

'Nick liked it this way.'

'You have not asked me how Markos is. You never do.'

You haven't asked me about your granddaughter. Val did not speak.

Yiannis sat back. 'Markos is a credit to the family,' he said, ignoring Val's hurt blue eyes. 'He is part of homicide now, a sharp officer.'

'Where is he?'

Yiannis tapped his chest. 'My son is in America.' He spoke as though sampling the delights of a five-course meal. 'A police conference and then backpacking in the Rockies.'

Beneath the window, shuttered against the lush blue of the sky, Yiannis's fax whined and licked paper into the carrying tray.

'Is there anything else?' he asked.

She could mention the contested will, the 'lost' jewellery, but all Val could think of was the proud way Yiannis had spoken of Markos: 'My son.'

The old jealousy took over. She rose and stalked past three empty desks to the door. 'I'll leave you to look at that – I'm sure it's more important.' Clasping the antique doorknob, she looked back.

Ignoring the fax, Yiannis's dark, grey-flecked head was bowed over the computer screen. He was humming the opening sequence of Tomb Raider.

'Goodbye,' Val told her surviving parent. There was no answer.

Six

Yiannis relaxed when he heard the door close. He had been disconcerted to see Valerie and now he was glad that she had gone. With her marriage and her deliberate exile overseas she was no longer family.

His father's choice of Valerie as his main heir enraged him. When had Carlo ever shown the interest in him that he had lavished on that girl?

Yiannis didn't want to play Tomb Raider any more. He walked to the window. Through the closed shutters he felt the heat of the sun, a clear, masculine strength. The moon, changeable and cold, belonged to women like his second wife Elizabeth, who would have left him, exposing him to ridicule, had she lived. Her daughter was just such another.

Shielded and warmed by the sun, Yiannis admitted that he disliked Valerie for the same reason that the heroes of Troy had hated Cassandra: her dreams. At seven years old, she had woken the whole house, shrieking that her mother was dead. Childish nonsense. But Elizabeth complained of a headache

28

and a stiff neck the next day and took a turn for the worse in the night. By evening, despite being transferred to Corfu hospital, she was dead. Meningitis, the doctor told Yiannis. Perhaps, if she had been brought in sooner, they might have been able to save her.

Yiannis never told Valerie what the doctor had said. Not that the child took any notice of him. After he told her that Elizabeth was dead, she stalked the street outside for the rest of the day, waiting for her grandfather. Carlo had been away in Italy when Elizabeth was taken ill.

'She dreams true,' Irene had said, pulling Yiannis on one side when Carlo walked into the alleyway to be greeted by a storm of weeping from his granddaughter. 'But the child is young; she will not remember. She will forget and say nothing, and so must we. Elizabeth is dead and can no longer threaten you with shame. It is over, my son.'

Yiannis leaned his forehead against the shutter, feeling the slats press against his forehead. In truth, he was never sure what Valerie remembered from that night. He knew she could remember a great deal.

The police report on Hilary Moffat: how much did Valerie remember of that? The old unsolved murder had been much on Yiannis's mind lately. It was ten years now since the English tourist, another sleek, luscious-lipped young woman like Elizabeth, had come to Corfu.

'A pity for her – and for me,' muttered Yiannis.

He flicked his motorbike keys to and fro in his fingers. Hilary was long dead, and the long-dead told no tales. Valerie was different, but he could leave her to his mother. Irene must find out what Valerie knew of Hilary.

Yiannis reached across the table for his cap. He had time, he thought, before the end of the siesta, to visit Valerie in Carlo's workshop, where she would have gone. There he would order her home.

She was not welcome, but she must come home.

29

Seven

Coming to herself again, Val realized that she had wandered in the wrong direction for the workshop and was approaching the café in the Liston where Nick used to buy her coffee.

In the afternoon haze she could see the parti-coloured awnings rippling above each colonnade. The Liston was named after the *Libro d'Oro*, the Golden Book, which listed the Venetian-Corfiot nobility allowed to stroll on the nearby wide pavement. Val thought of it as a caterpillar of cafés, their bright awnings linked by segments of glittering marble.

She found some habits hard to break, especially when the waiters recognized her and yelled smiling questions in the local dialect. Val was shepherded to a pavement seat, brought a ginger beer and a saucer of Greek delight 'on the house', then instructed to linger. 'You see, we remember your favourite drink. Now relax and enjoy.'

Touched, Val sipped her ginger beer and picked herself out two pieces of lemon-flavoured delight before putting the rest of the sweets in her clean hankie for Judith. Relishing the cool, sharp taste of her drink, she tried to remain upbeat, but was soon brooding over one of Corfu's most famous views – the green Spianada, the chic Café Capri opposite and the dusty, empty cricket pitch – absorbing little of their intimate, hospitable splendour. Her thoughts were of the past.

Yiannis had taunted her, calling her a boy. Hilary had also worn her light-brown hair in a short bob. In other ways, too – size and shape, age and interests – they had been similar. She and Hilary had shared more than the Corfiot police had ever known, more than she had told anyone.

What I knew then would have made no difference to catching

30

her killer, Val reassured herself, but an inner voice told her that was a lie. The harsh fact was that she had to be able to get on with her life, but Hilary had been murdered. If Yiannis and Irene had known that Hilary and Val – not Hilary alone – had arranged that day to meet a stranger on a blind date, they would never have allowed her out again.

Ten years earlier, when Val had been feeling trapped on the island, she and her grandfather attended the recital given outside the town hall by Stefan Gregory. At the interval Nonno patted her arm.

'I am going now. I will leave you during the second half.' His light-blue eyes were guileless but he spoke quite deliberately in careful English so that Val's neighbour would also understand. 'Mrs Christoforou's cello needs more *vernice*. You will find me at the workshop, *va bene*?'

His grey pointed beard nodded from Val to her neighbour, including both. 'You will be fine?' he asked, smiling at his granddaughter as he rose.

Val nodded. For the last few years, whenever she was home from school in Athens, she had scarcely been allowed out on her own. She had been told by Irene about 'That shame' – her mother's plan to leave Corfu and divorce her husband Yiannis. The older she grew, the more like Elizabeth she became in looks, the more the family seemed to fear her. Only Nonno sought to break through the tyranny of petty restrictions.

Now, happy to be out for the evening, she was soon answering Hilary's questions, delighted to be able to use her English.

'Yes, he's my grandfather. Signor Carlo Cavadini – instrument restorer.'

'You look a bit like him.' The girl smiled, showing dimples in a heart-shaped face. 'He's very good looking for a grandad.'

The men in her family were good looking, Val thought. No one had bothered to tell her what she was like.

'I'm Hilary, by the way. Hilary Moffat, music student.'

'Val Cavadini, also music student. Pleased to meet you.'

They were both excited. Hilary was backpacking through

the Ionian islands, and loved being able to talk freely in English 'to someone my own age who I don't have to fight off.'

Val was mesmerized. In the rest of the interval they covered Stefan Gregory's looks, the best way to tune cellos and Corfu's best beaches.

'I like the outfit.' Val cast envious eyes over Hilary's tight pink jeans and slinky aquamarine top. She liked the shocking pink lip-gloss, sophisticated jade ring and the red high heels, too.

After the recital, both agreed that a drink was in order. Val worried about revealing her ignorance of the bars and was relieved when Hilary linked arms with her and said, 'Let's go to Zeus's.'

Their rapid, light steps took them through the bustling, jasmine-scented streets in an easy ramble to the Liston, where others promenaded in the evening volta. Joining the young families with buggies, the youths riding pillion on ancient pushbikes, the mothers going home with bags of shopping, Val felt for the first time to be truly part of the town. The freedom made her giddy. She almost forgot Nonno, but not quite.

'Just one drink, okay?' she asked as they entered the classical facade of Zeus's on the Liston, shouting over the unrecognizable muzak.

'Sure,' said Hilary. 'What will you have?'

'I'll get them.' Val blushed, praying that she had enough cash on her. Every bar in the Liston was expensive: it was Corfu's place to be seen.

'I'll have a coke, please. That ought to be a little easier on the wallet.'

'Right, you grab us a table.' Val set off for the packed bar. When she returned with their cokes, Hilary had acquired an outside table beside the famous wide pavement, under a brightly lit lantern. Sipping her coke, wanting to make it last, Val settled into her seat.

'How long have you been at college?'

'Hang on,' Hilary warned. One of the svelte young bar staff was approaching their table, bearing two more cokes on a tray.

As he set them down, he nodded back towards the inner bar.

'From the man in the white shirt, with his compliments.'

Hilary glanced at the drinks and shook her head. 'Thanks but no thanks.' She nodded to the shadowy figure standing against the long black and gold chrome bar, his face and form obscured by the flashing interior purple lights that were supposed to represent Zeus's thunder and lightning.

'Take them back, please.' Hilary leaned against Val, whispering, 'I can't make him out, except for that white shirt. He might be a real horror.'

The barman whipped the cokes away but returned seconds later. 'He would like to meet you two charming girls here for coffee, tomorrow. Noon.'

Hilary smiled across at their unknown admirer. 'I don't think I've been called a charming girl before.' She nudged Val's leg with one of her high heels. 'Drink up. We need to make a mysterious exit. It should be fun. A blind date.' She giggled. 'He won't be able to hide what he looks like in sunlight.'

'Hilary, I can't promise I'll be here. At home, it's – difficult, I might not . . .'

'If you can't make it, I'll have him to myself, won't I?'

They walked arm in arm to Nonno's shop, where they parted. Val remembered Hilary walking back down the alley, turning once and grinning. 'Don't worry!' she shouted, causing one of the prowling cats to hiss at her. Laughing, Hilary stuck her tongue out at it and continued on her way.

Returning the following noon to Zeus's, Val found herself alone: no Hilary and no blind date. She found the barman who had tried to serve them the previous evening. He shook his head at her questions. No, the young woman had not returned this morning, and neither had the stranger in the white shirt. No, the young lady had not come back to Zeus's late last night. He had not seen the stranger leave. He could not remember the man's face, or age; possibly he was young, no grey. He did not know any more.

Still Hilary did not come. The hostel where Hilary was staying told Val that Miss Moffat had not yet returned. Growing anxious, Val phoned more guest houses and bars, each time drawing a blank. Two days later she read in the newspaper that Hilary was dead.

'I should have stayed with her. I should have walked her to the hostel.' Val lifted her head in the café that had once been the Zeus bar and was now an Italian-style *gelateria* and coffee house. She had returned to this bar and to their table through the years, hoping for some moment of revelation.

I should have been braver, Val thought. But at the time, shocked by Hilary's murder, she had told the police and her father only what she must. The stranger in the white shirt, yes, and her scandalous drinking in the Zeus bar, but she had contradicted the waiter's story, insisting that the man at the bar had asked Hilary alone on the blind date. Not her, too.

That tiny lie, that little sin of omission, would have made no difference to the investigation. But Val had never been sure. The only things she did know for sure were what she had read in that lifted police file.

Hilary's body had been washed. Posed under an olive tree close to the palace, she had been murdered sometime during the second evening after she had disappeared from Corfu town. In a ghastly irony, Yiannis had been summoned to the Achillion, some ten kilometres south of Corfu town, where he discovered her body and imposed some order on the crime scene.

Crime scene. 'She was Hilary.' Val drained the rest of her ginger beer. 'And I failed her.' She was still failing, doing nothing about the suspicions that Nonno had felt compelled to share with her, if only by letter.

Val understood why Nonno had written. Had he phoned or tried to speak to her anywhere close to her old family home, even from the phone in the workshop, someone might have overheard. Privacy was almost impossible. And this was not easy knowledge. Markos was his grandson. He told her by letter, too, to give her time for thought, for planning, although she had no idea yet what she was going to do.

When, exactly, had her grandfather written to her? Pulling out her mobile, Val phoned the lawyer who was dealing with Nonno's estate.

The man listened to her request for information – the date that Carlo Cavadini had placed his letter to her in his safe deposit box – and promised to find out.

'Thanks.' Leaving a generous tip, she walked out of the café that had once been Zeus's into the sticky heat of the Liston's broad pavement.

Eight

The jostling crowds along the top of Kapodistriou Street, the reek of cheap cigarettes, fried onions and frying meat that drifted down from the upper windows of the alley she was in seemed unreal. Chilled to the bone, Val wove through the shuttered lanes of the old town, past the massive electric pylon close to the church of Pantokrátor, with its baroque angel and stark square, a place she remembered walking across with her mother, just Elizabeth and herself.

The narrow streets of this part of town were being resurfaced and new wiring installed: broken pantiles, coils of black and blue wire, raised manholes and dust were everywhere. Feeling exiled, belonging nowhere, Val stalked past a modest jeweller's on the corner of Prossalendou Street and came to a tall ochre building with a black door and an iron shutter. She hurried up the two faded, whitewashed steps, unlocked the door and pushed it open.

In the foyer at the bottom of the inner staircase lay an old bike and rusting collection of fuse boxes. Immediately in front of her was an inner door, with a faded nameplate. Val opened this door with her grandfather's key and at last entered a world she was sure of: the large, high-ceilinged room of her grandfather's repair and restoration business.

Shrouded in cloths or gleaming with protective grease, Nonno's tools hung in racks above the great bench that dominated the workshop. The lathes were still straight, the largest of them covered, as always, by his black waistcoat. Val lifted the waistcoat off the lathe and cuddled it.

Whenever she thought of her grandfather she pictured his hands. Before arthritis had swollen each knuckle and bent the tips of the fingers of his right hand off at tortured angles, Nonno's hands had been elegant and shapely with fine, clean nails. When Val was tiny, the few silky, dirty-blond hairs growing on the backs of his hands had fascinated her.

His hands described shapes. The subtle swell and tapering of a piano soundboard. 'It is the instrument's throat, larynx and lungs, it is the place from which it speaks,' Carlo had told her. 'Feel the grain, Valerie. Can your fingertips taste the wood, the way the lines of growth run? Can you see the crown of the soundboard? Yes, that rise towards the bridge.'

'You have inherited my hands, Valerie,' he told her more than once. 'I pray that yours do not have the same fate.'

Nonno hated what arthritis had done to his fingers, but the disease had not prevented him from working. His restorations remained superb, for all that he was slower. 'The touch is still there, Valerie, but these fingers are so ugly.'

'Ugly,' he repeated, but Val said, 'Comforting hands, cradling hands.'

She was thirteen at the time, helping him in his workshop each day before or after school. It was the evening following the day when Markos had found her in church and she was grateful for the peace of Nonno's workshop.

Val remembered how Carlo Cavadini had looked at her then, how bright his eyes had seemed against his lightly tanned face. His fine straight hair, where it was not grey, was ash-blond. She considered him handsome and stylish, dapper even in his work overalls and waistcoat.

Now she gave her grandfather's waistcoat a pat and hung it back gently over the lathe. She remained still for another moment. Markos might scoff at the workshop but he did not appreciate the wealth of woods and veneers. The copy of an ancient Greek mask, hung as a good-luck charm above the box of violin bridges, was as valueless to him as the violin belly that Val had kept because it was the last piece her

36

grandfather made. She was glad that for Markos this place was without resonance.

'*Ciao, Nonno,*' she breathed into the dusty air. Her Italian grandfather had been an outsider in the family, as her mother had been. As she still was.

Hilary had been an outsider.

She had to find a way to stop this. Why was she dwelling on Hilary's murder? The investigation was cold; besides which she spent most of her time resenting the police, not wanting to help them.

Perversely, in her quest to suppress the grim details of Hilary's killing, Nick's death and her own personal grieving had been the most effective 'block' to her old memories. But now those memories were clear again and, though she did not want to admit this, her recurring dream was troubling her sleep more.

Nonno had warned her of Markos, but he had not expected her to pursue Hilary's killer. He had written that Markos was not capable of murder, but did she believe that? Val shook her head. 'Let the police do their job – they have all the facts of Hilary's death, leave it to them.' But so far, ten years on, the forces of law and order had no suspects, and why should they look at Markos, a policeman?

Val closed her eyes, breathing slowly. The workshop had its own notes to play: resin and pine, castor and olive oil, wood shavings and grease. The gentle rattle of the shutters, the slow drip of the tap over the stone sink in the corner of the room, birds calling under the eaves outside. The next-door neighbour singing along to her radio.

She should call on Voula, Val thought, wary of the obligation of courtesy to an old woman, another trap. Corfu was dragging her in.

Restive, she shifted and something snapped under her right foot. She glanced down at the crushed pistachio and knew who had been here – recently, too, by the satisfying crack of the rest of the shell.

Behind her someone knocked heavily on the black outer door, a knocking almost instantly repeated against her inner door. 'It's me, open up.'

Val unlocked the door and Yiannis came in, stepping sideways past a redundant keyboard positioned just inside the door.

'I see Markos has been poking around in here.' She was calm, but beneath that irritated.

Yiannis shouldered the door shut. He glared at the stone floor. 'Those damned pistachios that he eats.'

'What is Markos looking for, Father?'

Yiannis's arm strummed the middle keys of the upright board; they depressed without sound as he ignored the question. 'He doesn't disturb anything. Why should he not come? He is family.'

Val walked softly around the table. She knew that Markos would have told the family how much money could be made if the workshop was sold, but this was her domain. 'Nonno left it to *me*.'

'It's time you sold it, or moved back.'

'It's less than a year since Nonno died,' said Val quietly.

Yiannis jerked his shoulders up and down. 'Time you let him go, girl.'

She couldn't, not yet. The workshop had been Nonno's escape, as it was hers. 'I pay the bills. Deal with any problems through an agent.'

'I suppose he has keys, too,' muttered Yiannis.

'The agent doesn't come prowling. Tomorrow I'm changing this inner lock. I didn't think it was necessary, but now I see it is.'

Yiannis dropped his hat on to a crusted pot of glue and looked about for a chair. Reaching under the massive workbench, Val pulled out a tall stool for him. He settled on it without thanks.

'Why can you not get on with Markos?'

'You know why.'

Yiannis sighed irritably, slouching on the stool. 'Not that old thing about his kissing you.' He flicked the ends of his moustache, a habit of his when facing difficulty. 'Always the defiance,' Yiannis went on. 'You couldn't marry a Greek boy, could you?' He smoothed his moustache again. 'When you read that police file, was that another of your rebellions?'

'Perhaps.' Startled by the question and feeling a need for more light, Val wandered over to the shutters. She lifted the latch. To the shuttered homes springing into view from her newly opened window, she confessed, 'Hilary was like me, after all.'

'You told me and the police that you hardly knew her.'

'That's right.' It was easier to talk to her father about Hilary while watching the pigeons flapping overhead. Standing in the breeze from the window, Val asked, 'Why did you bring that file home, Father? Surely what you did was . . . unusual.'

With the word 'unusual' she thought of the giraffe piano and her god-daughter Chloe's silence. Her fear. Alexia had been convinced of it.

'I lost everything because of that case,' Yiannis said. 'They thought I should have found the killer but they didn't give me enough time or resources. My boss was gunning for me and that case gave him the perfect excuse to get rid of me. That's why I was transferred to the tourist police.'

Val rubbed her bare arms. 'Did you know Hilary?' she asked, a tactless question regretted as soon as spoken. Yiannis had found Hilary's body.

Her father raised his eyebrows and shook his head, an oddly subdued reaction for him. Val found herself following her first question with a second, more immediately relevant. 'What about Markos? Did he know Hilary?'

Yiannis pushed himself off the stool and removed his hat from the crusted glue pot. 'You should not be asking. You are not the police.' He walked to the door. 'My mother wishes to see you and the little girl. You will come to the house on Friday, after the siesta.'

Val might have argued, but the old desire to please him bit home. She was intrigued, too. Above all, there was Nonno's letter, with its reference to Hilary's jade ring. If she seized the chance of this invitation, she might be able to search Markos's room.

And if you find the jade ring, what then?

'Will Markos be back?' she asked, ducking her own question. If he was, she would be safer searching, although she would have to be careful of Irene.

39

'No,' Yiannis said, his face darkening. 'Why do you ask?'

'Only that it might have been useful to see him. It's been a long time.'

'Your doing, not my son's.'

'Of course.' Valerie inclined her head, hiding her face until she was sure she would appear calm. 'We'll be pleased to come.' She walked towards Yiannis to embrace him but he was already opening the door.

'I must return to the office. The siesta is over. Farewell.'

After he had gone, Val wiped a tear away and tried to concentrate on checking the workshop. Although she was intrigued by her father's admission about his enforced move to the tourist police, other ideas nagged at her. Nonno had been right – Yiannis also knew, or suspected, that Markos had met Hilary. For some reason Markos had also recently visited here. Why he had done so, Val did not yet understand.

Nine

Yiannis did not return to the office. He walked to the nearest bar. Standing at the bar he switched off his radio and tried to curb his temper.

He was sick of women. He missed Markos and feared for him. Had Valerie dreamed of Markos, jinxed his son and heir? Somehow she had sniffed out that Markos had possibly known the Moffat girl. A disconcerting idea, but he was reluctant to ask Markos direct. A man had the right to enjoy himself, thought Yiannis, shifting from one foot to the other.

Why had Markos gone into the workshop? Yiannis speared an olive and swallowed it, spitting the stone on to the bar floor. No one reproved him, a policeman. He finished his ouzo, tossed a few coins on to the counter and moved into the street again. He began walking back to Carlo's workshop, to find whatever Markos had been looking for. Or had Markos hidden something which needed to be recovered?

Oblivious to the other pedestrians and a seething moped driver, Yiannis stopped in the middle of the street, catching sight of a poster advertising Stefan Gregory's recital. 'The Achillion again,' he muttered.

Hilary and Valerie. He had always known that his daughter had met the girl, but until recently that knowledge had given him no more than a vague disquiet. Now, with Valerie back on the island, clearly obsessed with that old murder case he, and, it seemed, Markos, would need to be careful.

Yiannis turned about and marched off in the direction of his house. He would have to pick his moment to return to the workshop. Valerie's threat to change the lock was nothing – he had skeleton keys – but if he went back today, she would suspect. Instead, he lengthened his stride for home.

Ten

Val was prevented from working on the giraffe piano by Theo, who remained in his study until dinner. She had no chance to talk to Chloe, who was staying at Peritheia to take part in the wedding celebrations. After catching up on gossip over a leisurely evening meal of *bourdéto* with Alexia and Theo, she found that it was past eleven before she could coax a squealing Judy up to bed, and after three before she rolled sleepily into her attic room. On her way there she was joined on the grand staircase by Theo.

'Alexia will be up soon,' he said, falling into step. 'Before she does, I'd like to say again how delighted I am that you've returned to Cypress House. My wife is fond of you. And we do all seem to scurry about when you're here.' He smiled. 'If you need any help with that leviathan in my study, please ask.'

And you'll jump to it? Val thought, but wasn't quite bold enough to tease him. 'Thanks,' she said. 'I may just do that.'

They had come to a stop on the stairs, heads level as Theo was on the tread below hers. Val could see him clearly by the wall lights: a tall, lean man with long narrow features and, despite his headful of tight black curls, no discernible stubble. Theo was turning forty, but there was no grey in his hair, no excess weight round his middle. In many ways he was Alexia's masculine counterpart, tall, well bred and well groomed, someone whose very neatness of dress always made Val anxious of the shortcomings in her own.

'You've settled in? Do you all have everything you need?' he asked.

'Everything's very comfortable.' She was always a little in awe of Theo. Like Alexia, he was descended from one of the island's noble families. With him, Val was conscious of being an employee.

'I'll be as quick as I can be, dismantling the giraffe piano,' she promised. 'The thing is . . .' She found herself yawning. 'I'm so sorry about that.'

'Don't worry, Val. Sleep well.' Theo stepped past her on the stair and continued upstairs, turning on the first landing towards his study.

'Val!'

She turned and walked swiftly back down the staircase towards Alexia. The wan, distracted figure she had tried to reassure that morning was a glowing earth mother, kissing her on both cheeks.

'I've told him. He knows! Theo's over the moon – he's talking about asking Jessica to stay on.' Giddy with relief, Alexia plucked at Val's sleeve. 'You were right! He'll be on the phone first thing, bragging to his parents.'

Val hugged her. 'I'm so glad, Alex.' Shamefully, she felt like crying. She was delighted for Theo and Alexia, but there would be no more children for her and Nick.

She turned away so that Alex would not see her eyes moisten. In the stair panelling she spotted a 'face' in a knot of wood, a face her thoughts coloured with Harry's blond hair and light-blue eyes, a foolish idea. She'd seen him only a few days ago,

42

so she couldn't possibly be missing him. *Not even the chance to wrangle with him, or to feel superior?* I'm not superior, I just wish . . . Val's wish faded. Harry was miles away, in Fenfield.

Her mind plays tricks. Harry is here with her in Corfu. In the dream, he is as bright as an ikon. His blue eyes are rich with understanding. He runs to her through woods scented with jasmine and wild roses.

Val smiles. In sleep there is no story to be told but the true one, unacknowledged when she is awake but always waiting to be known. Perhaps a catalyst is needed, perhaps even a simple change of view, so that she and Harry see themselves liberated from their Fenfield past.

Hovering at the edge of wakefulness, Val almost stirs, almost remembers these thoughts, but then the scene changes. She is alone, without the sunlit woods and Harry's foolish, tender games. She is alone and then there is darkness. Sinking back into sleep, Val asks, *Where am I?*

An olive tree, in the garden of a great house – she can just make out the closed shutters of the house through the tangle of branches. An olive tree at the centre of a small arbour, bounded by a high wall on one side, supporting a flight of steps, and luxuriant shrubs and cypress on the other, with jasmine and honeysuckle on the wall. There is the statue of a woman's torso balanced on top of a curved marble seat at the base of the olive tree; both are under its friendly shade. It is noon, very hot, and a yellow butterfly flutters idly by her feet.

Val has seen this place before, for herself. Although the spot is not generally known and has never been made public as a place of murder, she has seen it before in her dreams. That, and clues gathered from odd comments from Yiannis when questioned on the case by Markos, led her here, many years ago, a pilgrim to guilt. She hoped that to see the site for herself would lay Hilary's ghost, for the villa behind the olive tree is a palace, and the grounds that the olive tree grows in are those of the Achillion.

A shadow falls across the naked torso of the marble woman and then across the marble seat. The shadow grows and deepens, takes on mass and detail. A young woman's face emerges. Music from an unseen accordion player silences the cheeping of an insistent young sparrow, demanding to be fed as it hops around the woman's feet. The accordion player is performing 'Mack the Knife'.

A dream Hilary looks up from her marble seat at Val. 'This should have been you,' she says.

In the dream, Val screams and the floodlights come on, the day changing instantly to night. But the olive tree and its marble seat and the marble woman are in darkness, because here there are no floodlights.

Footsteps are approaching, someone is rushing down the outside stair that borders and encloses this place. The killer has been bold, for any witness need only have been walking down the steps from the palace and peeped over the green iron balustrade to catch a glimpse of Hilary and her murderer, although the spot is shielded by the feathery leaves of the olive tree.

Gnarled and tall, its roots encased in rubble and concrete, its main trunk leaning over the shoulder of the classical torso, the olive tree has seen many things. It knows, as Val knows, that visitors rarely stray from the official staircase, that the little path running to this enclosed arbour is unmarked, unpaved and uninteresting. The killer has been daring but not reckless in striking at night, when the sightseers are gone.

In the dream, Hilary has vanished but the footsteps are still coming down the outside staircase, the sound changing as whoever it is steps on to the tiny unpaved track. Once he has rounded the corner of the staircase wall and has passed the rose bush and sprawling honeysuckle, Val will see him.

She wants to see, but finds herself running instead – the familiar nightmare dash across the grounds and woods of the Achillion. Val tries to stop herself, but the dream is strong and so she runs . . .

She had not expected to dream of Hilary's murder but the repeating nightmare woke her at 4 a.m. Angry at herself, Val heard a snatch of music at the edge of her consciousness. It faded even as she focused on it.

Aware that she wouldn't be able to rest again until she'd done something, Val put her laptop on the bare boards under the window. Checking the mosquito mesh, she opened the shutters. Moonlight guided her hands as she booted up the powerful little machine.

There were no emails apart from the usual spam and a brief message from the Greek lawyer to say that her grandfather had placed his final letter in his safe deposit box sometime in the early spring of the year he died. *Forgive me, Mrs Baker,* the email finished, *I can't say more precisely than that.*

Bewildered as to why her grandfather had not sent her the letter, Val was also disappointed. Not wanting to admit that she had hoped to find another message from Harry, she closed down her computer. Sitting cross-legged on the floor, she tried to consider what to do about her dream.

You don't have to do anything. She had been working hard these last few weeks, clearing the decks for Alexia's piano. Her nightmare had been a stress response, nothing more.

You dream true, Irene had said, and Val knew that was right. When she was fifteen, she had dreamed that her father fell up a step and broke his wrist. Yiannis scoffed when she tried to warn him, then blamed her when it happened. There had been other occasions, too, events which her sleeping life foretold. To Val's relief such dreams were infrequent. She had no wish to be a prophetess.

Her nightmare of Hilary's murder was different. It was a dream of a past event, and it recurred. But even so, until this last month she had dreamed of Hilary too rarely to bother with the trouble of therapy.

'Everyone has bad memories and they're not all rushing off to be psychoanalysed,' she said aloud. 'It's only an occasional dream.'

And she already knew why she dreamed that she was Hilary, why she always took Hilary's part. Good old-fashioned Greek guilt, the kind that Orestes had known. As avenging furies went, her little dream was nothing.

'Besides, talking doesn't work.' Val raised her head to the blind moon.

She uncoiled from her cross-legged position. Her legs fiery

with pins and needles, she lay down on the spongy mattress. It was a pity she could not hunt down Hilary's murderer. Perhaps if she did that she would find peace. If she could uncover the truth of Hilary's murder, would it stop her nightmare run across the grounds of the Achillion?

If she talked to Harry about Hilary, would it help? Val chewed pensively on her lower lip. To have someone to bounce ideas off was tempting.

'What ideas?' Val asked herself. 'You know no more about Hilary's final movements now than you did ten years ago.'

Nothing but the tantalizing notion that Markos had possibly known the murder victim. That and Nonno's warning.

Markos could not have hurt anyone, surely? She would have heard the rumour. Alexia would have known something.

That kiss in church had only been a kiss. It was the desire behind it, exposed for that moment, which Val had shrunk from. Markos's embrace had been a warning that she would have been foolish to ignore.

Markos had liked her looks, and not as a brother. Had he also liked Hilary's, so similar to her own? Had he done more with Hilary than kiss her?

'Too much and not enough,' Val said aloud. Leaning out of bed, she retrieved her laptop, hiding it under the bed away from Judy.

In the morning, back in Theo's study, Val shunted the giraffe piano away from the wall on to an old bedsheet. Before going further, she rummaged in the toolbox for a screwdriver and soon was absorbed in her task. Only a call of nature forced her to break off and leave the study.

From the second-floor landing, she heard a tinkling coming out of the music room. Could it be Chloe? She hurried downstairs.

It was the cleaning lady, dusting the piano. When she saw Val, she grinned and beckoned. 'Will you play something for me?'

'Yes, Val, do.' Now dressed, and carrying a vase of drooping lilies, her hair immaculate in a soft pleat, Alexia walked in from the dining room. 'Go on – I know you want to. Chloe won't be back for ages, and I know she never minds you playing.'

'Thanks,' said Val faintly, as Alexia, flower vase in both hands, disappeared downstairs determinedly humming a Greek love-song. She entered the music room with mixed feelings. The formal rooms of Cypress House were grand affairs and this space was no exception. The music room had buoyant dolphins in the Roman-style mosaic floor, oak panels and doors, and rococo mouldings around the fireplace and ceiling.

Uneasy at having an audience, Val crossed to the piano. Chloe's piano; that was another thing she found unnerving. Just off centre, close enough to the long balcony windows so that the pianist could have light, the black concert grand streamed off into the shadows. She had advised against a Steinway, but Theo had overruled her. She had already tuned this magnificent, powerful instrument, yet she remained immune to its charm. In her opinion, Steinways were heavy to play.

Of course, Steinways were good for some things, she conceded. The piece she had in mind, for instance. She would never play it properly, but it was a challenge, something she'd always wanted to try on a concert grand.

The score of Alkan's 'Allegro barbaro' filled her mind. She played the opening bars and was off – in control, but only just. The broad spreads crucified her hands as Alkan's ruthless virtuosity rang out from the Steinway.

'No, the third finger, not the fifth, or you'll run out – look, you have!'

It was Chloe, back early. Stealing into the house through a side doorway from the garden, her entrance into the music room had been masked by the volume of the piano.

'Move up!' She came straight in beside Val, a needle-like elbow catching Val in her stomach.

'This way!' Even before Chloe had sat down on the stool, she was playing, bending into the music.

'Darling!' Luminous with pleasure, breathless from running up from the kitchen, Alexia stepped over the threshold.

Chloe stopped, put her hands up to her face and began to sob.

47

Praying she had not made things worse, Val slipped down-stairs on to the patio with the cleaning lady, leaving mother and daughter together.

For the rest of the day Val worked on the giraffe piano. An uneasy truce settled over the villa; everyone was cheerful.

Val hoped it would last. There was no guarantee that Chloe would go on playing the piano. Looking back on what she had done, although accidental on her part, she was ashamed of pulling off a cheap trick.

She was still worrying late at night, when the house was quiet. Sitting on top of the sheet with the bedside light on, listening to the moths banging against the window mosquito mesh, she heard a gentle knock on her door.

'Come in, Chloe.' Val stopped her pretence of struggling with her business accounts and turned off the laptop. She patted the bed beside her. 'You're wondering how I knew it was you, but Judith never knocks and Steve sort of shoulders a door open. You know what I mean.'

Chloe laughed, and entered in a rush. Val moved the laptop off the mattress as her god-daughter bounced down beside her. 'Hello,' she said.

'Hello again yourself,' said Val. Chloe had been tall for her age, and sturdy, but now she looked almost weightless, floating like Ophelia through Cypress House. With her dark-brown ringlets, long-limbed, listless form and pale, studious face, she might have been returning today from a wake rather than a wedding.

'I'm glad you're here, God-mother.' Chloe's blush was visible even by the dim night light.

Val brushed her arm. 'How long have you been outside my door, dressed in nothing but a nightie and dressing gown? Get on in, silly.'

'I'm wearing knickers, too.' Burrowing under the sheets, Chloe flung the covers up around her ears. Lying in Val's bed, she looked like a slender odalisque, all eyes and eastern promise. Val wanted to rumple her silky hair, but Chloe might consider herself too old for that. Besides, her god-daughter was here for something.

'I'll put this out of the way and come in with you, if that's okay.' Val rolled off the bed and walked over to the painted chest of drawers. She busied herself with placing the laptop in the top drawer, giving Chloe the choice of whether to speak or not.

'Did Mother ask you to come here so that you could make me play?'

Val closed the drawer and turned to look at her god-daughter, wishing she could read her more easily. Apart from her full lips, Chloe had the face of a Byzantine Madonna, unreachable and old for her years. Yet somehow Val had to break through. She took a deep breath.

'Your parents would never make you do anything, Chloe. Neither would I.' She smiled. 'If I did, Judy would be practising scales and learning her notes. The thing is, I'm here because it's summer and you're family and your mother's promised me free rein over your giraffe piano.'

'The old thing in Dad's study?' Chloe chewed on a fingernail. 'It looks as if an elephant sat on it. Are you staying long?'

'The usual month.'

Chloe nodded. 'Steve, too?' she asked, elaborately casual. She and Steve had met at mealtimes, at the kitchen table.

'Him as well.' Val matched the tone.

'How old is— How much of the Alkan do you remember?'

Val was no longer smiling. She remembered everything, including being thirteen and smitten with feelings no one seemed to take seriously. 'I remember it all,' she said.

'His stuff is hard. It's great, though.'

'Intoxicating.' Val did smile now. 'Especially—'

'Don't! Not you as well,' Chloe interrupted, her naturally grave features taking on a rare sulky look. 'Mother's talked of nothing else but how pleased she is that I'm playing again, that I'm over my "little block".'

'Sounds like Greek plumbing to me.'

Chloe started to giggle at Val's feeble joke and then began to gasp.

'What is it?' Val climbed on top of the sheet and lay alongside the girl, putting out an arm to comfort and then stopping in mid-air, uncertain. 'What is it? Do you want me to talk to Alexia for you? Or your dad?'

49

Chloe was weeping silent tears. 'Come on, love,' Val whispered. 'You can tell me.' She laid her head on the pillow, close to Chloe.

Side by side, they lay for a moment in silence. Val felt the steady sleeping pulse of the house: Judith's fast, light breathing in the attic room beside hers, a mule or donkey outside yawning and shaking its ears.

Chloe said, 'Stefan Gregory says I've no talent.' There was a rustle of a tissue being drawn from a pocket. 'That's why I stopped playing.'

'What?' Val couldn't understand it. When had Stefan Gregory returned to Corfu? It couldn't be anything to do with his engagements at the Achillion – that was a far more recent development. How had he made time?

Chloe wiped her eyes and blew her nose. 'I don't really know why I bothered rushing into the music room today, except – except you were making so many mistakes.'

It stung Val that this brave little kid was trying to smile.

'You were awful.' Chloe smiled, but then sighed. 'He's right, though; he must be right. Someone like Gregory must know what he's talking about.'

'He's frightened of your competition.'

'It wasn't like that.' Chloe hid her scrap of tissue under the pillow and looked at Val with clear, pitiless eyes. 'He came to see Zennie – Mr Zeno, my new music tutor – a few weeks ago. I was there, having a lesson . . .' She gulped. 'I haven't told Mum.'

'I won't say anything. You can tell Alex yourself, when you're ready.' Val thought of Alexia's panic at the prospect of having to tell Chloe *her* news, and pitied them. It was a rotten situation for mother and daughter. She found one of Chloe's cold hands under the sheet and gently squeezed her fingers.

Chloe sighed. 'Zennie had me play for him. I knew it was going to be bad: Stefan Gregory sat completely still throughout, his fingers steepled together over his lap.'

'How peculiar.' Val was struck by the image.

'When Zennie asked him what he thought, he said my technique was "lacking" and that my musicianship was "stunted". He called me a presumptuous gnat.'

'God, how insulting! It's ridiculous to condemn you that way, after one piece. What did your tutor say?'

'Zennie didn't say anything until Gregory had gone.'

'You're sure that it was Stefan Gregory?' Surely a musician as sensitive as Gregory could not be so cruel, so stupid? 'Well, whoever it was, he's wrong, Chloe. Absolutely and completely wrong.'

Chloe shook her head. 'It was him. He left soon afterwards. I broke down – I couldn't help it. When Zennie came back into the room after seeing him off, he said we obviously had a lot of work to catch up on.'

'That's it? That's all he said?'

'No – when I carried on crying he said he wasn't sure if Stefan Gregory wasn't right. He said my going to pieces showed a lack of commitment. After that, I'm afraid I couldn't face it any more. There didn't seem to be any point.'

'He's wrong, Chloe. Both he and Gregory are wrong. Look how your music tutor has behaved. He should have told your parents what Gregory had said to you, the hatchet job he'd done on you—'

'I begged Zennie not to.'

'He should have said,' Val persisted. 'Just as he should have stood up for you with Gregory. You're his pupil, for goodness' sake!'

'Oh, he's tried to be more supportive,' Chloe went on dully, 'especially when Mother contacted him in a flap because I wasn't playing any more. But I know what he really thinks. He's after a fat lesson fee.'

'You should change your tutor. I always liked Mr Agostini.'

'So did I,' said Chloe. 'But Dad—'

'Would you like me to talk to your parents? I won't mention that fool Gregory.'

'Do you really think that?'

'Listen, Chloe.' Val brushed Chloe's hair out of her goddaughter's luminous eyes. 'I hear a lot of musicians in my business. I heard Gregory when I was about your age – Steve's age. He wasn't that special, believe me.'

This was an outright lie. Listening to Stefan Gregory playing outside the Corfu town hall had proved one thing beyond

51

doubt to Val. She would never have the talent to be a soloist. Gregory's bravura performance had destroyed her hopes. She had sat still and cold whilst those around her leaped and cheered.

'He left me completely unmoved – and he knew it.'

'Really? How brilliant!' Chloe was agog at that idea, and Val was glad that she was, although she knew Stefan Gregory would not have noticed her. An audience was a bobbing mass of faces.

Gregory would not have seen Nonno or Hilary Moffat, either, although Hilary had been sitting next to her at the recital.

Val frowned; why did she have to keep remembering Hilary? 'I'll talk to your parents,' she promised Chloe, wishing that she could live for ever in the present, without guilt. 'Will you leave it with me?'

'Yes, please.' Chloe's voice was very young, although her grey eyes looked old in her smooth face. She half raised herself, her body tensing as she moved. Her hidden hand fluttered under the sheet again.

'There was something else, a bit strange. The day after I'd been at that lesson, someone left an envelope for me at school. A big typed envelope, with my name on, nothing else. This is what I found inside.'

Chloe lifted her arm out of bed and opened her fingers. 'I think it must be some kind of joke. I didn't care for it at first, but it's been useful.'

Val stared at the thing on Chloe's palm and couldn't speak. Nestling in her god-daughter's unmarked, youthful hand was a pink novelty eraser in the shape of a pair of full, pouting lips.

Eleven

In the morning Chloe rushed up to the music room straight after breakfast to resume her practice. The young ones were off to the jetty, Steve even less coordinated than usual and Judy shrieking in delight as he and Jessica swung her along between them.

'Careful!' Val shouted, then, under her breath, 'The sea isn't going away.' She wondered whether to go alone to her father's, later on in the week, then pushed it aside.

'Why not ask Chloe if she likes Mr Zeno?' she asked Alexia, fulfilling her promise to Chloe to talk to her parents about her music tutor.

'I've already done that, but perhaps Chloe thought we'd be disappointed if she said she wanted to change.' Alexia nodded. 'Okay, I'll ask again – and I'll make sure she knows that it's what *she* wants that's important.'

Alexia closed the door of the dishwasher. 'Theo left early again this morning, but I'll warn him when he gets back.' She sighed and started the dishwasher. 'You were so clever to play for her. It goaded her into playing it better. So obvious, so *simple*. I wish we'd thought of it.'

'It was an accident, I'm afraid. I didn't know she was there, and certainly never guessed that she would burst in like that,' said Val lightly.

'What does it matter? Listen to her!'

Chloe was playing again, exuberant after her self-imposed break. Val hoped there wasn't an air of desperation in her music-making, then told herself not to be pessimistic.

Chloe had given her the novelty eraser last night. 'You can have it,' she'd said. 'It's naff. A joke.' The pink eraser was now in the drawer with Val's laptop and, as far as Val was

53

concerned, there it would stay. Chloe's parents had been through enough uncertainty these last few weeks.

Val blushed as she realized that Alexia was studying her. 'What is it?'

Alexia smiled. 'I'm just thinking what a lovely mum you are.' She laughed as Val pulled a mock scowl. 'You don't fancy telling your god-daughter *my* little piece of news, do you? Chloe's playing now, but . . .'

'There's no rush,' Val said. 'Talk it over with Theo.'

Alexia nodded. 'How are you getting on with the giraffe piano? Theo said last night in bed your estimate is tiny. You aren't making a loss?'

'No.' Val shook her head. 'And it's almost ready to go to the workshop.'

'Come on, you sad old duck.' Val was wrestling with the soundboard of the giraffe piano. She finished wrapping it in one of the old blankets she had borrowed from Alexia and leaned back on her heels to catch her breath.

'Hello? Are you okay?' Alexia knocked at the study door.

'Everything's fine,' Val called out. She had been working for hours and had no idea of the time.

'Isn't it rather silly to anthropomorphize a machine?'

'Try telling that to a musician who owns a Strad, Alex. Lots of them have names. The famous instruments. Besides, they all have a personality.'

'Yes, but they don't need to eat and you do.' Bearing a cloth-covered tray, Alexia glided over the threshold. 'You had hardly anything at breakfast and lunch is going to be late today. It's no wonder you're thin.'

Alexia heeled the door shut. 'You can also share this champagne with me. The bubbles will probably settle my stomach and, if not, the alcohol certainly will.' She smiled. 'Let's celebrate Chloe – and my other news.'

'How lovely!' Val was happy to celebrate. She stepped aside as Alexia set the tray down on Theo's desk and removed the cloth.

'Help yourself to some *tyrópittes* while they're warm.' Alexia began unwrapping the foil on the tall bottle and Val

54

ate one of the delicious cheese pastries as champagne fizzed into the narrow flutes.

'To Chloe,' she said, raising her glass.

Alexia touched her glass to Val's. 'To Chloe.'

They had taken a sip when the phone began to ring. Alexia made a face, put down her champagne and picked up the red phone. *'Parakaló.'* She listened, her scowl fading. 'One moment.' She handed the receiver to Val.

'It's for you. He won't say who he is, just can he speak to Val, please?' she said in English, a clue to the identity of the mystery speaker. Her tawny eyes sparkled with curiosity.

Val took the phone, her heart quickening. 'Val Baker.'

'It's me.' The line crackled. 'I'm in Corfu.'

'Harry. Harry?' Of course it was him, so why was she repeating his name?

'I know you're busy—'

'No, not really,' she interrupted, then wondered why she had been so quick to deny herself an excuse.

'Whatever, Val. I'm at the Demeter. If you fancy a drink one evening, this Friday, say, we could meet in the bar. Or I'll be happy to collect you, if you let me know when and where. I've hired a car.'

'It's Harry,' Val mouthed to Alexia, who was smiling and smoothing out imaginary creases in her silk sundress. 'He's staying at the Demeter.' Where Elizabeth had stayed all those years ago.

Alexia pursed her lips in a noiseless whistle.

'She's impressed,' Val inconsequentially told the disembodied Harry, wondering what her elegant friend would make of him in the flesh.

'She sounds like a nice lady,' said Harry.

'I'll tell her that. Are you on holiday?' *Don't be an idiot*, Val thought, *why else was he here?*

'Drink? This Friday? The day after tomorrow?' he prompted, as the phone popped in Val's ear. He was paying for this call and she was floating with her head anywhere but the task in hand. She'd never noticed before what a pleasant voice he had.

'Friday – yes.' An earlier command loomed in front of Val. 'Could we meet a little earlier?'

'Any time.'

'Would you like to see a real Corfiot home? The thing is, we're going to my father's on Friday afternoon just after the siesta; that's Judy, Steve and myself. You know Steve, don't you?'

'Yes, Val. I know Steve.' Harry's steady answer calmed her and she relaxed further when he said, 'Would you like me to go with you?'

Please, thought Val. 'If it's no trouble . . .'

'As I told you earlier, Val, no trouble at all.' Harry sounded as if he was smiling. 'Friday afternoon and a genuine Greek house. I'm looking forward to it. Do you want to give me the address of where to pick you up?'

He repeated the address, they agreed a time and Harry rang off.

'Bye.' Val stood with the receiver fixed in her palm until Alexia took the phone away and held up another glass of champagne.

'Earth to Valerie: beam down immediately.' Alexia waggled the flute in front of her. 'Here, drink. Loosen your tongue, my girl. Tell me everything.'

Twelve

Next morning the phone in Harry's hotel room rang early. He listened to Val's eloquent description of the hazards of driving in Corfu town.

'It's no trouble for me to drive to Komméno,' he said when she stopped for breath.

'Through Corfu town? I'm afraid you'll find it is. I'm only sorry I didn't mention it yesterday. Put that down to the heat.'

'Val—'

'I insist. We can walk to the family home from the Demeter.'

Val's old irritation with him had re-emerged in all its spiki-
ness, but then she sighed, adding, almost apologetically, 'I
need to drop off parts for the giraffe piano at the workshop,
anyway. Steve's helping me.'

So that had been that. Now Harry was waiting in the bar
of the Demeter and Val and her brood were thirty minutes
late.

Harry watched the businessmen and elegantly dressed
women sipping colourful cold drinks at low tables. He felt
out of place, a lone male unfairly laying claim to a three-
seater sofa, table and chairs. He had picked the spot because
it was in direct line of the patio doors that opened on to the
Demeter's pretty courtyard.

He plucked at his tie, aware that the new navy trousers,
jacket and white shirt were right for a family visit but uncomfortable in the heat. Staying in a former mansion had appealed
to his sense of style, but his surroundings were also a goad.

He had hoped Corfu might be a clean break for him, that
if he met Val here he would be free of ghosts. A ridiculous
misjudgement. What had he been hoping – that he could take
Nick's place? That if she walked round the little squares and
alleys with him his presence would overlay her memories?
When, since his divorce, had he ever got 'relationships' right?

Loosening his tie, tugging off his jacket and laying it on
the over-stuffed sofa, Harry drained his orange juice. At once
a waiter approached for his next order.

Harry glanced at his watch. She was three quarters of an
hour late. He drummed his fingers on the faintly slick surface
of his table, an overhead fan beating above him, stirring the
bristles on the back of his neck. Here came the waiter. Bearded
and solemn as a priest, he bent towards Harry, asking his
pleasure.

'Whisky, please.' Pointing across to the bevelled mirrors
and long, high table of the bar, Harry indicated the brand he
wanted.

Sitting on the sofa in the Demeter, he swirled the whisky
round in the glass. Val wasn't coming and the peaty, full-
mouthed Laphroaig was there: a kiss with a burning aftertaste
and no complications.

He raised his glass and drank, aware that once he started he could go on and on. Tempted, he forced himself to stop, ordering coffee and taking himself out into the small, sunken courtyard. A swift was there, weaving after insects, its wings stirring the leaves of the vines. Harry leaned against a white-washed stone wall and listened to a peal of bells.

'Harry, I'm so sorry. Judith was sick just as we were setting off in the car, sick over everything . . .'

Val was here with him in the courtyard, her feet light on the stone cobbles, her face dark with shame. '. . . We had to change all her clothes. And then Steve insisted on driving, even though he's only had a full licence for a month. We crawled from Komméno to the outskirts. We had to unload the parts for the giraffe piano, too. I'm sorry, I know you've been waiting ages.'

'Over an hour.'

He turned to look at her. She was closer than she usually came, her head bent right back so that she could see his face.

'You didn't get my message. They promised to let you know.' Bright and furious, Val swung round to the gaping black entrance behind the patio doors.

Touched by her fury towards the hapless barman who had failed to pass on her message, Harry overtook her in three strides. 'It doesn't matter,' he said, accidentally brushing his arm against hers. From the light shock of that touch, he felt her bristling indignation.

'Val, hold on, it's not important.' It was the most natural thing in the world to put his arms around her and, as her face came up to his, to kiss her.

She tasted of peppermint. The thyme of the courtyard seemed to have scented her hair, unless that was an illusion of his mazed senses. For an instant her mouth opened under his, the tip of her tongue flicking out to brush the soft underside of his top lip, more of a shimmer than a touch. Then they were both drawing away, shyer than teenagers on a first date.

Val bit her lip and said, 'You've been on the whisky again.'

Harry knew now where he stood. To Val he was unreli-able; for all her reaction, for all that she had shared confidences with him, that kiss might never have happened.

'Where's Judith and Steve?' he asked.

'Waiting for us at the bandstand.'

'Let's go.' Harry pushed through the door, retrieved his jacket and signed for the drinks. Silently, with Val trailing behind, he walked out into the swelter of the streets.

Thirteen

To Harry's surprise, Val slid her hand into his as they walked down Albana Street. 'It's Ionian Union Day today. Lots of crowds. We're going to lose each other, if we're not careful.'

'Fair enough.' Harry was careful not to squeeze her fingers. She thought him a whisky-sodden embarrassment. He wasn't going to grovel, but he was going to prove her wrong.

Curiosity overtook exasperation. 'Ionian Union Day?' he asked, as a cannon began firing from the old fortress. 'You mean the bunting isn't for my benefit?'

As he'd hoped, Val grinned. 'It does look festive – as it should,' she teased, glancing at the Greek flags hanging from the balconies of tall, ochre-coloured apartments. 'It celebrates Corfu's liberation from the British.'

'Oh, yes?' Harry stopped at a kiosk to buy a small Greek flag for Judy. Everyone was in holiday mood, locals and tourists flocking towards the Spianada. Marching bands, blasting their instruments at full throttle, seemed to be converging from every street.

'When was this "liberation"?' he asked.

'May 21st, 1864. That's when Corfu was united with Greece. It's a local holiday, when the army and sea scouts polish up their uniforms.' Val gave him an apologetic smile, ducking her head slightly as they joined the promenading families under the plane trees. 'Another reason why it's better to avoid driving in town today, unless you must.'

'Fair enough.' Harry thought that she'd apologized enough for their spat. 'Let's enjoy it, shall we?'

They were walking side by side under the trees along a crazy-paving path, passing bushes of pink oleander, yellow cacti and a stand of flowering mint with reddish-yellow flowers. Harry noticed a key-twirling local and envied the man the cigarette clamped between his lips, but was soon diverted by the blaring energy of the marching bands, the whiff of drains and the sea, a woman in a gingham dress peering intently at her euro change after buying a bunch of red tulips from a gypsy flower girl.

'Watch out!' He lifted Val's hand as they deftly avoided a toddler pushing his own buggy towards the main path. Through the shrubs and palm fronds Harry could see the wrought-iron bandstand topped with fairy lights, a place where children played tag and dogs chased each other's tails.

I could live here, he thought, relaxing into the mood of the place and its friendly, cosmopolitan feel, swinging Val's hand as they walked.

Winding round three flag-waving teenage girls in tight flared jeans and white gypsy-style tops, Harry and Val emerged from the shade of a brutally lopped plane tree on to the main path.

Judy pelted across the tarmac and launched herself into his arms. '*Thios* Harry!' She was scarlet with glee, half throttling him with chubby arms. He kissed her and she squirmed like a delighted puppy. 'Tickles!'

She tugged at his hair, to ensure she kept his attention amongst the cannon salutes. 'I've got a Lady Penelope,' she announced, as Harry watched a troop of soldiers line up by the white marble monument to the Ionian Union, the men shining in their scarlet uniforms and breastplates and cheerfully out of step in their marching. 'I was calling you Uncle in Greek.'

'I'm impressed.' Setting Judy gently back on her feet, he gave her the little flag he'd bought her and rumpled her auburn curls.

'You dropped this.' A sinewy hand tapped him on the shoulder.

Harry was ready for this younger mirror of Nick, but Steve's growing likeness to his father always struck him. The lean figure in blue jeans, with peach-fuzz-complexioned face, was Nick all over again.

'Good to see you again. Thanks.' He took the navy jacket that he'd lost in his whirl with Judy and slung it over his shoulder. He and Steve shook hands while Val knelt and tidied her daughter, retying her sash.

'How does this finish up like a corkscrew round your middle, eh, miss?'

Harry tore his attention from the pair. 'How are you finding Corfu, Steve?'

'Cool. Friendly natives.' Steve smirked at his stepmother's mock scowl. Harry laughed. 'How's your mum keeping?' He knew that Val wouldn't mind his asking after Penny.

'She's all right.' Steve was allowing Val to check his grooming, grinning but doing as she asked when she pleaded that he tuck his Iron Maiden T-shirt into his jeans.

'Please, Steve,' she said, with that strangely apologetic ducking of her head. 'It's flopping out all over your belt.'

'Relax, Val.' Steve darted after the pottering Judith to start a game of tag, disordering himself again as he and Judy sprinted towards the Maitland Rotunda, a relic of British rule now surrounded by scaffolding.

Val shook her head. 'They're going the wrong way.'

She was smiling, but Harry saw that deep V furrowed above her eyebrows. This coming family visit was an ordeal.

He took a step closer. 'Do I pass muster?'

She blushed, but answered at once, 'As a foreigner, you'll do.'

'And as a Corfiot?'

She grinned, putting a finger to her lips. 'Not quite. Rather more facial hair is required, and dark glasses, Gucci for preference.'

Steve was returning, carrying Judith upside down above several insouciant pigeons.

'Stop it, you two,' said Val mildly.

On her feet again, Judy scuttled across to claim Harry. 'Mummy calls me her little rascal.'

'Does she now?' said Harry, still watching Val. A shutter

seemed to have fallen across her face. When she spoke, her voice was colourless.

'Shall we go?'

They caught the mood from her, Harry noticed, Judith and then Steve growing quiet as they made their way back into the town, threading through packs of brightly costumed dancers from the islands. Judith's hand gripped tighter round his finger and he lifted the child to carry on his shoulders, worried that she might be crushed in this press of jostling bodies. Val was right – these streets today were hell for a driver, even a local.

He ducked with Judith under one of the lower arcades, envious of Steve walking ahead of them with Val.

'Careful overhead,' Val called back as a woman lowered a basket from a balcony into their alley to buy her vegetables from the street-level grocer. She glanced up at Judith, comfortable on Harry's shoulders and plaiting his hair with busy fingers. 'Is she okay for you?'

'She's no trouble. I imagine your father finds these streets difficult to patrol.'

'No doubt he did once. He's in the tourist police now. It's down there.' She stepped into a narrow cut between rows of windowless houses and crumbling grey walls.

'Yuk!' Judith's hands gouged anxiously into Harry's right eye and left ear. After the brightness of the Spianada, this was the underworld. There were no pots of flowers, no flags, no music from the fragile balconies above.

Val paused in front of a dark-green door set back into the wall. She extended a hand to indicate it and stepped sideways.

Harry lifted the silent child off his shoulders. Beside him Steve was tucking in his shirt.

'Hey, this will be interesting,' Val said, when Judy snuggled against her. 'You're going to meet Grandad Yiannis and a Greek grandmother – your great-grandmother. I'm going to be talking in Greek, because Granny doesn't know English. Don't worry! We don't have to stay long.'

Fourteen

V al lifted her hand to rap on the inner door, then stopped. 'They'll be out in the garden.'

She led them out of the tall narrow house, through an archway and round a corner to where a rough patch of ground ran along the backs and sides of other houses and parallel to a narrow cobbled alleyway. In this 'garden' were orange and lemon trees, both in fruit, a white iron bath, patches of scrubby grass and barley, a rose bush straggling out of a stone trough, a plastic table and several plastic chairs.

People had been here. An octopus, strung on a washing line to dry, was missing a peg and hanging at an undignified angle between the lemon and orange trees. A pile of crocheting had been left on the long, high, whitewashed step set along the sides of the house.

A lizard flickered under two plastic chairs before vanishing down a crack in the foundations of the three-storey houses. Judith had seen the creature too but said nothing; she was clasping Val's hand tightly now.

Val smiled down at her. She had already decided to do no more than her duty and then withdraw. At least she looked reasonable, her eyes hidden by sunglasses, her bobbed hair glossy, her poppy silk dress flowing in long smooth waves as she moved. Her other hand held a shiny parcel, bought a few moments before, almost as if she was coming here as a stranger.

'Sorry – the family must have decided to wait inside,' she said, turning to lead her party back indoors.

At the same moment Yiannis, dressed in casual jeans and a sweatshirt, ducked out under the lintel.

'Valerie.' He embraced her, patted Judy's head and shook

hands with Harry and Steve. 'The family are waiting inside,' he said. 'This way.'

With Yiannis's hand on her shoulder, Val strolled into the shuttered ground-floor area and entered the 'best' room. This was a large, bare square, with no ornaments on the corner table or on top of the wood-burning stove. The walls had been painted a lemon yellow, now faded to the parchment colour of many of the ikons that covered the walls. Dotted between these old gilt frames were photographs – with Judy and herself tucked away in corners.

A different family member hung in pride of place on the longest wall, beside a copy of part of Dionysios Solomos's national poem, 'Hymn to Freedom'. Strolling past the overblown photograph, Val went up to the poem and made great play of reading the Greek script. She already knew what Markos looked like. With Judy shy and silent beside her, she was conscious of black-robed women stealing into the room, followed by tumbling children.

Standing alongside her, Harry muttered, 'What now?'

Val wasn't sure. When she accepted Yiannis's invitation she had not expected to find all the extended-family members in the house. With so many people gathered here, she knew she would have little chance of searching Markos's room for Hilary's jade ring. Beside her, Harry was now wearing his interviewing face as her father reappeared behind a plump black pincushion of a woman, who wore the smile of a politician at election time.

'How are you?' Val asked her grandmother in Greek.

'Well enough,' said Irene.

'I think the family has grown since I saw them last,' Val said. 'One or two of my cousins have little ones – what are their names?'

Irene, her grey froth of curls the only relief to her black clothing and jewellery, muttered something, but made no move to introduce Val to her cousins or their new babies. Her dark eyes ranged over Val and Judith, as if probing for a weakness she could use. She carried a tray set with two glasses of ouzo for Harry and Steve, the male guests.

Irene's smile returned and never changed as Yiannis, the

man of the house, went through the formal welcome and Harry and Steve drained their glasses. Her father gave a little speech and Val's attention wandered. She had tried with her grandmother, but Irene refused to be charmed. She had not even said hello to Judith.

Val gave her daughter's hand a reassuring squeeze, aware of Yiannis staring at Irene and Irene ignoring him: the usual undercurrents.

'Come!' said Yiannis, and the family headed for the threshold, obviously relieved that they would soon be outside. Val was also grateful. She hoped to have a chance later to slip back indoors to look at Markos's room.

Stepping back into the garden, she joined Harry under the orange tree. Three of her female cousins wandered over, their faces all curiosity.

'Are you engaged to him?' asked the youngest in Greek, pressing a tall glass of lemonade into Judith's free hand. Val took a glass of ginger beer from another cousin, nodding her thanks.

'Harry's an old friend,' she replied in Greek, amused by the question.

'But he's not married to anyone else?'

Still alongside her, Harry was talking to her father in English, answering Yiannis's questions about the English police, but he broke off and smiled at her almost as if he knew what was being said.

Conscious of a blush creeping over her face, Val opened her mouth to explain, but her reply was lost in a roar of greeting.

'Markos!'

'Father.' Straightening theatrically after he entered the alleyway alongside the garden, Markos dropped his rucksack and suitcase into a patch of mallows and barley.

Yiannis plunged through the cousins and aunts and the pair embraced, clapping each other on the back. Cousins began asking excited questions about America, which Markos ignored. Instead, he shouted – in Greek and then in English – 'There has been another murder! The body of a young woman has been found at the Achillion.'

Val thought, *I dreamed of a young girl being murdered and*

the only young girl I know here on Corfu is Chloe. The first Achillion murder victim had her lips cut off, and now a crank has sent my god-daughter a tasteless pink eraser, lip shaped. Coincidences, that's all – but can I be sure?

She slipped past her excited relatives into the house. No one was interested in her except Harry and he was moving too, following her and Judy, his face stripped of its good humour so that she saw the iron beneath. Had it always been there? She was grateful for his presence, but remembered how the sweet taste to his kiss came from the whisky on his tongue.

'Excuse me,' Val said as she pushed past Markos into the best room, where she would not be disturbed. Taking a deep breath, she called Cypress House on her mobile.

'*Parakaló.*' Alexia's voice.

'Alex, it's Val.'

She could already hear Chloe, practising the piano in the background. It had to be Chloe. She listened to the beautiful, dancing chords, so alive.

'Yes, Val?'

'Sorry.' She snatched the first excuse that came to mind. 'We might be late. I thought I'd better warn you.'

'That's sweet of you, Val, but I do know what these family affairs are like. You mustn't fret about the time. After all, Harry's taking care of you now.'

Alexia rang off before Val could remonstrate. Not that she felt like scolding anyone as she dropped the mobile back into her shoulder bag. Someone's child was dead, but at least her god-daughter was unhurt.

Harry had come into the room. Swinging Judith up into his arms, he pointed out of the half-open shutters, saying, 'Would you like to play hopscotch? I think the other children are waiting for you.'

'Yes!' Set on her feet, Judy hurried outside to join in.

'Are you all right?' Harry asked. 'You look to have had a shock.'

'I'm fine.' Val walked to the window, smiling to see Judy playing.

'That's good. Is your workshop far?'

'A couple of streets away.' She had already been thinking of the workshop, her island of calm.

'I'd like to see it.' A smile hovered in his eyes. 'If it's no trouble?'

'No trouble at all.' Val stood back from the shutters, wishing they could go there now.

'You got through to the person you needed to speak to?'

Why did Harry look so keen? Had he ever looked that way in Fenfield?

'I did.' Val turned away, coming face to face with Markos.

He strode into the room, her father two steps behind. 'What's going on?' Markos demanded in Greek, but it was Harry who answered, almost as if he had understood the question.

'I was overcome with the sun,' he said in English. 'Val invited me indoors. I'll have that glass of water you offered, please, Val,' he continued. 'Then I think we really need to be going.'

'You are leaving?' Yiannis asked.

'Val promised to show me the British cemetery, where my uncle is buried.'

Val skirted round the men and escaped to the kitchen. She ought to have been angry with Harry, but she was too amused. A guest could not be denied; soon she, Judy and Steve would be away. It meant that there was no chance for her to scour Markos's room for the jade ring, but she would have had little opportunity now, anyway.

Keeping up Harry's shameless fiction, she was returning to the best room with a tumbler of water when Irene stopped her in the narrow hall.

Her grandmother stepped up as close as she could without having to touch Val and said, 'You should sell the workshop. Carlo should never have left it to you.'

Val said softly, 'The workshop is mine.'

'But Markos . . .' Irene snatched at the jet crucifix on her broad bosom, scurrying to keep pace as Val walked on.

Val presented the water to Harry. Across the rim of the glass, Harry met her brilliant gaze.

'Thank you, Valerie.' He took the glass, downing the water in a single swallow. 'And thank you for allowing me to visit your family. It has been an honour,' he said in perfect Greek, shaking Yiannis's hand and then Markos's with what looked to Val to be a fearsome grip.

The rest of the farewells were over quickly. Out in the garden, easing a path through uncles and aunts, Val collected a busy but sanguine Judith – happy to leave a hard game of hopscotch to her older cousins – and a bored Steve, and followed Harry to the top of the alley that bordered her old home. Out in the alley, Harry took her hand in his.

Fifteen

They returned to an arcaded street where they could stroll side by side, and Harry released Val's fingers. Perversely, Val was disappointed.

'Wait, please.' Harry crouched in the middle of the alley to retie one shoelace. Steve and Judith pushed round them. Judith, counting caged birds, called, 'There's another!'

Staring down at Harry, Val wondered if he was trying to put her off balance. Even as she thought it, he glanced up, straight at her. 'How about that visit to your workshop right now?'

'No cemetery?' Val teased back.

Harry laughed, but said, 'Or you go on alone there, if you want. Time in your own place.' He rose, looking her up and down, his face hardening. 'You've had enough today.'

Did she trust Harry? Could she really rely on him?

'Val.' Harry's voice returned Val to the middle of the alley. 'What do you say? A simple yes will do.'

Since when did he become so bossy? Val marvelled, uncertain what to make of this new Harry. She opened her mouth but was forestalled by Judith. Her daughter ran back up the street and cannoned into her legs.

'There's a poster round the corner of *Beauty and the Beast*! Can we go, Mummy, *please*?'

Val drew Judy out of the road and knelt in front of her daughter. Had she and Judith been alone, she would have happily gone to see her child's favourite film, but asking Steve or Harry to do so was unfair.

'Judy, I don't think—' she began, when Steve touched her arm.

'It's no problem,' he said, quietly. 'There's a film starting in about twenty minutes. Won't do me any harm.'

Harry took out his wallet and thrust a wad of euros at Steve. 'Have an ice-cream while you're about it,' he remarked, nodding at Judy.

Val admitted it made sense. Her workshop really wasn't the place for Judy and they all needed a lift after that family reunion.

'Right, but come straight back to the workshop as soon as the film's over. You're clear about the address? And you know where you're going?'

'You put Steve up to that,' she said, waving them off, watching until they had turned the corner.

'Did I?' Harry was looking past her, right over her head.

'What?' Val turned, her eye drawn to a poster celebrating the return of the 'International Performer' Stefan Gregory to Corfu. *Hear him live at the Achillion!* the poster proclaimed, a horrible irony. 'I need a newspaper, Harry.'

'There's a little shop three doors down. I'm sure they'll sell them.' Harry stepped round Val and was off. 'You'll translate the crime reports?' he called back. 'I still don't read Greek so well.'

Val trotted to catch up. 'Why do you want to know?'

Harry swung round. 'No, Val. The question is, why do you?'

'Why are you still thinking like a policeman? You're as bad—' Val stopped the rest of the complaint. She didn't want her father or Markos shadowing them, least of all Markos.

69

As bad as Nick, finished Harry in his own mind. Maybe he should go after Judy and Steve. The rest of this evening was going to be a bust.

'This is it.' Val set her shoulder to the workshop door.

'Good God,' Harry said.

'You like it?' Val was surprised. Most visitors to Nonno's workshop were overwhelmed. Nick had said, 'How do you move in here?' but Harry entered the room as she did, with a quiet confidence.

They breathed in together, sharing the scents of resin, polish and wood. His eyes were everywhere, taking in the disman- tled pianos, lighting on the old hard swatches of felt, sweeping to the stone sink in the corner and up the walls with their shelves and tools. He turned about in a circle.

'Whenever I picture you at work, I'll always see you here.'

Val nodded, swallowing. She was foolishly touched by Harry's sensitivity and ashamed of her earlier churlishness. 'I'm sorry.'

'Don't apologize. You say sorry far too much.'

She walked over to him. 'Bend down – you've got a cobweb.'

Harry half crouched and she lifted spider and web off the bronzing temple close to his left ear, marvelling at the Viking hair, the thick golden brows and eyelashes, pitying his slightly receding hairline. She dangled the spider on the closed shut- ters, startled by her own disappointment that Harry had made no attempt to touch her in return.

The heat's getting to me, she thought, turning from the shut- ters straight into Harry's arms.

'Hello,' he said.

'Hello back.' Aware that the next move must come from her, she transferred the local newspaper from her left hand into both hands, gripping it in front of her, and rested her head against his breastbone.

There was no sense of wonder, or fireworks, as there had been with Nick. Val was oddly divorced from her senses. She didn't want more than this floating peace. 'I can't—'

'Sssh. It's all right.' He brushed her jaw with his fingers, seeking her chin to raise her head. 'I only want to look at you.'

'You've seen me lots of times,' Val muttered at his stomach.

'True, but not here.'

'We're not in Fenfield,' she agreed, and lifted her face to his.

In the distance there was a knocking. Val didn't connect it with the workshop until Harry placed a warning finger on her lips.

'Let me in!' Markos hammered on her door. As Val tensed, he kicked the solid black wood of the outer door and left without noticing it was unlocked.

'That was lucky,' Val said, as his pounding feet faded away.

Harry spread a hand across the middle of her back and teased her closer. 'You've already told me about Markos, but am I missing something?'

Val batted him with the paper. 'Stop being a copper. It's not important.'

'Isn't it?'

'Leave it alone, Harry.'

'Fair enough, Val.' He released her and strode to the window, strumming his left hand down the length of one shutter. 'What about that newspaper report you wanted to see?'

Sensing that even this activity would be the prelude to more questions, Val spread the paper on the bench. Harry came to stare over her shoulder.

'Well?' he prompted above her, leaning on his braced arm, his palm spread on the bench amongst a tiny, forgotten pile of old wood shavings.

'It says very little.' Even as she scanned the pages covering the latest murder, she wondered just how much her companion understood. Not only about the body found at the Achillion.

'A young woman's naked body, discovered amongst trees in the grounds of the Achillion,' she paraphrased. 'No one seems to know who she is, what nationality. It says she died of a broken neck.'

'Her killer must be physically strong, then,' said Harry.

Val's fingers traced the lines. 'The paper speaks of other

71

wounds that the police won't disclose. It doesn't say she was raped, but people are already talking about the Achillion killer striking again.'

'How many times has this happened? Bodies of naked young women found in a well-known beauty spot?'

'I wouldn't call the Achillion beautiful.'

'Tourist spot. Whatever. What's going on, Val? When Markos trumpeted his news, you went white.'

Why did she feel tempted to confess? 'It was years ago,' she said, covering her confusion by folding up the newspaper. 'An English tourist called Hilary Moffat was killed here. She vanished from Corfu town and was found raped and murdered in the grounds of the Achillion the following night.'

'What distances are we talking here? Between Corfu town and the Achillion?'

'About ten kilometres. An easy road south.'

'So it's likely the killer had some kind of transport. And possibly an appealing manner, to lure the girl into it?'

'I should think so.' Val had considered these points long ago. 'It would be hard to snatch someone off the streets: too many people would see.'

'Were there any suspects the first time?'

Val shook her head. 'I don't know. The newspapers never mentioned anyone. No one was charged.'

'And the first victim was also naked?'

Val nodded, blushing as Harry looked at her, his head tilted to one side so that he could see all her face.

'You knew her.'

'She was a music student like me, that's all.'

She expected more – what, she couldn't say. More questions, possibly. Instead, Harry's face closed down as she spoke.

'I see.' He returned to his vantage point beside the shutters.

'What? What do you see?' Val became more exasperated as Harry smiled – and not a pleasant smile.

'Not comfortable, is it, being shut out?'

'I'm not . . . It's difficult . . .' Val stammered, alarmed by her unexpected wish to please Harry. 'I'm probably crazy, anyway. Too many dreams.'

Harry wandered back to her, reached under the bench and

lifted out her tall stool. 'Why don't we start again? You sit here and explain as much as you feel easy to tell me.'

Val sat on the stool and glanced at her watch.

'We've plenty of time. The film won't have started yet,' Harry coaxed.

'I know.' Anxious about confessing her involvement with Hilary, Val chewed on her lower lip.

Harry crossed the stone flags yet again and peered through the gap in the shutters. 'Nothing you say will change my good opinion of you— Hello! There's someone outside. He's coming here.'

A brisk rattling at the inner door.

'It's not Markos,' Harry whispered. 'Wait, he's coming back out into the street again. You can see for yourself.'

Val squeezed into the gap on the crowded workspace floor beside Harry and the window. Setting her eye to the crack, she inhaled.

'That's Stefan Gregory,' she said.

'The pianist? What does he want?'

Intrigued, Val opened the shutters.

Sixteen

Alerted by the creak of the shutters, Stefan Gregory turned.

'Mr Gregory?' Val spoke in English so that Harry would understand. Her 'plain' Fenfield policeman, who had recognized Gregory's name at once, stood in the lee of one shutter to listen. 'Is there something you wanted?'

The pianist marched back over the cobbles, his handsome face glowing. 'Ah, madam. I would be grateful if you could come with me and look at one of my pianos. To drive there will only take a few moments.'

Val leaned out of the workshop window. 'I regret, Mr Gregory, that I can't oblige you. I must collect my children.'

Gregory's lean, clean-shaven face grew longer, then the clouds on his long forehead chased away, leaving only smooth skin framed in neatly combed short black hair.

'But they must also come!' Gregory's English was oddly colourless and certainly not his first language, but his smile was charming.

'I think that would be tricky.'

'I could find Steve and tell him to get himself and Judy to my hotel when their film's over,' suggested Harry quietly. 'The Demeter's just round the corner from the cinema. There's TV and soft drinks in my room. Feta-flavoured crisps, even.'

'That's not fair on you,' Val whispered.

'It's no trouble to me.'

Bending out over the sill, Val spread her palms in an open-handed gesture that Harry knew well. 'I'm sorry, Mr Gregory. My children are at a film and I can't simply leave them. Do you need the repair for today?'

'Absolutely! For tonight.'

Val was too much of a professional not to help a musician with a damaged instrument, but she did wonder what would happen if she said, 'You hurt my god-daughter, now see how it feels to be let down.'

'Mr Gregory, it's a pity you didn't come to me earlier. Even simple repairs can take hours. Glues and resins need to harden, and so on.' This was true and it gave Val no pleasure to admit it. She was also puzzled. If Gregory had a problem, surely he would have spotted it sooner than the late afternoon before a recital?

'But it only began this morning! A distressing buzz. I have looked over the instrument and can find nothing wrong.'

'Has the piano been moved?' Val asked. 'Has anything been changed in the room?'

'My housekeeper placed a glass vase on a low table behind the piano. But that is several metres away.'

Val let out a breath. 'I think you'll find that the vase is the source of your irritating buzz, Mr Gregory. It may be resonating in sympathy with your instrument. I would go home and remove it.'

Gregory was shaking his head. 'Please come and see for yourself. I will naturally pay for your time.' He named a substantial fee, way beyond what Val normally charged. 'Please come,' he repeated, and, before she could answer, 'If you can repair it, will it need to be retuned?'

'I can tune it if you wish. I wasn't aware that you performed at home.'

'At my villa. A private recital, to which you and your family are invited. My first since my most recent return to Corfu.'

His first recital before his appearance at the Achillion, Val amended in her mind. 'Your villa contains many instruments?'

'Ah, yes, but, to respond to your delicate, unasked question, none of my other pianos is suitable for this recital. I will be playing Liszt and late Beethoven. I have a Bechstein, designed specially to withstand the demands of the virtuoso performers of the day.'

'You wish to play your nineteenth-century music on an authentic instrument?' A pity you did not show similar empathy to a fellow student of the art, Val thought. 'If it's not the vase that's our culprit, I may not be able to restore your Bechstein to full performing order today.'

'Please – if you could only do your best.' Gregory walked to the window, close enough for Val to shake his hand. 'Please? Otherwise I will have many disappointed guests. The mayor of Corfu, the chief of police . . . and that charming woman Alexia, whose last name I can never remember. I phoned her less than an hour ago and she was delighted to accept.'

Of course Alexia was delighted, Val thought, as the names of other dignitaries were reeled off for her to be impressed. Alex would love this impromptu recital of the big romantics. Perhaps it was fortunate, though, that Gregory did not appear to have connected his 'charming' music contact on Corfu with Chloe. Gregory had treated her badly and inviting Alexia to one of his recitals did not come close to restoring what he had done.

Gregory was still trying to persuade her. 'I have come to you because your workshop is known throughout Corfu. When

75

you are on the island, you are the *best*. Will you say, then, that you cannot help me?'

His question stung her pride, as intended, but Val found herself touched by the air of desperation that was stealing over Stefan Gregory. With the sun gone behind the tall buildings but its heat still grilling the streets, he was tired, hot and anxious. He was ten years older than when she had last seen him, and now he was starting to look it. He was also wearing odd socks: one grey-blue, one grey, a trivial detail that made him reassuringly ordinary.

Val checked the time again.

'You've got an hour,' Harry softly confirmed.

'Come in, please,' she invited. She felt she could not do otherwise. It was what her grandfather would have done, and it wouldn't be the first time that she had dealt with a client whom she disliked. 'I'll open the door for you.'

She was speaking to empty air. Gregory had entered through the unlocked outer door and crossed the foyer to her inner doorway.

'What a superb acoustic you have here,' he said, as Val held the door open for him. 'It must be a constant stimulus. I believe in such things, although some lessons are painful.'

'Is that so?' muttered Harry from the window.

Stefan Gregory ignored the interruption – or, more accurately, failed to register any other presence but hers, Val realized.

'It was you . . . It is you!' he said. 'I hoped that it was. My recital in the open air at Corfu town hall, seven, no ten years ago. You were there, in the audience with your grandfather, whom I knew, of course.'

Discomforted, Val realized that her earlier white lie to Chloe had turned out to have some basis in reality. 'I'm surprised you remember, Mr Gregory.'

'I have never forgotten.'

'Perhaps if you tell me more about the Bechstein?' she suggested.

'Why not see it for yourself? My villa is close.' Gregory strolled into the room. Without asking, he removed Nonno's black waistcoat from its lathe, smoothed it out and replaced it. 'I like to see clothes in their proper creases,' he remarked, smiling at Val's astonishment. 'But what do you say? I have one of those pretty little carriages waiting for us at the end of the street.'

Judy would love that, thought Val. Gregory must be doing well to be able to afford the rates of one of those carriages and just have it sitting, waiting, close to the alley.

'The carriage will naturally return you here.'

'Within the hour?' Val felt churlish, but she did not want to be too long away from Judy. Or Harry, she realized, with a touch of exasperation.

But Harry had other ideas. 'That's good, Mr Gregory. I'd welcome a ride in a carriage, just to have had the full tourist experience.'

Stefan Gregory shook a white handkerchief out of his jeans pocket, glancing from Val to Harry. 'You are not alone. I did not realize.' For an instant the handkerchief hid his expression as he wiped his aquiline nose. He turned to Harry. 'You are not a musician, I think.'

'I know music,' said Harry, utterly unabashed as he gave his name.

'Not a musician.'

'If we were all music-makers, you'd have no audience,' said Val, nettled by Gregory's dismissal. She caught hold of the outer door again. 'Shall we go to your piano, Mr Gregory? Time passes.'

Her first problem was the absurd dilemma of whether she should sit next to Gregory or Harry. As she hovered beside the four-seater carriage, Harry settled the matter. 'You must sit beside Mr Gregory, Val. You'll have things to discuss.'

She had picked up her chunky leather tool bag from the far end of the workbench, but Harry took it from her.

'Hey!' Her arm stretched after the thick brown bag. Harry simply offered his free hand to help her into the waiting carriage.

'This isn't Jane Austen,' she muttered, taking the proffered fingers and giving them a playful squeeze as she swung herself into the horse-drawn vehicle. Harry placed the bag gently on her lap, by which time Stefan Gregory was on the plush blue seat beside her.

They stopped almost at once, at the edge of the old and new towns, for Val to drop in at the Orfeus cinema. Soon Steve was standing in the right side-aisle of the air-conditioned auditorium, assuring her that he had got the message. 'Demeter after the flick. Room 314 – Harry's warned reception.'

'Now there are forty-five minutes,' Stefan Gregory remarked, when she clambered back into the carriage. Val nodded, opening her tool bag and checking its contents as the carriage turned to go down the coast road.

'What do you think of Corfu, Mr Gregory?' Harry asked. 'Do you know the island well?'

'I maintain a villa here: I have always enjoyed the island. For the rest, I know Corfu well enough to know that its public pianos can be a menace.'

That would explain his appearance on Corfu a few weeks earlier, Val thought, when he had treated Chloe to the 'benefits' of his opinion. It made sense: Gregory had many engagements in Italy, and the journey between Italy and Corfu was brief.

'So would you consider the level of classical musicianship in Corfu to be low?' Harry asked. 'There is surely a tradition of western music-making here, because of the Venetian influences.'

Val did not bother to listen to the reply. By engaging him in conversation, Harry had given her the freedom to consider Gregory at leisure.

The way he sat was instructive. The carriage was roomy, but the pianist had crammed his long legs into the corner farthest from her feet and had folded himself neatly into the smallest possible space. This was a huge contrast to his behaviour in the concert hall, where he played with complete abandon. His habitual expression off-stage, while he wrangled with Harry over the merits of modern Greek composers, appeared to be a frown.

Opposite her, Harry was clearly enjoying the ride, his fingers drumming the trot of the horse's busy hooves, his body rolling with the carriage. Stefan Gregory never stirred. He stared straight ahead, even when vehemently disagreeing. 'You cannot say that Greek music is more rhythmical than jazz . . .'

The highly strung virtuoso, fretting about his piano, Val thought. So why had he hired a carriage? A taxi would have been quicker. If he had done it to impress her, his behaviour became even stranger. By no sign did he acknowledge her presence. It wasn't shyness – even shy people glance at you occasionally, remark on the passing sights. Val was shy, and she knew what it was like. Perhaps it was focus: Gregory might be a man who could only deal with one thing at a time, people as well as music.

The black horse and carriage meanwhile brought them down a steep hill, past gardens full of palms and bougainvillaea, their flowers as delicate as tissue paper in the early evening light. With the sea and a view of mountains on one side and the Corfu Palace Hotel on the other, they ambled along the wide, level road. Val turned to watch the boats in Garitsa bay, floating between the wide blue of sea and sky. There was a warship in the bay, and on land, fast approaching, the off-white obelisk dedicated to Howard Douglas, once Lord High Commissioner to the Ionian islands. The carriage turned at the obelisk and Val relaxed as they trotted into the quieter streets in Garitsa. Here the horse picked up speed as they entered Mitropolitou Athenassiou road, with its modern flats and faded nineteenth-century mansions.

I am here, Val thought, enjoying the sun, the sparkle of the sea, the laughter of children playing on the swings, and another victim lies under plastic at the Achillion. Was it the same killer who had murdered Hilary? Was Markos somehow involved with this latest victim? No, that was impossible. Markos had only just arrived back from America – hadn't he?

A creak of the carriage wheels warned that they were stopping. She picked up her bag and stepped down in front of a large stuccoed villa freshly repainted in sandalwood, with black windows and doors. She wanted to ask if Gregory had chosen the decor, but he was still sparring with Harry.

79

'No! The finest flowering of Italian music must be the madrigal.'

Shading her eyes, Val admired the froth of wisteria spilling across the front of the villa. Behind her she heard the horse and driver crossing the road towards a green border of trees close to the sea, where they could rest in shade. She hurried forward to catch the driver to thank him, but found Gregory stepping straight in front of her.

Again, with that apparent selective blindness of his, he had not noticed her, but was pointing something out. Val also looked up, smiling at the graceful ironwork on the balconies but mystified as to what was being debated now.

She tuned in to Gregory's voice. 'You see the proportions, the striving for the golden mean? That is what, musically, I believe their madrigals were seeking to achieve.'

'Strange, I'd have said a celebration of death and sex: two universal obsessions,' remarked Harry.

He knew she was listening again and turned to include her. 'What do you think, Val?'

His action finally alerted Gregory, who took in Val and her tool bag as if seeing her afresh. She had half an hour now, although her own personal urgency had largely disappeared. Steve and Judy would enjoy poking around the room at the Demeter and since Harry had no secrets . . .

Don't be naive. You've been mistaken about this man for far too long.

She brushed the thought away. 'Mr Gregory, may I see the piano? You did say it was urgent.'

'But naturally! Follow me, please.'

Gregory led them with swift steps up a long staircase and into a first-floor drawing room that was strangely familiar to Val. She paused in the doorway. The plain white walls and those starkly elegant black and white floor tiles, with the walnut stock of the Bechstein glowing softly against the bare walls . . . No, it was not a Bechstein that she'd seen before in this kind of setting, but a Broadwood. Beethoven's Broadwood, housed in a recreation of his flat in Vienna. Stefan Gregory must have been there, too: his music room was clearly an act of homage.

80

There were differences between the two, Val noted. This room was larger, with a higher ceiling, and two French windows opening on to the balcony. At a distance from the Bechstein were several rows of straight-backed chairs, ready for Gregory's evening guests. The vase and occasional table set against the wall opposite the French windows looked out of place.

'May I try your piano?' Receiving a nod from the soloist, who had taken up a proprietorial position beside his instrument, Val tried a few scales. The buzzing began immediately. She broke off and turned to Stefan Gregory.

'Could we try removing the vase and table? The instrument is in the direct line of both. I think it's picking up their vibrations.'

'I'll phone from my study for the housekeeper.' Gregory stalked towards the door, but Harry intercepted him.

'You carry the vase and I'll get the table.' He moved to act on his own suggestion. 'Come along, Mr Gregory! This will be quicker.'

Val hurried round the grand. 'I'll help you with the table,' she began, but Harry shook his head.

'This is tiny. Will it be out of range on the landing?'

Val nodded, careful not to meet Harry's eye. She didn't want to succumb to a fit of laughter. 'If that's all right with Mr Gregory.'

'I don't care where it goes, so long as they are out of here.' Gregory almost skidded on the tiles in his haste to reach the vase ahead of Harry. 'This way.'

Harry strolled over to the back wall, picked up the table and caught up with his host.

Val returned to the keyboard. The gentle depression of middle C brought no buzz, only a warm, pleasing note. A scale of C sang. She was trying more scales when she sensed the return of the two men. Harry was grinning as if he had solved the buzz, but Gregory appeared thoughtful.

'I think that will see the end of any vibrations, but with your permission I'd like to check the piano over,' she said. 'It's a handsome instrument.'

Gregory glanced at Harry. 'Would you care to take a seat?'

'We won't be in your way, Val?' Harry asked.

'Not when I'm working.' Val opened her tool bag.

Forgetting her silk dress – it washed well – she checked and cleaned and tuned. The Bechstein was in beautiful condition: to do too much would be to gild the lily. Finally she had to admit she had finished. Reluctantly she packed up her things and rose to her feet. 'That's it.'

She had not expected effusive thanks and was not disappointed. Gregory had been trying hard to charm outside her shop; now that the job was done, the mystery solved, he was almost curt.

'My sincere thanks. You will come this evening, you and your children?' Stefan Gregory took her hand in a firm clasp, then released her. 'Mr Thompson, also?'

'Thank you, we'll be delighted. Now we must be getting back.'

Gregory nodded, homing in on the Bechstein. 'I will send you your fee.'

Don't bother, Val almost said. She picked up her tool bag and began crossing the tiles. Harry came to meet her, holding out a hand to carry the bag. 'No thank you,' she whispered.

'Mr Thompson,' Stefan Gregory called out, waiting until Harry and Val looked back. 'You asked me earlier if I considered there were any modern musicians worthy of the name in Corfu. I know of one, a charming girl, called Chloe.' Standing before the keyboard of the piano, Stefan Gregory stared at the keys. 'I may have been rude to her, but she must develop a skin to resist criticism, and quickly.'

'Surely that's not up to you?' said Harry quietly.

'I regret it now.' Gregory did not seem regretful so much as abstracted as he stroked the piano keys soundlessly. Val wanted to slap his clever hands, tell him he was wrong about Chloe.

'I suppose I was thinking of my father.' Gregory lifted his dark head to stare not at his companions, but at the blank white wall. 'He believed in "Cruel to be kind". I once gave a concert in Madrid that did not go well. Even before I had left the platform my father was on his feet in the stalls, condemning me.' He shrugged. 'He was correct. I had not prepared fully, so I did not do as well as I should have done.'

Now he turned, straddled his piano stool, sat on it and smiled at Val.

'People pay to hear me play. My father taught me a valuable lesson.'

Val imagined Yiannis condemning her in public. 'I'm sorry—'

Harry interrupted her. 'I think our horse will be well rested now.'

Gregory smiled and nodded. 'I look forward to seeing you both this evening. If you wish to bring a guest or friends with you, that is acceptable. My housekeeper will show you out.' Speaking, Gregory was also moving, swinging round to face the keyboard and adjusting the piano stool.

Dismissed, Val and Harry turned for the exit and left.

Seventeen

On the carriage trip back into town, Val sat with her tool bag next to her. Harry took the hint, bracing his body against the flimsy coachwork opposite, interlacing his fingers behind his head. Watching Val as she pointed out landmarks was almost as good as sitting beside her. Better, in one respect, because the impact of having her brush against him would have wiped out everything rational.

Amused by his predicament, Harry tried to distract himself by finding a madrigal to describe her. Gregory had been right about one thing: that marrying of sensual vocal lines and sensuous lyrics produced a form as startling as Val herself. The words and music of one recalled from his youthful repertoire suggested a part of how she made him feel.

Eyes serene and clear
You inflame me . . .

'What's that you're humming?' Val leaned towards him, blue eyes pensive, with that faraway look he found so appealing. 'It sounds like the bass line from Gesualdo's "Luci serene e chiare".'

'It is. Surprising, though.'

'That a sixteenth-century misogynist should produce such music?'

'No one said creative artists were saints. But did you hear Stefan Gregory say the madrigal is the perfect form? Rather unusual for a keyboard player.' Harry wished he had brought his sunglasses, then he could have stared at Val. He even loved the way the sun was starting to catch the tip of her nose.

Val saw through him. 'What are you needling about, Harry?'

Already back on the coast road, with a view of the old fort on its promontory, the carriage was jouncing along by the sea front and would soon be attacking the slope leading back into town. He had only minutes before Val would be swamped by Judith and Steve, and he was intrigued.

'Have you decided to forgive Gregory for whatever he said to Chloe? Don't worry,' he added, as Val coloured up. 'I doubt he knows you're connected. You hid that well.'

'Thanks.' Val hugged her knees, another habit which delighted him. *I'm a daft bugger*, Harry told himself, *but I don't care.*

'I'd say I was mollified – slightly,' Val said. 'He's a difficult person to make sense of, though. Perhaps lonely. Certainly obsessive. He told Chloe her musicianship was stunted. Can you imagine saying that to a thirteen-year-old? He seems sad.'

Nothing draws some women to a man, Harry thought, faster than a whiff of tragedy. 'Were you and Gregory ever introduced?' he asked. 'You seem to have made quite an impression.'

'No, it wasn't like that. I was stunned by his talent. I sat still and quiet while everyone else was cheering, leaping to their feet. I'm sure Stefan didn't notice. As he said, he knew who I was because of Nonno.'

Harry noted the 'Stefan' and registered Val's thoughtful expression between bars of black shadow thrown by tall tamarisk trees. He asked, 'How long ago did you say this was, again? Ten years?'

'I was Steve's age. I must have aged well.' Val laughed, but she sounded discomforted. 'Shall I tell you what I find surprising? That you hide your own tastes so carefully. Nick said you worked hard at being one of the lads.'

Her blue eyes were sparkling with amusement and something more. Val was teasing him, but she was also curious. Harry savoured her attention: even her mention of Nick evoked no awkwardness, only a grunt of agreement.

'In a police station it's best to blend in.'

'So how . . . ?'

'My choir days, when I was a lad? When I could reach top C without the operation?'

'Of course! I remember you talking—'

'That's when I got to know a lot of vocal music. We did Gesualdo for a competition. Came second.'

'Once heard, never forgotten. Why not join an adult choir?'

'On my shift pattern? I wouldn't be able to do it justice.'

Val sat back again in her seat. 'You're interested in justice, aren't you?'

Before Harry could ask her to explain, their driver leaned back on his high wooden seat, pulling lightly on the reins. Seconds later, the plodding black horse halted opposite the cinema. Harry tipped the driver and Val thanked him, both of which the man accepted with a '*Parakaló*' before cutting straight across traffic to return to the taxi rank close to the Liston.

'Now shall I carry that bag?' Harry asked.

Val grinned. 'I move grands around.'

Falling into step beside her, Harry took her free hand, as she had done his earlier that day.

Glancing down at the delicate fingers wound round his, Harry shook his head. Val's unexpected strength – a wiry toughness that was as much mental as physical – didn't surprise him, but her family had been worse than expected. Stefan Gregory was another odd one. Gregory in particular troubled him, and it was more than the gripe of jealousy. He wondered what would come out if the man were pushed.

'I don't think Judy and Steve are going to be interested in tonight's recital,' he said, strolling under the canopy of the Demeter. 'Why don't we take Chloe with us? Gregory did say we could bring along more friends.'

Val accepted the 'we' without a qualm. 'I was wondering that myself. Chloe might leap at the chance to come, although Alexia is going to be there, too, and that might be tricky. Chloe wants to tell her mum about her encounter with Stefan Gregory in her own time, and I have to respect that. I need to talk to Chloe, see what she wants to do. I don't think Alex needs to know about Gregory's rudeness just yet and I think it would do Chloe good to see Gregory perform, hear some of his inevitable wrong notes. It would give him a chance to redeem himself.'

Only if he's generous enough to take it, thought Harry.

'But Chloe might not want to face him, and she can't be blamed for that.' Val flicked Harry a look. 'In the end it may be just us.'

'Should be interesting.'

'Yes.' Val chewed her bottom lip. She was cool again, preoccupied. As they entered the foyer of the hotel, she detached her hand from his. 'I'd better go collect Judith and Steve. There isn't going to be much time to get back to Komméno, get Judy her tea and find out if Chloe and Alexia are coming. I do hope Jessica won't mind babysitting.'

'I don't suppose so. It's part of her job.' Harry touched Val on the shoulder. 'Do you want to wait here in the foyer? It might be quicker if I fetch them down – they'll want to tell us both what's been happening.'

Val nodded, stifling a yawn which showed how much the family visit had taken out of her. He was glad to leave her on one of the hotel sofas, and took the stairs to give her a few moments longer in peace. He also wanted a few seconds alone.

Stefan Gregory and madrigals. Harry kept returning to that as he took the oak stairs two at a time, the smell of dust and old polish heavy in his nostrils in the gloomy stairwell. Why would a solo pianist revere the vocal part music of madrigals so much?

Striding along the plush corridor to room 314, Harry wished that Gregory's favourite madrigal composer was not Carlo Gesualdo. The sixteenth-century renaissance prince had been a fresh and inventive composer, celebrated throughout Europe. Harry admired him.

He wondered how much Stefan Gregory knew of his idol's private life. What had he called him? 'A prince in life, a God of music.'

'Artistic exaggeration,' Harry muttered. 'You just don't like Gregory.' Which was true, except that Gesualdo, in the late 1580s, had murdered his wife, inflicting multiple stab wounds on her genitals.

It means nothing. Harry rapped at the door of number 314, hearing muted scuffles inside. 'Open up, police!' he called, and the scuffling turned to laughter.

Reunions complete, Harry walked Val and the others to their car. Val would return the tool bag she kept at the workshop later: right now there wasn't time.

Smiling apologetically at Steve, who had wanted to drive, Val slid into the driver's seat and turned the key in the ignition.

Nothing happened. She tried again, with the same result.

'I'll take a look.' Harry began checking the obvious: spark plugs, leads.

'Oh, no,' Val said, as he dashed his head on the inside of the bonnet.

'What is it?' he called, refusing to rub his skull.

'The lights were pushed on accidentally. It's the battery.'

Harry dropped the bonnet down. 'I'll drive you to Komméno. Don't worry about this – I'll sort something out. There isn't much time now.'

Transferring everyone to Harry's hire car took more time, with Steve wanting to sit in front with Harry and Harry insisting that he needed Val's navigational skills. 'In fact, why don't you drive – at least out of the town,' he suggested. She accepted with such alacrity that Harry was amused, although he was less so when he found Steve in the front passenger seat.

'Val knows where she's going,' Steve pointed out, waving impudently to Judith, who took no notice. Poised to climb into the small Fiat by one of the back doors, Judy turned to her mother. There was no child seat and she was clearly bewildered. 'Where do I sit?' she asked plaintively.

'You sit next to me in the back and show me how to work the seat belts,' Harry said. 'Here's the keys, Val. She'll be all right with me.'

'Thanks.' Val ducked under his arm and opened the driver's door.

Once outside the sprawl of the outskirts, where the car showrooms gave way to builders' yards and then views of the sea, Val began to put her foot down. Beside her, Steve was urging for more speed: 'Come on, Val, this is the Corfu motorway!'

Smoothly overtaking a bus, Val thumbed her nose at her stepson, who raised his ginger eyebrows just as Nick had done whenever she teased him. In her rear-view mirror, she saw Harry listening to Judy's exhaustive account of *Beauty and the Beast*. And behind them a red car, very close.

Belle had just reached the enchanted castle when Val roared the white Fiat past the Jungle Club. At this pre-party, pre-midnight hour, the place was deserted, shuttered and quiet. Seeing it reminded Val of her own evening engagement. 'Steve, would you like to come to Stefan Gregory's recital?'

'No thanks, but you can drop me off at the Jungle Club on your way back in.' Steve was watching a curvy blonde in a blue thong and tiny top strolling along by the highway.

'That's fine.' Val kept one eye on the traffic and another on Judith, checking for signs of car sickness. 'Have you cash for a taxi home?'

'When you give me some.' Steve grinned.

'Now that you've seen a couple of Corfu coppers, what do you think of them, Steve?' Harry shouted through from the back. They all had the windows open. Judith had become bored with the film story and was settling down with her thumb in her mouth. 'I know you're interested in joining the police, so were you impressed?'

'Not much. They fancy themselves.'

'I won't argue with that.' Val wrenched on the wheel to avoid a moped which shot out of a driveway of a low house straight at the Fiat's headlights. Perhaps more disturbingly, the red car had been following them closely for a while.

'But I do want to meet Yiannis again,' Steve went on. 'Maybe at his office, where hopefully he'll talk about work, and leave out superman Markos.'

Steve stretched both palms over the baking dashboard. He dipped his head under the sun visor, looking ahead and inland.

'Our turn coming up,' Val said. They had already passed the turn-off to the beach resort of Kondokáli.

Almost in answer, a gentle snore slipped from Judy's rosebud mouth, along with her thumb. Steve was looking about and Harry looked round, too, half turning in the short, sticky seat.

He couldn't miss the big red Mercedes now cruising inches behind. Its number plates were obscured by mud, and its closed windows were black tinted glass. He watched the red car as they turned off the main highway. The Merc was still suffocatingly close. Harry gestured to the unseen driver to fall back, his eyes catching Val's in the rear-view mirror. Neither spoke.

An olive grove, the first she had noticed since leaving the town, flashed into view in a wash of grey-green. Steve laughed at a fat paraglider drifting above them in the middle distance. Val watched the Mercedes.

'Here we go.' Steve flipped his baseball cap back on to his spiky curls. 'Our turning to Komméno.'

Val whipped the Fiat into the turn by the olive grove. In the back, braced so as not to roll on to Judy, Harry kept his eyes fixed on the wing mirror. Through the dust of their new road and against a tall hedgerow of what looked like blue bindweed, the red Mercedes rippled back into view.

Harry slipped out of his seat belt and hung his head between the front seats. 'How long has this guy been velcroed to our bumper?'

'Since we left the outskirts,' Val answered. 'Possibly before that, when we started out from the Demeter, but I can't be sure.'

'Anyone you know?'

'No.' Val accelerated past a lorry carrying building rubble and steered the Fiat around another sharp corner, attempting to put distance between herself and the stranger.

'Maybe they're driving to Komméno.' Steve didn't sound convinced.

'Let's get off this road.' She turned off the metalled road down a track signed for the little church in the Komméno bay, a church that Alexia and others at Cypress House could see from the house's gardens.

'We can't be being menaced by a car with black windows! That's Hollywood.' Steve flinched as the Fiat plunged into shadow, running between cypresses. 'Who knows us? Why would anyone bother?'

The Mercedes hit the back of the car, shunting it towards the water.

Val wrenched the Fiat into a corner where the track divided into two lanes separated by a line of small cypresses. Above Judith's wailing she heard the whine of the car behind them, then a squeal of brakes as the driver misjudged the turn.

She hauled on the wheel, driving the little car into the wild garden of a ruined villa through a narrow gap hidden from the main track by old olive trees and lush vegetation.

Judith was slipping from her seat belt, the straps too slack and high to secure the wildly kicking little girl. Harry lunged across and caught her as she fell from her seat. Everything seemed slower than it should be. *Please let him hold her safe*, thought Val, her fingers and arms turning numb on the wheel. No gunning behind them now. The red Mercedes was speeding towards the little headland church of Holy Ipapanti. It had lost sight of the Fiat on the last corner, Val's manoeuvre shielded by the stand of cypress. Now the big car was racing to catch up, its turbo receding into the distance as it roared past the overgrown entrance to the ruined villa.

The Fiat was slowing as Val worked down the gears, her eyes not on the choke of weeds ahead but on Judith and Harry, who must stay together.

She felt a judder as the car stalled, and was out of the driver's seat and round by Judith's passenger door the instant it stopped. Dragging the passenger door open, she stroked Judy's head and trembling body and Harry's braced arms.

'All gone, all gone,' she was saying.

By what looked to be a deliberate effort of will, Harry opened his hands and Val gathered up her daughter.

Eighteen

Harry drove the rest of the way. Judith and Val sat in the back, Judy on Val's lap. Steve gestured importantly towards the seatbelt. Val's eyes glittered.

'Leave it, Steve,' Harry said. 'They're mother and daughter. Come up here and show me the way.

'Come on,' he urged, as the young man drifted towards the rear of the Fiat to see what the Mercedes had done. Phoning the police could be done on the move.

Steve stalked back and Harry started the engine.

He could hear Val singing to Judith in Italian, a lullaby which she must have learned from her grandfather. Strangely, the simple, repetitive little tune soothed him, too, and he reversed the car from the garden of the ruined villa without any sense of foreboding.

The Mercedes was gone, and even if it turned round – as it must when it reached the headland where the little white church of Holy Ipapanti overlooked its side of Gouvía bay – the car would not catch them now. Driving back to the main Komméno road, Harry followed Steve's increasingly firm directions, picking up speed before stopping close to the ornamental urns that marked the turning to Cypress House.

'What is it?' Steve asked. Over the last mile he had watched how Harry drove, rather than craning this way and that in search of rogue cars.

'Come and see.' Harry opened his door and set off without

waiting for Steve. 'We're looking for skid marks, tyre marks, bits of dropped red paint, discarded cigarettes. You look that side.'

Steve stopped before Harry and stood in the middle of the narrow road, scratching a bruise forming by his collarbone. 'Doesn't seem to be anything. That's good, isn't it? That means the Merc driver doesn't know about Auntie Alex's house – or hasn't twigged that we're staying there.'

'Well done.' Harry smiled at the boy. Rattled, Steve looked as if he had been through a hedge.

'Go tell Val, she'll be pleased to know.'

Steve broke into a loping run, rather slower than usual. Harry spent another few seconds trying to convince himself that the Mercedes driver didn't know where Val was staying. So far as he could tell, the red car had passed here at speed, but that meant nothing. The driver could have already learned that Val was living here.

Harry returned to the Fiat. Val would not meet his eyes, which probably meant that she had drawn the same depressing conclusion but wasn't about to admit it.

'How are you?' he asked, sitting sideways in the driver's seat.

'I'm not sure.' Val was glowering, hollow eyed. 'Angry.' She kissed the top of Judith's head. 'That driver didn't care.'

'You did well.'

'So did you.' Val rocked Judith, the child stunned but sleepy, her tiny sunflower face losing its pinched look. 'Thank you for giving her back to me.'

They looked at one another. Steve was frowning at the mobile: Harry could see him but the young man seemed a long way off.

A donkey brayed somewhere on the Komméno point and turned the instant to comedy. Val squirmed slightly in her seat and Harry twisted to face forwards. Her voice followed him.

'You don't know yet, do you? It hasn't begun to smart. Shock, I suppose. But your waist . . .'

Harry had been aware, all right. The seat belt had left burn marks on both sides of his body. He lifted his jacket off the seat and put it on. He started the engine, embarrassed that

Val had noticed, not having realized that his shirt was torn.

'What's the number for the police, Val?' Steve called over the drone of the engine and steady *whap* of the tyres as Harry drove the Fiat through the back gates of Alexia's villa.

'Alex can be so surprising, sometimes,' Harry heard Val remark. 'She works like mad in her house to keep everything pristine, and yet in the garden she seems to adore the jungle effect. You can never really tell about people.'

'The police number, Val.'

'Don't bother, Steve.' Val shrugged. 'Sorry, but what can the police do now, except delay us with questions we can't answer? I want to go to my recital.' She grinned, shedding a dozen years. 'We'll call a taxi – this car's not going to be much use for a while.'

This car was never going to be the same again. Harry took a tighter grip of the hot steering wheel. Despite being a detective, he mostly agreed with Val about the police. They had no number for the Mercedes with its filthy plates, no description of the driver owing to the tinted glass. They could call the police at her friend's.

'I'm sorry about the car,' Val called through from the back. 'If you'd like me to come with you to the hire garage . . .'

She looked ashamed, apologizing again, and Harry hated that. 'I'll sort it,' he grunted.

'I'm sorry.' Val reached out to clasp Judith's foot. She was working her way over the child, touching each limb as if to convince herself that Judy really was unharmed. Her daughter basked in the sun of her attention, quiet but no longer troubled. By tomorrow, Harry guessed, this car journey would be a distant memory for his god-daughter.

Steve, older, understanding more, was the greater worry, particularly as he wanted to know why Val would not let him call the police. 'But that fucking Merc nearly ran us off the road! Don't pretend it was just a crazy Corfiot.'

'I resent that,' said Val. 'And watch your mouth, young man.'

'You're not taking this seriously!'

'We've got company,' Harry said quietly. He brought the Fiat to a stop.

Chloe was running along the track, her dark ringlets streaming back from her long face. Absorbing the view of her figure like a dry sponge in a rainstorm, Steve announced, 'I'm going with you.'

Shades of Markos and herself jostled in Val's memory. 'It's not your kind of music.'

'Maybe not, but it's hers.' Steve withdrew his pointing finger as though it had been burned when Chloe leaned in through his window.

'Auntie Val! I thought it was you. Hi, Judy! Hello, Steve.'

'Hello.' Steve's head was level with Chloe's bosom, so the poor lad was having difficulty concentrating. Val was relieved that he was no Markos, but she wasn't sure how Alex and Theo would react if they noticed this sudden attraction. She had started to introduce Harry to Chloe when Steve got out of the car and stood beside the tall, slender girl.

'There's a concert tonight – want to come?' he blurted out. 'It's a pianist, like you. Stefan Gregory. Val fixed his piano and he's invited us as thanks.' Steve was beaming, glad to have got his asking over, believing he was offering Chloe a treat.

'What?' said Chloe.

'He came to my workshop,' Val shouted through the back window, unable to join her god-daughter because she had Judith asleep on her lap. 'Chloe, listen to me, please. Stefan Gregory told me that he regrets what he said to you—'

'You talked about me? You and him? How could you, Aunt?' She marched away, straight from the track into the old olive and orange grove, her rigid back disappearing behind gnarled trees and sword-straight lilies.

'I'll go after her. Explain a bit.' Steve lumbered off in pursuit, tucking the Iron Maiden shirt into his baggy jeans without prompting.

Head in hand, feeling a million years old after Chloe's formal 'Aunt', Val heard him crashing through the under-growth. She groaned aloud.

Harry stared after the youngsters a moment, grinned and started the engine again. 'At least he's no longer in shock.'

*   *   *

Before calling the traffic police, Val told Alexia about their run-in with the Mercedes. Alexia was shocked and angry, but once she had railed against road rage and as soon as she had been reassured that everyone was fine, she put the incident behind her. For Val, things were more complicated.

Phoning the police, she discovered that no one there could do anything until tomorrow morning. Nothing this evening was going right.

'I'll take the Fiat in for them to look at tomorrow,' Harry said, resigned. 'Sorry to let you down again.'

'What do you mean?'

Alexia had left the kitchen by then, so they were sitting alone. With Judy drowsy on Val's lap and the twilight turning to gold about them, their situation echoed their conversations in her cottage kitchen back in Fenfield, but this was Corfu and everything was different.

'No fireworks.' Harry scratched his hair and sighed. 'No indignation against these traffic cops.'

Val kicked him under the table. 'If you're like me, you haven't the energy.' Their eyes had met in a moment of frustrated, weary understanding.

The police would do nothing tonight and neither could she. She had not been able to talk to Yiannis, she had not been able to look for the jade ring at her old home, and the thought of tackling Markos about Hilary Moffat did not make her feel any easier.

At least Alexia was happy. She was delighted to be going to Stefan Gregory's private recital, delighted that Val and Harry had also been invited, and intrigued by Harry. Now she returned to the kitchen and offered him a guided tour of the house.

'You must come, too, Val. I know Theo hasn't had time to show you round.' She nodded at Judy, limply asleep in Val's arms. 'Are you all right with her?'

'I'm fine.' With Alexia in the early stages of pregnancy, Val was relieved that her friend was not personally affected by what had happened to them and the Mercedes. 'I can always put Judy into bed when we go upstairs.'

'So long as you're sure.' Alexia, diverted by Harry asking her the age of Cypress House, was soon answering his questions. Evenings were always Alex's best time, especially at the moment. Energized by fresh company, she glowed. Her tawny eyes sparkled, her face was touched by the subtlest of pinks.

By contrast, a sense of foreboding dragged at Val as she slogged through the immaculate rooms, desperate not to show Alex how tired she was.

Transferring the sleeping Judith from one arm to the other as she followed Harry and Alex in and out of the music room, Val thought, I'm going to dream of Hilary tonight. She searched for the rage she had felt against the Mercedes, but found nothing. She wished she could talk to Chloe but, when she waved a greeting towards the orange grove, Chloe did not wave back.

Without Chloe's approval, Val knew she could not broach with Alexia the subject of her god-daughter's earlier, damaging encounter with Stefan Gregory, but by the time they reached the second floor of Cypress House, she had come to one decision she could manage. She touched her friend's arm. 'I think I'll put Judith to bed, Alex. She's had a busy day.'

'Good idea,' said Harry, smiling down at her.

Leaning over Judith's antique brass bed, Val touched the cheek of her sleeping child, then hurried from the room before she burst into tears.

On the attic landing she found Chloe and Steve. Both were hunched up under the sloping roof, and they had the bright look of fellow conspirators.

'We're coming with you to Gregory's bash,' said Steve.

'I want to sit on the front row and get in his face.' Chloe glanced at Steve to check that she had the slang right, and grinned.

Where was the shy, sturdy girl of last summer, the diffident girl of last week? Model slim and now model confident, Chloe was growing up. Val could only hope that the change was not too fast.

She made herself smile. 'That's marvellous. You know your mum is coming, too? Gregory invited her before any of us.' However much Chloe or Steve might consider Alexia's presence superfluous, Val thought that reminder was useful.

Chloe shrugged her shoulders. 'I know she's coming, of

course. I also know that when Dad finally gets out of work my mum is going to leave the recital reception and join him in town. She and Dad are going to the movies, one of those late showings of art-house films.'

Steve gave her a light punch on her arm. 'The cinema, nitwit! Chase you to the car . . .' Steve lunged at Chloe and she giggled and broke away.

'It's going to be a taxi,' Val called after them, reluctant to burst their bubble but wanting to remind Steve of other concerns.

'No problemo!' Steve's answer drifted up as the pair thundered off downstairs, leaving Val unsure whether Chloe had forgiven her.

Nineteen

Returning to Stefan Gregory's villa, only Harry witnessed the pianist's reaction when he spotted Val and Chloe amongst the guests.

Coming upon them as a waiter offered Chloe champagne, Gregory stopped dead in the foyer of his own house. Oblivious to the mayor's wife plucking at his sleeve, and to Alexia's broad smile, the pianist stared at Chloe. He stared for longer at Val, taking in her naked throat and arms, softly styled black silk trousers, gravity-defying high heels.

'Down, boy.' Harry hid his face behind a glass of mineral water, glad that Steve had gone to one of the bathrooms. He wasn't sure what to make of it himself, apart from approving of Gregory's taste in women.

After cocktails in the foyer and ground-floor former ballroom, the party retired upstairs for the recital. Gregory gave several encores, including his arrangement of Gesualdo's madrigal 'Languisco e moro': 'I languish and I die'. This he dedicated to Val and Chloe. Pointing them out on the second row immediately behind the mayor and his wife, he said of Chloe: 'If you think I'm wonderful, wait until you see her.'

Harry thought this an odd comment, possibly because of Gregory's uncertain use of English. The rest he was happy to applaud, still in a state of well-being after their 'escape' from the red Mercedes.

Twenty

Val stole downstairs from the attic. Judith was still asleep. Jessica, Chloe and Steve had retired. Theo and Alexia were clearing up in the kitchen after supper following their late night at the cinema.

Earlier that evening, Alex had been invigorated by Stefan's playing, saying that she could hardly wait for his second recital at the Achillion. 'You know I love music, and normally I do hear a lot of piano, including the big romantics, as you call them, but tonight – that was something else.'

'I'm glad you enjoyed it,' Val had said, conscious that Alexia did not know everything about Stefan Gregory and Chloe. She wished Chloe would talk to her mother. 'I'm glad he invited you,' she added.

'Naturally – I am a part of the scene here, you know.' Alexia's proud smile had faded a little. 'Do you think tonight helped Chloe? Inspired her to play again?'

'I'm sure it did,' Val answered, with a confidence she did not quite feel.

But Alexia's mood had not lasted. She returned from the cinema in high humour and sent Val off to find Harry, who was staying the night.

'He's walking in the orange grove. He says gardens smell better at night.'

Alexia smiled. 'I think that's a charming excuse to get out alone and a wonderful reason for you to go out now to find him.'

'Alex, it's quite true. He does like gardens at night.'

'Of course he does.' Alexia gave Val a brief hug. 'Go on, it's a lovely night. You're not still thinking of that Mercedes driver? He'll be long gone, probably dropping acid right now at a south-coast rave.'

'Is that supposed to give me confidence, Alex?'

Her friend shook her head. 'Don't always be so practical. The stars are bright, the orange grove smells of oranges – as it would – and there's a man wandering those paths who is dying for you to join him – it's romantic!'

As she let Val go, Alexia had one final instruction. 'While Harry is staying here, I don't want you working on that giraffe piano.' She gave a wide smile. 'Harry is our *guest*.'

Val found herself shy at meeting Harry. There was an expectation hanging over the end of the day which she was unsure whether to welcome or resent.

There were other things, too. The new murder victim found at the Achillion merged with Hilary in her mind as more details of Hilary's murder, successfully suppressed for years, battered on the inside of her aching skull.

Val bowed her head as she left the final step, crossing the cool tiles leading to the anteroom on bare feet, carrying her sandals in one hand. As she turned the handle of the door leading to the patio, she felt wetness on her hand. She lifted her arm and realized she was leaking tears. Rubbing both eyes, she turned the key. The air outside breathed fragrance, heady and cool.

She closed the door behind her, buckling on her sandals. Avoiding looking back at the ghostly outlines of Theo's orchids and bonsai, she darted along the patio. Once in the gardens, she unlatched a narrow gate and felt her way along the uneven wall until she reached the path to the orange grove.

Val started to run, trying to escape self-pity. A poppy, black against the darkness, bobbed along her arm and then was gone, back into the woody undergrowth. She ran between the orange trees. More flowers brushed against her as she approached a pergola overgrown with vines under the sooty shadow of a cypress.

Hilary's body had been found with flowers strewn about

her. Lilies, the ancient symbol of purity, with their stamens cut away, a part of their sex cut away as Hilary's had been.

No more . . .

A bat flickered out of the cypress. There was a swish of grasses, then a rush of movement as a shadow streamed over her head.

'Jesus, I always knew you'd wriggle,' said Harry, close to her ear. 'Sorry if I startled you.'

'It's okay.'

'Shall we go?' Harry gathered her in, lifting her in his arms. Stooping beneath the shelter of the cypress tree, he found the path back to the house.

'You know, you gave me quite a shock in that ghost outfit,' he said.

'My concert clothes were rather warm,' said Val, with an apologetic glance at the plain white sundress she had changed into since returning to Cypress House.

'I was joking.'

His arms were moulded against her as he drifted along the track, carrying her as easily as he carried Judith. Val leaned her head against the crook of his arm, no longer interested in asking questions.

'In Fenfield I thought you came to me because of Nick. Because I was Nick's widow and you were his best friend.'

'There was that, but it was never all of it.' He lifted her close and kissed her hand and arm, his lips hot and rough against her skin. Val could feel and taste his breath before she lifted her head, taking the kiss she'd wanted. It sent a wave of tingling heat from her scalp to her toes.

'I was wrong about you,' she said, when they broke off to breathe.

'But I wasn't about you.' He trailed a hand along her hip and thigh. His touch raised all the tiny hairs along her flanks and she pressed her breast tighter against his chest, feeling his ribs and longing to feel his flesh.

When they were halfway up the villa's grand central staircase, Val said softly, 'I can walk, you know. The attic rooms have low ceilings. You'll need to watch your head.'

Watching his head was the least of Harry's concerns, but he

set her down on the first landing, standing her off so that she wouldn't realize the aphrodisiac effect she was having on him.

Wrong move. He'd said she seemed like a ghost, but the body seen through that cotton sundress provoked a very human reaction.

'Come on.' He clasped her fingers and they moved for the next series of steps, Val stumbling in their mutual haste and he steadying her, he cracking his forehead on a beam and she pressing a cool hand against the pain.

'Do you think that Merc was just a crazy driver?' she said against his chest.

Harry tipped up her chin. 'Do you want to talk the serious stuff?'

She looked into his blazing eyes and ardent, tender face and wished that her mind and memory would be silent. A few steps away, through the first attic doorway, she could hear Judith snuffling in her sleep.

'We must,' she said.

In her attic room, with Harry standing watch in the window, head bowed towards the dark garden, Val told him about Hilary Moffat. As she recited the pathologist's report on Hilary's murder, she strode about the hot, narrow room on the balls of her feet, lightly, so that no one would hear.

She told because he had saved Judith and seemed keen to be burdened. She wanted him to know, before he became more deeply enmeshed, exactly how unreliable she was.

She told him everything. Nonno's warning letter. The lips cut from Hilary's murdered face with a razor. The pink eraser lips sent to Chloe. The ten-year anniversary of Hilary's death. Her recurring dream. Her father's finding of the body and interest in the case at the time. Yiannis's sense of failure in not solving the murder and his subsequent 'demotion' to the tourist police. A possible connection between Markos and Hilary, quite apart from Hilary's ring, which her grandfather had claimed was in Markos's possession. This second murder victim, found at the Achillion exactly ten years after the first.

'Don't they say some killers operate on anniversaries?' she asked, pleading almost for an answer.

'Ten years is a long time to wait.' Harry counted off on his fingers. 'Chloe's eraser seems nothing more than coincidence. She hasn't mentioned stalking to you?'

'No – but Markos called me Sweet Lips and Chloe was sent those lips . . .'

'Do you think Chloe is in danger?'

Val closed her eyes. 'No.'

'Where was Markos the night Hilary Moffat disappeared?'

'On duty – supposedly. A late shift. So although he could have been the man in the white shirt in the Zeus bar, it isn't very likely, seeing that he would have been due at work around that time. Unless he grabbed Hilary and took her somewhere, hid her . . . No, that's too fantastic.' Val was even more ashamed of her earlier suspicions.

'His time at the station will be logged.'

'I suppose so,' Val said. 'I've never asked. But there's still Hilary's jade ring. I believe Nonno did see Markos studying it, gloating – whatever – and I know he'd have recognized it for what it was.'

'Was his memory as good as yours?'

'Very nearly.'

Harry looked across at her from the window. 'What is it you want here, Val? Some kind of closure? People can suppress incidents in their lives for so long and then no more.'

'I don't know. Maybe.'

'Are you worried about that dream of yours, too?'

Val nodded. 'I suppose,' she murmured. 'The thing is . . .' She took a deep breath and admitted it. 'I was seven when my mother died. That was the first time I dreamed of the future,' she confessed through her fingers.

'What?'

'Two days before my mother became ill, I dreamed I was looking at her in her coffin.' Val lowered her head, hiding her face. 'A week later, I was.'

'Poor lass.' The endearment seemed wrung from him as Harry moved towards her, only stopping when Val motioned him away.

'No, let me say this and be done,' she said quickly.

'Do you often dream of the future?' he asked, resuming his place by the window.

'Sometimes. You don't seem surprised. The family resent me as a Cassandra, as well.'

'In police work you see everything. We do occasionally try using psychics to catch criminals. I've an open mind.'

'Nonno used to call me his weather glass,' Val said wonderingly, scarcely believing that Harry had understood, and accepted. More than that: he had not flinched from her. 'It doesn't make you nervous?'

Harry shook his head. 'I'm only sorry that it's caused you trouble. And perhaps, given what you've just told me, your dream is significant – but for whom?'

'I don't know,' Val muttered in frustration.

'Or is there more going on here that's to do with the past rather than the future, dreamed or otherwise? I know what Markos did to you when you were a girl was disturbing, but you're adult now. Do you feel it's time to bury the past, or confront it? Is that another reason why Hilary's death is haunting you? And do you wonder if Markos was driving that car this afternoon?'

Harry spoke to the window, but she saw his reflection in the dark glass and saw no judgement in his quiet, grave features, no condemnation.

Relief robbed her of speech, but she couldn't leave Harry as he was, banished at the other side of the room. She walked across to the hunched figure in her window, put her arms under his jacket, around the faintly sagging waist, and hugged him.

At her touch, Harry groaned and gathered her in, longing to soothe and silence, for the moment, the Neanderthal voice in his brain that had started up and was chanting, 'Get Markos'.

'I have to know what happened to Hilary,' Val was saying. 'Especially since my own family may have been involved. And now with this second killing at the Achillion . . .'

'That may be utterly unrelated.' He stroked her hair. She flinched and then relaxed against him. 'Sorry,' she said.

'No sorries needed.'

A bird began singing under the window. Further off, on the Corfu–Komméno road, a car backfired, loud as a gun shot.

They started, then laughed, embarrassed at revealing their tension.

Harry looked down at Val. In the last few moments he had been able to see her face more clearly. He ran his thumb along one of her shapely black eyebrows. 'Nearly dawn,' he said.

He tried to pull away, aware for the first time in hours of the bruises on his sides and waist. Val pressed against him. 'Harry?'

He wanted to say, *You don't have to do this as a 'thank you' for Judith*, but her blush and the unguardedness of her next confession were too honest for him to have any more doubts.

'I'm sorry, I'm not on the pill and I'm woefully out of practice,' she said in a rush, and Harry laughed.

'No worries, Val.' He ran his thumb over the swell of her breasts, tracing their abundant curve with his fingers. 'Let me take care of it.'

She tilted back her head and caught his face between her hands. 'No regrets, Harry – promise me.'

'No regrets.' Amazed at how she undervalued herself, Harry hooked an arm under those graceful legs and carried her to the bed.

Their first time was fast, a little clumsy, but glorious. Harry couldn't hold back – he had her now, and she was kissing and touching and saying his name until the last moment of speechless delight.

Afterwards, sprawled together, Val teased him for not having shed his socks.

'What about you, young woman?' He tugged lightly on her unbuttoned sundress. His other hand dived under the cotton to her warm softness, and her breath stopped.

'Someone may hear!' A blush swept over her face and breasts and arms again.

'Does it matter?'

A look of mischief crossed her face as she straddled him and stripped him, taking him inside her, fierce and tender, his Val. Except that in this searing instant of pleasure he was hers.

* * *

'Tell me again about you and Hilary,' Harry said later.

By this time they were both naked. Val lay on her stomach in the crook of his arm, blowing the blond hairs on his belly.

'I thought it was women who asked questions after sex,' she said.

'Or asked for favours after sex,' Harry teased. He cupped one of his hands over her bottom.

'Oh.' Val raised her hips in response. 'Harry, please, just don't do that, or I won't think.'

'This sounds serious.' He stopped stroking but kept his hand there. 'Yes?' he prompted, as Val remained silent.

'I do have a favour to ask,' she began.

'Go on.'

'You and Markos, you're both in the police, and I was wondering if, because of that, Markos or one of the police at Corfu station might be willing to talk more frankly to you than to me.' She shrugged.

'You mean, can I find out about the latest police report on that second murder at the Achillion.' Harry grinned at her, then added more seriously, 'I also think it's worth checking Markos's shift patterns, plus any DNA testing results from the investigation into Hilary's murder.'

Val frowned. 'Yes, but I wouldn't want you to think I'd use any part of what we've just shared, what has just happened between us to . . .' Her voice faded as Harry ran his hand between her legs.

'I don't,' he whispered against her throat. 'And I'll be happy to ask the local branch. Whether they'll share is another matter.'

He kissed her neck. The mystery of Hilary would have to wait.

Twenty-One

Just after first light, Harry retrieved Val's tool bag for her from the mauled boot of the Fiat, then came to hug her on the kitchen doorstep.

She tapped him on the chest. 'Remember, Markos is in homicide.'

'I'll be discreet,' he said. 'Leave it with me and I'll let you know what I find out.'

Val nodded, astonished at her ease of sharing, although after last night she ought to be beyond shocking. She had been wrong about the lack of fireworks between Harry and herself. This feeling had been there all the time, waiting for a catalyst.

No regrets, Val thought, waving Harry off, avoiding her face in a mirror. She and Harry had dressed, but she could feel that her dress buttons were wrong, and Harry's tie was in his jacket pocket. Neither of them had showered.

Had she shocked him? She hoped she had, then was afraid she had. Worse, she had smothered him with verbal goo, called him silly names. He had done the same.

Good for you, said Nick in her mind. She felt that he was on the stairs with her as she climbed back to the attic. Nick had always been generous.

Val lifted the latch of her attic bedroom and slid her tool bag into a corner. Knowing that Harry shared this state of expanded well-being, she shook her head. 'Crazy,' she said aloud.

Hoping to spot the hire car on the road above the villa, Val pressed her forehead against the window frame. A hanging cloud of dust marked where the Fiat had passed – no red Mercedes today. She looked out into the garden, marvelling at her sense of peace. She knew it could not last.

'Not past tonight.' She grinned and re-buttoned her sundress.

Her dreamlike state lasted until breakfast. Judy was hovering the honey spoon between her yoghurt and Jessica's black coffee as she twisted on her chair, tracking Steve. She seemed to have no memory of yesterday's car ride, but was going through a bout of hero worship brought on, Val suspected, by her awareness that Steve had been out to a recital with Chloe last night, and she had not.

'Careful, love.' Val jiggled the doll sitting next to Judith's cup. 'I think Lady Penelope is getting more freckles than you.'

'Definitely, sproglet.' Steve leaned across from his side of the table to rumple Judith's hair, almost sending his mango juice flying. At opposite sides of the table, Jessica and Chloe continued to munch croissants in puzzled amusement.

'Careful, Steve!' Val said. 'Alex, was Theo off early again this morning?'

'Afraid so.' At the head of the huge black kitchen table, looking tired again, Alexia was toying with her first mineral water of the day. 'Theo's very busy at the moment: I hardly see him.'

Val nodded sympathetically, aware that she had scarcely seen Theo on this trip. So far he had been gone by the time the rest of the household stirred. Apart from her first evening, she had hardly spoken to him. Theo had not spoken to Harry, either, beyond the formal how-do-you-dos – unusual behaviour in a Greek, even one as reserved as Theo.

'Are you going into town today?' Alexia went on. 'Oh, you will be, to the pol— to your workshop. Could I come in with you?'

'Of course, Alex, and welcome.'

Under the table, Steve's foot prodded hers. 'Don't you want the rest of that croissant? Can Chloe and I have it?'

'And me!' called Judith.

'Sure.' Discovering that she'd been staring at her freshly split croissant, Val mentally shook herself. She divided the warm half-moon into three, wondering again why Markos had been in the workshop. Had he been looking for something? Hiding something?

She did not hear Alexia until she repeated herself.

'Phone call for you.' Alexia held out the cordless. 'It'll work outside.'

Harry, already, thought Val, exasperated with herself for blushing as she thanked Alex and hurried out of the open kitchen door with the phone.

'Ms Baker? Stefan Gregory. How are you and Chloe this morning?'

'We're very well, thank you, Mr Gregory.' Val disguised her surprise. It was early for the musician to be phoning anyone.

'I insist you call me Stefan.'

'Thank you for inviting us to your wonderful recital last evening, Stefan.'

'My pleasure. But now, I would be honoured if you and Chloe would pay a second visit to my villa. You have heard my Bechstein, and I believe that you and your god-daughter would find my other pianos equally interesting. I would ask her charming mother, too, but I know Alexia is a busy woman.'

How did Stefan know that Chloe was her god-daughter, and that Alex was Chloe's mother? He must have been asking around. 'How many instruments do you have in your villa?'

'Here in Corfu? Just the three. But they are most worthy of attention. Will you and Chloe come this morning? Stay for a coffee, try the pianos, and then have my driver take you home? I apologize for not offering you lunch, but I have an appointment at twelve.'

'I'll need to check with Chloe.'

'Let me give you my phone number. I look forward to your call.'

Stefan rang off. Val phoned the police and was told that she could come in any time that day to make a statement. She walked back into the house, wanting to catch Alexia's eye before she said anything to Chloe.

Steve was less enthusiastic. 'Why you and Chloe? Why this morning?'

'He'll have a very tight schedule.' Chloe tapped her front teeth with a forefinger, rising at once from the breakfast table. 'I need to change.'

Steve put down his coffee cup, spilling the dregs into his saucer. 'You're not thinking of going?'

'Why not, Steve?' demanded Alexia, her eyes very bright.

'It's only for this morning,' Val said quickly. 'I'm sure it'll be interesting.'

Chloe was leaving but she gave a backward wave as she mounted the stone steps out of the kitchen.

'I'd like to see the other instruments he has,' Val went on, relieved that Chloe appeared to be acknowledging her again.

'Oh, well, you have to. It's your job,' said Steve. 'I bet Harry won't be impressed.'

When Val returned Stefan's call, the pianist said at once, 'Let me have your address. I am working at present. My driver will come and collect you.'

'There's no need, Stefan. We can easily make our own way.'

'No, I insist. My driver loves to show off.' Stefan gave a small laugh. 'Rather as I do. Until later?'

'Until later.'

Chloe was still changing, and Val also went upstairs. In the privacy of her attic bedroom she used her mobile to call Tattooed Spiro, a piano tuner in town. Spiro was planning to retire next year, but he knew everyone in the music business on the island, and she had often traded him favours. Val was also aware that he was delectably indiscreet.

'What can you tell me about Stefan Gregory?' she asked, when they had finished with their how are yous.

'A man worth knowing.' The old man coughed as he drew on a cigarette. 'He never forgets Corfu: has a house here and returns every year to perform.'

'Do his public recitals tend to be at the Achillion?'

'No, he rarely goes out of Corfu town. But he's a good bloke. Harsh but fair. Last year he bawled out a young pianist at the summer music festival, one of those recitals they hold in the new fortress, and then the next day the pianist took delivery of a beautiful new Steinway – a gift from Stefan Gregory.'

'Gregory shouting at a fellow musician doesn't seem professional.'

'No, but I chatted to the pianist later and he told me Stefan was right. He hadn't practised nearly enough and some of his runs weren't all they should be. He wasn't complaining – he'd been sent an incentive to do better.'

So Chloe wasn't the only person to have suffered from Stefan's double-edged nature, Val thought.

'I knew him as a boy, you know,' her contact continued. 'Stefan and his father.'

'They're from Corfu?'

'No one's sure where they're from, but I remember Stefan giving a recital in the new fortress when he was only a little kid. You'd only have been a baby then, Val, so you wouldn't know the stir he made. He was amazing; a real prodigy, like Mozart. But he was a very natural kid, unaffected. His father was a slave driver, a real misery, but Stefan was great. I remember the first time I tuned his piano, he came scampering up to me and gave me a huge hug. Most kids his age were scared of my size and my tattoos, but not Stefan. He seemed to have a feeling for the underdog – and that hasn't changed.'

Spiro rang off, leaving Val feeling foolish for asking about Stefan at all.

Stefan was waiting for them at the entrance to his villa. He was dressed in denim, head to foot, with black shiny shoes. The shoes touched Val – Stefan was trying so hard to be casual, but that fashion mistake made him human, brought him down from his musical pedestal.

Throughout their visit, Val found him not only charming but endearing. He allowed Chloe free rein over the Bechstein and patiently answered all her questions. His other pianos were equally fascinating to Val. Both were in a ground-floor room at the back of the villa, close to a narrow corridor, which, Stefan explained, ran directly to the kitchen. 'I must have coffee whilst I work,' he said, his warm eyes crinkling in a self-deprecating smile.

Val did not bother to explain that tea did the same for her. She was drawn into the plain, high-ceilinged room by the two great instruments. One was an early Broadwood and the second an Erard, modelled on the highly gilded and ornamented piano made for the French king Louis XV.

'I saw the original of this in Versailles,' Stefan admitted, with that slight lifting of his close-cropped head which Val took to be a characteristic gesture: one of shyness, not arrogance as she'd first assumed.

'Beautiful action,' she remarked, watching the hammers rise and fall as Stefan played the opening bars of a Schubert duet.

'Beautiful tone!' Chloe exclaimed, needing no further invitation than a nod from Stefan to sit beside him and begin to play the top part of the duet.

They played the rest of the duet, Stefan calling, 'Rubato!' 'Crescendo!' and apologizing when his hand slapped against Chloe's. Watching their intent faces, Val felt not excluded but privileged.

They finished with a triumphant series of chords, watching each other's flying fingers, and Chloe burst out laughing.

'You're wonderful!'

'And you are superb.' Stefan took hold of her left hand in both of his. 'What I would give for this hand – and you are still so young! You will have all the plaudits I once enjoyed as a prodigy, and you will deserve them more.'

Too soon, the driver was hovering in the doorway to the lower music room, politely reminding the maestro of his noon appointment.

In the car, on their return trip to Cypress House, Chloe was jubilant. 'Can you imagine? Stefan, jealous of me!' She raised her left hand in triumph. 'Someone like him, jealous of me.'

And big enough to admit it, thought Val. She wished now that they could have spent more time in his company.

111

Twenty-Two

Back at his hotel Harry changed, bagging up his torn shirt for the traffic police. It was easy to resist a shower, not because the police might ask for more but because this skin was the skin Val had touched.

Easing his way round the one-way system, he made for the Palace of St Michael and St George. The headquarters of the tourist and traffic police were in its west wing. Harry was planning that both should see the damage. The wrecked Fiat might remind Yiannis that he had a daughter.

He'd be civil to Yiannis: the man was Val's father. He steered round a boy pushing a cooker on a handcart and turned along the seaward side of the Spianada, accelerating past the taxi rank and cricket pitch.

'Valerie-Chloe.' Harry enjoyed saying her full name. There was an ornate gilt medallion of St Spyridon, the island's favourite saint, suspended from the Fiat's driving mirror. As he stopped for an elderly tourist, he touched the trinket where it had brushed against Val's forehead. He set off again, ignoring a gesturing bus tour driver behind him, and glided into a parking space outside the palace.

'Remember. This isn't your patch.' He smacked his left hand against one of the off-white pillars of the colonnade. He thought of Val and Judy in the back of the hire car, the two of them colder and paler than this limestone. If Markos had been driving the red Merc, there would be hell to pay.

At the centre of the colonnade, opposite the statue of Sir Frederick Adam in a toga, Harry strolled through the open doors of the tourist-police office. Yiannis was manning the desk furthest away from the door and had no one with him.

112

There were three other desks and chairs, but only the desk closest to the entrance was occupied.

Harry watched as a junior officer tried to deal with a dishevelled street entertainer who could not be persuaded to take a seat. Instead, clinging on to two dusty suitcases and a bunch of garish balloons, the young woman, dressed in clown's make-up and baggy pants, leaned over the desk and berated the harassed tourist policeman in an urgent undertone. Although he could not make out what language the clown was speaking, Harry was surprised that Yiannis had left his younger partner to flounder.

He queue-jumped a trio of backpackers and homed in on his target, wondering if Yiannis enjoyed working in this monument to nineteenth-century British colonialism. Its classical outer facades and lavish interiors – marble flooring and heavy chandeliers – reminded Harry of his bank in Fenfield.

In his buoyant mood, he might have been tempted to laugh had he not seen Yiannis's bored face tighten at his approach.

'Mr Cavadini! Good to see you again!' He spoke in English, to give himself the advantage. 'Val sends her good wishes.'

Yiannis closed the book he had been reading and laid it cover up on the desk, his face expressing something between irritation and curiosity.

'How are you, Mr Cavadini?' Harry sat opposite Yiannis, stretching his long legs under the table. 'Is Markos about? I was hoping to have a word.'

'Markos does not work in this building, Mr Thompson.'

'Harry, please. I insist.' By the smallest of hand movements, Harry indicated that this informality was mandatory.

'My son is a busy man.'

'I know: the Achillion case. This won't take long.' Harry rested an arm on the warm wood of the desk, aware that behind him the backpackers were glaring. His neck prickled in response. 'How's the investigation going?'

Yiannis said nothing.

'You may be able to help me,' Harry continued. 'You'll probably know the name of the garage which services and repairs Markos's car, his red Mercedes. If you can direct me, I can take Val's hire car to the same place.'

Puzzlement broke through the mask of Yiannis's expression. 'What has happened? What has Val done?'

'Val's car was rammed yesterday afternoon.' Again Harry waited, ready for the questions that any natural parent would ask: was Val all right? Was anyone hurt?

'I don't understand.'

'Come and see the damage, before I talk to your traffic police.' Harry walked out with Yiannis and the junior tourist policeman, who had slipped out to see what his boss was doing. Harry had hopes of using that curiosity later, if he could detach the young officer from the heels of his grim superior.

No fun running into you on a dark night, Harry thought, as he glanced back to check that Yiannis was still following. Big as he was himself, Harry recognized Yiannis as a tall, tough customer like his son. Either one had the strength to kill in the way of the first Achillion murder, and Yiannis was displaying an unnerving air of detachment when it came to other people – except Markos.

Last night when he'd asked Val about Markos's whereabouts on the night Hilary Moffat had disappeared it hadn't seemed tactful to question her about her father as well. Last night questions about Yiannis had seemed irrelevant – he was just a straight copper, on duty the evening Hilary Moffat vanished and on duty the following night when she was murdered. Harry had assumed that Yiannis had been summoned to the Achillion from a distress call of some kind – the palace was off his usual beat – and had found her body and secured the crime scene.

Yiannis appeared to have been the one who found the body, since Val hadn't mentioned any other witness, but last night Harry hadn't wanted to question her about the hows and whys of her father discovering the body. She'd clearly accepted that her father had been deeply affected by it all, and Harry had respected her feeling.

Last night he'd been a lover, but today he was an investigator, watching Yiannis through professional eyes.

Was Yiannis a suspect? He was the first at the murder scene, in the classic tradition of the lingering killer. He had plenty of means – he'd have had police transport and he could have written up his shifts to cover any activities with Hilary. He could have fixed the crime scene as he wanted, removed forensics, added confusion. There was the problem of the twenty-four hours, though: the gap between Hilary's goodbye to Val and her eventual reappearance as a corpse in the grounds of a palace ten kilometres south. Where could Yiannis have kept the girl, undetected, for that length of time? Or had he picked her up in town, or close to town, much later, possibly just before the start of his shift? Yet if that were the case, why hadn't Hilary appeared at the Zeus bar, as arranged?

Another puzzle. Why had Yiannis been transferred to the tourist police? Had it been a demotion, as Yiannis himself saw it? Why had his superiors been unhappy with his performance in the Moffat murder case?

He needed to find out. Local newspapers of the time would have some pointers, but police files and details – if he could extract any – would be better. First, since it directly concerned Val, there was the damaged hire car.

'Here it is, just past these cars.' The cars had been parked after his, crammed in to any available space, and so hid the back of the Fiat. Harry strode ahead, keen to take in Yiannis's reaction. He was glad of the second tourist policeman: he was also a witness to whatever Yiannis did, or said.

So far what Yiannis was not saying was turning out to be the more interesting, he thought, turning sideways as if studying the mangled bumper and car boot but really watching Yiannis with his peripheral vision. The man had not denied that Markos owned a Mercedes. Nor had he voiced the least anxiety for his daughter. He had been altogether too careful in not revealing anything, especially of the tangled family relationships that must operate in his household.

Harry suppressed a frown. Waiting for Yiannis to face up to this mass of crumpled metal, he wondered how many other families had been blighted by the favoured-son syndrome. What else had Markos done? What else had Yiannis covered up for him? Were they operating together in some way?

'Saint Spyridon!' The young tourist policeman had spotted the boot of the Fiat. 'Were people hurt?' He knelt, his round brown eyes scanning the sheared-off bumper. 'The traffic police must see this.'

'I'm seeing the traffic police next,' said Harry.

Beside him, Yiannis had put on sunglasses.

You're expected to say something, Mr Cavadini.

'This is terrible,' Yiannis said finally, with all the emotion of a weatherman reporting a light shower.

'Get closer. It's obvious what's happened,' Harry urged.

Unlike his associate, Yiannis would not crouch or kneel. He touched the back of the younger policeman with the tips of his fingers. When the man looked round, Yiannis motioned towards the offices of the traffic police.

The junior officer said something, scrambled to his feet and raced off.

'The boy has gone to fetch the traffic cops,' Yiannis explained.

'Judith was riding in the back of this car,' Harry said quietly.

'Valerie was driving the car?'

'She was.'

'But you were also in the car?'

'Val knows the Corfu town traffic system better than I do.'

'Not well enough, it seems.'

Yiannis kicked a stone out of the way – his first genuine action, Harry thought. He removed his dark glasses, peering at the flakes of red paint peppered liberally across the back of the Fiat. 'No doubt it was an accident. My daughter has not driven here for many months. She stops suddenly for a minor hazard . . .' Yiannis spread both hands in an open-fingered gesture of resignation. 'Women drivers often have problems on Corfu.'

Harry felt himself growing cold. He'd need to watch his temper. 'We were deliberately rammed by a red Mercedes.'

Yiannis brushed a speck off his charcoal grey trousers. 'Yet you came here to ask the address of my son's garage for repairs. That doesn't sound as if you were too disturbed.'

'My first priority is the traffic police, but seeing as you work in the same building, I thought I'd call in. I thought you might be interested.' Harry was careful to keep his voice even. 'And, of course, I'm after information.'

Yiannis's chin came up at that. 'What kind?'

'I'd like a garage to give me an independent assessment of the damage. If we end up paying, I'll have to take what the hire company tells me about costs as the gospel truth, and I think that's unwise.'

Yiannis smiled, his dark-blue eyes narrowing into slits. 'You are trying to take the place of her husband by being useful. This I understand. Nico was very much of a man to my daughter.'

Harry had always been envious of Nick, but Yiannis's words ignited a flare of jealousy in him. He could not compete with the dead.

'Certainly, I'd never hope to take the place of her family,' he replied, his voice deliberately soft. 'Especially not her grand-father. Val speaks of him often. And of course his workshop contains many treasures.'

Gratifyingly, Yiannis's tanned features, so contained that they might have been cast in bronze, remoulded themselves into a furious scowl.

'The Mercedes – that's not Markos's.' He turned away from the wrecked boot of the Fiat, straightening at the approach of rapid footsteps. 'Here are the men from traffic. I will explain to them.'

Harry blocked Yiannis with an arm. 'I will tell them.'

For a second, Yiannis wore a mutinous expression reminding Harry of Val's stubborn look and then the traffic police joined them.

To his disappointment, the two new officers were not accom-panied by the young tourist policeman, but, unlike Yiannis, they asked about the red Mercedes, Val, Judith and himself. They promised Val sympathetic treatment. When Harry reminded them that he had been injured, they wanted photo-graphs of his back and sides, as well as his shirt.

'Give me thirty minutes, okay?' he said. 'I promised Yiannis that I'd buy him a drink – he's had a shock this morning.'

Yiannis said nothing. The traffic investigators plied him with questions about Val, whose name had cropped up in their conversations, along with *kóri*, 'daughter', several times. They hadn't been aware of that relationship yesterday evening, but today they were. Harry was unable to follow all the rapid-fire

Greek, but guessed that Yiannis had been asked his own where-abouts yesterday afternoon. The man flushed a brick red and spat back a reply, jabbing both arms towards the palace.

So Val's father had been at work when the Mercedes had tried to run them off the road. Harry was thankful for it and relieved at Yiannis's anger. Surely it meant that he wasn't indifferent to his daughter, but maybe there was another conclusion. Yiannis was busy protecting someone else.

Twenty-Three

Val was planning to take the number seven bus into Corfu town. Her hire car was still in the car park of the Demeter, although she had organized for a garage to recharge the battery and deliver it to Cypress House.

She packed the young ones off to the jetty for the day with a picnic. Agreeing to meet Alexia in the foyer to travel into town, she instantly felt underdressed in her white sundress when Alex reappeared in a linen suit and sun hat.

'Lunch with the music festival committee,' Alexia explained, amused by Val's stricken expression. 'I know it's horribly formal, but the other members do like to put on a fashion show and Theo loves me to look my best.'

'As ever, Alex, the picture of elegance. But . . .'

Alexia wandered over the tiles to give Val an inelegant tap on her shoulder. 'Come on, Valerie! Out with it.'

'I was going in by bus.' Val waved a hand at Alexia's suit. 'Is that okay?'

'The bus suits me fine. I loathe driving in town on a Saturday.' Alexia picked Val's tool bag off the foyer floor, setting it down just as quickly. 'Must you drag that thing in with you? It'll almost take up a seat on its own.'

'I can carry it on my knee.' Val's mind flashed back to her

carriage ride with Harry and Stefan, a pleasant thought in a whirl of dilemmas.

'Have you heard anything I said?' Alexia demanded, hands on hips but with a decidedly playful lilt to her voice. Alexia was certainly restored today: her skin had lost that translucent look.

'Sorry, Alex,' Val said, taking up her tool bag. 'Would you like to run that by me again?'

'It's Theo and Chloe, what else? Theo has no idea when I should tell Chloe about this.' Alexia spread her hands over her flat stomach. 'He's leaving it to me. There's something going on where he works, but he won't talk about that, either. All I know is that he's away half the night these days.'

'You did have that trip to the cinema.' Val had noticed Theo's absences, but his absence during the night was something she hadn't really considered. 'It's to do with work, yes?'

Alexia sighed. 'So he says. But when I ask what, he bites my head off. I don't know why I'm uneasy. He's had busy times like this before. He's always at the office when I phone. He even smells the same.'

'What?' Val couldn't help smiling.

'It's supposed to be one of the clues – you know, according to those dreadful articles in women's magazines: "Is your man having an affair?" A new aftershave is supposed to be significant.'

'I presume Theo isn't using different cosmetics?'

'That's right. And there's never a whiff of perfume on him.'

What was she saying? Val wondered. That Theo was being careful? 'So what do you think?'

'I don't know. He seems to have so many long business lunches.'

'Perhaps the lunches are part of this new work he's doing.'

'Maybe. He's more distant, somehow—' Alexia broke off with a flush of alarm as a door banged in the kitchen.

It was the handyman-gardener, his boots echoing on the stone flags, his voice an indistinct growl as he chatted to the cook. Alexia waited another moment to be sure the youngsters had not returned.

'And look now,' she went on. 'Chloe's playing again, but

not today. She's flitted down to the beach with Judy and Steve.'

'The odd day off won't hurt her,' Val said, with a smile, going along with the sudden change of subject. 'She's only just thirteen.'

'And Steve is seventeen.'

'Steve's very protective, you know. Judy adores him.'

'Judy is four years old,' replied Alexia patiently. 'Chloe is at a highly impressionable age. Her talent has made her older than most of her contemporaries in musical terms but she's very much younger in other ways. Remember, too, that Steve is English. There will be a certain cultural gap. After all,' Alexia concluded with raised tawny eyebrows, 'it's your country that has the highest teenage pregnancy rate in Europe.'

'All that, based on a day at the beach?' Val asked lightly.

'It's best to be forewarned, I think.' Sometimes Alex could look quite snooty, every centimetre a throwback to her aristocratic ancestors.

'I'll talk to Steve today,' Val said.

'Let us hope you can get him to listen,' Alexia replied, losing her earlier glow as Val looked steadily at her. 'I'm sorry,' she said. 'I know that I'm probably over-reacting. Only' – She opened the foyer door, squinting out into the day's dazzle – 'I haven't forgotten you and Markos.'

'Steve isn't Markos.' *But at thirteen you thought Markos was handsome, Val,* her memory reminded her. Had his kiss been less demanding . . .

Val's usual grace left her for a moment and she stumbled towards the open door. 'Come on, we'll miss the bus.'

Slipping round Alexia, she was in the sunlight, feeling a welcome breeze from the orange grove, when her mobile went off. It was the lawyer who was dealing with Nonno's estate. He was elated.

'Mrs Baker, I know!'

'Slow down,' Val pleaded. 'Nonno's lawyer,' she explained, as Alexia gave her an enquiring stare. 'I'm not following you,' she told the man. 'Start from the beginning.'

The lawyer was delighted to comply. Did Mrs Baker recall that she had asked when Mr Cavadini had placed a copy of his final letter to her in his safe deposit box? He had assumed a date around winter, eighteen months ago, because that was the last time he had seen Carlo, but yesterday he had learned more. Eleni, one of the office staff, returning after maternity leave, had just told him that Mr Cavadini had been into the office much later than the winter. Only Eleni had been present, but Carlo had appeared during the siesta of June 7th and placed the letter in his box. Eleni remembered because Mr Cavadini had spoken to her, joked about the postal service being so slow that his granddaughter would probably read it first from here, rather than by mail.

June 7th, the day before Carlo died: no wonder Nonno had never had time to post the letter on to her.

'Thanks. Yes, I'm delighted you told me. I really appreciate it.'

'Now we really will have to hurry,' she told Alexia when she had cut the connection.

'What was that about?'

'I'll tell you on the bus. Shall we?'

They had hurried a few metres along the track when there was a crash in the undergrowth.

Val stepped ahead of Alexia. 'Who's there?'

'Chill, Val, it's us,' Steve called back. The low-hanging branches of an olive tree seemed to explode apart as he and Chloe hurtled from the half-wild garden.

'Can you get us something from town?' he went on. 'We'd like a—'

Whatever Steve was going to say was blotted out by a shout.

'Mrs Valerie – wait!'

The plump, elderly gardener appeared on the drive in front of Cypress House, hurrying so much that his floppy hat came off and rolled over the gravel. Alarmed by his rapid change of colour, Val ran back to meet him.

'Wait,' the wheezing gardener pleaded. He handed Val a small brown jiffy bag. 'This was left at the villa gates by the Komméno road this morning. I don't know who left it. Sorry.'

To Valerie, the typewritten label read, in English and in Greek.

'Thank you.' Val felt a premonition crawl over her and thrust the tiny parcel into the pocket of her white sundress.

Steve had already dashed along the track to meet her.

'My watch,' Val lied, showing her wristwatch. 'He kindly brought it out for me. I wouldn't get very far using the buses today without it.'

'Right. Chloe and me will be off then – her mum knows what we want.' He and Chloe vanished back into the olive and orange trees, Chloe clearly having decided that she was not speaking to her again.

No change there for a while yet, Val thought. She prayed that her instincts were wrong about the jiffy bag. Perhaps she should have opened it at once, but if it was nothing then not showing it to Chloe and the others didn't matter.

She checked her watch: there was time before the bus came. She crouched and removed tweezers and scissors from her tool bag. Spreading a clean handkerchief on the dust, she set the small package on the white square and set to work on the bag, piercing a hole in the opposite end to the one that had been stapled and sellotaped. Maybe there would be fingerprints on the tape, a forlorn hope but one she couldn't ignore.

Alexia, who had been shaking a pebble out of her sandal, came to stand beside her. 'What on earth are you doing?'

'I'm sorry, Alex, I know I shouldn't be doing this, that I ought to let the police see it, but I'd feel such a fool if it turns out to be nothing.' She felt the point of her scissors touch whatever was lodged inside the jiffy bag.

A colourless glass paperweight, in the shape of a pair of pouting lips, dropped on to the handkerchief.

'How peculiar.' Alexia stared at the paperweight, her sensitive face puzzled but not fearful.

'Alexia.' Val wondered if her voice sounded as strange as she felt. 'Could you possibly bear to cancel your engagement and have a morning in the gardens instead? There's something I need to tell you and Chloe.'

On the lower terrace closest to the strip of shingle, while Jessica took Judith to look for more shells, Steve listened to Val's account with amusement. When Val produced the glass lips and the pink-lipped eraser he wanted to laugh out loud – a stalker sending fake mouths had to be nothing more than some harmless old fart. He'd have said something to that effect had Chloe not been taking it seriously. The poor kid was picking up bad vibes, Steve decided, helping himself to a slice of cold pizza. Sitting round in a circle under the pine trees, none of the others was eating, so he was working his way through the picnic.

He was on to the halva and baklava when Chloe also joined the confession session, recounting a disjointed story about Stefan Gregory. Taking it in with half an ear, Steve decided that Gregory must be your typical uptight classical musician.

'Why not talk to the police?' he dropped into the first available lull in the conversation. 'Give me your phone, Val. I'll talk to them.'

'Hang on there, Steve.' Val again, saying what she usually said.

'Yeah, Val?' Now that he was looking at her, Steve realized that his stepmum was pretty pale. The fact that she was worried but trying to make light of it began to intrigue him.

'You want to talk to Harry, right?' he said, partly to make her blush.

The blush came, but Val surprised him with her answer.

'I think it's right for Harry to know this, before the local police.'

'Why?'

She waved off his question. 'I'm afraid there's something else.' Val looked away from him to Alexia and Chloe. 'I don't know how to say this. I may be jumping at shadows. Corfu's a small island. The police are still looking for whoever killed that poor girl at the Achillion.'

'But what has that got to do with these things, Aunt?' Chloe pointed to the eraser and glass paperweight, placed on the sand on a paper bag.

'Remember not to touch them,' Steve warned.

Chloe smiled at him, but tilted her chin at Val. 'Well, Aunt?'

Val went scarlet. 'I don't know,' she said, hugging her knees, 'but it's strange. I've never had anything like this given to me before. Have you?'

Chloe shrugged. 'I still don't see the relevance.'

'Chloe, you must see that it's sensible to be careful,' Alexia dropped in quickly. 'These packages are peculiar. In fact, I'm rather surprised you didn't mention yours earlier. Or that affair with Mr Zeno and Stefan Gregory.'

'Don't go on about it, Mother!' Chloe snapped, flicking a tendril of curly hair away from her neck. 'Neither were that important. Stefan's fine now – we simply got off on the wrong foot with each other. And you don't tell me everything. Why should I tell you?'

To Steve's astonishment, Alexia ducked her head, the large brim of her sun hat shielding her expression. Val's look of guilt, on the other hand, was visible for everyone.

'I'm sorry,' she said again.

'Don't dare apologize to her on my behalf.' Chloe scrambled to her feet. 'Everyone says how mature I am as a pianist, but off-stage you still treat me like a child!' she burst out. 'I'm going to join Jessica and be with the other little kid – that is, if you think I can walk across to the jetty!'

She ran off towards the terrace steps, spraying dust over Steve's halva. Devouring it regardless, Steve went after her. 'Wait!' he shouted.

She turned on him, her lace-trimmed, flared jeans tight in all the right places, but that sneering look of rage turning her into a modern avenging fury. 'Why aren't you with the grown-ups?'

'I bloody well am, you bitch,' Steve shot back.

'Nerd.'

'Bitch,' said Steve without heat.

'You used that before,' said Chloe, yawning into the sun. 'Tosser.'

They were jogging side by side, overshooting the steps and continuing into the private woods bordering each side of Cypress House, their hands almost touching. Showing great enterprise on a metre-wide strip of sand and rocks, Judith was building a castle under a yellow and green striped parasol, while Jessica read in the shade of the parasol. Steve didn't bother looking round to check what Val and Alex were doing: he could guess.

'I bet Mum and my Aunt Val are talking now.' Chloe hugged her elbows as she slowed to a saunter.

'I thought Val was hiding something,' Steve admitted.

'So did I,' Chloe agreed. 'She's probably telling my mother.' She kicked a pine cone off the path, her long narrow face looking longer in disapproval.

'It's the Achillion murder,' Steve said, thinking back over Val's reluctant conversation. 'Something connected with those dumb lips.' He smacked a fist against his palm. 'Maybe the victim was sent fake lips, too.'

Chloe shivered and Steve put an arm around her. 'Don't worry. Once the police know about this, they can do all sorts of tests – DNA and that kind of stuff. They'll find a suspect fast.'

'I don't want Auntie Val hurt.' Chloe leaned her head briefly against Steve's shoulder.

The contact made them forget everything but each other. Shielded by the pines and cypress they stopped walking and embraced.

When they broke apart Chloe's pale face was a mottled scarlet and Steve felt as if his entire body had been charged with electricity – he was conscious of his groin and, eerily enough, his mouth.

'I think you'll make a good policeman,' Chloe said, speaking to the dust at her feet. 'Have you always wanted to be a detective?'

Steve made a big effort to think. 'Yeah.'

As he spoke, Steve realized something else: that he didn't want Chloe hurt and that he wanted to do something. 'Jessica has a mobile, hasn't she?'

'Yeah,' said Chloe. 'A brilliant one: music, emails, pictures. You can go on the Net, too.'

Steve snatched hold of Chloe's hand. 'Let's join the two Js and I'll use it to call Yiannis.'

Twenty-Four

'I cannot accept your invitation,' Yiannis said, when the two traffic police had left. 'I must return to my post.'

'I insist,' Harry countered. 'You look as though you need a drink.'

Yiannis was looking down the hill towards the Liston. 'Here is my son!' Jubilant, he seemed to shed years and grow backbone in seconds, thought Harry, sour as he strode across the tarmac between the cars to pump Markos's hand.

'Hello! How's the Achillion case going?' Harry asked, determined to speak before Yiannis could warn Markos. He stepped aside, giving Markos his first clear view of the Fiat.

Accustomed to interpreting nuances of expression, Harry saw the one thing in Markos's face that he had not expected: bewilderment.

'What's that wreck doing in here?' he asked.

'It's your sister's.' Yiannis spoke rapidly in fractured English – keen to show that he'd nothing to hide. 'She was rammed yesterday, driving on the Corfu–Komméno road. The traffic police are dealing with it.'

Markos swung round. 'Was she hurt? What happened?'

'What I said. *He* was there.'

Markos turned to glare at Harry.

'No one was hurt,' said Harry quietly.

'She is okay?' Markos seemed genuinely concerned.

'Not much fazes Val for long. Except, of course, she's upset by this new murder. She knew the first Achillion victim quite well. She and Hilary were similar in age – in height and looks, too, from what Val tells me.'

Not a flicker from either man. In the sudden, heavy silence, a heron slid down a thermal to glide over the fountains and pools of the Spianada.

'The silver swan,' said Markos, mistaking the large bird and grinning at Harry's double-take. 'We are not savages, Mr Thompson: Valerie acquired her culture from her family. I have said the title correctly.'

> The silver swan, who living had no note,
> When death approached unlocked her silent throat.

Harry ran through the first two lines of Orlando Gibbons's madrigal in his head, uneasy at Markos's clumsy attempt to change the subject. 'Val still likes that part song,' he said, unconcerned whether she did or not. 'But tell me, were you a part of the original investigation? I can find it in the records, but I'd rather hear it from you.'

'My son was not part of homicide then,' said Yiannis slowly.

Maybe wine would loosen their tongues faster, Harry thought, wondering whether to extend his offer of buying drinks for a third time.

'But two police in the same house – you would have talked.'

'We did not discuss the case.' Markos raised his head and smiled. 'That would have been wrong.'

I bet, thought Harry. 'You will have read the first case by now, though: to see if there are any similarities in the killer's MO, and so on.'

'Of course he has,' Yiannis said, parental pride overcoming discretion.

'And are there any points in common? Is it possible that the person who had your father taken off the original case has had a hand in this one?' Harry persisted, trying to exploit old grudges and resentments.

Yiannis's mobile began chirruping in a high-pitched monotonous tone that had the pigeons starting up in answer.

'Excuse me.' Yiannis turned his back on Harry to take the call.

Irritated by the interruption, Harry decided to be blunt. 'Is there a serial killer, here on Corfu?' he asked Markos, while straining to catch Yiannis's muttered responses.

'This is not a good time,' Yiannis was saying in English. 'Go on, if it's vital . . . Yes, that must have been unsettling for them. You were right to phone me. I'll inform the proper authorities.'

Harry frowned at the sarcasm in Yiannis's voice, especially as he said 'proper authorities'.

'What do you think?' Markos flung the question back.

'I really couldn't say without studying both case files,' Harry replied.

'I'll be in touch.' Yiannis closed his mobile with a snap.

'Who was that?' Markos asked in Greek.

'Spiro,' said Yiannis, extending an arm to guide his son to one side, away from Harry and out of the path of an oncoming taxi. Markos and Yiannis put their heads together for several moments, gesturing and almost shouting at each other in fast, colloquial Greek.

Harry followed only odd words, but he heard 'Go' and that word *kóri* again. He wasn't surprised when Markos turned back to him and said he would have to leave.

'And you, Mr Thompson, have an appointment with the police photographer, so my father tells me.'

'That's right. I'm going there now.' Harry nodded to Yiannis. 'Good to see you again. Pity about the drink.' Without waiting for a response, he strode towards the shaded portico of the palace.

Harry felt their eyes on his back as he crossed the road by the triumphal arch. Never changing step, he reached the entrance to the museum of Asiatic art and, in a small room off a grand colonnaded antechamber, the office of the traffic police. Checking that Yiannis was not following, he pulled his mobile out of the pocket of his jacket.

The shiny new phone, bought that morning before he drove to the palace, was easily handled. Harry rummaged a second time in his other pocket for the number of Val's mobile.

'Don't be switched off,' he said, wishing aloud as he dialled. 'Spiro? I don't think so.'

Waiting for the mobiles to connect, Harry drummed his fingers on the nearby wall. Spiro was as common a name on Corfu as John was in Britain. Yiannis would surely have added more, to let Markos know which Spiro was calling him. And if a Spiro, why had they spoken together in English?

Harry had his suspicions, most of them centred on a certain young man who wanted to be one of the 'proper authorities' in his own country. Steve hadn't thought much of Yiannis or Markos, but that didn't appear to have stopped him from rushing in to tell Yiannis about something that had happened this morning.

'Playing detective,' Harry grumbled, stepping closer to the wall as a new batch of backpackers wandered into the foyer and up the grand staircase leading to the state rooms and the museum of Asiatic art. But that was unkind: Steve was idealistic – he probably believed that, as Val's father, Yiannis would be only too happy to help them.

'Help who?'

'Sorry – I must have been talking to myself. Listen, Val, I realize this might seem a bit strange, but has something happened at the villa?'

'How do you know that? Has Steve phoned? I told him I'd let you know as soon as I could. I'm sorry, Harry. It's a mess.'

She seemed to think he knew what had happened. 'It's okay,' Harry said. Conscious that Yiannis might wander into the foyer, he wanted to warn her. 'You may have a visitor calling later this afternoon. I overheard your dad and Markos talking just now. They spoke in Greek, so I'm not sure, but I think Markos knows. I think he's driving out to Cypress House.'

'My God, Harry, how could you tell him? I'm sorry – that wasn't fair. You didn't know, did you? Alex is giving me one of her killer glares.'

'Easy, Val.' The 'how could you tell him?' hurt, but he was glad Alexia was with her. He wondered where they were.

'No wonder Steve's looking so pleased with himself.'

'He'd be trying to help,' said Harry. 'Val, what's happened?'

Hearing Yiannis calling just outside the entrance, Harry said, 'Talk to you later. Be careful, love.'

He cut the connection and wrapped his fingers protectively around the slender phone as Yiannis marched inside, clearly amused. 'Lost, Harry? Let me show you the way.'

Twenty-Five

Alexia shifted position on the pine needles. Her smart linen suit was crease resistant, but her body was holding up less well.

'Are you sure you're all right?' Val asked, alert to her slight movement.

'I'm fine,' Alexia lied, sitting down again on the gritty needles. Her bottom was numb, but comfort could wait until she had more answers.

'I am really sorry about Stefan Gregory,' Val went on. 'But Chloe's right about him. He is very generous, once you get to know him.'

'You promised Chloe you'd say nothing,' Alexia said, understanding useless guilt only too well. Chloe's line about not telling her everything was true. Watching her daughter flounce off, Alexia had felt a mixture of exasperation and pity and the unworthy wish, just for an instant, that Chloe was male. Had Chloe been a boy, Theo wouldn't have been able to leave all the difficult stuff to her and hide behind work. 'I shouldn't have said what I did,' Val was saying, and Alexia broke in briskly. 'Maybe not, but you can kiss and make up with Harry when you see him. For myself, I'd appreciate a little more candour in future, Valerie-Chloe.'

Her reproof had the desired effect. Beside her, sitting on her heels like a Japanese geisha, gathering up sandwich wrappers scattered by Steve, Val frowned. Dropping the rubbish into the cool box, she raised her eyes. 'Alex . . .'

Alexia leaned across and shook her friend's arm. 'That was a joke. But I do have questions, and I hope you won't be inhibited, shall we say, by my present condition. I know you

130

try to spare me worries, but I think now I need to know all that you know, because of Chloe.'

'Yes.' Val's face cleared, then grew sad. 'I didn't think you'd ever have to know.' She shook her head. 'Even now, I'm not sure—'

'If there's a link between Chloe and the Achillion case?' Alexia could not bring herself to say murder.

'I'm not sure.' Val leaned forward and scooped up a handful of pine needles, scattering them on the dry ground. 'It's horribly tenuous.'

Listening to the soft cooing of pigeons and the distant, occasional voices of Chloe, Judith, Jessica and Steve, Alexia thought how far the picture they would present to the world, of a happy family, picnicking in a private wood and garden, was at odds with the reality.

'In a creepy kind of way, it's a marvel,' Val said, picking up on the same idea. 'We must look as if we haven't a care in the world.'

'But you think we have?'

Val slowly nodded. 'What is this thing with the lips? Why have Chloe and I been sent these fake lips? And why would anyone connect us with a murder at the Achillion?

'Are we talking about the latest killing, or the first?'

'Hilary Moffat.' Val sighed. 'I knew her. So, it turns out, did Markos.' She rose to her feet. 'This is such a nuisance. He's coming out here.'

'Really?' Alexia allowed Val to help her up. 'Well, you don't have to gather your brood up to meet Markos yet, if you don't want to. It's at least a thirty-minute drive from Corfu town and he'll have to get through the weekend traffic first. I'd say we've a good hour, so let's use it.'

Alexia felt revitalized. She loved organizing, and Val was in need of direction. 'We'll leave the scamps where they are – they can come when they're ready. I'm longing for civilization, at least a tonic water and some decent mezes. We'll go back to the villa and you, my friend, can talk to me.'

Climbing along the terraces and up the stone steps through the wild garden, Val explained everything she knew and suspected about Hilary's death. Hilary's lips had been cut from her in death. Chloe had been sent an eraser in the shape of lips, and now she had been sent a lip-shaped paperweight. There was the red Mercedes, and Hilary's ring, and Nonno's warning letter, placed in the safe deposit box only one day before he died. Whether these matters were linked solely in her imagination or through a more sinister reality, Val could not decide. Perhaps in the end it was all folly and her responses had been coloured by her recurring dream. Listening to her confession, she thought that if these elements were the signature of a serial murderer, then a soundboard and a set of pedals made a Steinway. Embarrassed by the analogy, she fell silent.

'I think after that I need something more bracing than tonic.' Alexia pushed open the big black door to the kitchen cellar. 'Excellent! Cook has slipped off home for her break, so we have the place to ourselves.'

She walked over the stone flags and pulled out a stool. 'Sit there, Val. I'm going to fix us a madrigal.'

Val sat down in sheer surprise. 'Madrigal?'

Flipping off her hat and allowing it to roll slowly over the large centre table, Alexia crossed to the display cabinet set against the back wall. 'That's Theo's name for a drink I invented late last summer. My madrigal cocktail is kumquat liqueur, sparkling wine, kirsch and grape juice, measured out as the fancy takes me into a large water glass.'

Alexia removed a tall, dark-blue, transparent pitcher from the display cabinet. 'It always pours so prettily out of this.' She stopped and sighed, passing her free hand over her stomach. 'I suppose this seems rather heartless, my prattling on about cocktails while you've been telling me about poor Hilary, but we both need a touch of everyday, trivial glamour.'

'Can everyday be glamorous?' Val's spine cracked as she stretched both arms above her head, a trick she'd watched Harry indulge in for years.

Alexia flashed her a look. 'Sometimes triviality is essential – it stops you going mad over things you can't control.' She took a bottle of grape juice out of the fridge and poured it into the jug. 'I'm glad you swallowed your pride and told me. This could be a lot riskier than simply looking foolish.'

This was Chloe's safety they were talking about. The

realization made Alexia feel foolish herself and then a strange wave of heat, both scalding and icy, passed through her. 'I feel rather queer.'

Val sprang off the stool and caught the tall dark-blue pitcher as Alexia rocked. Dragging the stool with her feet, she guided her friend on to the seat and gently urged her to put her head on her knees.

'Don't you dare say sorry,' Alexia muttered, moving so the weight of her skull rested on her forearms. She felt as fragile as glass and then wished she hadn't thought of that metaphor. 'Fake lips. I wonder if the sender likes Isabella Rossellini? I remember going to see *Blue Velvet* with Theo.'

'Where's the coffee grinder?' Val responded, lifting the pitcher out of Alexia's reach. 'No, I think your madrigal will wait, don't you? What I really fancy is a coffee.' Val tilted her head, her dark-blue eyes glittering in the light from the open door. 'I think a few olives and so on would do some good, too.'

Under Alexia's direction, Val worked her way through the fridge and food cupboard, bringing out olives, plain bread rolls, sweet bread, oranges and a bowl of morello cherries. As the mini feast was spread before her, Alexia began picking at pieces of bread, tentatively at first and then with more gusto. She ordered Val to put more coffee in the grinder: 'None of your Fenfield dishwater here, my girl.'

After grinding the fragrant Colombian beans, Val took out her mobile and dialled Yiannis's number.

'I'm driving into town right now. Would you like to meet me at the café where Nick and I used to go, in the Liston? I'd like to talk to you about the workshop,' she added, crossing her fingers under the table at the lie. She didn't really want to see her father. She was after Markos.

'I can't manage it today,' said Yiannis gracelessly. As Val relaxed against the table he added, 'But Markos is coming out to see you.'

'Really? Then we'll probably miss each other on the road.'

'Phone him on his mobile: tell him what you're doing.'

'Can you do it for me? Only driving and phoning isn't so

133

easy for me here in Corfu.' She allowed that reminder of the red Mercedes sink in. 'Could you ask Markos to meet me at the Liston in two hours? I know that's quite a wait, but I have to find somewhere to park in town.'

'Of course! I'll tell him. Excuse me, Valerie, I have to go now. *Addío.*'

Alexia munched on a piece of sweet bread stuffed with raisins. 'Run it past me again why you don't want Markos coming to Cypress House,' she observed. 'I know the one about Chloe's pink eraser and the "Sweet Lips" Markos called you when you were Chloe's age, but I must tell you, Val, that the only Markos my daughter has ever mentioned in the last couple of years is a rival pianist at her school.'

Val snapped the phone shut. 'I don't want him to question Chloe or Steve, and I certainly don't want him near Chloe, or Judith. Markos might indulge the girls or scare them: he's perfectly capable of either.' She pushed a plate of mezes further away from her across the table. 'However he behaves, I think he's an unwholesome influence.'

'Isn't that a bit harsh?' Alexia was fingering her long rope of pearls.

Val felt herself going red. 'How can you think that? I told you, he probably knew Hilary, and if he does have her jade ring, how did he get it?' Unable to keep still, she left the table and marched up and down the stone flags beside the sink. 'I don't trust him.'

'You don't want Markos handling the evidence.' Alexia dropped an olive stone on to her plate. 'If Markos arrives here, takes the eraser and your paperweight and then they conveniently "disappear" from police property, that's two possible clues gone.'

'You do see it, don't you, Alex?'

'I also realize that if you meet Markos in town you can drop the eraser and paperweight off at the police station first, to an officer who will be more impartial than your brother.'

'Half-brother.'

'Yes, Val,' said Alexia with a sigh, 'I know that, too.'

Twenty-Six

Val's hire car had just been returned to Cypress House and left by the garage. Since Alexia had recovered, she loaded her tool bag into the car boot and drove out again on to the Corfu town road.

Alex had elected to stay home. 'For some reason I don't fancy lunch,' she said, a tease which Val could only agree with. She had no appetite either, just a series of unanswered questions.

Was her friend's marriage in danger? Theo was possibly the perfect age for an affair, hovering on the cusp of middle age. She walked him through her mind, admitting that, apart from her first night at Cypress House, on this visit she had missed his usual indulgence towards her.

'He loves early music, including madrigals,' she said aloud. For some reason, possibly connected to her recurring dream, this point seemed important; instinct warned that it was so. Could he have met Hilary? 'Don't be absurd. This is Alex's husband, Chloe's father.'

Why had she and Chloe been sent those lips? Val squinted into the sunlight, wondering what connections existed between her and her god-daughter. Apart from the family relationship and their involvement with music, they weren't the same height, shape, age or colouring.

'It's a crank thing, just coincidence,' Val said aloud. Whoever had sent the lips was unlikely to be the driver of the Mercedes. She and Harry had one obvious suspect for that, and she sensed that Alex had been right. Markos wouldn't know Chloe if you put her in a line-up.

She's not his type, insisted an unwelcome voice in Val's mind. *Not like you or Hilary.*

She had stopped checking in her rear-view mirror for the Mercedes when Yiannis telephoned her again. 'You will meet Markos at the Palace of St Michael and St George,' he ordered. 'From there, go into the west wing—'

'And take in the museum of Asiatic art?' Val interrupted, before Yiannis could suggest that she and Markos wander into the office of the tourist police to see *him*. 'I think that's a marvellous idea. Thank Markos for being so considerate.' She pressed the end call button, smiling at the thought of Yiannis's expression.

As she entered the museum, on the first floor of the palace, Val regretted her impulsive choice of venue. Yiannis might not leave his desk, but Markos might insist that they join him. She didn't want to have to deal with the pair of them.

Weaving round the tourists and the display stands, Val decided that the museum was a good place to meet: it was neutral territory and there would be safety in numbers. At that moment there was a coach party in the gallery, visitors in brightly coloured shirts. Light seeped companionably through the shuttered windows. The floorboards creaked uneasily under their feet and there was a smell of overheated bodies.

Val was fascinated by crafts. Normally she would have lingered but today she walked around the masks, ceramics and bronze statuettes with scarcely a glance, wanting to see Markos before he saw her. This was why she had arrived early, to give herself an advantage for their encounter.

She was moving towards a stand of Samurai armour, wondering if here was a good place to watch for Markos, when she found herself staring at the top of his head. Turning, sidestepping a young woman carrying a tiny baby in a pink sling, she concentrated on a beautifully patterned kimono.

Ahead of her Markos was studying one of the swords. Staring at the long, curved weapon, his face was as bright as the blade.

To find Markos staring obsessively at a Samurai sword made Val uneasy. This was a weapon subtle enough to inflict precise, fatal injuries. Val closed her eyes, but could not stop herself thinking of the razor used on Hilary. It was easier to look again at Markos.

In his well-pressed uniform his long muscular body was shown to great advantage. He had the wavy black hair and flawless olive complexion admired in the Mediterranean as well as further north. He had removed his sunglasses, the better to see the exhibits, and Val noticed that several young women who passed that showcase slowed down, trying to catch a more complete look at him. With a faint shudder, Val recalled the taste and texture of his mouth, now narrowed into a hard line of concentration.

Markos looked what he was: formidable. But still appealing and strangely reassuring to women, Val recognized, and no doubt charming when he chose to be. Had he been the shadowy figure in the white shirt in the Zeus bar? That wasn't impossible, even though he had been on duty. Hilary would have gone with Markos without a qualm.

Markos raised his head, his eyes flicking through the glass. He saw her and snapped into motion, striding around the display case.

'Valerie.' He kissed her lightly on both cheeks. 'Harry Thompson told us – that crazy driver.' He held her a moment longer, then released her. 'Would you like a coffee? The art café next door is pretty good.'

He was speaking in Greek, a tongue rich with associations but no longer her first language. His manner was bluff, but Val had sensed the faint tremor in his body when they embraced. Pity, the last emotion she expected, welled in her. Not for the first time, she wondered why her brother had never married. *Do you think that you alone were wounded in the cathedral, when you were thirteen?* She had gone on to leave and escape the family, while Markos had stayed. Perhaps the weight of their father's love was more of a burden than a blessing.

Disconcerted, Val answered in Greek, 'A drink would be welcome, thank you.'

'This way, then.' Markos strolled beside her, neither of them hurrying.

'You like swords?' Val found herself trying to strike up a conversation.

'Not particularly.' Her brother grinned down at her. 'I prefer guns.'

'Yes, I suppose you would, seeing that you wear one.'

'No doubt you'd prefer a blade, for the craftsmanship.' Markos paused before the kimono she had admired earlier. 'The woman who wore this would have been about your height . . . and used that fan as a weapon.' He smiled. 'In her battles with other ladies at the imperial court.'

They were being careful with each other, Val knew, and part of her relaxed for the first time in years. She was English, but she was also half-Corfiot, and it was hard for her to remain estranged from her family. 'How is Dad?' she asked. 'Really?'

'He is upset by this second murder.' Markos's eyes swung away from Val to a nearby plinth, topped by a serene brass Buddha. 'As are you. Thompson has been asking questions about the killing, but I told him nothing.' His eyes were on her again. 'What is it you want to know?'

'Nothing much, just morbid curiosity, because I knew Hilary,' Val said. 'It's such a weird place, the Achillion. Almost like a film set. I keep wondering: how did she come to that place?'

'Valerie.' Markos was shaking his head. 'Why did you not come to me? Even Nico's boy has the sense to realize that this sort of thing is best left to local men. Have you them with you now? The packages? I would like to see them.'

I bet you would. 'I dropped them off at the police station on my way here.' She had also given her statement about the Mercedes: the traffic police had an office in the main station close to San Rocco square in the new town.

'What are they like?' Markos asked.

'A pink eraser and a glass paperweight, both in the shape of lips.'

'Just the lips? You've not had anything else – neither you nor Chloe?'

'That's right.'

138

'Good!' Markos drummed two fingers on top of a display case full of netsuke. 'Good, and the police have them.'

Was that relief she was hearing? 'Markos.' She lifted her face frankly to his. 'May I ask you something else? It's been preying on my mind.'

Her brother spread both hands.

'How was Nonno, the day before he died? Was he any different?'

Markos found her hand. 'I know his death was a shock to you, Valerie. It was to all of us. Carlo was always so vigorous. How did he seem? Much as usual. Quieter, perhaps, but he went out to his workshop at the same hour as always and came home at sunset. He did that on the day before he died and, yes, on the day he died. His usual pattern.'

'His usual pattern.' Hearing that made Val's skin creep. It was only a casual police term that Markos used quite unconsciously, but for an instant it sounded as if Nonno had been watched by someone with a separate agenda.

'When did he die?' she asked.

'Around nine, just before our meal. He had fallen asleep in his armchair. Grandmother tried to wake him and found she could not. But you know this, Valerie: you have asked our father these things.'

And been given the same answers. Val recalled her questions to Yiannis of almost a year ago, when her father had telephoned her at Fenfield to tell her that Nonno had died.

She jumped, sensing a light touch upon her left hand. Markos brushed his index finger over her plain gold band. 'You still wear your wedding ring. I'm surprised Thompson does not object; he has an opinion on everything.'

'It's nothing to do with Harry.' The instant the words were out, Val felt as if she'd betrayed someone: Nick or Harry or both, she wasn't sure.

'Not yet, eh?' Markos dropped her hand and moved away from the display of silks, a swagger in his step.

He really was a mixed-up character, Val thought, caught between amusement and pity and an older guilt. Every day on this working holiday so far, she had thanked fate or God that Steve and Judith, also half-brother and half-sister, were straightforward with each other. *Innocent*, that unwelcome inner voice said, and Val ignored it.

'What is it you wish to know about the latest Achillion murder?' Markos repeated. 'Whether you and Chloe are in danger? I would say not.' He pointed to a silk screen. 'Do you see the painting of the sleeping girl on that screen? The girl discovered at the Achillion looked as . . . undisturbed as that. Her face was unmarked.'

Val covered her mouth with her hand. 'I'd like that drink, please,' she said, through her fingers.

Sitting in the open-air café of the modern art gallery next door to the palace, Val stared from beneath a fig tree across the crowded tables. She wasn't looking for anyone, but her heart quickened each time she picked out a tall, fair-haired man moving towards them through the palms and banana trees. Turning to the sea and mountains, a warm breeze on her face, she drank deeply from her glass. The taste of her youth was no longer so appealing, but she had ordered cola from the young waiter without hesitation.

Markos had not reacted. Did she really think he would confess, 'Yes! I was the stranger ten years ago in the Zeus bar who offered you and Hilary two cokes'? She'd never thought of Markos in that time or place during all the ten years since Hilary's murder. But, of course, it was only this summer that she'd been sent Nonno's warning letter, and only now that their father had admitted, by omission, that Markos had known Hilary. And where was Hilary's jade ring?

'Val? Dad said you wanted to talk about the workshop.'

'Sorry, Markos, I was wool-gathering. Dreaming.' She had no intention of discussing her inheritance, however much her family disapproved of Carlo Cavadini's will, but since her brother was so free with their father's name and implied authority, Val decided to use it to her advantage. 'Yiannis told me that you've been in the workshop recently. Anything in there caught your eye?'

Markos drained his cappuccino, wiped his mouth and neat beard with a napkin and took another slow drag of his slim black cigarette. 'I'll show you. We could go there now.'

Out in the sea below them in the strait between Corfu and Vidos island two passing ships blew their horns in greeting.

No, warned the part of Val's memory that was forever thirteen, while her older self calculated the likely advantages. Perhaps in the workshop Markos would be more forthcoming. Perhaps he would show her something, quite unconsciously.

'We could,' she admitted. She had done what she'd half threatened Yiannis she would do, and had the lock to the workshop door changed, but she decided it would be tactless to mention that. 'My keys are locked in my tool bag back at the car. If we go back—'

'No need to go out of our way.' Markos laid a copy of her new workshop key on the table between them. 'The locksmith's a friend of mine. I also have a spare for the outer door.'

'You can't resist showing off, can you?'

Markos smiled and, leaning towards her, gave her hair a tug, as he had done when she was living at home. 'Don't be a bad loser, Valerie. I am a policeman here, and your brother.'

Half-brother, Val amended in her thoughts, ashamed of her own pettiness, and feeling uneasy. Because Markos had keys, she felt less in control.

She reached across the table to pick up the workshop key, but Markos pocketed it, blowing out a stream of smoke as he settled back in his chair. 'Let us finish our refreshments,' he said, patting the jacket pocket where his key lay.

Twenty-Seven

With Markos hovering Val stood and, taking her time, strolled past the tables of gossiping art students.

They walked by the modern art gallery with its vases of flowers on window-ledges and the scent of lilies swirling in the air. Nervous, she was unable to stop herself trying to assess Markos's mood, a habit from her teenage years, but told herself not to be ridiculous. The only danger was in allowing her imagination to run riot.

Too soon, it seemed, she was standing on the outside steps to her grandfather's workshop, watching in irritation as Markos opened the doors to her world.

'Val! Val Baker!'

Stefan Gregory rose from where he had been sitting on one of the doorsteps on the shady side of the alley. In his classically cut, dark Italian suit and old-fashioned fedora he looked like a being from another time. Val was delighted to see him again.

'Mr Gregory – twice in one day.' She held out both hands, an impulsive gesture of welcome. 'How is the Bechstein?' she teased.

'I have told you before.' Stefan Gregory wagged an elegant finger under her nose. 'Stefan, please. The piano is splendid: thank you again.'

'It was nothing, really.'

She was about to ask Stefan, in polite, general terms, how his midday appointment had gone, but, stepping past her into the foyer, Markos unlocked and thrust open the inner door to her workshop with such force that the hinges groaned.

'Come, Valerie, we should go in.' Standing within the foyer, but in clear sight of Stefan, Markos struck the inner door a second time.

'Markos, please,' Val murmured, embarrassed by his macho posturing.

Stefan gave a small cough. 'This is a different man from the one I saw you with yesterday,' he said, looking Markos up and down.

Val remembered Stefan's singular view of the world, seeing only one thing or person at a time. 'No, this—'

'Forgive me.' Stefan threw up a hand. 'I apologize for being nosy.'

Turning on the step, Val prepared to make the situation clear. 'This is—'

'Markos Cavadini.' With his key in the lock and the inner door fully open, Markos stepped back out into the street. 'We are close,' he said.

'He's my brother,' Val said. 'Half-brother.'

Markos raised his eyebrows. 'I'm sure you see a strong resemblance,' he said, smiling as the pianist's dark eyes ranged over his height and breadth and Val's small, slight figure.

'I see.' Stefan's suave face was suddenly impossible to read. 'Good afternoon, then.'

Leaving whatever he had been going to say unsaid, he set off down the alleyway at a pace Val would have found hard to match.

She rounded on Markos. 'What in God's name were you doing?' she demanded in Greek. 'Stefan is one of my clients – how dare you interfere? He probably thinks we're not related at all! Why did you do it?'

Markos laughed. 'Relax, Valerie. I was merely clarifying our relationship.'

'I don't think Stefan got that message.'

His face darkened. 'That man is strange.'

'What you did was intolerable.'

'No.' Markos struck the folding metal grille of the work-shop with the flat of his hand. 'That man is strange. You should not encourage his company.'

'He's right,' called a voice from one of the upper windows overlooking the alley. 'Listen to him, girl, and do what he tells you.' A second-floor window shutter closed before Val could register the speaker's age or sex.

By now Val also wanted to leave. Markos and herself alone under the ringing of church bells at noon recalled her meeting with Markos in the cathedral. Except she was no longer thirteen.

There was no way she was going to allow Markos into the workshop, stamping his rough path through everything.

'Shall we get on?'

'Wait.' Glancing down the street in the direction that Stefan had taken, Val saw a wizened bird of an old woman hobble out on to her doorstep a few doors down, clutching an antique brass mirror. As the widow began to polish its metal surround, sunlight flashed on its surface.

Inspiration struck and Val knew what to say. 'Markos, can't we leave the workshop until later? I'd rather you took me back to the police station, and you can look at the glass paper-weight I was left this morning. You did say you wanted to see it.' She dropped her voice. 'I'd appreciate it.'

Markos studied her open expression and then nodded. 'Very well.'

He locked both doors and they walked off down the street, a smile teasing at the corners of Markos's mouth as they passed the old woman.

'What is it?' Val asked.

'Harry Thompson. He was coming this way from further along the street until he saw your little performance just now. No, Val, don't insult me by denying it. When you smile that way, you're after something. Thompson will know that, too, or he is a greater fool than I thought.'

'He's no kind of fool at all.' Val looked round, but the cobbles behind them were empty apart from the widow.

'He must have slipped down another alley.' Markos hooked his thumbs into his gun belt. 'Perhaps he did not like the way we looked together.'

'Don't be ridiculous,' Val muttered. 'I don't believe you.'

Markos's smile broadened. 'In that case, shall we go?'

She and Markos were within sight of the police station at the corner of Romanou and Alexandras streets when a police car swung over to the curb a few yards in front of them. The driver yelled through his open window, in a broad Athenian dialect, 'Hey, Markos! Get yourself in here! The boss has been looking for you for the last hour and if he spots you with your girlfriend he'll have your balls in a meat grinder!' The policeman flapped a hairy arm at the startled pair. 'Come on!'

'He's new,' Markos explained, stepping away from Val with a shamefaced expression. 'Transferred from Faliraki. Doesn't know anything about us yet. I'll have to go. Will you be okay?'

'Of course,' Val said, touched by his question, one Yiannis never asked. 'You go on, I don't want you to get into trouble. We can talk again.' She wanted to ask him for his spare keys but it seemed unkind and then there was no more time.

A horn blast, another shriek of tyres and Markos was gone, the police car hurtling along Alexandras towards the Douglas obelisk.

Twenty-Eight

Val wished she knew what Stefan had wanted. Stefan was in town right now, and they could meet and talk if only she knew where he was.

'Tourists!' an old man muttered as he limped past with his shopping towards the blue bus terminus in San Rocco square. She was standing in the middle of the pavement, staring after the police car. She felt ridiculous but did not move. She wanted to gain something out of this wretched day, so what should she do? Find Stefan? Find Harry? Go to the police station?

No. She had already given her statement and the glass paperweight and novelty eraser. The two officers had been attentive but not very concerned. A mild case of road rage and curious gifts for a young woman and girl were scarcely going to stimulate detectives dealing with violence and murder.

145

Neither made any connection between the lips and the post-mortem injuries inflicted ten years ago on Hilary Moffat. She had waited for them to suggest it, and then mentioned it herself. Gently, but dismissively, they had instructed her in the standard habits of serial killers.

She was back with Hilary again, and Markos. It was so easy – and so wrong – to think of Markos as a monster. She was no longer a child, seeing life in black and white.

What had Markos meant to show her in the workshop? Val squinted into the sunlight reflected off the modern buildings that surrounded her. Then she turned, her choice of direction made.

Back in the workshop, Val only glanced at the parts from the giraffe piano. She was going to search this place. She would recognize anything that did not belong here.

She placed her bag in the middle of the workbench. Looking down at her sundress, she smiled, aware that soon it would no longer be white.

Keeping unnecessary movements to the minimum, she looked up into the eaves, tracing the length of the beams of the roof. She was hunting for broken cobwebs, fresh scratches along the timbers, snagged fibres from clothing – although would Markos go to so much trouble if he was hiding something? Looking for something would have been different.

Val lowered her eyes, searching for signs of disturbance amongst the racks of tools above the great workbench. The planks of wood and sheets of veneer, the frames of larger instruments leaning against the wall, the mugs in the bottom of the stone sink were as they had always been.

Voula was hanging washing over the narrow street: Val could hear her neighbour's loose-fitting shoes rattling on the floorboards over her head as the widow moved. Val had phoned her local agent and asked him if he had heard or seen any of her family lurking about the workshop and been told 'Never!' but Voula, a neighbour, might know better.

It would mean calling in, the rituals of gift-taking, the receiving of hospitality. Voula would expect her to stay, as a matter of courtesy. Val frowned, feeling that today she had

146

not the time to indulge in such a visit. Better to keep on searching for pistachio shells. She crouched and peered over the length and breadth of the stone floor, watching out for glints and gleams along the cracks in the flags, for the odd piece of paper – an envelope, perhaps – or a lost and forgotten earring. On the night she was killed Hilary had been wearing a pair of long jade earrings to match her ring.

The problem was, Val realized, turning on her heels in a crouch, she had no idea what she was looking for, and there were so many nooks and crannies. Soon she would have to clamber amongst the piano legs and soundboards, and shine the powerful workshop torch into the soundless keyboard standing beside the door. Whatever she was looking for could have been dropped, by accident or design, into the belly of a cello or guitar.

Val snorted and stood up. She walked back out to the foyer to the outer door and locked it, aware that her sense of security was misplaced, seeing that Markos still had keys, but feeling easier as she returned to the maze of tools and woods. Boosting herself with her arms, she sat on top of the workbench beside the biggest lathe and Nonno's black waistcoat, swinging her legs as she searched her grandfather's pockets.

Nothing. Val sat on her hands, allowing her thoughts to wander.

What if Nonno had decided to leave something in here for her to find? Something perhaps to go with the letter he had thought important enough to copy and guard in his safe deposit box. Where in this room would he secrete such an object? Val glanced about and then she knew.

Stretching forward, she unhooked the copy of an ancient Greek mask hanging above the box of violin bridges. Nonno knew she had always been fascinated by this grinning gargoyle, and it was before her and everyone else in plain sight, the best kind of hiding place.

Running her thumbs across its high cheekbones, she turned it over. Strapped to the inside, along the bulge of the nose, was a small cardboard tube. Removing the tube with a pair of tweezers, Val peeled back the two brittle strips of masking tape covering one end of the tube.

Several pieces of tightly rolled paper dropped on to the bench. She could already see the tiny handwriting covering the paper and her eyes filled, knowing what such crabbed lettering would have cost her grandfather in pain.

Taking a pair of fine cotton gloves from a drawer, Val put them on and then unrolled and read the message her grandfather had intended her to find.

Valerie, it may be that Markos received the jade ring from Yiannis. From your father! My son!

Markos was not at work for the entire evening that Hilary Moffat disappeared, but was instead two hours late coming on to his shift. I know this, because I talked to a friend in the police, someone who did not know why I was asking. A simple soul. If only our family were the same.

Petro – let me call my friend Petro – has recently retired from the police. I called on him today and loosened his tongue with wine. I had hoped to learn more of Markos, some final sign of his guilt or innocence. Instead, I have heaped confusion upon confusion.

Petro remembered the Hilary Moffat case well. 'A sad misfortune for your son and the second night of missed opportunity for your grandson,' was how he described it. When I asked him to explain about Markos, Petro was surprised. 'The evening that the English girl went missing, Markos was late in to work – have you forgotten, Mr Memory?' he teased me. 'Markos had a bad stomach upset and was two hours late on shift, so he wasn't there to help break up an early rowdy crowd out by the Jungle Club nightclub. He was usually so keen to get involved that he was teased a good deal. Your Irene was ready to come down to the station to complain about his "victimization", but my wife happened to meet her while she was shopping in the new town and she persuaded Irene to let things go.'

'Now that you remind me, I remember Irene mentioning something,' I told Petro, although that was not true. I had known nothing of Markos's supposed bad stomach. Markos must have persuaded his grandmother to lie for him. I say

148

this because I know that Markos was not in the family home for those two hours when he was late for his night shift. Irene had telephoned me several times at the workshop during that period, complaining about being left alone. This after she had told me that morning that she was looking forward to having some time to herself!

But my wife's changes of mind are not the issue. Why was Markos two hours late on to his shift? He was not at home, so where was he? Why did he feel it necessary to embroil Irene in his cover story?

I do not blame Irene. She has been taught to do and say everything and anything for the menfolk of our house. But Markos is a policeman: he should know better.

I asked Petro to remind me of Markos's second missed opportunity.

'Isn't that obvious?' Petro said. 'It was your son, not grandson, who found the girl's body. It was Yiannis who was given the chance to show off his skills. Markos was stuck out on another call, somewhere in town. No one saw him for most of that shift; he missed the excitement.'

Petro could not remember what call Markos was out on, and he became puzzled when I pressed him for answers. 'Markos missed the murder discovery and so never got to be part of the investigation – what of it? Is that still eating the boy, after all these years? We all have lost chances, cases we'd have killed to be part of, but weren't chosen. Tell Markos it's happened to all of us, he's not unique.'

So, Valerie, there it is. Markos was off duty for part of the night of Stefan Gregory's recital, when you walked out in the town afterwards with Hilary. We both know Markos was also out that night and the night after – the night Hilary's body was discovered at the Achillion. But it seems no one in the police force knows exactly where he was on that second night, and there is the missing two hours to consider, plus the fact that he did not return to the family home on either night until late the following morning.

Val sighed, remembering, with more than a touch of bitterness, how intently Irene had monitored her own comings and

149

goings, while Markos could use the house like a hotel. No one had ever questioned Markos's whereabouts.

Petro told me bluntly that it would have been better for Yiannis if Markos had been part of the team investigating Hilary Moffat's murder. 'Why do you say that?' I asked, but Petro needed no prompting. My old friend seemed eager to talk, as if certain matters had preyed upon him for too long.

'Yiannis would have had someone to watch his back,' Petro told me. 'As it was, Yiannis's boss had it in for him, wanting him to account for every moment, especially the night of the English girl's murder. I saw Yiannis, you know, when he came off at four, a few hours after he'd discovered and called in about the body. He was whiter than marble, but that miserable bastard Dinos still wanted Yiannis's report before Yiannis left the station, wanted it on his desk for five. Dinos loved to play the big tough boss-man.

Val felt as if she had plunged into icy water. Yiannis might have finished work at five in the morning after he had discovered Hilary's body sometime around 11 p.m. of the previous night, but he had not returned to the family home until noon of the following day. Markos, too, had not returned until long after midday. Both had claimed they had been forced to put in abnormally long shifts because of Hilary's murder, but Markos had never been part of the case and Yiannis had actually finished work at dawn. Where had he been and what had he been doing in the seven hours between leaving work and going home?

Val read on, and now Carlo was quoting Petro's words.

'Of course, Dinos and your son, Yiannis, never got on. Dinos was one of the old guard: very pro the generals. Yiannis called Dinos "the Fascist Fossil". I tried to warn Yiannis, remind him that old Dinos was retiring in another year, but he wouldn't listen. He and Dinos were always oil and water. In the end, Dinos got him.

'It happened this way. Only the day before Yiannis discovered that English girl's body, he and Dinos had a

150

huge argument. Yiannis had come into the station at the end of his shift, bragging about how all the foreign girls found him irresistible, about them being turned on by guns and uniforms. He claimed that one English girl had thrown herself at him just as he was coming off duty. "A pert little number, gentlemen, with an arse to die for, tits and lips to wake the dead."

'I swear to you, Carlo, that is what Yiannis said, or something very like. The men were laughing and urging him to say more. Markos wasn't in the station then. No, I'm wrong about that; Markos was there but he walked out. Afterwards, I did wonder if he'd been embarrassed, although Yiannis wasn't saying much. Just men together.

'But then Dinos appeared at the front desk and he soon put the dampers on. He accused Yiannis of making sexist remarks and wanted to know if the rest of us hadn't anything better to do than to stand around gossiping like old women.

'As Yiannis left, he muttered, just loud enough to be heard, "That fascist has just contradicted himself, but never mind. He wouldn't know a sexist remark if it ran up his leg and grabbed his prick." Something like that. I tried to remember it, because at the time it made me laugh. No one liked Dinos very much.

'That was the problem: Dinos remembered what Yiannis had said and how Yiannis had bragged. Dinos was looking for a chance to get him. So it was bad luck for Yiannis, how he found the English girl's body forty-five minutes before he was officially on duty.

At this point, Carlo had written, *I told Petro I didn't understand.* Val discovered that she did not understand either. She had never questioned Yiannis's finding of Hilary's body. Her father was in homicide and Hilary was murdered and that was that. Now, Val realized that she had always assumed that someone else had spotted something in the grounds of the Achillion and phoned the police and Yiannis had been sent out to investigate. But surely anyone finding a body would have called a local officer, rather than one from Corfu town. Val raised her head from her grandfather's papers. How strange that she had never considered that. Almost as if she'd deliberately suppressed it.

She focused again on Nonno's tiny writing. Carlo, like Val, had never thought to question why it was that Yiannis had found Hilary's body, but his old friend Petro had supplied the answer.

Yiannis had not been on duty when he'd found Hilary's remains beneath the olive tree in the grounds of the Achillion. Two hours before the start of his shift, Yiannis had driven ten kilometres south of Corfu town to pay his respects at a police leaving do, a party taking place in the restaurant close to the palace. Yiannis had been driving past the heavy gates of the entrance to the palace when he had noticed that one of the gates was ajar. He had stopped to see, gone into the grounds and, finding a second inner garden gate unpadlocked, walked up the outside staircase. Because he had been looking carefully and using a flashlight, he had spotted Hilary's body posed on the marble seat beneath the olive tree.

'A leaving do,' Val marvelled, torn between pity and disquiet.

As you see, Valerie, my son's connection with the case was unconventional from the very beginning. Details of how Yiannis had stumbled upon the body were kept from the press, but Dinos lost no time in arguing that your father was too shocked by this unexpected event, too emotionally involved to be effective. It wasn't long before Dinos had Yiannis transferred out of homicide, with the embittering of Yiannis that we have all seen.

Forgive this crude, unvarnished account. I set things down as quickly as I can. I fear that my old friend Petro's semi-drunk ramblings are merely part of a greater and more rotten whole. So far, I have seen a dead girl's ring in the hand of my grandson, heard my wife and son quarrelling only yesterday about a 'morbid token' and had Yiannis visiting me in the workshop and lingering there while I walked out to my lawyer's office – two things Yiannis never usually does.

When I returned to the workshop at the end of the

152

siesta this afternoon, I found Markos, balancing halfway up a stepladder. He said he thought he'd spotted a rat moving along the rafters and had climbed up for a closer look. I am not convinced by this excuse. I am going to look amongst the roof beams myself, in case Yiannis, or possibly Markos, has hidden something up there.

To conclude: I have hidden this account here, in the hope that I will discover more, one way or the other, and then act upon it myself. I pray that you and Irene need never be troubled, and that these papers, which I have placed in a spot in which only you or I would look, can be destroyed without your ever having to read them.

But if you are reading this, Valerie, it will be because I have failed. I am sorry beyond all words. It is in your hands now.

The letter broke off, with no farewell, but the date was there: June 7th, the day that Carlo left his first letter to Val in the safe deposit box, the day before he died.

Twenty-Nine

Val returned the papers to their hiding place, a mechanical action born of shock. She understood Nonno's fears, because she could so easily share them. She sat on the workbench, her head in her gloved hands.

Her mobile began to ring. Val tried to extract her phone from the mask, realized what she was doing and burrowed into her shoulder bag. 'Yes?'

'Val?' asked Harry. If he had seen her 'performance', as Markos had called her behaviour in the street, he had not been affected by it. 'Are you all right?'

'I'm in the workshop. Where are you? How did it go with the traffic police?'

'Fair enough, though they ignored questions about Markos's work shifts. There's nothing much in the newspapers from the time, either.' Harry cleared his throat. 'Of course, I was really stuck with reading the English one, the *Corfiot*. I've photo-copied the Greek papers: you'll probably find a lot more refer-ences that I've missed.'

Again, his trust moved her.

'Is that okay?' Harry was asking.

'Yes,' she mumbled, fighting an absurd desire to cry. 'Did the traffic police believe you?'

'Yes.'

'I've found some more of my grandfather's papers. They're important—' In the street she heard footsteps; someone was approaching who sounded like Harry. She jumped down from the table. 'Are you there?'

The footsteps stopped outside the window. A snatch of music, too faint for her to recognize, filtered through the closed shutters.

'What is it?' Harry demanded over the phone. 'What's going on?'

He was too loud. Instinctively, Val cut the connection. Had she locked the black outer door? She heard the catch being tried, then released.

'. . . *morte* . . .' A word from a song, thin and tinny beyond the outer door. Whoever was there had been listening to music on a personal stereo: the earphones must be round his throat now.

She heard the snap of a release button as the stereo was switched off. The figure outside was breathing rapidly, which was strange after his measured steps.

How do you know it's a man? Val questioned herself, but she did know, just as she knew it was safest for her to keep still and silent.

The man beyond the door inhaled, as if trying to track her by scent.

'. . . *amore* . . .' His voice, too low to be distinct.

Val heard a rapid drumming of fingers on the black wood

154

of the outer door, and then the faded ochre wall. He was walking away, his footsteps quieter than those stiff, insistent fingers.

Edging round a stack of veneers, Val unlocked her inner door, stepped through the foyer and reached the outer door. Stripping off her gloves, she took hold of the large iron key to the apartment block in both hands. She inched it slowly from the lock. She would need to hurry to see anything, but also be careful – she did not want the stranger to realize she was there.

She peeped through the keyhole. Someone was standing directly in front of the outer door, dressed in blue denim. Startled, Val dropped the key. She lunged after it but was too late: the key bounced along the stone flag, disappearing between the narrow but definite gap between the bottom of the door and the worn step.

She heard a faint click as it was set into the lock. Failing to lock the inner door with the new key, she armed herself with a long screwdriver and pointed it at the door, gripping it with both hands.

The man walked in and Val lunged at him without looking up. He stopped short, hands in the air. 'Christ, Val, I surrender.'

'Harry!'

'I saw your other visitor leave and wondered if you were still here. I did call out.'

'I didn't hear you.'

'No, I couldn't be too loud, in case Mr Anonymous came back, and I didn't really expect you to be answering any knocks.' Harry's hand gently closed over the shaft of the screwdriver, drawing the tool down and away from his body. 'I'm sorry,' he said.

'I thought you were someone else.' She knew too many men, Yiannis and Markos among them, who wore blue jeans for preference.

'That's obvious.'

Val allowed him to take the screwdriver. Feeling her skin break out in gooseflesh, she clasped her arms. Part of her wanted to hug Harry, to wallow in his muscular comfort, part of her was determined to calm down. She strove for lightness.

'No harm done. Who was it, out there?'

'A man in a grey tracksuit with the hood up. He went off down the shaded side of the street. I'd have no chance picking him out of a line-up.'

Harry was beside her now, grim faced, his ready colour blazoned across his cheekbones and forehead. He rolled the screwdriver out of reach across the workbench. 'I ought to have gone after him, made sure I got a proper look, but I had to know about you first.'

'Apart from almost disembowelling you with my best screwdriver, I'm fine. Why are you hiding your hand?'

He was quick, but she was quicker, catching his forearm in a firm grip before he could tuck his fist into the pocket of his jacket.

'You're bleeding!' She had intended no more than a warning with her undirected stab but the point of the screwdriver had scraped along Harry's palm, drawing blood in the fleshy part of his hand, close to the wrist.

'It'll stop in a second.' Harry unwound her fingers from his arm and drew her to him. 'I've got good healing skin.'

'I remember.'

'Of course you do. But you won't remember this.' Harry kissed her. 'I wanted to do that at the time, after you'd bandaged my hand,' he confessed, raising his head after a long embrace. 'You looked so worried about me. Back then, that was a heady experience.' He gathered her closer. 'These days, I'm getting used to it.'

'Really?'

Val tried to answer in the same teasing way, but as she drew in breath to say more, Harry ran a finger tenderly over her lower lip. With one arm lifting her, he leaned towards the work bench. Using his free hand, he swept a space clear, pressing her bottom gently against the warm wood. 'Don't do that,' he said. 'You're looking anxious again. That V line over your forehead.'

He bent and kissed it, then her eyelids. 'That worried look of yours drives me crazy – sexy and serious all together.'

His need ignited hers. In seconds, all thoughts of the track-suited stranger and Nonno's letter vanished. Hilary was dead but she and Harry were not. In a mixture of defiance and anger and spiralling excitement, Val chose life.

Thirty

S omeone was spying. Someone guessed their lovemaking. Someone watched as Harry opened the shutters halfway, standing in the window space as Val moved about the workshop. Glimpsing her through the crack in the shutters, the watcher saw dark shadows across her stomach and breasts: dust marks, showing up starkly against her white sundress.

Her companion also noticed, and pointed.

Val laughed, pointing back, saying something. A few moments later the pair disappeared from view.

The watcher was patient, waiting out the time, hearing gentle scuffles and serious voices, the words blurring in distance and traffic noise. They seemed to be looking for something within the workshop, but without haste, breaking off frequently from their search to talk.

Finally, Val pushed the shutters right back to their wall catches and the watcher saw her again. She smiled and nodded at something her companion said, the Englishman coming to stand beside her to look out into the street. Leaning out over the window-ledge, she seemed shameless with happiness.

From the shadows the watcher cursed her and slipped away.

Thirty-One

Val and Harry had found nothing more in the workshop. No jade earrings, no more notes or clues, no more discarded pistachio shells. They had talked and each knew what the other knew, although their reactions were very different. Val was still struggling with the idea that Yiannis or Markos could have murdered Hilary. Harry was altogether more sceptical.

'What have you got as real evidence?' he demanded. 'No murder weapon, no witness. All you have is a finger ring which may have belonged to the dead girl, and which seems to have gone missing. That and a letter and this scribbled note from your grandfather.'

'It's very far from being a note and it's not scribbled.'

'Okay, I'll give you that, but the content remains pretty thin. So what if Markos was "missing" for two hours on such and such an evening and Yiannis "missing" for seven the following night. It doesn't follow that either of them abducted and murdered that girl.' Harry took her hand in his, as if seeking to soften the impact of his next words. 'Have you thought of asking yourself why your grandfather was trying to drive another wedge between you and your family?'

They were sitting on the workbench, Val swinging her legs companionably against Harry's. As he spoke, she felt the hairs on her shoulders and arms prickling.

'You don't – didn't – know Nonno. You never met him, so you don't know.'

'Fair enough. That's all it was, Val. A suggestion.' Harry released her squirming fingers and nodded towards the open shutters. 'Think about this, too. There are tens of thousands of tourists visiting Corfu town and the Achillion every year.

There are over one hundred and twenty thousand Corfiots crammed into this island. That's a lot of possible suspects, quite apart from Yiannis and Markos.'

'I thought you didn't like them. I thought you were with me.' Val couldn't quite believe what she was hearing. Harry had already refused to react on hearing about the glass lips, saying quietly, 'Go on.'

Her mobile shrilled into the stiff silence and Harry waved a thumb towards her bag. 'Are you going to get that?'

'You're just avoiding giving me an answer.'

'Christ, you're worse than Gilda with this "we stand together" stuff. I'm with you, now answer the sodding phone.'

Val leaped off the bench and scooped her phone from the detritus of her bag. '*Parakaló.*'

'Val – Steve. No worries, the doctor says she's fine, but the poor kid wants her mum. To be honest, I need someone to talk to, too.'

'Who is it? What's going on now?'

Feeling a tiny spiteful flush of satisfaction, Val held up a hand against Harry's questions. She hadn't liked his comparison: it seemed disloyal to herself and to Gilda. As for his statistics, it didn't matter if he was right; with her own and Chloe's safety at stake she couldn't afford to be wrong.

'Harry,' she said, 'it's Steve.' Then, 'Steve, can you explain a bit more? I must have missed something.'

'It's Judith. She's fine now – temperature dropping and all that and the doctor Alexia called is quite happy. She's tucked up in bed, smothered in calamine, and Jessica's reading her stories . . .'

'What's wrong with her?'

'Chickenpox. Started feeling funny on the jetty after you'd gone off to town and went downhill from there.'

'I'll be there in twenty minutes. Tell Judy I'll be home as soon as I can.'

'Great, Val. See ya.' He cut the connection.

Val clutched the receiver. 'I have to go. Judy has chickenpox.'

'What's this twenty minutes? Chickenpox isn't fatal.'

'Yes, but she needs me.'

'In one piece.' Harry gave her a little shake. 'Come on, I'll drive us back. Just remember, we've all had chickenpox and lived to tell the tale.'

'I haven't had it.'

'Then you might catch it from your daughter. I caught it off my older brother Peter when I was about Judy's age. Once the spots came out I was okay. I paraded my pimples for the little girl next door.'

'You must have been a horrible child.' Foolish as Harry's recollections were, his account made Val feel easier. She remembered that Steve had said Jessica was reading to Judith. If she was enjoying stories, Judy couldn't be as out of sorts as she'd been with her last bout of tonsillitis.

She turned back in the doorway. Harry was closing the shutters. 'Thank you,' she said.

'*Parakaló.*' He picked up the big iron key and waved it at her. 'Go on, Mrs Whiz. Don't you be worrying so much.' His smile faded. 'At least, not about chickenpox.'

While Val was stepping down into the shaded side alley leading to the bigger, sunlit street, Steve phoned a second time.

'It's me again. Judith's not that sick – she just ate a pot of yoghurt.'

'Thanks for letting me know.'

'Thing is,' Steve's voice dropped to a growl, 'Chloe and Alexia have gone off into town. An all-girl shop-till-they-drop session, or something.'

'Right,' Val answered. Poor Alex, having to look after someone else's poorly child while she was struggling with morning sickness and the dilemma of when to confess to her thirteen-year-old that she was pregnant. If she was speaking to Chloe now, Val prayed that it was all going well.

Another thought struck her. Had Alex had chickenpox? She didn't know. 'Has Auntie Alexia been dealing with Judy?'

Steve gave a bark of laughter. 'Not when there's Jessica, covering herself in glory as super-nanny! What's with the "Auntie Alexia" bit?'

'Sorry.' Val hoped she sounded contrite, although Steve's sense of injury made her inclined to smile.

'You are on your way? I really need to talk to someone.'

'Harry's locking up the workshop for me even as I speak. We're coming back now.'

'What's eating Steve?' Harry asked, handing her the keys as Val tucked her mobile back into her shoulder bag. 'Usual teenage angst?'

'Don't be rotten.' Val glanced up at the cloudless blue sky and the cheeping birds hanging in cages from balconies. Missing lunch, she hoped her stomach wouldn't grumble and then started as she heard a definite tummy rumble.

'No-lunch blues.' Harry patted his own stomach. 'Do it good.'

'We could pick up something on the way.' About to reel off some local specialities as they hurried to her car, Val caught a flicker of movement from the corner of her eye. She turned, coming face to face with the next-door neighbour, Voula, who was trotting towards them from another of the tall, narrow houses.

'*Kyria* Baker, I've caught you!' She was gasping, a wrinkled hand pressed to her bosom, her squat frame quivering with effort.

'Voula, how are you? What can I do for you?' Val asked in Greek, speaking slowly to include Harry and to give the scarlet-cheeked widow time to snatch her breath.

Voula was beckoning. 'Come with me. I have something of yours. I have kept it almost a year. You were already gone last summer when Carlo gave it into my hands and made me promise to keep it for you. Come. I have it safe, but it will take time to retrieve it.'

Sensing that no one was following, the widow looked back. 'What is it? Why the drooping shoulders? Do you think my house is too poor for you?'

'No, of course not. But, Voula, my daughter is not well . . .'

'Then you must see her as soon as possible.' Voula shook her pewter-grey curls. 'Go now – your little one needs you. He can help me, instead.' She gave Harry an unblinking

161

appraisal, showing loose-fitting dentures in a mischievous grin. 'Let my neighbours gossip! He will do very well. Go on. I will take excellent care of him.'

Her laughter surrounded Val, bouncing off the alley walls. Val arranged to meet Harry back at Cypress House, and strode along the street towards the tiny triangle of rough ground where she had parked the hire car. Between the cries of the caged birds, she could still hear Voula's throaty chuckle.

Thirty-Two

B ack at Cypress House, Val met Jessica coming out of the second attic bedroom. Before she could speak, the blonde nanny placed a finger over her own mouth.

'She's just gone off to sleep,' she whispered.

Conscious of Jessica's status, and deeply grateful for all that she had done, Val touched the door latch but did not open it at once. 'Would it be all right if I take a peep? I'll be very quiet.'

'Of course.' Jessica's calm persona fractured slightly as she bit one of her fingernails. 'Please don't think I'm trying to exclude you.'

'I know that.' Impulsively, Val stretched towards the tall, slim figure and kissed Jessica's porcelain cheek. 'Thanks for everything this morning. Judith couldn't have been in better hands.' Conscious of a blush of guilty shame as she admitted this, Val was grateful for the gloom of the landing – especially since she'd not had time to change from her dust-striped sundress.

Val spent some time watching her sleeping child. When she eventually stole out of the bedroom, Steve ambushed her on the landing.

'Chloe and Alex are still in town,' he protested, as Val fastened the door latch. 'What do you women find to shop for?'

'Come and have a drink,' Val said. Hunched uncomfortably under the low ceiling beams of the sloping attic roof, Steve looked more restive than his half-sister. His ragged hair, raked up with impatient tugging, was standing straight up over his head in mini cockscombs.

Steve followed Val to her room, sprawling on her bed as she handed him a fresh bottle of sparkling mineral water, thoughtfully provided each day by Alexia. Steve drank the bottle in one go, flopping back against the pillows with a huge belch.

'Thanks. I needed that. How's the sproglet?'

'She's fine, though her head's covered in spots. I've no idea how I'm going to comb her hair – her scalp is one mass of blisters.'

Val wandered to the window and peeped out between the shutter slats. After all, whoever had left those parcels for Chloe and herself might return to check how the 'gifts' had been received. Wondering about the second murder, Val rubbed her arms and asked with feigned brightness, 'Have the morning papers arrived?'

'I think Theo went off with them, first thing.'

'Pity.' Val scanned the empty track. Her attic window did not show her all of the orchard where she and Harry had walked.

'Is Chloe's dad always this way? You know, striding about like he's got the world on his back when he's here and hardly around for most of the time.'

'There's the siesta here,' Val reminded him, and herself.

'Until midnight every day?' Steve slithered off the bed and rose to join her. 'And do you know what's going on with Chloe and Alexia? It's a bit more than a girlie shopping session, isn't it?'

Wishing that she knew as little as Steve, Val shook her head.

'It doesn't matter. I can understand if you didn't want to tell me anything.' Steve's face turned scarlet. 'I told your father about the paperweight and eraser,' he went on, tossing the empty water bottle from one hand to the other. 'I thought it would move things on.'

'That's a good thought.'

'You don't really believe that. Otherwise you'd have phoned Yiannis.' Steve glanced longingly towards the open door. 'I'm sorry if I've messed things up.'

'You haven't, Steve,' Val said. 'I'd like to tell you more, only I'm not sure of all the facts myself.'

'You're worried that Yiannis or Markos won't do anything. Or are you afraid of what they might do?' he added, in a disconcerting flash of perception.

'I don't know what you mean,' Val floundered, stopping when Steve touched her arm.

'Think about this: if Yiannis and Markos are inept or corrupt, then isn't that all the more reason for people like me to get involved?'

'I'm sorry,' Val said, touched by her stepson's mixture of pragmatism and enthusiasm.

'Actually, it'll be safer for me to know more. Whatever you're afraid of is a potential threat to Chloe, and there's Judith and Jessica to think about.'

Tempted to explain, Val decided that Steve was certainly ready for more responsibility. 'There is something you can do – it's very important. See if you can draw Chloe out a little more. She won't talk to me, not properly.'

'That's true.'

'See if she remembers anything else, anything at all, about the eraser she was left. Any small detail about the packaging, how and when and where it was left – you know the sort of thing police look for.'

'Yes, I can do that. How about you, Val? Can I draw you out?'

Why don't you ring? Val mentally demanded of her phone and the doorbell. Both remained silent and she sighed, wondering where to begin. With Hilary's murder, or earlier, with how she was treated by Yiannis at home? Should she say anything about Markos and herself? How could she account for their tangled relationship?

164

Misinterpreting her sigh, Steve straightened, giving a dismissive shrug. 'Forget I asked. I'll spare you the trouble of fobbing me off, Val. See you.'

Lobbing the plastic bottle on to the bed, Steve stalked out. 'Steve, please . . .'

Hurrying after him, hoping to apologize and start again, Val heard a plaintive, 'Mummy,' from the second attic bedroom.

'Hello, sweetheart, how are you feeling?' She went in to her daughter and knelt by the bed, touched as Judith lifted her spotty face and gave her a huge smile. Val swept her close, hugging and kissing.

'That tickles,' Judith said. Absent-mindedly, she scratched at a large red blister on her forehead.

'Careful, love.' Val took Judy's fingers away from the spot and shook the calamine bottle in front of her daughter's widening blue eyes. 'Let's have a finger-painting session, eh? You can dabble your toes.' She handed Judith a wad of cotton wool soaked in calamine.

Judy lost no time in squirrelling herself deep into Val's lap, where she happily dabbled and dropped lotion over her feet and the floorboards. Val was glad to allow Judith to do as she pleased; she would clear up later.

'Mummy,' Judith began, as Val lifted up her Mickey Mouse nightshirt to smooth calamine over her chest, 'can I have a kitten? Jessica's mummy and daddy live on a farm with cats. Jessica says I can have one.'

'A paintbrush might be better than cotton wool for this job,' Val said under her breath. Judith's words caught up with her and she groaned.

Two floors below, the house phone began to ring.

'*Kyria* Valerie!' the cook shouted up the stairs.

'Coming!' Releasing the folds of Judith's nightshirt, she lifted her daughter on to the bed.

'No!' Judith clung around her neck, half smothering Val with wiry little arms. She was pink with temper and effort but tears spilled from her eyes and Val could not bear her to be so unhappy.

'Sssh,' she whispered against Judy's burning ear, 'You're

coming, too. If it's Uncle Harry, you can tell him about your spots.'

Silent now, Judith snuggled into the crook of her mother's arm as Val strolled with her out of the attic and down the steps.

Val followed the cook's pointing arm into the first-floor dining room. The massive oak table was being set for a formal dinner, glinting with glasses and cutlery. Picking a way round an assortment of mismatched chairs, Val walked over to the marble fireplace. The kitchen phone handset was waiting for her on the mantelpiece, and the cook withdrew from the room, taking a wineglass and polishing cloth with her.

Keeping a supporting arm around Judith, Val lifted the handset. 'Sorry to keep you waiting,' she began in Greek.

'No matter,' came the clipped reply in English. 'It is not always easy to find someone in a mansion.'

'That's right.' Val placed a warning finger on Judith's lips. This wasn't Uncle Harry. 'How can I help you, Stefan?'

'I am pleased you remember my name, amongst so many other clients.' His voice carried an edge of annoyance after his encounter with Markos. Tonight, as you know, I am giving the first of my recitals at the Achillion.'

She had forgotten.

'I would be deeply grateful if you would consent to attend my performance, and also join my party after the recital

Val glanced over the dinner table, freshly polished and set, and guessed that Alexia, who had accepted Stefan's invitation to his second recital, was also holding a party that evening.

'I'm sorry, Stefan, but I'm afraid I have another engagement this evening.' Val took hold of Judith's free hand, which was hovering towards a particularly angry-looking spot on her chin, and beat imaginary time with it.

'No matter. My next recital is in three days, also at the Achillion. You must come to that, and afterwards there's a party at the mayor's villa. My driver will come for you at six. If that is convenient?'

Although she disliked the Achillion as a venue, a mayor's party sounded harmless enough, and Alexia would be there too. It would be interesting to find out more about Stefan. 'That would be lovely, thank you.'

'Good. It is settled then. Until the twenty-fifth.'

'I shall look forward to it.' Val slowly waltzed her daughter around the dining room, hoping that Stefan could not hear Judy's heavy breathing: it lent their entire conversation a faintly surreal aspect.

'As will I.' Stefan rang off.

Singing 'Teddy Bears' Picnic', Val danced Judith towards the kitchen, where she replaced the phone and set about finding her daughter a cooling drink.

Thirty-Three

Harry spent a couple of productive hours being led around like a tame bear by Voula – productive for the old lady, that is. Trailing after her flapping apron strings, doing odd jobs as they 'happened' to come upon them, Harry admired her enterprise. He was amused, too, and once pitying, when Voula asked him to straighten the large, fading photograph of her son in her cluttered living room.

'I would do it myself, but my knees – ah! They are not what they were, when I could dance the Easter dances. Would you hand it down for me to dust? Since you are here, and it is so simple for you . . .'

'No trouble at all,' Harry said in English, lifting the photograph off the citrus-yellow wall. He and Voula were managing to communicate, in a mixture of mangled Greek, English and gestures.

Voula cleaned the photograph in a series of jerky flicks of her dusting cloth. 'My son. He is in America. He sends money, but what is that to me?' The widow's face was still for a moment. 'I would rather he came home.'

Voula's wrinkled eyes were suspiciously bright, but then she handed Harry her duster, asking him to clean the top of the shutters. 'I cannot reach them without a chair, but you, being so tall . . . I may have put Carlo's keepsake in that top cupboard. When you look, you can pass me down the china dogs. Only a few, but they need washing.'

A few turned out to be twenty porcelain Dalmatians. One had been repainted blue with yellow spots.

'My boy did that when he was five,' Voula explained, giving the unique Dalmatian a pat before placing it with the others on an occasional table already crowded with pyramid-shaped cigarette lighters with 'A Present from Las Vegas' emblazoned on their sides.

Glancing over the cigarette lighters and wishing he could borrow one, craving a smoke, Harry shook his head and flapped the cobwebbed cloth out of the open ground-floor window. So far, using him as her labourer, Voula had dusted her sitting room, shaken five mats, had him scrambling in the foyer to replace a light bulb over her door and spring-cleaned two cupboards.

But Voula knew men, or male irritation at least. At the exact instant when Harry's polishing fingers began to clench around the scrubbing brush that she had exhorted him to use on her third cupboard top, Voula vanished into her kitchen. Returning just as Harry was stepping down from a footstool which creaked ominously as he stood on it, Voula shook the thing in her hand, careless of the ash being scattered over her newly washed china dogs.

'Here! I hid it in the old brazier. I knew I'd put it some-where really safe.'

She dropped it into Harry's hand, clacked her dentures together cheerfully and waddled back towards the kitchen. 'Coffee. You will stay?'

'Thank you, I will,' Harry replied, conscious of the weighty brown paper bag in his hand. He resigned himself to another wait.

Finally Harry extracted himself from Voula's, allowed himself to be escorted through the foyer and marched off down the street. Turning the corner, he waited several moments then looked back.

Voula had returned to her house and gone inside. He could slip into the workshop again, and there, away from prying eyes, decide what to do.

Anything Yiannis or Markos knew about forcing locks or easing open doors Harry also knew, from long contact with Fenfield villains and Fenfield homes. Within three minutes he was inside the workshop.

He knew he should wait for Val to open Carlo's latest offering, but professional curiosity, coupled with professional caution, were very strong. Val was naturally preoccupied with caring for Judy and he wasn't entirely sure that she saw all members of her family as clearly as she should. No, that was a patronizing idea. Harry tried to shrug it off as he crouched beside the workbench, his face level with that seductive paper bag. No one need ever know, especially Val, busy as she was. Somewhere in this tangle of disembowelled instruments were the giraffe piano parts she was working on.

Harry smiled, drumming his fingers against the bench leg in an abstracted way as he allowed his thoughts free rein. 'Disembowelled' was a good word, and Val's accurate use of it after their tussle showed one thing starkly. Despite personal loss, she was no one's victim.

So where do you fit in her life? She doesn't need you. After this time on Corfu, what then? Harry stood up, longing for a whisky and a cigarette. His roving eyes fell on the Greek mask. Increasingly in his mind he saw Carlo Cavadini wearing it. Were these hidden clues and letters, as Val believed, the desperate cry of an old man who, against his own feelings, suspected his family of terrible crimes? Or was it a false trail? Carlo, after all, had met Hilary Moffat at the town hall recital. Val had never said where her grandfather had been the night Hilary had been murdered; she had obviously never thought it necessary to consider. But Carlo would have had the strength and the tools and the skill, especially for those post-mortem injuries.

Who was sending Val and Chloe those lips? Who was the lurker in the grey tracksuit today? These things couldn't be anything to do with Carlo Cavadini, could they? Was there any real connection between Hilary Moffat's death and the recent killing at the Achillion? Anything linking Yiannis or Markos to the new Achillion murder? Was that second murder in any way a homage to the first, or even an attempt by someone to divert the Corfiot police from pursuing an inquiry that might place Carlo Cavadini in the frame for Hilary's murder?

Then there was the music, and the words, that Val had heard outside the workshop door. *Morte* and *amore*, death and love, the area of perverted sexual obsession and deranged longing but also the special province of the madrigal, more particularly of madrigal composers such as Gesualdo. Harry cracked his knuckles together, unable to move freely in this space of sturdy tools, delicate woods and irreplaceable bows, bridges and sounding boards.

'Sod it!' He seized a pair of narrow pliers, cleaned them on the inside of his jacket and began opening the bag.

It hadn't been sellotaped. The top had simply been twisted closed by a hand. Easing it free with the pliers, Harry found himself grinning: he had the strong impression that he wasn't the first to have sneaked a look into this unlikely Pandora's box. In fact, he'd be prepared to put money on the idea that Voula had peeped in.

Or was he trying to justify his own action? What he was doing risked contaminating forensic evidence. Yet these paper folds were suspiciously free of dust.

Harry snorted: who was he fooling? He wasn't thinking or acting like a detective. He should have made a far closer inspection of the bag, instead of the cursory glance he'd given it. Had Carlo deliberately set out to use an anonymous container, he could scarcely have done better than this.

'Forget the old man,' Harry muttered, catching a new smell in the dust and resins of the workshop. Fighting off an urge to look over his shoulder, he grasped the pliers in his left hand.

He smelled it again – a mixture of lemon juice and basil, seeping in through the window shutters. Footsteps marched past the window, stopping at the black outer door.

'Get out here and face me, girl!'

Irene, breathing hard from her furious pace, pulled herself on to the doorstep and thumped on the outer door. 'Get out!' she shouted in English. 'Get out, or I will come in to you.'

Good, Val's grandmother couldn't pretend not to understand him, Harry thought, stuffing the brown paper bag into his jacket pocket, its contents still unknown. From her threat, it was clear that Markos had provided his grandmother with a new spare workshop key, but Harry wasn't about to make it easy for her.

He tugged open the outer door, blocking the view. 'Val isn't here, Mrs Cavadini.'

Sometimes, his size was useful. Irene looked as if she had taken a swig of vinegar. Taking advantage, Harry stepped past her into the street.

'You've been making souvlaki, or the marinade for souvlaki,' he said amiably. Irene's apron was smudged across her middle with green and the aroma of garlic, lemon and basil was very strong. Such a hasty departure from her house suggested more. 'I'm surprised you found a place to park. I know it's the siesta, but even so.'

'There are always places to park if you know where to go.'

Harry nodded. So Irene knew how to drive. Interesting.

'Where is she? The workshop is the only thing she cares about!'

'And her daughter.' Harry was delighted to disabuse this malicious old woman. 'Val has gone back to Cypress House. Judith has chickenpox. She's not particularly sick,' he continued, unsure whether Irene would understand 'chickenpox' and ignorant of the Greek equivalent, 'but Val was concerned.' He looked straight into Irene's flat dark eyes. 'She's a good mother.'

'Not her! She's not fit to have a child! Be warned: she is a cold, devious creature. She cares nothing for the family.'

'Your husband didn't see her that way.'

'Carlo didn't see her as she truly is – that was always his blind spot. But I know her and I tell you this: Valerie cannot go on as she is, making a mockery of the family, stirring up trouble.'

Irene shook the creases out of her black skirt and tried to

171

leave, but Harry blocked her path. 'What kind of trouble?'

'She knows! And she must stop!'

'Is that a threat?'

Irene's double chins shook and her throat was suddenly as red as fire. 'Let me pass! You have no right, Englishman. This is not your concern.'

Bold words, but Irene's eyes were flicking up and down the alley, watching a distant Vespa rider at the end of the street, passing over a giggling quartet of slim Danish girls strolling towards them linked arm in arm. Looking for moral support, Harry guessed, but he was beyond caring what the neighbourhood might think. He stooped over the foot-tapping widow, closing on her until Irene took an involuntary backward step.

'That's where you're wrong,' he said quietly, 'and the next time you try to ram us with that Mercedes, Irene, I'll be coming after the lot of you. *Katálave?* Understand?'

He felt obscenely gratified when Irene flinched and walked off.

Halfway down the street, he remembered the old woman's ragged breathing and felt ashamed. Then, tempted to go back, speak to her gently and ask why she disliked her granddaughter so much, he heard Irene yell after him, 'She must be stopped, that one – you men are blind!'

Thirty-Four

'I don't understand her any more,' Alexia said. 'I can't reach her. We spent all that time together in town, and when I told her my news it was like talking to a stone. She says she's going out with Steve tomorrow to Mount Pantokrátor. She seemed disappointed when I didn't protest.'

The kitchen telephone interrupted her.

'Can you get that?' Alexia was up to her elbows in flour and eggs, impatient at being broken off, but hoping that it might be Theo.

It wasn't. Frustrated again, she listened to Val's side of a conversation.

'. . . Voula gave you a brown paper bag? . . . No, Harry, I don't mind at all. I can't resist a mystery. So you've not been able to have a look in the bag . . . Yes, we can look together . . . Irene? . . . My God . . . No, that isn't anything to be proud of, but I do understand . . . Judy's doing well. She's painting on the patio with Jessica. Strictly speaking, Jessica's painting with watercolours, Judith's daubing herself. It'll wash off. See you.'

Val put the phone down and gave Alexia a smile. Alexia found herself smiling back. Harry was good for Val. Her colour was high. Had Harry finished on a tease, or an endearment?

It made Alexia herself feel lonely. None of her family wanted to know about her. She felt the silken texture of the pasta dough beneath her fingers. She was cooking her favourite 'grand' dinner tonight, partly as a statement of family solidarity in the face of so many elusive troubles, partly as a celebration of her own fertility, which she intended to declare in the dining room that evening. Now, in the light of Chloe's indifference she saw the meal as an act of hubris. Everything was going wrong.

'What should I do next?'

Val's innocent question eerily echoed her own ragged collection of thoughts. Glancing across the kitchen table, Alexia saw that Val had chopped the walnuts and fresh herbs. The knife she had used was already washed and returned to the knife block. Val was not usually so cautious: she handled blades with casual expertise. Hilary Moffat's death coloured everything.

'Do you ever get over it?' Alexia asked.

Val walked towards her around the table. Her every step made Alexia feel more uncomfortable.

'Val, I don't know why I said that . . .'

Her friend gently squeezed Alexia's arm. Her dark-blue

eyes were steady, her whole face composed into a kind of patience.

'Don't worry, Alex, I understand. What happened to Hilary is here with us now; I'm only sorry you ever had to know about her. Maybe I shouldn't have told you, but after what was left at the gates this morning, I felt I should.'

'Yes, you told me that already,' Alexia said. The kneaded ball of dough seemed to weigh on her fingers. She dropped it into the nearest clean mixing bowl and covered it with a towel. Strangely, once that was out of the way she felt easier, a sense that increased as she realized that Val had changed the subject.

'This holiday's transformed Harry, unless it's me who's changed.' Val hugged herself. 'I don't care. I know Nick wouldn't mind. It's been five years.'

'You don't have to justify yourself,' Alexia broke in, afraid of Val's overdeveloped sense of obligation. Besides, Alexia liked Harry very much, whereas Nick remained little more than a name to her. Harry was different. If Harry was in any way responsible for the new glow that had settled over Val this summer, then Harry could stay. Alexia was still very pleased that she had instructed Val to stop work on the giraffe piano while he was with them.

'Harry is staying tonight, I assume? And you're both coming to my dinner party this evening?' The idea of playing cupid appealed to Alexia, but Val seemed not to have heard her questions.

'So many vanished people,' she said, raising her hands as if to count them off on her fingers. 'Nick and my grandfather and Hilary.' She shook her head. 'Steve's about Hilary's age now.' She walked across the stone flags and lifted down the pasta maker from the shelf.

'I don't need that yet,' said Alexia. 'And just because that young man wants to join the police doesn't mean that he has any right to drag my daughter into it. She was with him, no doubt egging him on, when he phoned Yiannis, you know.'

'I know,' Val said promptly, 'but if he and Chloe are off for the day in the mountains it means that they won't be involved in anything foolish in Corfu town.' She gave a sudden grin. 'I didn't know teenagers still went fell walking or anything so mundane.'

Alexia felt her stomach tremble and wondered if it was the baby, but of course it was far too early. Feeling slightly nauseous again, she said lightly, making a joke, 'And what do you know about teenage hobbies, eh? That grandmother of yours never let you out into the street without an escort.'

Val replaced the pasta maker on its shelf. When she turned back, Alexia became very still.

'I detest her.' Val's earlier glow had gone. 'Harry's just encountered the full force of her charm in the street outside the workshop. He's feeling guilty because he threatened Irene after he realized that it was my grandmother who had rammed my car.'

'What do you mean?'

'Irene drove her red Merc into the back of my car and tried to run us off the road. It had slipped my mind that she could drive, and I certainly didn't know she owned a Mercedes, but there it is.'

'But what on earth for?'

'Probably as a warning. She must have seen me driving in Corfu town while she was in her car and decided to make the most of the moment. Irene doesn't need much to get angry, and she doesn't believe in holding back.'

Moving slowly for her, Val made her way to the stairs leading out of the kitchen into the main part of the house. 'Harry and I would like to stay for dinner tonight,' she said quietly. 'I'm sorry I didn't answer you earlier.' She climbed the first step and then stopped. 'Would it be all right if I grab a quick shower? I'd really like to change out of these clothes.'

Alexia had noticed the dust marks but said nothing. 'Take your time, Val. We'll be eating late.'

After Val had gone, Alexia made herself a cup of sage tea and sat for a while in the herb garden, trying to make sense of what she had heard, trying to make sense of Theo and herself. Failing, she distracted herself by choosing wines for the evening's 'celebration' menu.

Thirty-Five

As she washed her hair, Val ran through the apologies she could give to Alexia, her voice dissolving into the rush of the shower. 'I'm sorry I dumped my psychological hang-ups on you. No, that's not right. I'm sorry I dumped . . . horrible word. The thing is, Alex, my relationship with Irene is difficult.'

Val flicked her black fringe out of her eyes. 'She knows that already. Damn!' She retrieved the soap, straightened and tried to lose herself in the ritual of cleaning her body. Whenever memories of her grandmother became too pressing, she had discovered that taking a shower helped. She could imagine Irene's malice flowing away down the drain.

Today the trick wasn't working. Val knew why Irene had tried to intimidate her on the Corfu–Komméno road. She knew something about Yiannis or Markos and, as usual, was protecting her men at the expense of others.

Had Irene known that Judy was in the back of the hire car? 'She can't have seen her.' Val raised her head to the warm cascade, closing her eyes to feel the shower beating softly against her face.

The memories were just under the surface. They played against the blank screen of her eyelids in brilliant tides of colour. There were noises, too, in particular the rasp of Irene's complaints.

Her mother all over again: cheap . . . useless . . . a filthy liar . . . sly . . .

When she was very young, Val had been afraid to tell Nonno the words that Irene used against her in case he, too, turned against her. When she grew up she was too proud to admit anything.

Although Val had always fought her own fights with her grandmother, her grandfather had known that Irene was not indulgent towards her. Whether Carlo ever spoke privately to his wife was impossible to say. In the workshop, soon after Val had protested at home at how Markos had treated her in church, Nonno had tried in his own way to explain.

'I realize that your grandmother seems strict to you and cold, but you must understand, Valerie, that she was made that way. Before I married her, Irene's life was wretched. Her elder sister died in childbirth, a despised and humiliated unmarried mother, and the women in her village told Irene that she would never marry, because her father walked with a limp and no Greek man would want that defect passed on to his sons. Irene knows at first hand about being publicly shamed. She does not want the same thing to happen to you.'

'Why should it?' Val countered. 'I'm sorry for Grandmother, yes, but that was years ago, in a remote village. We live in Corfu town, in the capital of the island. And you were not put off – you married her.'

Nonno smiled, his kind blue eyes full of private memories. 'I was an outsider: an Italian, and a travelling man, going from village to village repairing instruments. I was called gypsy and worse. I laughed it off. I was young, and full of fire and pluck. I had an eye for good wines, good violins and handsome women. Irene was handsome. Brave, too: she married me when I had no house, no land. We lived in rented rooms in the winter and she travelled the roads with me in the summer. Wonderful times!' He sighed with pleasure, then gave Val a piercing look. 'So do not judge your grandmother. If she seems over anxious about the appearance of things, of custom, it is because of her own past.'

'I understand,' Val had said quietly.

Yes, I do understand, Val reflected, returned to the present by the distant throb of rap music escaping from a speeding car on the Corfu–Komméno road. Over the years, her understanding had put a brake on her tongue. Whatever Irene's taunts, Val had never retaliated with mockery. She had told herself again and again that Irene undervalued herself because she had been taught to undervalue herself.

'She had a good marriage, a loving husband, an attentive son. In her mountain-village terms, Irene has been a huge success. So what else does she want? Why is she so dissatisfied?'

Coughing as she inhaled water at the end of her angry speech, Val turned off the shower. She felt less sweaty but no cleaner.

She dressed in her red silk sundress and hurried downstairs to help Alexia prepare the evening meal. Coming to the first floor, she heard Alexia calling her from the music room.

'These bouquets have just arrived,' Alexia told her as she crossed the threshold. 'One for Chloe and two for you and all from Stefan Gregory. You seem to have made an impression there.' She pointed with her scissors.

Following the scissors, Val saw a sparkling mass of cellophane and multicoloured ribbons, topped with a froth of yellows and greens. A tiny chill ran through her. This pattern of yellows and greens: she had glimpsed it before, long ago, in a dream. A dream of no obvious sense, merely a swirl of these colours and a mood of deep disquiet. She had been glad to wake up and find herself in her cottage in Fenfield.

'What messages are with the flowers?' she asked.

'"To Val". "To Chloe". Nothing more. But he must have spent a fortune.'

Unsmiling, Alexia turned back to arranging the tall stiff stems of white lilies into a heavy crystal vase. 'I decided to bring them up here: it saves me having to clear the marinade ingredients off the kitchen table and the light's always good in this room.'

She turned the crystal vase on the polished surface of a small oak table, checking the overall shape of the bouquet. 'These lilies are Chloe's. I'll tell her the aquapack was leaking and I didn't want her flowers to wilt before she could decide what to do with them.' Tweaking the final stem and a few glossy leaves, Alexia went on, 'I'm going to leave them for her in here – it may remind her that she has a piano. Who knows? She may even want to play it again, if she can drag herself away from the jetty.

'But you haven't looked at your flowers,' she went on, with an obvious effort at changing the subject. 'They're lovely.' Her tawny eyes sparkled. 'Harry will think he has a rival.'

With a satisfied 'Yes!' Alexia stepped back from Chloe's vase of white lilies and turned to her friend. 'I've brought my largest vase for your flowers from our bedroom,' she went on. 'You can keep it in your room for the time being. Unless there are objections from certain parties.'

'I doubt that,' Val said mildly, her mind on anything but flowers.

To divert Alex's unspoken questions about Harry, Val walked farther into the music room. Quite apart from their oddly disturbing colours, she was reluctant to look at the tribute from Stefan. In a strange way she felt guilty at receiving them. She was wary of extravagant gestures.

The flowers were beside the vase, standing on the mosaic floor in the shade of the piano. As she approached, her sense of disquiet grew more insistent. She picked up the two bunches and prepared to make a swift exit.

'Thanks, Alex. I'll take these up now and come back for the vase. I don't want to get water or clippings over this floor.'

'It doesn't matter,' Alexia said, handing Val the scissors she had been using to trim the flower stems, 'but if you feel easier up there, that's fine. I'll see you downstairs, okay?'

'Fine,' Val said, grateful that her voice sounded normal. Her throat felt clammy and she wanted to run from the room. Smiling at Alexia, carrying the bouquets, she forced herself to walk steadily across the dolphin mosaic.

Safely inside her attic bedroom, Val waited for her heartbeat to settle. For several moments in the music room she had been uneasy, but apart from an ancient dream she could think of no real reason why.

Had she reacted badly to the sight of Chloe's white lilies, Val would have better understood her fear. Lilies had been found with Hilary, arranged over her body, lilies with their stamens cut out. Chloe's flowers had been ripe with pollen and scent, so perhaps that was why they had not troubled her, and their alabaster, slim sweetness and stately poise would have no doubt recommended them to Stefan as a suitable symbol for a young girl at the beginning of her musical and emotional life.

Stefan's flowers for herself, now lying beside the glass vase under the shuttered window, were far more opulent. Tall nodding day lilies, narcissi and yellow iris, surrounded by a froth of yellow jasmine and the bolder sunbursts of sunflowers and yellow daisies. The spiky scent of French marigolds mingled with that of yellow roses and tuberoses. As contrast to the blazing warmth of these yellows and oranges, there were the broad glossy leaves of laurel and sweet bay, while threaded in amongst like long silky spiders-webs were the delicate winding strands of marjoram. The only jarring note were the wide crimson ribbons, but men liked red.

Val sat on the bed. When she saw this, Judy would say 'Pretty!' and the two bouquets were certainly that. Dramatic, too, exploding into this shuttered attic like the brightest of fireworks.

'That can't be how he sees me, surely,' Val said, touched and a little disconcerted. She couldn't live up to this energy and optimism.

Perhaps that was the core of her disquiet – a feeling of inadequacy? Or a sense that Stefan had misjudged her, missed her essence?

'Reading messages into flowers – I'm going crazy. The florist probably picked them: the tuberoses alone must have cost a concert fee.'

Frowning over what words she could possibly use to thank Stefan when she phoned him, Val put that off for now. Picking up Alexia's flower scissors from where she had placed them on the bedside table, she set to work, the scent of the flowers drowning her in honey as she arranged them in the large glass vase.

Thirty-Six

After thanking Stefan by phone, Val telephoned Harry. Quickly she brought him up to date, ending with Stefan's dinner invitation and flowers.

'I've just phoned him to say thanks and he said, "From the heart to the heart." But you needn't worry,' Val went on. 'It's a quote from his hero – not Gesualdo, this time. It's from the original manuscript of the *Missa Solemnis*. Beethoven wrote that line over the top of his score. I don't think Stefan means anything by it, apart from the usual artistic hyperbole.'

'Be glad he isn't lighting candles to you.' Harry was at the hire garage, explaining the wreck of the car, and Stefan Gregory's choice of musical quotes was not a major concern. 'See you soon.' An optimistic prophecy.

Later, riding out to Cypress House in a blue taxi, Harry blocked out the car hire hassle and brooded on the concert pianist. To say he was jealous of Gregory's attentions to Val was putting it too strongly, but he wasn't happy.

In the cellar kitchen of Cypress House, Val and Alexia were preparing fresh figs baked in Mavrodaphne wine. Judith and Jessica remained painting on the patio and Chloe and Steve were windsurfing from the private jetty. Theo was strolling back to his office to glance at a few more files and to let Alexia know that he would be in good time for dinner.

In a different part of the city, meanwhile, Markos was at work. His father was riding his Kawasaki motorbike, a Vulcan Classic, home from work.

Yiannis was not looking forward to returning to his house. His mother had already embarrassed him, phoning the tourist police station to share her worthless news. She was fretting that Valerie and her English lover might press charges against her, seeing that they, like Markos and himself, had guessed how she had used her red Mercedes. Irene had claimed it as a moment of weakness, an overwhelming anger born of her love for her son and grandson.

Yiannis was weary of her. Letting her stew in her anxiety, he had not troubled to explain to Irene that Valerie was too proud to make a complaint against her own grandmother. Even if she did, he still had contacts and the report would be somehow lost.

From those contacts he knew that the second murder at the Achillion was nothing like the first, whatever the newspapers might be saying. As his old priest would have put it, the second murder victim was a girl no better than she should be, and the so-called second Achillion killing was a tragic, messy case of erotic asphyxiation. There were several likely suspects amongst the victim's Corfiot and foreign boyfriends, and forensics had gathered several DNA samples. The police would catch their man, or men.

Markos was involved in the case and, according to Yiannis's contact, was proving to be a good interrogator. He had been arguing for the facts of the case to be released to the press, to stop speculation in the papers about there being a serial killer loose on the island. Yiannis knew that the detective in charge of the case would be revelling in the press coverage, which would fade away once the full unsavoury details were known.

The newspapers had raked up the first Achillion killing and Valerie was doing the same. So long as the newspapers assumed a connection between the first Achillion murder and the second, Valerie and that damned policeman lover of hers would keep peering into matters that were best forgotten. So far there had been no action, nothing but talk. Yiannis knew that so far his secrets were safe. But for how long?

Slowing for a sharp corner under the landward triumphal archway of the Palace of St Michael and St George, Yiannis kicked a tin can out of his way into the gutter. Should he let Valerie know that there was no link between the two murders? Would that make her less wary of Markos and himself? Would she believe him? He scowled; he had no access to the kind of proof that even Valerie must accept. Markos was naturally concerned to watch his own back in the department: he could be of no help.

Irene had been of no use to him, either. He had hoped she could have persuaded Valerie to talk about her evening with Hilary Moffat, a close, informal chat, where all sorts of interesting confidences and new details might emerge. But no – his daughter had been haughty during her single visit home, in spite of the reminder of her family obligations provided by his inviting her cousins and aunts, and his mother had done nothing to break down that irritating reserve. Quite the reverse.

Nor did he know what Markos had been looking for in the workshop. He had his suspicions, but Markos had shrugged off his concern and questions with a blunt answer. 'That place is good real estate. Once Valerie hands it over to the family, we can sell it on, but we'll lose money if the structure's gone. If I keep looking it over, it's only to ensure her agent is doing his job.'

Yiannis remembered how he had been forced to placate his son, when a part of him had wanted to warn Markos. 'Valerie is clever. She may guess.'

'Let her,' Markos had answered.

'You should beware,' Yiannis said aloud, shaking his head at a youth doing wheelies on his moped along Arseniou Street, where Corfu town stopped and the sea began. So far, thought Yiannis, Markos had acted with the utmost discretion over certain, regrettable, events which were now more than ten years in the past. Yiannis could only hope that his son would continue to act wisely. It was hard for him not to demand more absolute assurances, especially as Val and that goddaughter of hers had been left those unnerving lips. He, and he suspected Markos, knew too much about lips. If only he dare ask his son outright – but he was wary of the answers.

His mother was urging him to act. Irene wanted him to go to where Valerie was staying to demand that she return home with him. According to his mother's view of the world, the family should settle their outstanding issues once and for all and, if necessary, impose their ruling on those family members

183

who would not submit. 'It would be,' Irene told him, 'for the good of the family.'

Irene would like the secrets to remain hidden. 'The shame would kill me,' she was fond of saying, especially when she was crossed. 'Shame destroyed my sister – I will not allow it to happen to me.'

When she talked like this, Yiannis was glad that Irene was his doting mother and not an enemy, but these days he could be sure of no one.

What else had Irene gabbled to him? Turning into the second side street along Aghias Theodoras, nodding abstractedly to a neighbour mopping her house step, Yiannis considered the matter. That Valerie had returned to Cypress House because of . . . what was her name? Judith. She had some childish ailment and Valerie had rushed to her bedside in the kind of domestic panic that women indulged in from time to time. Judith was of no real interest to him, but her sickness could provide a useful excuse. He could call in at Cypress House, ask how she was. Then he would see Valerie.

If he waited until tomorrow, Markos could go with him, Yiannis decided, freewheeling his motorbike round a pile of steel cables laid down one side of the alley. For once their shift patterns had coincided and they both had a free day. They could drive out together to Cypress House, make a play of concern over the child. Perhaps suggest that Judith stay with her family until she was recovered. No, Valerie would never agree to that. But Nico's boy, Steve, he had already proved a handy dupe. Perhaps there were ways to reach Valerie through Steve.

Yiannis rode the rest of the way home in a better humour.

Thirty-Seven

'A sumptuous meal.' Sitting at the far end of the huge dining table, Theo raised his glass in salute. Over the top of his designer spectacles, his eyes seemed to flicker in the candlelight, and he smiled at Jessica on his right. 'We were going to have lobster, one of our local specialities,' he went on. 'But Val protested, even though, as we know, they are destroyed without pain, die without languishing.'

Alexia gave him the tired smile of a wife used to her husband's stock of habitual quotations.

'Ask a lobster,' Val said, disquieted by Theo's last words, taken directly from Gesualdo the murderer. To the twisted mind that had conceived and carried out Hilary's murder, even her killing might be described as 'without pain, without languishing'.

Across the table, her troubled eyes met Harry's. He, too, recognized the quotation, having spent the hour before this late-evening meal browsing through Theo's CD collection in the study. There he'd found the Gesualdo CD. Preoccupied with Stefan Gregory, he'd read the sleeve notes, picking up on the 'die without languishing', and those recurring words, *amore* and *morte*.

'The thing is, we shouldn't make too much of this,' Val said later, when she and Harry were taking a midnight stroll down the garden terraces. 'In spite of the movie cliché, not everyone who likes classical music is a murderer. I've always found Theo a warm, enthusiastic kind of man, with a sharp sense of humour. Alex complains of his being distant, and it's true that he hasn't been quite as chatty to me this trip, but Alex also mentioned that he has problems at work. I know he's been working until late at night,' she finished lamely.

'Money or women?' Harry asked at once.

'But he was so delighted about Alex's pregnancy,' Val said sadly.

'Macho pride. Doesn't mean he's not indulging himself elsewhere. You said yourself he's a man of enthusiasms.'

'Yes, but Alexia is so elegant and clever and caring.'

'All the wifely virtues. Maybe Theo is after a few more thrills.'

'I don't want to think about it.'

She and Harry walked in silence. Val was thinking of Theo: his bright brown eyes, quicksilver smile and crisp black hair, his spare frame and rapid, faintly prissy way of walking. Those neat designer spectacles and dark, classic suits of his. His orchids, tirelessly tended, and the ever-youthful, clear-cut planes of his face, which had not changed in all the years she had known him. His attentiveness to Alexia this evening – was that the concern of a hopelessly busy man for his wife, Theo snatching quality time when he could? Was it the play-acting of a guilty man?

'What do you think of him?' she asked.

Harry touched the flower of an asphodel, a wild lily, growing close to the path. 'Does he always wear a suit and waistcoat for dinner?'

'Always.' Val had heard the gardener opening the main door for Theo in the formal receiving room but had not seen his return to Cypress House earlier that evening; she had been busy in the kitchen. 'He always changes for dinner.'

'I wonder what he was wearing earlier today?'

Val's dark suspicions began seeping into the forefront of her mind. 'What do you mean?' she whispered, aware of the sweet, heavy fragrance of the asphodel as Harry's brief handling of the tall flower released its scent.

'Only that your friend's husband strikes me as a highly self-contained individual. Those types, when they lose it, tend to really explode. That chap in the grey tracksuit was tall and lean enough to be Theo.'

'He likes lips,' Val muttered, thinking of Alexia's comment about Isabella Rossellini and the print of *The Bower Meadow* in Theo's study.

186

Harry gave a snort of laughter. 'I can't see Theo sending fake lips.'

'Neither can I,' Val admitted, relieved to have her instinct confirmed.

'Has he any kind of police record? I only ask because these murders – these two Achillion murders – aren't the usual "domestic" kind. These are cold-headed killings, which have to be planned – and that usually leaves a trail. Small offences to begin with, increasing over time in violence.'

'Theo's never been in trouble,' Val said, adding, 'Anyway, if you think he's the sort to explode, wouldn't that rule him out as the cold-hearted killer?'

'Unless he can put himself into a state beyond his immediate feelings.' Harry let out a long breath. 'To be honest, I don't know what to make of Theo, but I can't see a woman like Alexia choosing a murderer for a husband and the father of her two children.'

All of this was what Val had told herself and what she wanted to hear, but, playing devil's advocate, she said, 'People change. Maybe he has.'

'Not that much, surely!' Harry broke off as they strolled around a marble urn, a relic from the garden's formal past. 'I wish this was straightforward.'

'Yes.'

'At least with the red Merc we know what happened. So much of the rest is insubstantial.'

'Yes, it is.' Reminded of her family, Val was forced to accept that Theo remained an unlikely suspect, certainly when compared with Markos or Yiannis.

'First Gregory and Markos, now Theo.'

Harry was staring up at the stars as he spoke, his face resigned. Val assumed she must look much the same. In her room they had opened the brown paper bag that Carlo Cavadini had left in the keeping of his neighbour and had found only a small screwtop jar with a strip of paper inside it. Nonno had written on the paper, *Look in the favourite place.*

'What did he mean by that?' Val wondered. She was tired of riddles.

'What did who mean?'

'Sorry, Harry. I was thinking of Nonno. You said something . . .'

'It'll keep.'

'No, you first.'

'No, you.' Privately, Harry considered Carlo Cavadini's hints and messages at best tiresome, at worst malicious, but overall the work of a disturbed mind. Whatever else Carlo had been doing when he'd left this latest message with his neighbour, he'd not been thinking straight. A man operating under stress.

'I'm bewildered,' Val admitted. 'Why leave anything with Voula? I mean, she's trustworthy and no gossip, but why her? Did Nonno act in haste? Was he intending to go back and retrieve it? Was it simply a stop-gap measure because perhaps Markos or Yiannis – or both – had returned to the workshop and my grandfather wanted to leave a message with a neighbour, just in case? Perhaps he had no time to devise anything better for that moment?'

'And then he . . . passed on, unexpectedly.'

'Who expects to die? But Nonno was worried that his son or grandson might be a murderer.' They were dancing around other alternatives to her grandfather's sudden death. At that moment, more than ever, she understood Nonno's hints and letters as a sign of the desperate yearning of a man hoping that his suspicions were wrong.

'If he found something important in the workshop after he wrote his letter to me, why not simply leave whatever it was with Voula?' Val's question was really to her grandfather, but Harry answered it.

'Would you leave anything with Voula and rely on her not to touch it? You say she's no gossip but she's still curious. My guess is that your grandad knew it was too much to expect Voula not to look or touch – and if it's the jade ring we're talking about here, she might have contaminated evidence. He's hidden it somewhere you both knew, and left Voula a message, just in case.'

Val frowned. 'What do you mean about Stefan and Markos and Theo?' she asked, returning to their earlier conversation.

'Madrigals. That poster of the Prospero Singers in Theo's

study and now Theo's madrigal drink and reference. Markos quotes "The Silver Swan" at me. Gregory tells me it's the greatest art form. Then that prowler outside the workshop. What else could he have been listening to, except a madrigal?'

'And?' Val prompted.

'I don't know.' Looking down into the bay at the little church of Holy Ipapanti and beyond that gleaming patch of silver where tiny lanterns floated over the sleek darkness of the sea as lobster-catchers fished from their small boats in Gouvía bay, he said, 'I've been reading up again about Gesualdo.'

'Again?'

'The first time I came across anything about him, I was in my teens. I read on then because of the sex.'

'Oh, yes?'

Harry smiled but said seriously, 'How much do you know about him?'

Val counted off on her fingers. 'Italian count and composer. Lived in the sixteenth century. Wrote six volumes of madrigals, many using highly erotic texts. I believe he killed his first wife, although that didn't stop another woman from marrying him and having his child.' She looked up at Harry, her eyes narrowing. 'That's over four hundred years ago; rather a long time for a link to the present murders, don't you think?'

'He murdered his first wife, the noted beauty Princess Donna Maria, because of her infidelity. He burst into her bedchamber where she was lying with her lover and killed them both, stabbing them to death. After Donna Maria and her lover were dead, he carried on stabbing, mutilating them both. True, another woman married him, but he mistreated her, too.'

'I really can't see any relevance—'

'Carlo Gesualdo was a sexual sadist who killed with a blade, who mutilated bodies after death and who had the naked body of his first wife displayed, not to say posed, on the grounds of his estate.'

'Hilary Moffat was no one's wife,' Val replied crisply. 'There was never any suggestion of a boyfriend, even.'

'But supposing someone considered himself to be a

189

boyfriend and then fancied himself betrayed, like Gesualdo? Look at the fellow's weird life – look at his music, full of sex and death.'

'As is the music of many other composers. Why aren't you suggesting that the Achillion murderer was "inspired" by them as well? And speaking of post-mortem wounds, did Gesualdo cut off his wife's lips?'

'No, he didn't. You're right: it's a crazy idea and I'm clutching at straws.' Harry glowered at the fragile bobbing lights in the bay. 'I wish I could have got more information out of the police.'

'Would they protect one of their own, do you think?' Her next question slipped out without thought. 'Would your people, at Fenfield?'

'Not murder! Not a killing like Hilary Moffat's. Or this latest one, especially if it's the same MO. Which we don't know.' Harry struck an olive tree in frustration. 'I used to think my family were dysfunctional, but yours . . . Sorry.'

Val stepped closer and hugged him. 'When I was younger, I used to pretend I was an orphan,' she confessed. 'If the old— if Irene knows something, which I'm sure she does, she'll never tell me.'

Harry was holding her gently but she could feel the burn of his anger. 'What kind of woman tries to force her grand-daughter's car off the road? What else has she done?' He stroked Val's hair and the side of her throat. 'I don't want you going back to that house on your own.'

Because he spoke out of love and for her protection, Val allowed his peremptory tone to pass. She blew on his fingers and he smiled to show he wasn't annoyed with her. They stood a moment together, beguiled by each other and the blood-warm dark, the bright stars.

'Chloe was pleased with her lilies.' Val paused, debating whether to mention her disquiet at seeing her flowers for the first time and deciding it was too foolish.

'Steve wasn't happy. He looked as if he was chewing on a turd.'

'Harry!'

'Sorry.' Harry removed a fallen pine needle from Val's

190

shoulder strap. 'I'm glad those two are off gambolling in the mountains tomorrow, out of the way. Do you think Judy will be fit enough to tag along as chaperone?'

Val gave him a sharp look, realized he was joking and responded with her own tease. 'Maybe. She was already much brighter this evening than she'd been in the afternoon. But don't you think that's a bit unfair on Chloe and Steve?'

Harry laughed. He smoothed the slender strap off Val's shoulder and kissed her collarbone. 'You always smell so good,' he said.

Returning late to Cypress House, they made love again, a defiant celebration of life, then slept sprawled together in the Victorian-style, brass-headed bed, where Val began to dream.

She dreamed of the Achillion. It was a summer's day, early morning before the cicadas had begun their relentless drumming. She was strolling in the palace grounds towards the marble statue of the fallen Achilles and Chloe was with her. Chloe was humming the soprano line from the Gesualdo madrigal 'Luci serene e chiare'. She was wearing an Alice band in her hair, made up in a pattern of black and white piano keys, and dressed in a flowing yellow robe that shimmered in the sunlight and showed shades of citrus, orange and rose as she moved. A gnat hovered around her lips and Chloe, still singing, blew it away. The fly returned and settled on the girl's forehead, walking across her eyebrows.

Val brushed her own forehead with a hand and woke. As in her dream, it was early, just after dawn. She lay a moment, trying to make sense of her dream and failing. She watched Harry sleeping beside her and then swung her legs carefully out of bed.

What should she do about Nonno's latest message, or anything else? she wondered, slipping into Judy's room to check on her sleeping daughter.

Judith's forehead was cool. Spreadeagled with one hand curled protectively around Lady Penelope, who lay in a homemade nightdress on the thin pillow beside her head, the child appeared tranquil and remote, like a Pre-Raphaelite angel.

Nick had looked this way when he was sleeping. The same

tumble of brilliant curls, the same close-lipped, serene expression. Judith's chickenpox spots were not fading yet, but they were less angry. With the natural resilience of children, she was recovering fast.

Val looked at her daughter and remembered Nick, and a disloyal sense of doubt stole over her. Had he lived, would they still be together? He had loved his work so much: the longer the hours, the more challenging the quarry, the greater the kudos Nick had fought for and won. He had been relentless in pursuit, as single-minded as herself.

With Harry on Corfu, though, she was not rushing obsessively to return to the giraffe piano. It wasn't only because Alexia had given her leave, or because of the Achillion murders or those strange 'gifts' sent to Chloe and herself that she found she was less engaged than usual in the restoration. Harry was different from Nick, just as committed but interested in people more as individuals than as criminal types.

Startled and a little saddened by her thoughts, Val turned away from her daughter and walked slowly from the room.

Later that morning, dressed in her favourite blue sundress and a long white blouse, Val took breakfast on the patio with Harry. Alexia had insisted that her guests rise when they please, and she and Harry were alone. Chloe and Steve were no doubt still in bed, whilst Judith certainly was. Jessica was in the kitchen, exchanging pizza recipes with the cook.

'What time is it?' Harry asked, spooning sugar into his coffee. They had carried their empty yoghurt pots and plates back to the kitchen but lingered over their drinks, sitting on the marble bench with a cheerful array of cups and cafetières between them.

'Just after ten.' Recalling Alexia's virtual order that she do no work on the giraffe piano, Val smiled, grateful for her friend's generosity. She and Harry had been able to make love again, play, shower, take their time.

'We're with the lotus eaters here. I suppose we are close to Odysseus' island. Ithaca is just down there.' Harry stretched a pointing arm across their 'table', tousling Val's hair on the way.

'Hey! I'll do a Circe on you, turn you into a lion.'

'I thought Circe did pigs. Besides, you're more of a Penelope.'

'A stay-at-home, fiddling with the loom?'

'Penelope's more than that – look how she fights every way she can to keep her home and family together. And she does trick Odysseus into revealing himself at the end.'

'You're incorrigible.' Val looked away from Harry and the dazzle of the sea. Half turning on the bench towards the house, she glanced into the dim anteroom, wondering how Alexia was feeling. Although it was Sunday, Theo had already gone off to work – or wherever else he might be going – and Alexia had long since eaten what breakfast she could keep down. Through the half-open patio doors Val could hear her friend moving somewhere inside the house.

'Do you think—?' Her thoughts on whether Theo had even noticed how out of sorts Alex was in the mornings were interrupted by the sound of an approaching car. A taxi, its engine idling, was rolling down the track to Cypress House. Val rose to her feet and shielded her eyes, the better to see who was coming. A second, startled glance confirmed both passengers.

'It's my father and Markos. But what on earth is my father doing in uniform? I can still remember their work rotas and it's their rest day today.'

Harry shrugged and drained his coffee. 'Any idea why they're here?'

Val shook her head. 'None whatsoever,' she said, struggling to maintain her light-hearted mood as old resentments began to churn within her. 'They've never taken the trouble to come out here before.'

Harry rose and dusted a few crumbs off his lap. Still in bare feet, he sat down again, making no move to go indoors to fetch a pair of sandals or trainers. 'Maybe they're just calling in for a visit.'

'Yiannis hasn't set foot in Cypress House, not once in five years.'

'Fair enough. But there's always a first time.'

The taxi had reached the portico in front of the house. Val

could just make out Alexia's voice, raised in greeting. In a few moments Alex would be directing Yiannis and Markos through to the patio.

Embarrassed at the clutter, Val began putting their breakfast cups on to the tray. Harry touched her arm. 'A few bits of china don't matter. They know you're on holiday.'

Val sat down again, hearing Alexia say in Greek, from within the anteroom, 'I'll join you in a moment, gentlemen. What was it again, two coffees?'

Yiannis's reply was inaudible but Val could hear his and Markos's heavy shoes on the tiles. Soon she could see them through the half-open patio door, Markos smiling and nodding. He stared about frankly, taking in the splendour of the house with open curiosity. He was dressed in casuals, dusty trainers, blue jeans and a purple sweatshirt. In contrast, Yiannis was stiff and sweating in his uniform, his eyes hidden by dark sunglasses, his bronzed face stripped of every expression but his customary look of scarcely suppressed irritation. He did not smile.

Val rose to meet the visitors, aware that Harry had also risen and was leaning back against the marble balustrade like a statue posed in a study of nonchalance. A tiny lizard basked on the warm flagstones close to Harry's bare feet, a sight which made Val feel strangely tender and optimistic.

'Hello, Father. Markos.' She greeted them in English, giving each a warm smile. Close to her, Harry exchanged a courteous 'good morning' with the two men, although neither Markos nor Yiannis made any attempt to shake hands with him this time.

'Hello. How is your daughter? How is Judith?' Yiannis fired back at her, his Greek curiosity sounding brusque in English.

'She's much better, thank you, Father,' said Val, unsure what to make of this concern. As usual, Yiannis had not embraced her, and although he smiled everything he said sounded like a complaint.

'These childhood ailments can be treacherous. She is not feverish? You have not allowed her to become too hot? You have not given her too much to eat?'

'I'm sure that Valerie will have done everything that was necessary, including summoning a doctor,' Markos dropped in smoothly.

'She did,' Harry agreed, a bland lie as he turned to follow the flight of a citrus-yellow butterfly tumbling away from the bougainvillaea on the patio and fluttering over the balustrade. 'He told us that Judith was over the worst.'

'That is excellent news!' Markos turned to Val, his handsome face enlivened by interest. 'May I see her? I have a toy I meant to give her at the family gathering, but there was no time.'

'I'm afraid Judy's still asleep.'

'That's a pity.' Markos took something from the top pocket of his sweatshirt and held it out. 'Here, give her this when she wakes. Tell her it's from her *Thios* Markos.'

Lying in the middle of his palm was a tiny doll in Corfiot national costume – the kind of toy Judy would love, Val thought, with a pang. Conscious of Yiannis's watchful eyes, she skirted around her father and walked up to her brother, receiving his gift with a soft, 'Thank you,' in Greek.

'*Parakaló*,' said Markos, smiling down at her.

Yiannis walked to the edge of the patio. Leaning over the balustrade, he inhaled deeply. 'The boy, Steve, your stepson,' he said, straightening up, ensuring that his police cap was still on his head, 'he is not sick?'

'Father!' Markos laughingly protested. 'Steve is a young man.'

'Besides, he tells me he's already had chickenpox,' Val said, grateful for Markos's timely interjections. Yiannis's curt behaviour was familiar, if hurtful, but Markos was no longer the frightening bully of her adolescence – he had never been just that, she was forced to admit. She realized that if she owed Markos an apology in some ways, she owed her father very little.

She fell into step with the pacing Yiannis. 'Last year Judith had mumps while we were staying here. None of the family felt compelled to visit then.' Her lie was delivered flawlessly and it was easier to hold Yiannis's shaded gaze than his naked eyes. 'Not that I'm not grateful to see you today,' she went on, leaving her father to puzzle out the double negative, 'but

I am wondering why you are in your uniform, Father.'

'I thought Steve would be interested to see it,' Yiannis muttered. 'Here is our hostess.'

Val turned, catching sight of Alexia's wan, determined face behind the opening louvred doors. The pale morning sun lit up Alex's loose, flowing hair in a river of fire, but the rest of her was as drab as widow's black: a severe, charcoal-grey suit with black trim, black sheer tights and black low-heeled shoes.

'Your coffees,' she said, in her most formal Greek, giving Val a faint smile as Val lifted up the tray containing her and Harry's used cups. She set the new tray down smoothly on the bench in its place and said lightly to Val, 'Would you mind coming back to the kitchen with me for a moment – Harry, too? Just a tiresome question about menus. Please, gentlemen, help yourselves to coffee and cake while we're away. I won't keep Val longer than necessary.'

'Of course,' Markos said. Yiannis was already homing in on the cake.

Leaving them to it, Val and Harry stepped through into the anteroom. 'What is it, Alex?' Val asked, carrying the tray and hurrying to keep up.

Alex stopped at the inner door to the anteroom, touching a hand to her forehead. 'Chloe and that stepson of yours, what else?'

'Have they gone off on that mountain trip Chloe was talking about?'

'The mountain trip doesn't matter!' Alexia waved it aside. 'What matters is where they're going *after* that. They're using the whole trip as a means to sneak off – I've no idea where, or when they'll be back, and I can't get hold of Theo at work. All I get is the answerphone, and his mobile's switched off again.' She thrust a scrap of paper at Val. 'Read this. Harry can read it, too – my daughter's obviously practising her English.'

Val put the tray down on the tiles and scanned Chloe's breathless computer-printed note.

Mom, this is so cool! Steve and I are going to the mountain top, which is going to be okay. Steve keeps talking about ideas to stalk the stalker – to get after and unmask the Lip Man. (That's Steve's name for the saddo who has been leaving me and Auntie Val those lips.) Steve wants to run a few more ideas past me today, while we're out walking. Steve says he does football training runs back home and they stimulate thought. He says that walking up in the hills will clear our minds and allow fresh ideas to flood in. We'll find new ideas about the Lip Man that we'll be able to pass on to the police.

'Oh, yes?' said Harry over Val's shoulder. 'A one-man detective force.'

'So far, so idealist,' Val said. 'Nothing here to worry about.'

'Read on,' Alexia said grimly, tapping a foot. 'You obviously haven't reached the really exciting part yet.'

As I say, that will be okay but what is really, really ace is where we're heading after we've hit the top of Pantokrátor. You know Markos Stephanides, my jazz rival? In school last week he told me about an evening barbecue and all-night rave that's happening on the mountain this weekend. He'd wanted me to go with him – but no way was I going to an all-nighter with him! Can you imagine it? He's shorter than I am!

But now everything will be great. I can go with Steve!! It'll be so cool. There's Stella, of course, who's going out with a soldier who is eighteen, but nobody else will have a foreign boyfriend. It'll be wonderful – away in the mountains, in a place miles from anywhere and no one to complain. There'll be ancient ruins and music and loads of atmosphere – there's a full moon tonight. It'll be great. Markos said when I phoned him to check that it was still on that the DJ's coming specially from Athens.

We've borrowed Jessica's mobile and I've got my party kit. Other people are bringing wine and stuff. Markos said something about a Mexican barbecue but when I phoned Stella she said he'd got that all wrong – as usual.

See you and dad sometime tomorrow – probably very late!!

Chloe

'Cheeky little madam,' Alexia said. 'At her age I was having sleepovers at girlfriends' houses, not going to all-night raves! God knows what drugs will be circulating – coke and ecstasy will probably just be the start.'

'Maybe it won't happen,' Val said. 'I'm sure they'll be fine. If tonight's bash is with her schoolmates I can't see it being too wild. Where are Corfiot thirteen-year-olds going to get drugs?'

'You'd be surprised.'

'Chloe's a sensible girl,' said Harry.

'I wish I could be so certain,' said Alexia. 'I've just tried to phone them but the mobile's been switched off. It's the deceit that really annoys me: Chloe knows I disapprove of things like raves—'

A tapping on the patio doors made her break off. Val turned as Yiannis put his head through the gap in the doors. 'Hello?' he was saying. 'Is everything all right?'

'It's nothing,' Alexia said. 'My daughter, Chloe, who's thirteen, has taken it into her head to go to an evening barbecue and all-night party. Not alone,' she added. 'Val's stepson is with her. I know it's silly of me to worry, but I'm disappointed that my daughter has gone behind my back.'

'Yes, that is upsetting,' said Yiannis, careful not to look at Val.

'But forgive me, Mr Cavadini,' Alexia went on, with a rapid glance at Yiannis and then, through the half-open louvre door, at Markos, 'I apologize for my poor welcome.' She walked to the door and opened it fully, extending her hands towards the two men. 'You have come to see Val.'

'We are policemen, *Kyria* Alexia. We are always ready to listen and to help others.' Yiannis stepped through the patio door, removed his hat and strolled to the balustrade to sit down on the marble bench.

'Come,' he said, patting the warm stone. 'Tell us more about this party. Is it going to be in a private house? No? Then tell us more. My son Markos knows every disco and nightclub in Corfu town and many more over the rest of the island. He will be able to set your mind at rest.'

Alexia gave Val a look which meant *Don't dare mention*

the rave and stepped through into the sunlight. Val picked up the tray and took it in to the kitchen. When she returned to the patio, Alexia was still explaining. She was sitting beside Yiannis on the marble bench and looking up every few seconds to check on Markos's reactions. Standing staring out over Gouvía bay with his hands clasped behind his back, Markos looked in need of a cigarette, Val thought. But he was paying Alex close attention, as was Harry, who was back in his favourite position of leaning against the balustrade.

'There are many isolated farms on Pantokrátor,' Alexia was saying. 'I presume the party will be in one of those.'

'Chloe mentions ruins,' put in Harry.

Yiannis waved that idea aside. 'Typical girlish romantic fancies. Still, a barn in a farmhouse should be safe enough. Did you say that all her class are going?'

'I don't know,' Alexia admitted. 'I could ring some of her friends, talk to their parents, but of course if I do that Chloe will be put out. Though, yes, that's what I should do.' She swallowed and a spasm of distaste crossed her delicately handsome face.

Val wondered, where is Theo? Why was he not taking part in this discussion? Why couldn't he be reached at work?

In the instant she thought that, a memory of ruins, not ancient, but atmospheric and probably wonderful under moonlight, rose up in her mind. She said, 'I know where it's going to be.'

On the patio everyone stopped talking to look at her.

'They're going to hold it at the deserted village.'

'Old Períthia,' said Markos. 'Of course.'

Catching Harry's look, Val explained. 'It's on the northern slopes of Pantokrátor – you can drive right up to it now. The people moved from the village down to the coast in search of work, but I think there's one taverna left open there.'

'Chloe's ruins,' said Harry, nodding. 'Well done, Val.'

'And you can reach it from the summit of Pantokrátor,' Val added. 'There's a clear path.'

'So there you go, *Kyria* Alexia.' Yiannis crossed his arms above his head. 'I will stay and see my granddaughter when she wakes. My son will look for Steve and your daughter at

199

Old Períthia and make sure that this "party" is all that it should be.'

Clearly taken aback by this offer, Alexia turned a puzzled face to Markos. 'Oh, I couldn't possibly expect Mr Cavadini to do such a thing. Mount Pantokrátor is scarcely the edge of the world. As I've already said, I'll simply phone Chloe's school friends, starting with Stella—'

'It would be my pleasure.' Wreathed in smiles, Markos straightened and flicked at his jeans. 'I have no other duties today and I often go hunting in the hills. I will hunt today and at twilight I'll make my way back through Old Períthia, see Chloe and Steve and let you know all is well.'

'Fell walking: an excellent way to keep fit!' Harry announced. 'I do it myself, every weekend.'

Alexia was looking happier, although Val did not recognize fell or any other kind of walking as one of Harry's hobbies.

Markos glared at him. 'Let us go together, then, to the mountain.'

'Why?' asked Harry. 'Surely you're not being serious about this? You can't think that Chloe and Steve need chaperoning?'

'Certainly not on my behalf,' Alexia put in, with an embarrassed laugh.

'I do not go to the mountain for the young people,' Markos said. 'Steve is a man: he will take care of the girl.' Turning to Alexia, he gave her the smallest of bows. 'Have no fears, *Kyria* Alexia. I shall find them.'

Markos had contradicted himself and Val wasn't prepared to leave it at that. 'Why are you going to Pantokrátor?'

'To hunt, of course. As I told you earlier, Valerie, I was planning to hunt today, until I was asked to come here by our father. Now I will go – and Harry will come with me.' Markos looked straight at Harry, his expression openly derisive. 'Unless it is too much for you?'

'I'll come,' said Harry at once, leaving Val seething at the masculine inability to resist a challenge.

'Be—' Val began, and then stifled the rest. One thing she knew about policemen was their pig-headedness; she didn't need him with her and she wasn't about to argue. 'Take my mobile,' she said.

Harry shook his head. 'I've my own phone, remember? And I've done this before.'

Val watched as Alexia withdrew into the house again, having offered a second coffee and been taken up on her offer by Yiannis.

'Where have the young people set out from?' Markos asked.

'What do you hunt?' Val wanted to ask in reply. 'Why have you and our father offered to do anything for Alexia? If you find the barbecue and rave going on at Old Períthia and there are drugs – what then? Will you arrest my stepson and god-daughter?

'Valerie?' Markos prompted, walking towards her. Harry stepped in front of him, giving him Chloe's note.

'They didn't tell us. See for yourself.' He smiled. 'I think they'll probably go straight for the summit, glance at the monastery, then find a taverna to while away an hour or two before they take the stroll down to Old Períthia to eat burned sausages and party the night away.'

So why go there, Val thought. Harry and Markos clearly had their reasons, which were nothing to do with Steve and Chloe, although Harry was now saying, 'When we see them, I'll let you know. They needn't see us.'

'I suppose that's all right,' Val said. She'd no wish to spoil Steve and Chloe's pleasure, but if Harry was able to reassure Alexia that might be useful. She remembered when she was expecting Judy. In the early stages she had burst into tears at nothing.

'Valerie,' Yiannis called to her. 'Come and sit with me.'

Wondering what was coming next, Val crossed the baking flagstones to join her father.

Thirty-Eight

Yiannis rose and looked over the gardens and orange groves. Being outside on the patio, waiting for *Kyria* Alexia to bring more coffee, was no hardship.

An hour had passed since he and Markos had arrived here. Since then Markos and Harry had left – it had been a good move of his to suggest the mountain trip, get them both out of the way. *Kyria* Alexia, less pale than before, had telephoned the mother of one of her daughter's school friends. The woman mentioned a schoolgirl sleepover party at the nearest farmhouse to Old Períthia. When *Kyria* Alexia had rung off and repeated the conversation to Valerie, she laughed.

'At least Chloe had the good sense not to try that on me – it wouldn't work, not when she has Steve in tow.'

'But it is Old Períthia,' Valerie said.

'It looks that way,' Alexia agreed, turning to go back into the house to check on the brewing coffee. She had said more to Valerie in English, something about her driving into Corfu town – Yiannis thought he'd caught the words 'music festival committee' and 'Stefan Gregory', but he wasn't concerned. With everyone gone he would be able to press Valerie to come home. For Markos and himself, it was more than their careers at stake. He had to find out what his sly, clever daughter knew.

She was sitting beside him now on the stone bench, asking yet another question. 'Why are you so interested in Steve? I can't understand . . .'

Yiannis blocked out the rest, wishing that Valerie would be silent. Her voice was like that of her mother, Elizabeth, long dead, who had been preparing to desert him. It was because of Elizabeth that he had divorced Markos's mother.

Ah, Lefkosia! A young bride, so pretty, so good. His first wife. His true wife, in the eyes of the Church.

Yiannis raised his arms to heaven and stood motionless until he felt his shoulders crack. He coveted this orange grove, with its tumble of wild flowers and those delicious wafts of scent. Lowering his arms, he turned away from the gardens. He was not here for pleasure.

'Quite apart from this party, *Kyria* Alexia is anxious for her daughter. Why is that?' Yiannis was mildly curious and he enjoyed parrying Valerie's question with a question. He was the professional interrogator, not her.

Valerie sighed. 'I presume Markos told you about the strange paperweight that was left for me by the back gates of Cypress House? Before that, Chloe was sent an eraser. I took both to the police in Corfu town. They didn't seem interested, but you remember Hilary Moffat.'

'You told Alexia about a ten-year-old murder?'

'A ten-year-old unsolved murder, where the killer showed an unhealthy fascination with lips. Chloe and I were left packages of false lips. For us both to receive such "gifts" is surely odd, and a good reason to be careful.'

'So you worried your best friend.'

'I thought Alexia should be told.'

'Why? What threats have been made against you, or this girl?'

'None against Chloe, thank God! You know about mine.'

Yiannis said nothing. Valerie twisted on the stone bench, resting her forehead against the cool marble balustrade. 'Chloe's only thirteen.'

'But today Steve is with her and Steve is seventeen. Like Markos and yourself.'

'Markos knew exactly what he was doing.'

A second, more absolute silence fell between them. Cursing his idle tongue, Yiannis decided that the only way to puncture Valerie's infernal self-possession was to goad her. 'Thirteen and seventeen, at an all-night party: I can see why *Kyria* Alexia is concerned. Young passions heat quickly – it would be a shame if Chloe were spoiled.'

Valerie jumped to her feet. 'You are shameless!' she spat

at him in Greek, walking away towards the house.

How dare she turn her back on him! Forgetting that it had been his intention to provoke, Yiannis went after her, seizing Valerie's arm as she opened the patio doors.

She looked at him, her face high coloured and unyielding, Elizabeth's battle face. 'I must see to Judith,' she said in English.

'Don't be always fussing. The girl is recovering.' Yiannis broke off as Valerie's eyes narrowed. For a second he felt to be in the heart of a thunderstorm and he automatically let her go.

'That's what your mother told me when my mother was taken ill. When you and Irene ignored all warnings, all my own pleading. Even at seven, I knew she was sick; I remember her white face . . . So do you think that I will let you or any of the family come anywhere near to my child? And before you admonish me again for my faults, Father, should you not look to your own? I know you have done things which you regret.'

She left him on the threshold. It was a second before Yiannis could collect himself to speak. She was already halfway through the foyer, passing between huge pots of tall orchids; Yiannis hated the orchids, with their unearthly flowers and cloying scent.

'Don't you want to know why I'm interested in Steve?' he called out to her disappearing back.

Amazingly she stopped and looked round.

'Steve reminds me of myself at the same age,' Yiannis mumbled. He had no intention of admitting his true reason: to pump the boy for all that he knew about Valerie and her ghoulish interest in the Achillion murders – that and other matters which should not concern her.

He decided to elaborate. 'Your grandfather didn't want me to become a policeman, did you know that? He remembered the police under the fascists in Italy and he thought it was too dangerous a profession.'

Valerie was coming back, her short bob casting a shadow on her narrow shoulders. For an instant she put him in mind of Hilary Moffat, but Valerie was solemn and intense, where

Hilary had been merry and smiling, at least at first.

'Nonno never told me that,' Valerie said slowly. 'We talked about many things in the workshop and he told me all kinds of marvellous stories, but he never mentioned that. What did you do to change his mind?'

She was talking to him again, but her tender smile of remembrance drilled into an ancient jealousy that Yiannis was reluctant to acknowledge.

'I wrote him a letter – what do you think, girl? We spoke together as men and it was settled.' Yiannis heard a door further inside the house opening. Soon, Alexia would be returning; he had not much time. 'When are matters between us going to be settled, Valerie? The workshop, these suspicions you seem to have of Markos. It is not right.'

Refusing to answer, Valerie cupped a small pink orchid flower. Her head bent, she appeared to be examining its petals, fascinated by its structure. His father had been the same, forever poring over things, scratching about in the insides of objects, wanting to know how and why they worked.

Perhaps that was the means to ensnare Valerie, thought Yiannis, smiling as Alexia strolled towards them, bearing a tray of her excellent coffee.

He spoke. 'At home I have a half-strung guitar that Carlo was working on before he died; its age and origin were a mystery to him and he treasured it all the more. I believe it was his favourite piece. Why not come home with me and see it? Perhaps you will do better than he did in working out when and where it came from. I'm sure he would be pleased.'

Valerie's head came up at that and Yiannis wondered if he had been too extravagant in his appeal, but then she smiled. 'The favourite place. Of course. I should have realized that earlier.'

'Piece, not place.' Yiannis could not resist correcting her, but she still looked at him and nodded.

'Very well,' she said.

'You will come home today?' Yiannis could not believe it.

Valerie's blue eyes were filled with that dreaming, pensive expression he disliked for being so distant, so damn other-worldly, but she said, clearly and distinctly, 'Yes. I will come today.'

Thirty-Nine

Val held the door open for Alexia to carry her tray out on to the patio, then walked upstairs. She would have several moments while Yiannis was drinking. Before going to see Judy, she folded the photocopies of the Greek newspapers into her bag for later, then took an old metal coat hanger from her attic wardrobe, bent it in two and hid it in her large handbag.

As she picked up her handbag, she spotted a blond hair on the bed coverlet. Harry had said he didn't want her going back to her old home by herself, but Harry was wandering in the mountains with Markos. She guessed that both men had seized on the trip as an excuse to size each other up. Whether that would be useful or not Val could not say – dealing with her family had never been easy. She picked up her sun hat and went out.

Jessica had just come out of Judith's bedroom, carrying the little girl wrapped in one of the bedsheets. 'She wanted to get up just as she is, and since her nightshirt is cool and loose I thought that would be all right,' Jessica said quickly.

'That's fine.' Val wished that Jessica would be easier with her. Had the nanny had some tricky moments that made her always eager to explain?

'Mummy.' Judy stopped rubbing her eyes and held out both arms.

Val took her, tucking the trailing bedsheet around Judith's chubby bare legs and feet.

'Mummy, where's Steve?'

Oh dear, Val thought. 'Steve's gone out walking early this

morning, love. Very early. Before you or any of the rest of us were awake.'

Judy tugged on her bottom lip. 'Where's Chloe?'

'Chloe went walking as well,' Val said, tightening her grip slightly around her daughter's middle.

'They went without me! That's not fair!' Judith pummelled Val's shoulder and began to howl, causing Jessica to cover her ears and Val almost to drop her down on the steep attic steps.

'Hey, Jude.' Val whispered Judith's favourite nickname against her daughter's scarlet ear. 'You and I are going somewhere special later today.'

Judith stopped in mid-wail, the tide of instant molten fury draining from her blotchy face. 'Uncle Harry, too?'

'If you invite him. Of course, Uncle Harry is helping someone today, so he won't be home until late this afternoon,' Val went on. 'You'll be able to do your drawing again, and keep Jessica company while Auntie Alexia and I go food shopping.' A tiny white lie there, but Val knew that Judith hated shopping for anything except toys.

Judith stared at Jessica, who was quietly keeping pace with Val on the wider part of the main staircase.

'Yes – they left me, too,' said Jessica with a smile.

'Ohhh.' Judith lunged forwards to hug her tall, slim friend, who received her with a startled, 'Watch out for your mummy, darling: she's not made of iron and you've got very sharp elbows.'

'That's okay, I'm used to them by now,' laughed Val, passing the bedsheet over to Jessica as her daughter snuggled into riding against her nanny's hip. 'I think it's the kitchen for you, young lady, for orange juice.'

As she and Jessica strolled over the tiled floor of the main entrance towards the kitchen, the inner door opened and Alexia beckoned. Her delicate features were flushed and she was chattering into her mobile.

'We'll say no more about it now, Chloe, except that your father and I are disappointed . . . Chloe,' Alexia mouthed unnecessarily at Val. 'Yes, we'll talk about it tonight.'

Alexia scowled at the receiver and then came up close to

Jessica and tickled Judy. 'Be thankful yours is still at this age,' she told Val.

'What's this about talking tonight?'

'It's all off, apparently. Barbecue, rave and all-night party. That's what she told me when I was finally able to get through to her.' Alexia pulled a face at Judith, provoking a fit of giggles.

'What's happened? Chloe's note seemed so certain . . .'

Alexia smiled, then gave up trying to contain her delight and laughed out loud. 'It turns out that Chloe jumped the gun. Her little friend Stella has just phoned her in floods of tears to say that the Athens DJ has given backword, that Markos Stephanides has broken his arm and is in hospital having it set and that the sound system they were going to use has been commandeered by somebody's older brother. Oh, yes, and five of their closest friends have been grounded this weekend because their parents didn't believe the story about the all-girl farmhouse sleepover.'

'And that's the end of it?'

'The wheels have dropped off,' said Alexia happily. 'Although of course Chloe is trying to salvage some of her cool. She tells me that she and Steve are having a brilliant time *walking* and that I shouldn't be so prehistoric.' Alexia glanced at Val through a fall of tawny hair, her rich brown eyes sparkling with mingled relief and exasperation. 'I do believe my young madam was going to say "anal", but fortunately she didn't. I told her Harry and Markos were also coming to the mountain – I did stress to go hunting – and she got quite snippy with me.'

Alexia looked at the phone in her hand. 'I'll tell Harry not to bother tramping down to Old Períthia.' She laughed and held out the mobile. 'On second thoughts, I imagine you'll want to do it.'

'Thanks,' said Val, as Jessica and Alexia wandered on through the foyer towards the patio, Jessica still carrying Judy. Pausing beside a tall flowering orchid, she dialled the number of Harry's mobile. He answered on the second ring and she told him about Chloe and Steve and the non-rave.

'Okay, I'll let Markos know before we leave town. Listen, Val, I'll talk to you later.' He rang off.

A little sad for Chloe and Steve, Val walked into the sunlight on the patio. Jessica had set Judith down on the flags and Yiannis was calling to her.

'Come, little one, this is for you,' he was crooning in English, leaning forward on the bench with the doll nipped between forefinger and thumb.

Judith, her bedsheet wound about her in an untidy toga, glanced at the smiling Jessica and then padded towards her grandfather.

Yiannis plucked Judith off the flagstones and settled her on his knee. Fascinated by her present, Judith ran her fingers over the stiff petticoats and began to strip off the doll's tiny lace apron. Absorbed, she did not see Yiannis's self-satisfied smirk.

Jessica did, and she cast a puzzled glance at Val.

Val made the introductions. 'This is my father, Yiannis Cavadini. Father, this is Jessica MacTeer.'

'You are my granddaughter's nurse? Do you enjoy it here? Do you like working for my daughter's friend?' Yiannis fired these questions at Jessica, who, flustered by this seemingly aggressive beginning, stammered, 'Yes, I like it very much . . . thank you.' Jessica took a step backwards, into the shade. 'I'll go fetch Judith some juice, shall I?'

Alexia, who knew more of Val's family and regularly met Markos and Yiannis in town, took over the small talk. 'More coffee, Mr Cavadini?' She indicated his half-filled cup balanced on the balustrade.

'No, thank you.' Yiannis lifted his sunglasses on to the top of his head. Keeping his glinting blue eyes firmly on Val's face, he encircled Judith's middle with an arm, drawing her backwards so that her body rested more fully against his. 'Did I hear a phone just now?'

'Alex's mobile.' Val held out the phone to her friend, who took it from her with a smile.

'It was Chloe, Mr Cavadini,' Alexia explained. 'Or, rather, it was me phoning Chloe. She's not going to the barbecue and party tonight after all, because both have been cancelled. She is quite—'

'So where are they now?'

Alexia blinked but began to answer. Why not? thought Val. Yiannis wore the uniform even on his rest day: he was supposed to be a protector and upholder of the law. Only she knew that her father would lose no time in telling Markos.

What harm can Markos do to Chloe or Steve? Val pushed the question away.

'. . . They're taking a taxi to Petália and walking to the monastery up on top from there.' Alexia's voice returned Val to her own dilemma: how to get Judy away from Yiannis. The last thing she wanted was for her father to suggest that Judith came home with them to see Irene. Judith's presence would inhibit her.

'The tourist route,' rumbled Yiannis, and Val started, surprised that he and Alexia were still discussing Steve and Chloe. 'I have not walked up there myself for many years,' Yiannis continued. 'Perhaps, when I have more time.' He clambered slowly to his feet. 'Thank you for your hospitality, *Kyria* Alexia.'

Lifted in his arms, Judith regarded him solemnly. 'Are you my grandad?' she asked, eyeing his moustache while pressing a finger against one of his bright uniform buttons.

'I am.' Yiannis wriggled his moustache and Judith laughed.

'You live where I played hopscotch?'

'Let me take her – she's making your uniform sticky,' Val said.

'Take her, then.' With only the slightest hesitation, Yiannis handed Judith back to Val just as the child accidentally dropped her new toy on to the stone bench. Val scooped it back and returned it to her daughter, saying, 'Auntie Alexia would love to see this. What are you going to call her?'

'Jessica,' said Judith, staring up at Yiannis as he offered Alexia a stiff handshake, a brief smile and another formal thank you.

Forty

Early that morning Markos and Harry had called another taxi. Val wondered if Markos would use it for their mountain trip, then dismissed the thought. The good thing about the two men using a taxi was that she was now driving Yiannis into Corfu town in her hire car, so would be independent of him for the journey back.

Yiannis had not spoken so far. Val, with her mobile in her lap in case Harry, Alexia or Jessica contacted her, concentrated on the late-morning traffic.

Joining the main road from Komméno, she was driving alongside the twisted olive grove that bordered the junction when her mobile began to ring. Staying behind a cement mixer and slowing down as it began to pull away, Val took the call.

'Stefan Gregory,' said Stefan, at his most formal. 'Is dinner this evening still convenient?'

'Pardon?' Val was so startled that she did not ask how his first recital at the Achillion had gone.

'Our dinner arrangement for this evening,' said Stefan, in tones of absolute patience. 'I will be at Cypress House for seven to collect you.'

'Stefan, you suggested the twenty-fifth – that's another two days from now,' said Val gently. One thing she remained sure of was her memory. 'Your recital and the mayor's party? Your driver to pick me up at six?'

'Who's that?' Yiannis demanded. Val heard Stefan's hiss of surprise and knew that he had heard the male voice, if not the question.

'I'm out with my father,' she told the pianist, 'and I doubt very much if I will be back in time for dinner this evening.

It's a very pleasant thought, Stefan, but we must have misunderstood each other.'

'So you say. But I have already sent you the flowers. Flowers, dinner – is that not the accepted way for a man to make closer acquaintance of a young woman?'

It was on the tip of Val's tongue to say, 'You forgot chocolates,' but she did not want to be unkind to Stefan, who seemed to be having great difficulty in accepting that there had been a simple mistake. His manner to her was incredibly stiff, compared to the easy way they had been with each other at his villa, only yesterday. Perhaps he wasn't happy talking on the telephone, Val thought. 'I'm really sorry,' she began, changing down a gear as the cement mixer in front of her began to signal that it would be taking the next left turn. Behind her, a driver blasted his horn.

'He wouldn't do that to me, if I were driving,' snarled Yiannis.

'Who is that with you?' demanded Stefan.

'My father,' said Val, irritated at having to repeat herself. She swapped the phone receiver from her right ear to her left. 'I've already told you, Stefan. I thought I was going out with you to the mayor's party on the twenty-fifth of this month. I knew nothing whatever about any dinner invitation for tonight. I'm sorry to have to disappoint you, but I can't come with you, not at such short notice.'

'You make that perfectly plain. Until—'

Val did not hear the rest. Less than a car's length in front of her, the cement mixer began to turn off the road, then the driver changed his mind and veered back again on to the main highway. She swerved to avoid it and Yiannis blasted the car horn.

'Don't!' Val protested, appalled. She accelerated around the vehicle, calling, 'Hello?' into the phone, but Stefan had rung off. Steering one-handed, she displayed the number Stefan had been calling from and dialled it, tucking her mobile back under her chin.

A computer voice informed her that the phone she was trying to reach had been switched off.

'Marvellous,' said Val under her breath. She had no idea

what Stefan had been saying; possibly he had cancelled their plans for the twenty-fifth, which would be no great loss. Just at the moment she had enough going on in her life without having to cope with an artistic temperament as well.

'Who is Stefan?' Yiannis asked, as Val dropped the phone back into her lap.

'The pianist, Stefan Gregory. I met him this summer when I restored his Bechstein,' Val answered, thinking that restored was scarcely the right word in those queer circumstances. *I have already sent you the flowers. Flowers, dinner – is that not the accepted way for a man to make closer acquaintance?* Why did he not simply ask her out?

'He was the man you and Carlo heard outside the town hall.'

'Yes,' said Val, surprised that Yiannis remembered. Taking her eyes off the busy road for a moment, she glanced at her father. 'You already knew who Stefan was, so why ask?'

'I like to be sure.' Yiannis drummed his fingers on the dashboard. 'You will tell your daughter that the doll is from Markos?'

'When she's better, Judy will be writing him a thank you card.' Val reflected bleakly that it ought to be easier to talk to her father while she was doing something else. The road surface thundered under her wheels and sunlight flashed on the multiple road junctions and the huge car garages. Soon they would be in the heart of the town and conversation would be impossible.

'You are changing,' said Yiannis. 'Becoming harder, even less respectful. No doubt because of that new man in your life.'

'Not because of Harry,' said Val.

Yiannis hunched forward and switched on the car radio, pushing buttons. Schubert's Unfinished Symphony reverberated over the speakers.

'Music appropriate for you, given the state of the workshop,' Yiannis called out, leaning his head against the padded backrest and closing his eyes.

Val was too wise in the ways of her father to respond to that remark. He was right about one thing, though: she was

213

changing. She was no longer so anxious to please him, nor so keen to build any emotional bridges between them – a thought at once sobering and liberating.

'I am not a monster,' said Yiannis, without opening his eyes.

Val looked at his head rocking, at his hands folded together over his slight pot belly, at the faint pink marks close to his aquiline nose where the dark glasses had pinched him. He was her father, and a stranger to her.

'Is Irene expecting us?' she asked.

'When we are in town I will use your phone to let her know we are arriving.'

'This wasn't planned, then?'

Yiannis's closed eyes flickered. 'Let me listen to the music.'

Val turned up the volume.

Yiannis did not borrow Val's mobile to alert Irene to their coming. Val dropped him off at the end of several narrow streets, leaving him to go on ahead to the family home while she parked the car. She could have left it where her father had instructed, in the square below Pantokrátor church, an area which several families, including her own, used as a car lot. Instead, to avoid seeing the red Mercedes, Val parked near the workshop.

Walking back to her old home gave her time to think. Common sense told her that she would not be allowed into Markos's or Yiannis's rooms to search for evidence that might link them to Hilary Moffat or to the more recent Achillion murder. Instinct warned that such a search would probably be fruitless and possibly dangerous. Perhaps it was no longer so important – much depended on whatever Nonno had hidden away in the favourite place.

Checking that the coat hanger was still in her handbag, Val knocked on the dark-green door. No one came out of the house to greet her.

Irene, making one of her points? Val called out in Greek in as natural a manner as possible, 'Grandmother?' She rarely addressed Irene that way, so was intrigued to see what would happen.

The alley remained empty, the house still. Val wondered if there were eyes peeping at her through the closed window shutters of the 'best' room, but decided not to speak again. If Irene and Yiannis were inside, their silence suited her own plans.

Without looking up at the first-floor balcony or the second-floor windows, in case someone was watching, she walked round the corner into the garden.

Alert in every sense as she moved, skirting round the plastic chairs, she could smell the sea and, more prosaically, the stink of drying paint. She could hear the cheeping of caged budgies from one adjoining property and, further off, the click of knitting needles. Unusually there were no voices, but as she listened she caught the drone of a Vespa engine suddenly cut off as its driver coasted down one of the narrow arcaded alleys.

By now she had reached the orange tree. Conscious of the low branches, heavy with fruit, curving over her head, she hurried through the narrow gap between the tree and the back walls of the houses. Here in the corner, close to the broad white step where people would sit and chat in the cool of the evenings, was where Yiannis parked his motorbike. There was also the big black dustbin, the old iron bath, part of a toilet seat and a stone horse trough.

In the trough flourished one of the marvels of Val's childhood, a wild rose. Growing taller than a man in this shadowy, musty world, the rose had pink blossoms, a sweet, heady scent and lethal thorns.

A few wizened scarlet hips, survivors from the previous summer, flicked Val's face as she stepped around the rose and knelt beside the crumbling low wall of the ancient family well, positioned in the gap between the walls of the houses and the stone trough.

She would only have a few moments before her father or grandmother came looking for her. Her explanation was ready, but first she needed to recover something. Luckily, the wild rose would shield her from the windows and balcony of her former home.

If she was right, Val thought, Nonno had chosen his hiding place well.

She reached with her hand down over the lips of the old well. Closing her eyes to enhance her sense of touch, Val remembered this place as it had been when she was a child. The rose had been there then, but the other clutter had not and the well itself had been covered with an old carved wooden cover. She had sat upon it, her feet dangling down over the built-up neck of the well, watching Nonno picking hips from the rose. In her memories, it was always early evening, sunset and bells and the pungent scent of Nonno's pipe, which Irene forbade him to smoke indoors. Sometimes, Nonno would remove the well cover and allow Val to peer down, drop a pebble into its dry, dark shallows – the well had been partly filled in, stopping at a depth of two metres.

'It still counts as a wishing well,' Nonno had told her.

'This is one of my favourite places,' she'd replied, tossing a drachma into the old well and wishing, with tightly closed eyes, that her father would, one day, be proud of her.

Nonno had remembered, Val thought, opening her eyes as her stretching, searching fingers discovered a loose stone. She eased it free, her face pressed against the rough brickwork of the rim of the well.

She lifted the stone out, laying it by the rose roots before trailing her fingertips down the mossy inner surfaces of the well, back to the gap. For an instant, fear of scorpions or watersnakes made her stop. Val straightened a second time and removed the bent coat hanger from her bag, using it to investigate the gap in the well wall. She heard the faint chink of the metal against something smooth, possibly glass, and then the click of low heels and Irene calling, 'Where are you?'

Letting the hanger drop into the well, Val lifted out a small glass jar. Dropping it, cobwebs, dirt and all, into her bag, she rose to her feet.

Forty-One

Harry was irritated. By now he'd expected Markos and himself to be on their way to the mountains, but they were still messing about. They had taken a taxi back to the Liston and walked up through the older, narrower streets to collect a family car – in this case Irene's.

Markos had parked the red Mercedes in Pantokrátor square, close to the baroque church, under the shadow of its stone angel. Unlocking the doors of the gleaming car – freshly repaired, repainted and repolished – Markos stood back, ready to enjoy Harry's reaction.

Staring at the hulk which had almost run Val and her family off the road, Harry wanted to tear off its smirking metal grille.

'The repair was quick.' He was using English, so Markos would miss his suppressed anger.

At this point, Val's phone call turned out to be a godsend. Hearing her talk gave Harry the chance to rein himself back.

'That was Val,' he said, snapping down the cover on his mobile. 'Chloe and Steve are fine, and the Períthia party is off, so we can leave them to it. I was wondering . . .'

Markos pointed with his thumb to the passenger side. 'It's open. My hunting gear's in the back. Let's go.'

Harry ducked forward and opened the door, leaning against the car body. 'I'd like to take a look at the Achillion.'

Markos snorted but said nothing as he dragged his door open and sat in the Mercedes.

'I think a trip out there would be useful.' Harry settled into the cream upholstery. 'Yiannis did discover Hilary Moffat's body in the grounds, and with this latest killing it would be good to get a real picture of the scene. How about it?'

Harry was disappointed when Markos's mobile phone began

to ring and frustrated when Markos said nothing but 'Yes' and 'Okay' in Greek.

Markos tossed his phone on to the back seat. 'Nothing important.' He started the engine with a roar of the accelerator, rammed the Mercedes into first and shot out of the square. A small dust cloud rose behind them as they rounded the corner. If they didn't crash on the way out of the old town, Harry thought, he might shake a little more out of this rather jumpy customer.

'Have you and your father been asked to give DNA samples for elimination?' He paused, letting silence do its work, aware now that neither Yiannis nor Markos had given DNA – if they had, Markos would not have been able to resist proclaiming their innocence. 'By the way, why was Yiannis cruising the grounds of the Achillion palace the night he stumbled on the body? Rather off the usual tourist-police beat, isn't it?'

'He was not part of the tourist police, then,' Markos said. 'He was going to the restaurant close to the Achillion. One of the officers was hosting a leaving party there – the restaurant belongs to his cousin. My father was driving there when he passed the palace gates and saw they were open. He stopped to see why. The rest you know.'

'Very commendable.' Harry knew this already from talking to Val, but it was useful to have facts confirmed by a hostile witness. So far Yiannis did have a plausible reason for being in the grounds and, if those missing seven hours of his could be tracked down, possibly a perfect alibi.

Markos cleared his throat. 'Why is Valerie so interested in the Hilary Moffat case?'

Here we go, thought Harry. 'Val knew Hilary. And the case has never been closed. Are they the same MO by the way? Hilary's murder and this new case?'

He withdrew his elbow quickly from the window-ledge as the Mercedes skidded round a blind corner. Finding an empty horse-drawn carriage in his way, Markos stood on his brakes and blew his horn.

'I'm not at liberty—' Markos thumped the horn again as a woman ran her moped straight out in front of them without a backward glance. 'Tourist!'

Harry couldn't tell how he knew – the woman was wearing a heavy coat and boots: an outfit he would have been melting in.

'Why aren't the police concerned about Val and Chloe being stalked?' he asked.

The answer he could have supplied himself, from Fenfield. 'It's not been established that they are being stalked. We haven't the resources to look into every piece of crank mail that people get sent.'

'Even your sister?'

A vein was pulsing in Markos's temple. Ten minutes later, he turned the Mercedes on to the coast road.

Glad that they were out of the worst of the centre traffic, Harry tugged down his sun visor. 'The Achillion's not far, is it?'

'I'm not going to the Achillion. I'm going north, to the mountain.' Markos grinned at him. 'It's my day off and I want to hunt.'

'Is it the season?'

'If it bothers you, I can drop you off.' Markos rolled down his window, flipped open the glove compartment and brought out a bag of pistachios, tossing one into his mouth and spitting the shell out of the window. His unspoken contempt filled the space between them.

Even without the embarrassing possibility of encountering Chloe and Steve, the idea of Markos striding about Pantokrátor with a shotgun wasn't amongst Harry's favourite images. But since Markos seemed to think that he was testing machismo, and as there was the issue of trust to be resolved between them, he decided to stay.

Know your enemy, Harry told himself, especially when you're not sure if your lover's half-brother is an enemy. Val was safe today at Cypress House, looking after Judy, safe amongst others, and if she upbraided him afterwards for seeming to fall for Markos's clumsy challenge, so be it. He wasn't going to pass up this chance and all these hours to pump Markos for any information he could get. They had a day ahead of them, and in that time Harry was certain he'd learn something useful.

219

'Does Yiannis hunt?' he asked.

Markos gave a bark of laughter. 'My father, out of the town? Not in a thousand years.' He cracked another pistachio shell between his teeth.

'What about—' Harry stopped himself, though not before he felt utterly ridiculous. He couldn't possibly ask, What about Irene? 'Is hunting a popular sport on Corfu? Do a lot of men go out at weekends or their days off? The family Val's staying with, for instance: does Theo hunt?'

'Maybe.'

'You don't keep a police record? In Fenfield we keep lists of hunters and farmers with rifles.'

'Why should we do that?' Markos flicked him a malicious look. 'We don't have your problem with guns.'

'No, I can see that.' Harry was happy to agree if he could extract a little more information. 'Back in Fenfield you have to be a model citizen to own a firearm, so if Theo came into my station I'd be checking him up on the computer for any misdemeanours . . . you know the kind of thing.'

Alert to the slightest sign of recognition, he sensed no reaction from Markos. Either the man had glacier meltwater in his veins – and Harry knew that wasn't so – or Theo, the possibly straying husband, had no kind of form.

Alexia and Val would be glad, Harry decided, unsure himself whether he was disappointed or not. He wanted to know who was sending Val and Chloe those strange tokens and he thought it likeliest that it was someone they knew. How else would that paperweight have turned up at the back gates of Cypress House, at the same time as Val was staying there?

'Did Carlo hunt?' he asked, more as a way of introducing Val's grandfather, and his workshop, into this rather one-sided conversation than because he was interested in the answer.

'Of course.' Markos also appeared bored with questions, or at least with this one. Harry didn't expect him to say anything else on the subject, but as they roared past a wayside shrine set slightly back from the main coast road, Markos roused himself to add, 'Carlo left me his hunting rifle – a good one, if rather heavy on the trigger.'

'I understand your grandfather died suddenly,' Harry

remarked, glancing at the passing signs for the beach resorts of Kondókali and Gouvía. So far as he knew, the most direct route to the summit of Pantokrátor from this side of the island was by the mountain road to Spartilas. That turning wasn't for several kilometres yet, so he could concentrate on Markos. 'Val was wondering if there were any unusual circumstances.'

'She would!' Markos seemed both bitter and amused. 'Valerie adored Carlo; she would have wanted him to live for ever. Me, I would say he had a good death, a clean one.' He tapped his head. 'Fatal stroke in his sleep, the doctor said.'

'Had he had any shocks? Bad news – anything like that?'

'Has Val got you on that line too?' Markos now was pitying. He shook his head. 'No more than the rest of us.'

Harry let the matter drop for a few kilometres and left Markos to wrestle with the coast-road traffic. Only when the car was powering up a steep hill, with the junction to Spartilas emerging out of the heat haze, did he ask, 'What kind of man was Carlo?'

'A moment,' Markos grunted. He brought the Mercedes off the main road and round the sharp turning to Spartilas, coming to another dead stop a few metres farther along when they encountered a goatherd with a flock of long-haired goats. As Markos edged the car round the bleating goats, the goatherd cursed in a dialect so thick Harry could make no sense of it, but Markos bawled back in ripe Corfiot, flooring the accelerator as soon as the Mercedes was past the man and his flock. Now the red car leaped up a dusty, fly-blown road that climbed sheer in places, twisting almost back on itself. Aware that he might be one reason for this display of dash, Harry sat quietly, showing no reaction as the car thundered by several roadside shrines, each one erected in memory of a fatal accident on this road.

Markos was a good driver – Harry was forced to concede that. He warmed to the man a little more when he slowed to a crawl to pass a trio of weary walkers, stopping the Mercedes by the leader of the party to ask if the little group were okay.

'I can give you a lift to Spartilas,' he offered in English.

Squinting into the car, the leader of the party, immaculately turned out, stared at Harry's unshaven face and crumpled clothes, his brawny forearm resting on the car window-ledge. He shook his head.

'Here, then.' Markos passed the man a large bottle of water and pointed to the sun. 'Try not to be out in this at midday, eh, my friend?'

They drove off, Harry wincing at the stricken expressions of the other walkers.

'You were asking about Carlo,' Markos continued. 'Carlo was a private man, a loner. This is unusual in my country, perhaps less so in yours. He carried many secrets, I think.'

Including a guilty conscience? Harry wondered.

'He was the head of our family but always separate from it. That used to make my father unhappy: he never knew what Carlo wanted from him.'

'Rather like Val with him.'

'Indeed.' Markos's mouth snapped shut. They drove through the ancient village of Spartilas without speaking, Harry watching as the terraces of olives and vines were replaced by stumpy bushes of broom, heather and holm oak, all growing in the direction of the prevailing wind. The landscape colours were different here, too, the soft greens and blues of the coast giving way to burned-off grass and stark greys, the foothills of the mountain bare and stony, a litter of skeletal white stones threaded through by spiny ribbons of gorse and bare animal tracks. Overhead a bird of prey rode the thermals with lazy ease. Below there seemed to be no animals at all, only more cars ahead of them on the hot tarred road, their engines busy on the steep incline.

Harry saw no other houses until the tiny hamlet of Strinalas, whose car-filled square was dwarfed by a massive elm with dusty, tattered leaves. Young tourists sat outside the tavernas, but he couldn't see Chloe or Steve. He half expected Markos to stop, but he kept on driving, easing through the narrow street leading out of the settlement.

'We will go on to Petalia – that's where the young ones have started from,' Markos announced.

'It was Yiannis who phoned you earlier, telling you where they'd gone.'

'Of course.' Markos swerved to avoid a pothole in the new road, his eyes gleaming with amusement.

'You said that call wasn't important.'

'It wasn't – I knew I'd be coming up here.' Briefly, Markos took both hands off the steering wheel, cupping his fingers in a gesture that seemed to be inviting applause. 'If we spot them, that's a bonus.'

For whom? Harry wondered, but he said nothing, showed no surprise when, after they had climbed a couple more kilometres, Markos parked the Mercedes off the track in front of a broken-down wall, just outside the village square.

'They will be long gone by now,' Markos said, stepping out of the car and walking round to the boot.

The lunar summit of Pantokrátor, with its ugly radio masts, brooded over Harry as he squashed his sun hat down over his ears. He joined Markos to take his share of the burden: a rucksack with water bottles, socks, maps and insect repellent; two boxes of shotgun cartridges; a telescopic sight; a light tripod; a pair of binoculars. The ground where they were parked was strewn with empty shotgun cartridges and dead flies. Everywhere he looked, Harry saw rising bare ground, dotted with tiny pockets of trees or broom. The *maestros*, the prevailing north-westerly wind, beat on his face and snagged his hair, threatening to flip his hat into the nearest gorge. From further down the slopes he heard the boom of gunfire: hunters spraying any likely target.

Several pilgrims, tottering from one of the tour coaches that had stopped in Petalia village square, said 'good morning' in Greek as they passed Harry on their way to the monastery crouched under the radio towers. Closer still, he heard the whine of a horse fly and tugged up his shirt collar.

'You take this one.' Markos tossed him something from the boot, which Harry automatically caught, bracing his arm against the weight. Markos took a more modern version of the same hunting rifle from the back of the Mercedes, slinging it over one shoulder as he slammed the boot lid. 'We'll go on foot from here.'

'I'd never have guessed,' Harry muttered, turning the unfamiliar weapon in his hands. He slung it over his shoulder and waited. Whichever direction they were headed, there was no way he was going to walk in front, with Markos carrying a firearm and breathing down his neck. 'After you.'

Markos pointed to his feet. 'Boots would be better: this is snake country.'

'I'll bear that in mind next time.' Harry decided that the warning was genuine. Perhaps it was the effects of the altitude, but he didn't feel quite as antagonistic towards Markos as he had done earlier that morning.

Perhaps Markos felt the same. He moved off confidently, still on the road but striding out towards the village centre. 'I know a good place close to Lafki,' he threw back over his shoulder, not adding whether he meant it was a spot for hunting, viewing, finding Chloe and Steve or simply walking. Falling into easy step a few paces behind, Harry decided to wait and find out.

Some time after they had gone through Petalia they left the tarred road for scrub-bounded tracks and stretches of grassland thick with flies and spring flowers gone to seed. Watching his feet in this landscape more suited to goats, Harry glanced up every now and then to see Markos's shoulders working. Above his unshaded, dark head there were distant purple patches, the northern islands of Mathraki, Erracusa and Othondi. Later, when they turned north-east, the dark blue gleam of the sea became more visible, and the cloud-topped mountains of Albania across the strait.

As a scramble Harry thought it easy enough, although the dive-bombing flies were a pest. Trigger-happy hunters were a nuisance, but at least the one he was with seemed harmless enough, using only his scope to check this arid, stony cover for game.

He smiled. 'Harmless' was not how he would describe Markos.

'Look,' said his companion, pointing up towards the mountain summit.

Harry saw the two bright, scampering figures and knew at once who they were. Markos, following them with his scope, confirmed it. 'They're fine. He's talking and she's listening.' He chuckled, lowering the scope. 'Not any more.'

Harry guessed that Steve and Chloe were kissing, up on the

track above them, within sight of the monastery, but the haze and distance made it impossible for him to pick out details by eye alone.

'A tall girl for thirteen.' Markos stepped back to come alongside him.

Harry, who hadn't thought about Chloe's height in any particular way, said nothing. He sensed that Markos was about to say more.

'When I first saw her, Valerie was thirteen.' Markos cleared his throat. 'She was pretty then, and prettier now.' He straightened and glared. 'She deserves the best.'

Brotherly warning, or something more tragic? Harry took the simpler meaning – it was kinder that way. 'I know it,' he said.

'She has been unlucky. It was a pity, Nico dying, leaving her alone.'

'Val was never left alone,' said Harry.

'So you do care.'

'What business is that of yours?'

Markos began to polish the gun scope with the front of his casual shirt. 'Valerie would say none. Perhaps she is right – but could you stand by without trying to know more about her new man?'

Was that the reason why they were up here, so that Markos could quiz him, man to man, about his intentions? For an instant, Harry was furious, then, seeing behind Markos's bluster to the bewildered hurt beneath, disconcerted. 'Do I pass the test?' he asked.

'Do you expect me to answer that?' Markos resumed cleaning the scope with added ferocity. He, too, seemed uncomfortable with the subject, but unsure how to bring it to a close.

Nothing had really changed, but in that moment Harry felt closer than he ever thought he could to Markos. 'How about a drink?' He lifted the rucksack off his back, relieved to be looking down into the pack rather than at Markos's rather too naked expression.

Standing silhouetted against the clouds, the two men drank from their water bottles. Harry drained his as Markos set the gun scope to his eye a second time, watching Chloe and Steve. Or was it more than watching? The man was careful enough to be the controlled killer who had mutilated Hilary Moffat. Always, Markos used the scope alone, his raised hand as still as stone, never training the rifle itself on the young couple. Utterly correct.

Harry wished that he could dislike Markos as heartily as he had earlier. Instead, he was discovering on this trip that one of Val's family wasn't a complete creep, that they could rub along, as long as he didn't think about Markos in relation to Yiannis. Or – and Harry faced this squarely – in relation to Val.

Uncomfortable, he changed the subject. Instead of asking Markos where he was on the evening Hilary went missing or the day and evening she was murdered, he decided such questions were futile and would only put Markos back on his guard.

'You know anything about the pianist Stefan Gregory?'

Markos turned, his face genuinely puzzled.

'He sent Val and Chloe flowers this week,' Harry went on, astonished and rather ashamed of his own jealousy. 'Val's were pretty spectacular: sunflowers, yellow roses, yellow lilies.'

'What about Chloe's?'

'I believe lilies again. White lilies. Where I come from, they're popular at weddings.'

'But no yellow flowers for Chloe?'

'Not so far as I know.' Harry wasn't sure what reaction he'd expected: these thoughtful questions weren't supposed to be coming from Markos. 'What is it?'

Markos scowled, squinting into the sun. 'Nothing – let's go.'

He stalked off along the track.

Forty-Two

'Someone might see! Don't!' Chloe giggled, but the slap she gave Steve stung quite a bit.

'I thought you liked it.' Steve withdrew his hand from her breast. 'Christ,' he said, noticing her trembling bottom lip.

'We're within sight of the monastery! On holy ground, almost!'

'Sorry.' Steve raised a hand in mock surrender. God, Greek girls were a pain. He'd wanted to ride up here on a couple of hired mopeds, but Chloe had vetoed that as well. Some blather about her having to be careful with her hands. She wouldn't even share a Vespa with him. 'I've seen you windsurfing,' she'd said, as if that explained everything.

Still, even though the rave wasn't happening, it wasn't all bad news. They'd shared the taxi that morning with a couple of blonde Swedish babes. They'd been giving him the eye, and if Chloe hadn't been sitting there . . .

You look after her. Val's voice: an unwelcome conscience. He scowled.

'Steve?'

'Will you look at this view,' he said, flinging out an arm in the vague direction of Italy.

'We can go back. There's woods, lower down. I could let you, you know . . .'

'Right,' he grunted. He wasn't bothered about the monastery, and the last thing he wanted was some gun-toting Greek accusing him of molesting his second cousin, niece, or whatever.

'Steve?'

To be honest, Steve thought, staring at the long hilly flank of Albania, what he fancied were a few cold beers in a mountain taverna and maybe another crack at the two Swedes.

227

Blondes were cool, sexy. Thirteen was much too young.

'Steve?'

'What?' Don't let her start on about whether I still like her. As he reluctantly looked back, he saw her pointing arm – a silken, shapely arm, with glowing, touchable skin.

'I've just seen Harry and Val's brother,' she said, an instant antidote to eroticism.

'What?' Steve shaded his eyes, irritated that he did not see as far into the rippling wall of heat as Chloe.

'Over there.'

'Wow!' He had spotted them now. Automatically he grabbed Chloe's wrist, dragging her behind him. 'They've got guns! They've actually followed us up here with guns!'

Chloe touched his shoulder. 'That's my mother's doing,' she said. 'She'd do anything to get me to practice.'

'Nice one, Chloe.' His face bright with excitement, Steve patted her fingers. 'Keep walking as if we've not seen them.' He threw an arm about Chloe's shoulders. 'Excellent! Keep going towards the monastery. They won't dare follow us in there. We'll beat them at their own game!'

Steve was in his element, Chloe thought, matching her steps to his long stride. He was pleased with her again – but would that last? Once their remaining project – to unmask the 'Lip Man' – was over, how long would they be together? What had they in common?

How can we track a man the police can't find? the realist in Chloe insisted, but she glanced at Steve's keen face and knew she would not ask.

They were crossing under the shadow of the radio masts, the iron struts radiating reflected heat and light. Chloe racked her mind for something to say before they entered the monastery grounds and she was awed by the setting. Steve would never understand that, the quality of still silence such holy places inspired in her, in all Greeks.

Thinking of silence made her remember its opposite. She had thought in sound since she was a child. Stefan Gregory's lilies for instance – they were the beginning of Chopin's Raindrop Prelude. Her parents, the two sheltering arches over her life: Schubert for two pianos.

228

Chloe stopped directly beneath the massive electrical pylon. *I miss my piano.*

'Come on,' Steve urged.

Chloe thought of her Steinway, black and sleek and hers to command, with Stefan Gregory's bouquet standing as audience.

'Why flowers?' she said softly. Why flowers for her and Auntie Val, and why these strange gifts for them both, too?

'That relationship. Music. Pianos,' she muttered, falling naturally into her native tongue.

Steve stepped in front of her, giving her a tiny shake. 'If I didn't know better, I'd think you were *on* something.'

Chloe looked between the iron legs of the radio mast to the ridge where Steve had spotted Harry and Markos. They were gone, but she caught herself saying, in English, 'Blonds and redheads.'

'What about them?'

'Val likes foreign men and so do I. There must be something we have in common, but I can't see it, apart from the musical connection. We don't dress the same, and our hair, hands, eyes and faces are all different.'

'Different body types,' said Steve, his eyes lingering over hers.

Chloe ignored him. She was thinking hard, applying the same concentration that she did to her practice. *I must get back to that soon.* Perhaps her own dedication to practice was another similarity between her and Auntie Val.

'A need to impress?' Steve put in, surprising Chloe with his insight.

'Perhaps.' Chloe tapped her teeth with a forefinger. A need to please would be more accurate, but that thought was too revealing for her to share.

Steve grinned and playfully grabbed her hand, drawing it away from her lips. 'What about mouths?'

'Dad once said I had a mouth like a Cupid's bow. Let's get out of this sun.' She wanted to be away from prying eyes, and not only those of Harry and Markos.

'For a lot of what you've said, the guy must know both of you.' Steve brushed a speck of rust off her nose, then tugged her forward.

Once in the bare grounds of the tiny monastery, Chloe took a pink chiffon scarf – one of her mother's – from her bumbag, to cover her head while on sacred ground.

She was forced to admit that she'd been unkind when Mum had told her about the new baby. With a twist of shame, Chloe remembered how her mother had blushed pinker than this scarf. Mum had wanted her to be pleased and all she had talked about was this mountain trip.

Chloe stared at the soft scarf, wondering how her mother was now. She would have another brother or sister. All her friends would be intrigued. She'd be able to shop for cute clothes, sit her baby brother or sister at her piano. It would be great to show a little one the notes, like discovering the piano all over again.

Thoughtfully, Chloe knotted the chiffon under her chin. As she did so, her mind flew back again to her piano and from there to Stefan Gregory. At his villa, showing off his instruments, Stefan had been lavish with his praise, which made his first, cruel comments about her playing all the stranger.

'She plays like a pink cloud,' Stefan had said, smiling at her over his long, steepled fingers. 'Precision is what's needed.' He had brought both hands down on to his knees with a slap, causing Chloe to blink through her misting eyes.

With a daring she blushed at to consider, she had stammered, 'But, *maestro*, I am precise—'

'Pah!' Stefan had clicked his fingers. 'The precision of a woodworker, as bald as a clockmaker. No artistry. No suffering.' He had risen to his feet and turned his back on her.

'I could learn.' Remembering, Chloe crossed herself. A stride ahead, Steve marched on, oblivious. She wanted to forget, but the rest of that first encounter with Stefan rattled on like some nineteenth-century piano concerto to its predestined end.

'Perhaps,' Stefan had said, examining his fingernails. 'Perhaps you, among others. Those who have listened and not learned. How many chances do you give such a one?'

'Poser!' muttered Chloe in Greek, and walked after Steve into the warm, dark heart of the monastery church.

Forty-Three

Irene's face twitched. 'Why are you out here?'

'No one came when I knocked at the door. I went to see if anyone was in the garden.' Val reached up to the arching wild rose, brushing a crinkled leaf. 'I came to see this, too. Nonno would be pleased it's still flowering.' How it thrived in this scrap heap was a marvel. 'He always loved this rose.'

Irene's black eyes took on a stony look. 'Come with me now!' Her jet crucifix bounced on her ample bosom as she left the garden and strutted back under the arch at the end of the alley.

Val followed her. In her handbag was the thing she had come for: Nonno's last message. Why not make her excuses and go? Harry doesn't want you in this house on your own, her conscience nagged, but Harry was with Markos, the other suspect Cavadini. These were her family. Surely that should count for something?

Already she was back at the house and to stop seemed foolish. She caught up with Irene as she marched into the 'best' room.

To her surprise, Yiannis was not there. Even so, this formal room evoked no happy memories. The eyes of the many photographs seemed to follow her across the bare room to the shuttered window. Taking her accustomed place, determined by many family gatherings when she had been thrust away to stand against the window-ledge, Val turned and waited. A tiny breeze, flavoured deliciously with cinnamon coffee, wafted in, a welcome link with the normal outside world.

There was never any offer of coffee for her, she thought unhappily, watching Irene sit down on one of the upright chairs, with the ancient wood-burning stove, unlit and cold, between them.

'We must wait for your father,' her grandmother said.

'How are you?' Val leaned against the shutters. 'Did my father tell you that Judith has chickenpox?'

'Harry told me.' In Irene's mouth, the name became a curse. She did not answer Val's question, nor did she ask about Judith.

'How is my father?'

'What do you care? You're only here because you want something.'

'Really? What do you think I want?' Meeting her grandmother's black eyes, Val asked herself: how much does Irene know? At once the answer flashed back: everything. Perhaps not the details, but enough.

'Your kind always want something. Like your mother before you.'

Val remembered her mother in this room, standing with her back to the shutters as she was doing now. Elizabeth's picture was not in the family gallery. She had been expunged. When her mother had been left to suffer and die she had been able to do nothing, but she could do something now: a kind of vengeance for Elizabeth, and herself, and, she hoped, for Hilary.

'I already have what I need from this family,' she said. 'I have it in a safe place.'

Irene shifted on her chair. 'If you will talk nonsense—'

'Something small. Quite precious.' She could mention that the object had been in Markos's hands, but that would be a risk. Irene might not know about the jade ring.

'You're lying!'

Val smiled, her heart hammering under her breastbone. There was a perverse satisfaction in using Irene's hatred against her.

Gripping the open iron door of the stove, Irene levered herself to her feet. Her face had turned the same dull parchment colour as the faded lemon walls. 'You cannot have it! Ah, you must think me stupid! What are you trying to do, girl? Have you one of those infernal recorders in your bag?'

She lurched forward, stepping round the stove and

232

approaching with surprising swiftness, her feet making the same padding sound that Val had heard on the cobblestones outside her workshop, when the grey-hooded watcher had run away. But that couldn't have been Irene.

'Give me that!'

Irene snatched at her shoulder bag but Val lifted it out of her reach, saying, 'There's no recorder! What do you think I am?'

Even as she twisted away from Irene, Val glanced at the bag. It had only a single clasp fastener in its middle and its contents could be glimpsed: the dusty glass jar and her mobile. She didn't want to engage Irene in any undignified scrabble but at the same time she was determined that the glass jar remain undetected. She brought out her phone.

'*This* is what's in my bag.' As she flourished the mobile, Val walked away from Irene. She was tempted to walk out but from upstairs she heard the creaking of old mattress springs and then rapid footsteps as a powerful body rushed down the narrow internal spiral staircase.

Her father, who had been lying on his bed, from the direction of his charging feet. If she tried to leave now, he might prevent her. Better to bluff it out.

From habit, she checked her phone. A text message was displayed on the small screen. *Workshop. 4 to 7 tonight. Or no more sweet breezes.*

'I will take that.' Yiannis closed a large fist over Val's hand, squeezing her fingers until she released her mobile with a sharp cry of pain. The phone clattered on to the polished wood floor and Irene carefully retrieved it.

'No need for you to hurry now,' said Val, despising herself. She had only meant to show the mobile as a feint. Now she had no idea who had sent that text message.

She held out her hand. Feeling had only just started to creep back into her fingers. 'May I have my phone, please?'

'How does this work?' Irene demanded, jabbing buttons as she spoke.

'I need it for my work.' Val looked at Yiannis, not expecting any help from that quarter but compelled to try. 'Judy might ring.'

'Mother.' Yiannis snapped his fingers, adding wearily, when Irene showed no signs of relinquishing the phone, 'If you will.'

Irene handed it to her son, who slipped it into his shirt pocket. Val almost moaned aloud, then cursed. Let them think that was all she had of value in her bag.

'I need to know who is texting me.' The truth gave her voice an urgent sincerity.

Yiannis chuckled. 'It will surely wait, for it cannot be your daughter. She will not know how to write yet.'

'Judith can write!'

'Not, I think, text messages.'

Val stood her ground. 'May I have my phone, please?'

'Later. We do not wish to be disturbed, do we?' Yiannis walked to the main easy chair within the room and sat down. 'Are we going to have coffee?' he asked his mother. 'Or perhaps wine?'

Irene sat down again, wheezing, on the chair behind the stove. 'I do not give hospitality to family traitors.' She snatched at her jet crucifix. 'Ask her what she means to do.' She swung the end of the crucifix at Yiannis, almost seeming to aim it at him. 'I warned you: bad blood will out. It always does.'

'So you have told me. Often.'

'She has found what Markos was looking for!'

'Lost by me and my son and found by her?' Yiannis stretched his legs out in front of him. 'With help from Carlo. Yes,' he went on, when Val said nothing. 'That would make sense.'

Val licked her dry lips.

'You're thirsty?' Yiannis asked. 'So am I. We shall drink wine and water, like the ancients. From the best glasses. A small way to mark your homecoming.' Without giving Val a chance to respond, Yiannis motioned to his mother. 'Do it for me, for this time, Mamma,' he cajoled in Greek, using the diminutive and smiling broadly – probably in relief – when Irene seized hold of the stove pipe and hauled herself to her feet. Impatient for her to be gone, Yiannis waved his fingers at her back.

'I'll help you.' It was one of the few times she could

remember that Val found herself eager to join Irene, but Yiannis barked, 'Sit down!' To her confusion and shame, she folded on to the seat her grandmother had just left, its wood still warm from Irene's body.

'So I can still command you. But now you are on your guard against your Greek instincts and the next time I ask something you may not do it.' Yiannis beckoned. 'Bring your chair in front of the stove. We cannot discuss what needs to be said with half this room between us.'

His words were a mockery and a challenge but Val hesitated.

'As you wish.' Yiannis dismissed her lack of action as of no consequence. The grumbling of Irene in the kitchen filtered through to where he was sitting. 'She will be struggling with the wine cork,' he said.

'Shouldn't you help her?'

'It will do her good to vent her spleen on an inanimate object for once.' Yiannis turned in his chair and pointed to a tiny photograph in the dimmest corner of the room. 'When you were your daughter's age, you were fair. It doesn't show up so well in that picture, but seeing her today reminded me of you when you were six.'

Anxious to draw him out, Val did not remind her father that Judy was four.

'We were a family then,' said Yiannis.

'I don't remember.' Val refused to succumb to nostalgia.

'Who knows you are here?'

'Everyone,' Val said at once. It was good to see Yiannis finally on the defensive, but she must be careful. Her mind flashed to the pathologist's report on Hilary, a gruesome warning of what she might be dealing with.

But if Yiannis was involved in Hilary's murder, what was she going to do?

'Harry knows,' Val lied. One task at a time, she told herself, chanting the restorer's creed. See the whole but concentrate on the detail. 'Markos knows, too,' she added.

Under cover of the curved sides of the stove, she checked the time: 11.08 a.m. She had several hours before her mysterious summons to the workshop.

'He took the ring from Hilary Moffat's hand. Carlo.' Yiannis

235

crossed one leg over the other, leaning back in his seat as if he had reached the conclusion of some long internal wrangle. 'I don't know what trash Carlo told you, but Irene threw it into the sea.'

'Why should I believe that?'

'It was Carlo who killed Hilary.'

Forty-Four

Yiannis waited for furious denials. He had spoken on impulse. He wanted her precious mental image of Carlo, her hero, to come crashing down.

Valerie glanced at the most recent photograph of Carlo on the walls.

'May I see the guitar Nonno was working on, before he died? That *is* why I'm here, isn't it?'

'I lied. The day after my father's funeral, the owner came and took it away. But he didn't ask you to complete the repair, did he?'

Valerie was smiling, that annoying half-smile. 'I can understand that. The touch of each restorer is different.' She straightened on her chair. 'Some things are better for not being restored.'

A gasp of triumph from the kitchen warned Yiannis that Irene had won her wrestling match with the wine cork. 'You don't believe me about Carlo.'

Valerie leaned her elbows on the cold stove and settled her face on her hands. 'Convince me. Why did Irene remove Hilary's ring from Markos's room?'

'She believed the ring could be used against the family.'

'So she removed it to protect her husband?'

'Irene and Markos know their first loyalty is to the family.'

'What about Hilary? What about her family?'

'Markos hid the ring in Carlo's workshop.' Ignoring awkward questions, Yiannis dropped another piece of tailored history into his clever daughter's ears. To receive information you sometimes had to give. 'He thought the workshop would be the last place Carlo would look, amongst his own things.'

'And you're going to tell me that Markos forgot where he had stashed the ring, in that maze of woods and veneers and tools?'

'We don't all have your memory.'

'Markos looked for the ring in the workshop and found it again and *Irene* made sure it was gone this time by tossing it into the sea? Why not do so earlier?'

'How should I know? But remember Carlo went out again on the night that you and he went to that recital at the town hall. He said it was to continue work on a cello, but what if he really went out to find Hilary again? He'd seen her earlier – he'd even sat beside her. He could have taken the car and picked her up, driven to the Achillion.' Yiannis paused, allowing the tension to build. 'You know the rest.'

'And the man Hilary and I saw in the Zeus bar? The stranger in the white shirt who tried to pick us up?'

'A nobody.' Yiannis waved him away with an imperial sweep of his hand. For years he had wanted Val to see Carlo's faults as well as his virtues – well now she could, with a vengeance.

Val was staring at him with stricken eyes. 'Nonno kept his word. After we came home, he did go back to the workshop that night.'

'So he said. But none of us was with him.' Yiannis inhaled deeply. In the kitchen Irene was slicing figs. Was she preparing his childhood favourite, fresh figs with *mizýthra* cheese? 'Not even you were with him overnight – my mother had you helping her with the washing.'

'Yes, because our washer had broken down and Markos wanted his football kit clean for the next day but said nothing until eleven at night! He was out supposedly working, probably enjoying himself . . . somewhere, but he still phoned Irene for her to instruct me to scrub his dirty washing! I was up until three in the morning.'

'As was your grandmother, girl, so don't whine.'

Valerie's rosy colour deepened, but when she spoke again her voice was calm. 'Nonno was at the workshop all night. In the morning, when I walked down to the workshop to see him, he showed me Mrs Christoforou's cello, with its coats of varnish, new strings and restored bow. To do what he did, Nonno would have had to have spent all night in the workshop.'

'So you say.'

'Why are people bad?' Valerie said. 'My daughter asks me that. And I wonder at you. Why are you so spiteful about your own father? Are you envious of him? I'd no idea that you were quite so malicious.'

Her words stung, but Yiannis said nothing.

Valerie hung her shoulder bag on the back of the chair, drumming the fingers of her right hand against her cheek. 'The night Hilary was murdered, Markos was out all night and he did not return home until long after midday of the following morning. Isn't it more likely that he took her ring as a trophy? That Irene threw it into the sea because someone saw him looking at it?'

This was so close to the truth that Yiannis felt his face colouring in anger.

'Unless Markos didn't have the balls to kill Hilary.'

'That's not true! But my son is no murderer.'

'Not man enough?'

Yiannis turned away from the blazing face and bright, goading eyes. 'No. Yes. Not man enough, as you put it. Not for that.' He put his face in his hands.

'I realize this is hard for you, but do you think that it's easy for me? I know we're estranged as a family but I'm still concerned for you all. Even Markos. I do still care.'

Yiannis heard her stumble on the final word. Now that he was not looking at this living mask of Elizabeth, he sensed the deep sympathy and confusion in the young woman. Valerie was only a few metres away, but there was a mountain of distrust and misunderstanding between them. Yiannis felt too weary to climb it.

He scratched at the ends of his moustache. 'I've not been sleeping too well these days.'

'What is it?'

Yiannis looked up, remaining still in his seat as Valerie left hers. Her features still transfigured by that earlier brightness, she came sure-footedly across the room and drew up the second easy chair. She sat opposite him, their knees almost touching. 'I will know everything, in the end,' she said softly. 'But I would also like to understand.'

She was close enough for him to notice the faint tremor in her limbs. Valerie had compassion and, more worthy, courage.

'I will try to do the right thing,' she said. She leaned away from him, her hands resting on her thighs. 'If Markos is no killer, how and why did he come by Hilary's jade ring? We can't pretend that he didn't, Father. Matters have gone too far for that.'

Unsure what to do or say, Yiannis was silent.

'Shall I tell you what I think?'

Self-interest warred with curiosity in Yiannis. In the end he told himself they were the same and nodded.

'I think Markos did take Hilary's ring, but not, as I claimed earlier, as a trophy. Markos is not stupid. Had he removed the jade ring from Hilary's strangled and mutilated corpse as a trophy he would have kept it hidden for ever. He would never have brought it out to study, not even ten years after Hilary's death – and yet that is precisely what he did. He brought the ring out from wherever he had hidden it. Why? As a warning to the real killer? But why should the killer remember an insignificant piece of jewellery, unless he had taken it first, as a dark memento? Is that what happened, Father? Did you take Hilary's ring and then lose it to Markos? How long was it before you realized that Markos had it? And did Markos, in spiriting the ring away from you, really attempt to hide it – only to lose it – in Nonno's workshop?' Valerie's thick black eyebrows came together in a frown. 'Poor Markos,' she muttered. 'So many problems.'

She looked past Yiannis to Irene, who stood rigidly on the threshold, carrying a tray loaded with glasses, a bottle of the rich local wine and a plateful of fresh figs and cheese. 'You suspected, Grandmother. You know much of what goes on in this house. Which is why, of course, my grandfather attempted to resolve it from his own territory, the workshop.'

Yiannis was experiencing profound feelings of dislocation. 'My father . . . ?'

'I told Markos at the time that it was a mistake to keep the ring.' Irene walked into the room, and conscious of the antique Venetian glasses on her tray lowered it to the floor. 'Markos never expected Carlo to notice or remember that foolish girl's trinket. He intended it, as *she* has guessed' – a baleful glance at Valerie – 'as a warning to you. My Markos has studied in the police force. He knows that anniversaries are important.'

Yiannis was remembering. 'The date of the Moffat girl's murder . . . Markos would always be with me that day, *all* day, *all* night. We'd go to a football match or the cinema, or take in a concert. I thought it was just a coincidence!'

'Except that last year something else happened to make Markos wonder afresh about the first Achillion murder?' Valerie looked at Irene.

'Ask Markos,' Irene snapped.

'So Markos began to wonder,' Valerie said thoughtfully. Her eyes returned to Yiannis, who was struggling to come to terms with what his son had obviously told his mother. Twelve months ago, prompted by a glimpse of that damned jade ring and Markos's persistent questions, he had explained much to Markos. But Markos was his son, another man, who would understand what had happened between himself and the Moffat girl, would understand how things had got out of hand. The thought of Markos and Irene discussing it was intolerable.

Valerie was speaking again. 'It's said you found Hilary's body in the grounds of the Achillion the night she was murdered. Is it possible that you had cut yourself, perhaps, and so bloodied Hilary's ring? That you removed the ring because you were innocent of her murder and the presence of your DNA at the crime scene would only confuse matters?'

'Such things are between Markos and myself,' said Yiannis, furious at this interference.

Irene clicked her tongue. 'The girl has given you a way out.'

240

Yiannis blanched – they were all turning against him. 'It's done with, finished!'

'If you believe that, you're a fool.' Irene stalked up to her son and jabbed at his shoulder. 'She knows better than that, just like Carlo!'

'My father knew? What? When?' Suspicion grew in Yiannis's mind. 'Was this just before he was taken ill?'

'Carlo's blood pressure had already been troubling him,' Irene said, shaking her hands in denial. 'You must not think—'

'That I caused my own father's stroke?'

'No, no, my son.' Irene broke off, gasping.

'Why not? I'm certain Valerie believes it!'

Yiannis was shouting. His blood thumped in his ears. For an instant his eyes seemed unable to focus. He saw a Valerie sitting bolt upright across from him, partially superimposed upon a Valerie stripped of all facial colour.

'What do you think I am, a murderer twice over?' he roared. 'The little bitch was asking for a smack in the mouth but I never touched her again. She got out of my car, alive, on the southern coast road and that was the last I saw of her, until her body turned up dead in the grounds of the Achillion.'

'Yiannis! That's enough!' said Irene.

Around Yiannis, the faces in the photographs seemed to be fading. The walls seemed to be dropping away at the edges, the light growing dim. Through the open door of the room there came a new shadow, the black double of one of the tall buildings that filled the cramped alleyways of the old town.

'I believe I will have that drink.' Valerie rose out of the chair. Black as tar, the noon shadow swept over her feet and knees and waist, casting her face into semi-darkness. 'Will you join me?'

Her invitation included both Yiannis and Irene but Yiannis was aware only of her. The silhouette of her small, pert figure. Her graceful walk – surely more flowing than he remembered? But this was Valerie, he reminded himself. Valerie, not Hilary. Valerie-Chloe, the family Cassandra, his daughter.

'Were they your handcuffs?' she asked, moving away, her back to him. 'The pathologist's report mentioned bruising around Hilary's wrists "indicating possible use of handcuffs". Did you use yours on her?'

'Why do you take the girl's part?' Irene demanded. 'She is nothing!'

'Not to you, certainly.' Valerie half turned and flicked her eyes towards Yiannis. 'But you. I know that she has haunted you, as she has me.'

There it was again, that look of possession, as if her face was not hers alone. As if the darkness across her eyes and lips was more than a simple shadow. 'You're not her!' He threw up an arm, shielding his face from those eyes, that accusing mouth.

'I'm here for her,' said the silhouetted figure. 'If I do not take her part, who will? When the police themselves—'

'Don't say it!' Leaping to his feet, Yiannis sent his chair crashing against the wall behind him. 'Don't say the police were corrupt! We looked for her killer. I ran down every lead I could.'

'To cover your own back. That's why you copied the pathologist's report – to make sure there were no clues in it that would point to you.'

'That's a lie!'

'Then tell me what really happened.'

'No!' Irene's breathing was rough with tension. 'The girl is dead; nothing can change that. Some silences must be kept!'

Yiannis heard the implied threat in Irene's words. 'Wine,' he ordered, licking his parched lips.

He watched the shadowed form of his daughter crouch before the tray and pour a glass of the rich wine, dark as blood. Lifting the glass, she deliberately tipped some of the liquid on to the floor, almost as if she was offering a libation to the dead. The hair on his shoulders and neck crawled.

She straightened and came towards him, her face still in shadow. Yiannis took a step back, then stopped. Wordlessly, she offered him the wine and he accepted it. Only then did she speak.

'Tell me,' she said. 'If not for Hilary's sake, then for your own peace.'

Forty-Five

Markos struck the dashboard with the fist that held his phone. 'Val's mobile's still switched off!' He threw the phone behind him, spinning the wheel into another steep downhill corner.

Silent so far in the passenger seat, Harry glanced back at the rapidly receding mountain and at their rifles, bouncing and jarring together on the rear seats. They had slogged along the mountain trails for less than an hour before Markos turned about. Returning at speed to the car, Markos had unceremoniously tossed the rifles into the back, then started the Mercedes and set off while Harry was still closing his passenger door.

'Are you going to fill me in?' Harry asked.

'A couple of years ago I dated a girl who worked in a florist's shop. Nice girl, but very scatty. Blonde. Beautiful brown eyes. Tall. Loved jewellery. Not my usual type.' Waiting at the junction to pull on to the main road, Markos looked Harry squarely in the face. 'You know the kind of girl I like.'

Get on with it. 'So she was nice, Markos. So what?' A bit harsh, that, Harry decided. 'It didn't work out between you?'

'She was besotted – that the right word? Yes, besotted with flowers. Her blooms, as she called them. She could talk at Olympic standard and most of it was about flowers. Theodora might forget where we were supposed to be meeting but she never forgot to condition her blooms. New colours, new arrangements. Japanese style. American style. Kinds of ribbons. We'd be strolling round the town in the evening before dinner and she'd spend her time flitting in and out of other florists, checking out the competition.' Markos sighed as a van carrying a load of bottled water went trundling past on the main road. 'It got to the point where I could recite the prices of the special and deluxe aquapacks and tell anyone who might want to know which bloom symbolizes secret love.'

He spotted the gap in the traffic and shot out on to the main carriageway, accelerating away from a white Lotus with a self-satisfied grin.

'It's yellow acacia, if you're wondering.'

'Don't know how I managed to live without knowing that,' said Harry.

'My thought exactly, so goodbye, Theodora.'

'What's this to do with Val?' Harry asked, glad of the Merc's tinted glass as they drove through the glare of the sun.

'Probably nothing.'

Harry punched Markos lightly on the shoulder. 'Come on, Markos. You can do better than that.'

'Okay! Okay. But if you laugh . . .'

'Hey.' Harry spread the fingers of both hands, wishing that Markos would keep his eyes on the road. They were weaving through heavier traffic now and it wouldn't do them or Val any good if they ended up under a petrol tanker before they reached the outskirts of town.

'Flowers are all about colour. Shapes, textures, scents but most of all colour, according to Theodora. That's how she put together her blooms. And, again, according to Theodora, every colour has a meaning.'

'Like the yellow acacia,' said Harry.

'Exactly!' Markos rapped the steering wheel in agreement. So far on this return trip he hadn't eaten one pistachio, perhaps a sign of anxiety.

'Funny you should mention yellow.' Markos ran a red light, ignoring horns and hand gestures. 'Theodora told me yellow flowers often have quite dark meanings – roses, for instance, usually mean love, but yellow roses symbolize the lessening of affection.

'I may be worrying about nothing,' he went on. 'Red roses are considered a bit obvious these days and yellow flowers do look great in masses. I've seen enough to know,' he added, with a touch of bitterness.

Harry thought of Val's flowers from Gregory, all yellows

and oranges, like exploding suns. A tribute to her energy, surely, and nothing more sinister?

'If you can't reach Val's mobile, why not try Cypress House?' he asked. 'Someone's bound to be there. They can fetch her to the ordinary phone.'

'I've already done that.' Markos kept both eyes fixed firmly ahead. 'The cook told me that Val's gone off with Dad into town. They were going back to the family home. The cook had no idea why.'

'I see.' Dropping his left hand below the car seat, out of Markos's line of sight, Harry clenched it into a fist. He wanted to yell at Val for being so obstinate, so independent. He had warned her not to go back there alone.

Forty-Six

Val watched her father drain his wine. He held out the glass and Irene poured him more, bobbing down to the tray and up again like a black robin. She pointed to the armchair and, when Yiannis did not move, lowered herself into it, her breath coming in sharp gasps.

'Stop that,' Yiannis said. 'That asthma trick might have worked on Markos but not with me.' He stalked across to the window and stood with his back to them, the light through the half-open shutters glinting on his uniform buttons.

Val crouched and poured another glass of wine, which Irene refused. Giving Yiannis time, she took the glass and walked back to the window.

Still with his back to her, Yiannis began to speak.

'I was on shift that night but it was the quiet time, before the Greeks leave the restaurants after dinner and before the English drunks spill out of the bars. The others on my shift I won't mention, because they had their own affairs to attend

245

to. One was sorting out an awkward waiter at his brother's taverna – I remember that. Our business was close to the centre. We had our radios and could gather fast if there was trouble. Not that there was.

'I'd parked on Kapodistriou, near the Liston. I'd just walked back there, after a sneaky listen to part of that recital which you, Valerie, had been able to attend. I was sitting in my police car, enjoying a cigar, when a young woman came dashing across the street from the Liston. She was looking behind and shouting in English, "I'm not going back to the bar alone with you, so why don't you bugger off?"'

'Hilary, dealing with our man in the white shirt? So it wasn't Markos?'

Yiannis shrugged his shoulders, clearly irritated by her interruption. 'Go on,' Val said quickly, praying that he would – and he did.

'I stepped out of the police car, my hand on my gun belt. The creep who was pestering the girl never stepped out of the shadows; I never saw him.

'As I crossed the street, Hilary Moffat yelled and felt at her back. "It's okay," she told me, when I reached her. "Cheeky bugger threw something at me." She pointed and then crouched down into the gutter. "There!"

'It was a pair of fake plastic lips. Red lips. Hilary picked them up. "God, how tacky!" she said, and laughed.'

'Thrown by the man in the white shirt, who you said was no one,' said Val, who could hardly believe what she was hearing.

'He was a tourist with a solid alibi,' Yiannis snapped. 'The night I met Hilary, he was later picked up by the police in a punch-up. Your man in the white shirt spent the next day and night in a cell.'

Val stared at her father's back. Hearing him accuse Nonno had been bad enough, but this was worse. 'Why didn't you tell me?'

Yiannis swung round to face her. 'Why should I tell you anything? Your interest in the case was already unhealthy. I thought the fastest way you *might* forget was to give you as little information as possible.'

'Had he thrown the lips at Hilary?' Val persisted, feeling her fingers tight about the wineglass, her throat and mouth clammy.

Yiannis shrugged. 'He said he knew nothing about them. The girl herself assumed he had and treated it as a joke. She gave them to me.'

Yiannis paused, his face slackening so that for an instant he looked much younger, almost vulnerable. 'She was a very sexy girl: lovely figure, great big eyes, beautiful lips. Very grateful. She thanked me, gave me the fake red lips, kissed me on the cheek. We exchanged names. She asked me if she could buy me a drink, in thanks. I offered her the bottle of retsina we kept in the car to moisten our mouths through the long night watches.

'She came and sat in the car. Drank some retsina. Stroked my arm. Asked me to show her my firearm.

'I drove her out of town – there were too many crowds where I was parked. I flipped off the radio. I could always say it had broken; some minor electrical fault. We drove along the south coast road: Hilary wanted to see a beach at night. She talked about finding a secluded spot, somewhere unspoiled. I knew then what she was after.

'We stopped close to one of the watersports places. It was deserted. The moon was up and she walked along the beach with me, barefoot, carrying her shoes, wriggling her behind in those slutty jeans. She wanted me to take off my boots and socks. We'd brought the retsina with us and she drank more, straight from the bottle.'

'Cheap,' said Irene.

Rising from the chair and removing a duster from her apron, Irene began to wipe down the photographs, beginning with the large picture of Markos. Val, remembering Hilary laughing and alive, dreading what Yiannis and Markos might have done to her, took her empty wineglass and placed it carefully on the window-ledge behind her father.

'I gave her a kiss,' Yiannis was saying. He had closed his eyes, as if visualizing the scene. 'She never objected. We got into a little chase and tag; each time I caught her, I took something off her. One shoe, then the other. Her handbag. Her necklace and earrings and then her jade ring. I think that, between us, we must have left her earrings and necklace on the beach, where they were probably picked up by another tourist. I never saw them again. I put the ring in my breast pocket and buttoned it down – I was going to give it back later, with the rest of her gear, but I forgot.

'She was giddy by then – too much wine, she said. Next time I caught her, I told her I was going to do a strip search. It was play – you know the kind of thing.'

Val felt as if something cold had touched her. Now that Irene's flapping duster had been momentarily stilled, she could hear only her own breathing. Ashamed of Yiannis, afraid of what else he might say but determined to hear it all, she leaned back against the wall.

Standing in the half-light, trim and gleaming, still handsome, her father did not open his eyes. He seemed to be reliving the experience, almost enjoying it. 'The girl struggled a little, not very much. She kept trying to push me away. I took her down on the sands with me and asked her what was wrong. She said she wanted to go back. Maybe she was crying then, I don't remember. I told her she owed me, that she should thank me properly.

'But then the little tease broke off and ran back to her clothes. When I moved to go after her she started screaming. She shrieked like a banshee the whole time she was tugging on her underwear. She screamed louder if I tried to get near. I was tired of it by then. I told her I was going back to the car and that if she wanted a lift into town, she should shut her mouth and hurry.

'I drove her back to the outskirts, her snuffling the whole time. By then I'd had enough of her whining, so I dropped her off at the start of the Garitsa district and tossed her a wad of drachmas for her to get herself a taxi. Then I drove back to the town centre and finished my night shift.'

'And the next time you saw her?' Val asked quietly, willing her father to open his eyes, to face what he'd done.

'It was the following evening; early, before the start of my shift. I'd gone out to a restaurant close to the Achillion – one of the traffic cops was having a leaving party there. The drive took me right past the palace grounds.'

Val saw Yiannis take a deep breath.

'I didn't think of murder when I saw that the gate into the grounds was unlocked and hanging open,' he said. 'I drove into the car park. I noticed that one of the gates to the gardens was also unlocked, so I went up the staircase to investigate.

'It was very dark, even with the floodlighting. I had to use my torch. She – the body – was in the grounds. I saw what I took to be a rubbish bag at first, stashed under an olive tree close to the palace. I was on the staircase above. I think it was sound that made me look closer. Rustling in the undergrowth.'

'The killer?' As Irene paused again in her dusting, her grey head close to Markos's photograph, her eyes were bright. Val could hardly bear to look at her. Beside her, close enough to touch, Yiannis shook his head. He still had not opened his eyes.

'An animal, probably a bird,' he said. 'I leaned over the railing and saw her. I realized what it was and who it was. She was draped in a sheet and there were flowers round her. Then I saw what someone had done to her.'

Yiannis shuddered, the first truly human reaction Val had seen in him. 'I had to call in the crime, secure the crime scene, write a report. Afterwards, when I came off duty, I don't know where I went. I walked the streets until I felt alive again. I couldn't cope with seeing her like that.' He opened his eyes and looked straight at Val. 'You were always my Cassandra. Can you foretell what will happen now? What will you do?'

'What will *she* do?' Irene burst out. 'It is you who must act! The girl you saw that night is dead, but you did not kill her! My son, the silence must be preserved. Think of your career. Think of Markos's career. Do not let these things be destroyed.'

Val held her breath but Yiannis merely wiped his eyes. He drained his glass again and Val, anticipating his need, poured him another. Their eyes met. In his she saw anger and shame, but also relief.

'That is no longer my choice to make,' he said.

Val nodded. 'But we have not finished,' she said. 'I also said that I would like to understand.' She paused, waiting while Yiannis took the first sip of his new drink, then gently placed the wine bottle on the floor. 'You took, or more accurately kept, Hilary's jade ring. So how did Markos come by it?'

Forty-Seven

Yiannis sighed, conscious of Valerie's small, stiff figure beside him. 'I'd forgotten the ring. The evening I met Hilary, I finished my shift, returned to the station. A few of the younger cops were there, the ones who always bragged about their romantic encounters.'

'Romantic!' snorted Irene, dropping her duster on the flags and leaving it there.

'I told them a little about my time with the girl. It was pleasant for me to be telling them. Markos was there for part of that and he saw me again later, when we were both at home. I was stripping off in the kitchen, piling my clothes into the wash tub. The ring bounced out of my pocket on to the flags. Markos picked it up for me.

'"A token from your evening?" he asked and I said yes. I took the ring back and put it with my cufflinks in my room.' Yiannis did not voice his secret wish of that night, that the girl might seek him out at the police station. He wanted the chance to buy her a coke, kiss those luscious lips and make up.

Valerie walked closer to the window and turned to face him. 'How did Markos react when you reported the murder the following evening?'

Yiannis frowned at Valerie's question. His daughter should have been a cop. 'I don't know how he reacted! I didn't see him until the siesta of the next day, when he barged into my room. When he realized how shocked I was, he didn't ask me much, just was I okay and things like that. He didn't mention the ring but I told him that I'd return it to Hilary's family. Markos must have been satisfied.'

'What changed after that?'

Yiannis ran a hand through his hair. Not looking at Valerie, he muttered, 'Afterwards my boss started getting after me, saying rubbish. That I had a thing about women's lips—'

'Which you have.'

'So what? If you'd seen what the beast had done to that girl. But enough! With Dinos on my back, I could not hope to return Hilary's jade ring to her people without awkward questions.'

'You kept the ring.'

Yiannis nodded. 'For nine years. Why not? It wasn't part of the crime scene, it was of no use to the investigation. But then last year Markos got a letter from Hilary Moffat's mother. It was addressed to *Kyrie* Cavadini and it went to him by mistake. She was writing to me; she knew I'd found her daughter's body.

'Markos came home that evening with the letter. He'd opened and read it, although it was addressed inside to me. The mother was asking questions: whether there had been any developments, any leads, whether Hilary's jade ring and earrings had ever been found. Markos came to my room and demanded to know more.

'I told him the full story of that night, not just the pretty bits I'd shared with the men at the station. He seemed nearly as straight-laced as you, Valerie, but in the end he said he believed me. He demanded the ring, though. He said he'd return it to the mother.'

'But he didn't and Nonno saw it and remembered it.'

'I didn't know anything about that,' snapped Yiannis. 'I supposed Markos did nothing because he saw the same problem as I had: too many difficult questions from the rest of the police. I do know that when I asked him later if he'd sent on the ring – this was just before Carlo died, around the tenth anniversary of the girl's murder – he was evasive. Something about irregular posts to England. By then I didn't like to ask too much.'

251

Valerie glanced at Irene. 'This was all at home. You over-heard them.'

Irene's head came up. 'I listened to them talking! I am not afraid to admit it. When I learned of this morbid trinket, I questioned Yiannis, but he said nothing. So I looked for it. I finally found it in my grandson's room, soon after *you* had returned, asking questions, making trouble. So I took the ring and threw it into the sea.'

Valerie surprised Yiannis then. She smiled, a sad half-smile that quickly faded. 'Nonno knew you well,' she said. 'He heard you arguing, too. But for me, to be so close to the ring after all those years . . .' She chewed on her lower lip, head down for an instant, and then she straightened again. 'My grandfather never had the ring.'

'No.' Yiannis was reluctant to admit more but Valerie was clever. She had already guessed.

'But your father had the other thing Hilary gave you.' Valerie's face cleared and then darkened again. 'You tried to hide it in his workshop, away from the family.'

Away from her and other prying women, thought Yiannis.

'And Nonno found it. And he wasn't sure if you or Markos had tried to hide it, but he knew it was important, because he knew Markos had Hilary's jade ring and he remembered how she had been mutilated after death.'

Yiannis flinched and Irene broke in. 'What thing? What is this, girl? Yiannis, what is she jabbering about?'

'You don't need to know,' Valerie said, a neat re-turning of one of Irene's favourite phrases to her over the years.

'What!'

'Mother,' said Yiannis, amused by his daughter's response. He glowered at Irene until she subsided.

'That was what Markos was looking for in the workshop,' said Valerie. 'He saw more than the jade ring, didn't he, when you stripped off in the kitchen all those years ago. I presume you told him that Hilary had given you the red lips as a joke – and he believed you at first, particularly when you were so obviously distressed at finding Hilary's body. But then over the years as no other suspects were found Markos began to doubt you.'

'I suppose,' Yiannis grunted.

'After he received the letter from Hilary's mother, did you decide to hide Hilary's fake lips in Nonno's workshop – only to lose them there?'

Yiannis would not give her the satisfaction of an answer, but Valerie, his Cassandra, knew.

'My grandfather found you in his workshop, found Markos looking for what you had tried to hide and found them himself.' Valerie's mouth trembled, the only sign she showed of any natural feeling. 'You should not have used his place,' she said.

'Don't lecture me,' growled Yiannis.

'No, that's way too late.' Valerie hugged her elbows and paced up and down the length of the shuttered window. When she stopped again, she had recovered that damnable self-possession of hers, resuming her relentless restoration of the past, of things best left to rot.

'Markos had seen the fake red lips. That was why he has been disconcerted by the fake lips sent to Chloe and myself. But you have not seemed so troubled.'

'I did not think they were relevant.'

'Yes, I suppose with Hilary being killed less than twenty-four hours after receiving her "gift", you assumed that Chloe and I were safe, seeing that no similar attempt was made against us. How very convenient that must have been for you, Father! Did it remove all sense of obligation for you? Or did you think that if you watched Markos closely enough you might prevent him from moving against us?'

'Markos suspected you and you suspected him, didn't you?' Valerie's shoulders shook. For a second Yiannis thought she was crying, but then he realized that it was laughter. 'What a marvellous, wretched mess you have made between you!'

'He is my son,' Yiannis began, but Valerie cut across him, striking straight at the heart of the matter.

'Why did you begin to doubt Markos?'

Her questions were intolerable but Yiannis found himself answering. It was a relief to speak, a catharsis he had yearned for over the last year, since his father's sudden death. 'When I guessed he had not returned the ring to the girl's family. When I remembered how eager he had been for details of my

253

evening with her. When I checked the work records and realized that Markos had worked alone for much of the evening when Hilary disappeared. When *you* appeared, asking questions about him . . . Damn you, girl!'

'Say it, Father. I want you to admit it, just once.'

Yiannis sagged in his chair. 'When I realized Hilary looked like you.'

'And why did you keep the red lips? Why take the risk?'

Because otherwise he would have had to explain to that smug bastard Dinos, thought Yiannis. They were a guilty reminder of things he and Hilary had shared that Hilary had not wanted. He knew about killers keeping grisly tokens. All these reasons, and the most compelling: 'Because she gave them to me. Hilary gave them to me.'

Valerie nodded and walked across the room for her bag. She passed by him, saying very softly, 'Goodbye, Father. I must think, so I will be alone for a while in the workshop.'

'I understand.'

'You may not have murdered Hilary, but you made her an easy prey. You left her on the road to the Achillion.'

'Yes,' said Yiannis, acknowledging the truth that Markos had spared him but that he had always known. His Cassandra was braver than his son: she spoke it aloud.

'Stop her!' Irene shouted.

But Valerie continued walking and Yiannis let her go.

Forty-Eight

Yiannis was sitting on the whitewashed step, staring into the garden. Harry did not waste time with greetings. 'Where's Val?'

'Gone. Long gone. I've lost her.' Yiannis drained his tin cup and poured another measure of red wine, squinting into the bottle to check the level. 'I've lost her and Markos lost her and you will lose her, too, Englishman.'

'He's drunk.' Markos jerked his chin at the house. 'Go look inside for her. I'll talk some sense into him.'

'No.' Harry was less suspicious of Markos but not that trusting. 'See if your grandmother will make him some coffee.'

Harry waited until Markos disappeared indoors, then took the bottle from Yiannis's unresisting fingers, sniffed it, checking the alcohol level. He set the bottle on the wide step. 'I'll use your toilet.' Once in the house, he could look for Val, but his instincts were telling him that Yiannis wasn't lying.

Ten minutes later, when he'd gone through every room, checking for signs of a struggle, he was satisfied. Val had walked out of her old home alone and unharmed.

Markos and Irene were bickering in the kitchen. They ignored him as he searched. Harry caught a few Greek words – 'shameless', 'disloyal', 'ruin' – and left them to it. He found Yiannis refilling his cup from the near-empty bottle.

Yiannis tilted his head. 'My mother wouldn't let me use the Venetian glass for this.' Close to, he seemed shrunken, suddenly aged.

'Listen, Yiannis,' Harry said. 'I know you're not as drunk as you're pretending to be.'

'I'm working on it.' Yiannis peered at him. 'Maybe you would know.' He laughed. 'You've had dealings with the creatures that drive us to drink. Women!'

Harry spotted the mobile bulging from Yiannis's top pocket. 'I'll have that, it's Val's.' He snapped his fingers, holding his palm flat until Yiannis complied, slapping the phone into his hand.

'All this technology,' Yiannis complained in a low sulky voice. 'Why she need it?'

'Where's she gone?' Harry asked.

Yiannis raised and dropped his shoulders. 'Shopping, going back to Cypress House, meeting her lover – who knows?'

'What lover?'

'Ha!'

Harry ignored him and checked Val's phone for messages.

There was a garbled text message, plus a recorded one from Gregory.

'Looking forward to seeing you again. You are always as fresh as a daisy, a Chloris. Until later.' The message ended with a click.

'That came in almost as soon as I switched her phone back on. Her friend the concert pianist.' Yiannis kicked at a pebble and grinned. 'What chance have you against him? My daughter has already had one policeman.'

Shut your mouth, old man. Uncomfortable thoughts and memories stirred. Val and Gregory sitting together in the horse-drawn carriage. Val's second visit to Garitsa. Gregory, calling her as fresh as a daisy.

'Like mother, like daughter.' Yiannis tipped back his head to take another drink.

Watching him, Harry realized how much he wanted a drink himself. He craved whisky, a large Laphroaig.

'You jealous? Or is there no hot blood in those sluggish veins?'

'She will betray him!' Irene yelled from the kitchen, in perfect English.

Harry felt through his pockets and found the workshop address and phone number. His call was answered almost at once.

'*Parakaló.*'

It was Val, safe and as prickly as ever, asking in Greek, 'Who is this?'

'Me. Harry.'

'Oh!'

'I'm at your father's.'

'I see.' No explanation of why she went to Yiannis's home first, against his advice. 'I'll come down and join you,' she said.

'No! No, that isn't necessary. I'll be finished here soon, anyway, and then I'll hurry back.'

'That's fine. Love you.'

The dial tone was her only answer. He hadn't even had time to let her know that he now had her mobile. Harry stared at it. An image of Stefan Gregory's smiling face flashed across his mind, followed almost as swiftly by a memory of Val's rapt expression when she had been working on the Bechstein. A piano and a pianist.

Yiannis chuckled and poured the dregs of the wine bottle on to the yard floor. 'I need another.' He lurched to his feet. 'Want to join me?'

Harry had a mental image of himself sitting here several hours later, empty bottles around his feet.

'Something stronger?' Yiannis waved the empty wine bottle in front of Harry's face.

Harry thought, *I wonder if he's got whisky?*

Forty-Nine

Val stared at the dusty glass jar on the bench. She felt drained of her usual energy – a state she had existed in for months after Nick's death. Harry had been there then to help, but now Harry would be ashamed of her. Hearing his voice had made Val aware of how impossible it was. Bad genes or bad luck, they brought the same result.

'Grandmother was right. I am tainted,' Val said aloud.

'You were always my Cassandra,' Yiannis had told her. 'What will you do?'

She did not know what she would do. Her mind was a hurricane. If she went to the police with what she now knew about Yiannis, would Harry despise her? 'Harry detests disloyalty,' Nick had told her. 'He believes in looking after his coppers.' If she informed on Yiannis, would Harry see it as an act of betrayal?

This is your father, the Greek part of her argued. *There could be no grosser act of treachery.*

Hilary was dead. Informing on her father would not bring Hilary back. Yiannis would be publicly reviled and Markos with him. The family would be notorious, avoided in the streets.

257

Her father's dream of a peaceful retirement would be shattered. Markos's career in homicide would stall: none of his bosses would dare promote the son of the disgraced Yiannis Cavadini.

She could fly away and leave the whole mess behind her.

'I know I've not treated you always as I should have done,' said Yiannis in her head: an imaginary Yiannis, to whom she could talk. 'You must have longed to be revenged. Now I have given you the means.'

If she told she would lose the last vestiges of her family's respect and make reconciliation impossible. If not could she respect herself?

Val walked over to the shutters and strummed down the slats with a sweep of her fingers, hurting her hand. Anything to stop these thoughts.

If she did not tell, was she failing Hilary a second time?

The workshop phone was ringing again, and she forced herself to answer it.

'Sorry, wrong number,' a voice apologized and she was alone again.

Val reached for her handbag and brought out the photocopies of the Greek newspapers. Any insight, however small, would be welcome.

A CD insert dropped out of the photocopies. Notes and lyrics from madrigals by Carlo Gesualdo, the fruit of Harry's reading the previous evening, gathered up with the copies by mistake.

Val scanned everything, the old newspaper reports and the CD notes. There was nothing in the Greek newspapers that she did not already know. The clear eroticism of the lyrics used by Gesualdo would have intrigued her, had she the leisure to listen to the music too.

She walked back to the dusty glass jar. For several marvellous, mind-numbing seconds her attention was concentrated on easing open the jar without smearing her fingerprints over what might be conclusive evidence.

This should go to the police, Harry scolded in her thoughts, as she deftly turned the top with narrow pliers, cradling the base of the jar on a nest of cotton wool stuffed into a brown paper bag that had once contained violin strings.

'Nonno left it to me,' Val answered, and that was enough.

Val felt her eyes fill and lifted her head, staring at the high ceiling, anxious not to cry on the jar and impatient with herself. She blinked and opened it. Using her tweezers, she lifted the covering wad of cotton wool from the glass jar and peered inside.

As she had expected, full red lips, plastic and tacky. A trivial novelty item, taken by Hilary as a bad joke and never mentioned by her father. When Markos saw them and learned the details of Hilary's death, he must have been horrified.

Markos must have suspected Yiannis of terrible things, but had never confronted him. Even with the jade ring, it seemed that Markos had not been able to bring himself either to hand it in as evidence or dispose of it, so he had hidden it away. He had made himself a burden and carried it in silence.

Or was Markos the one who had hurled the fake lips at Hilary? 'Surely not,' Val whispered, but she could not be certain.

It was the same with her father. Even with Yiannis's disturbingly frank confession she still was not sure if he was Hilary's killer or not. She did not think so – she desperately wanted to believe that he wasn't – but neither he nor Markos had behaved like innocent men.

Val gently tipped the jar, causing the lips to shift on their bed of crumpled tissues. She lifted them out. There was something written on the inside of the plastic.

Scratched on the red inside, two words: *Farewell, Chloris.*

An epitaph, thought Val, and now, finally, she knew who had written it. Images from her most recent dream hovered before her eyes. The gnat hovering around Chloe's lips, and her dream Alice band. The flowing robe, its colour swimming and blurring. The soprano line of the Gesualdo madrigal that Chloe had hummed. In all these images and sounds her dreams, her prescience, her subconscious, had tried to warn her, but she had not understood until now.

Time to go to the police.

Fifty

C hloe wandered about the monastery church of Pantokrátor, walking with Steve but thinking about Stefan Gregory. She stared at the fading frescoes, trying to decide if she should tell someone about what else Stefan had said to her when they first met at Mr Zeno's.

'You play with the precision of a woodworker,' Stefan had said and, 'How many chances do you give to those who listen but don't learn?'

He sent me flowers, Chloe argued with herself. But her unease persisted. She remembered how he'd said he was jealous of her, called her a prodigy, said that she was receiving the compliments he had once enjoyed when he was younger. Did Stefan resent her for that?

Leaving the monastery grounds, she expected the sunlight to dispel her thoughts, but instead, as she hurriedly tucked her mother's pink chiffon scarf out of sight into her rucksack, Chloe was reminded of the pink eraser she had been left. Another disquieting puzzle.

'Steve, can I talk to you about something? It's rather embarrassing.'

Steve took her hand and squeezed it. 'Sure, Chloe, whatever.' He smiled at her as they began the return walk to Petália.

After that, Chloe found, it was easy for her to speak about Stefan.

Fifty-One

Harry stood up, uneasy about the atmosphere in this house. The tensions were visible on Yiannis's haggard face and audible in Irene's wheeze of complaint. He walked to the door and shouted for Markos.

There was an answer from inside, but before Harry could shout back that he was going to the workshop, Val's mobile went off. Harry cupped the receiver with a hand so that Yiannis would have no chance of overhearing.

'Val? That you?'

'Hang on, Steve, I don't think Val's got that low a voice.'

'Harry? Where's Val? This is her mobile. Can you put Val on?'

'She's at the workshop. Will I do instead?'

After several heavy breaths on the other end of the line, the phone traded hands and he found himself talking to Chloe. What she said didn't make Harry feel any better about Gregory and it got more complicated when Steve took the phone back.

'Hi, Harry. Listen, Chloe's slipped off between the rocks for a moment and I think I better tell you this. She also told me that her dad, Theo, used to talk about her cupid bow lips, whatever that means. I don't know if that's important, but, you know . . .'

'Thanks, Steve.' Harry rubbed at his forehead, wanting to be off the phone and out of Yiannis's house.

'Yeah, well, I thought it might be. Uh – gotta go, Chloe's coming back.'

'Good,' said Harry into the dead receiver, keen to leave. He needed to see Val.

Fifty-Two

S tanding on the edge of the mountain road, her feet sticking
to the warm tarmac, Chloe checked the mobile and shook
her head. 'The credit's run out and the charge is down far too
low. We can't use it again.'

Steve snapped his fingers. 'I warned you that latest phone
call to your mother was going on too long.'

'Here, then, Mr Smart.' Chloe virtually threw the phone at
him.

Checking the mobile for himself, Steve swore aloud.

'This is useless.' He whipped round on his heels and glared
over the landscape, jabbing a finger at the tall communica-
tions masts on the mountain summit. 'Those don't help, and
we're stuck in the middle of nowhere. I need to phone Val at
the workshop.'

'So let's go back to town,' Chloe suggested crisply. 'Flag
down the next taxi. Look, there's one coming.' She thrust out
an arm and waved.

'Anything to get off this dump,' muttered Steve. No
barbecue. No rave. No blondes. No booze. And no Lip Man.

A sullen taxi ride later, Chloe and Steve had reached the
outskirts of Corfu town.

'We should split up,' Steve was saying. 'Have the taxi drop
us at the palace. I know the way to Val's old home – I'll go look
there. You go to the workshop. We can meet up at the Liston.'

'Fine,' said Chloe. She needed to be free of this gangling
English boy for a while, free of thirst and stickiness. When
the taxi pulled up, she watched him march away, mobile in
hand, then turned and crossed the Spianada in search of a cool
drink.

*   *   *

In the dusty ochre streets near Val's workshop, Chloe opened the can of iced tea and took a long swig.

'Chloe! I looked for you at Cypress House. I thought I would have to delay my plans when you weren't there. How are you?'

Chloe did a double-take. What was Stefan doing here, in a car parked in a section where cars were banned?

'Are you going to see Val?' Stefan leaned his head out of the window. 'I'm hoping to speak to her, too. Help me out, would you? I know I can get my car closer than this to her workshop, but I'm not sure of the way.'

He was smiling, and speaking flawless Greek. 'Would you like to hop in?' he asked. 'We can chat on the way. Did you like the flowers?'

The car was as green and inviting as a fresh apple, and Chloe could hear its air conditioning. It would be cool inside.

'Very much, thank you,' Chloe answered, picturing the white lilies, so elegant and statuesque, so far in spirit from the tacky pink lips.

'I chose them to represent your playing,' Stefan went on. 'Do you remember the duet we played together?'

'At your villa?' Chloe's free hand closed on the passenger door. She glanced at the can of peach tea, unsure what to do with it.

'May I have a sip?'

Chloe giggled. This was the Stefan she knew from his villa in Garitsa, not the cold, harsh stranger of their first meeting, when they had both misjudged each other. She knew him, and now she was ashamed of her earlier fears. Of course Stefan was interested in Auntie Val. He wanted Val to do some restoring work on his pianos.

'Here.' She passed him the drink through the open passenger door, her heart quickening when their fingers touched on the chilled metal surface.

'Thanks.' Stefan shook the can very slightly. 'You must tell me what exercises you do for that wonderful left hand of yours.' He grinned, suddenly looking as young as Steve. 'Or is it your secret?'

'Of course not.' Chloe felt proud and empowered. This was Stefan Gregory, asking her about making music.

263

'Good! I'm envious of that left hand.' Stefan patted the passenger seat, inviting her inside, then tipped back his head, drinking deeply.

Chloe climbed into the car, luxuriating in its air conditioning as Stefan closed the windows and started the engine.

'Finished,' said Stefan, crushing the empty tin can against the steering wheel with the heel of one hand. 'Fortunately, I have some cola – it's behind my seat, Chloe. Would you mind?'

Chloe reached for the large bottle wedged between two stacks of sheet music. 'Wow! You're tackling the *Transcendental Studies*?' She tightened her two-handed grip on the bottle. Of course Stefan would be playing the Liszt: it was a virtuoso piece.

'Have some,' said Stefan kindly, misinterpreting her blush as a touch of heatstroke.

Glad to be doing something and to be hiding her face, Chloe lifted the tall bottle and drank deeply.

'Look,' said Stefan a moment later, pointing at two figures directly ahead. 'Doesn't that child look like Valerie's little girl? Who is she with?'

Chloe peered through the windscreen and wondered vaguely if the man was her father. Then she gave up on the glare and haze and closed her eyes. Just for a moment.

Fifty-Three

Following local custom, Val left the door of the workshop unlocked, with a note inside for Harry. Hurrying down the street with the jar in her shoulder bag, she was almost running as she reached the first street junction.

She did run when she spotted her car, safe and shaded under its usual palm tree, close to the high wall. Opening the driver's door and sitting in, she turned the key in the ignition.

Nothing happened. Not even electrics. Dead. With no choice but to walk, she set off through the old town, picking her way towards the police station. The street took her back to the workshop. As she passed she noticed that the door, left unlocked, was now partly open.

Someone's gone inside the apartment block, she thought. Someone who may be entirely innocent, a visitor for another flat. Or maybe a visitor for me, maybe Harry.

As she walked closer, a shutter on one of the workshop windows was eased halfway open. Hanging from the latch of the shutter, on a long string so that it dangled beneath the window-ledge, was Judith's Lady Penelope doll.

Transfixed by the sight of the hanging doll swinging slowly to and fro on its string, Val was too shocked to speak. That icy moment saved her, for when she did move, an instant later, she was also thinking. She glanced at her shoulder bag, then at the half-open door and came to a decision. Judy could never have reached high enough to hang anything on the shutter. Whoever was waiting for her in the workshop, she couldn't afford to allow her bag, with its evidence, to fall into the wrong hands.

There were no cars nearby, no mopeds, no one she could appeal to. Instead, hobbling along the shaded part of the alley, Voula was returning from the fishmonger's.

Moving into deeper shade, Val scribbled a second note. It was hard for her to turn and walk away from the workshop, but she needed to speak to Voula as far as possible from the half-open door. Voula had a carrying voice.

Afterwards, Val walked the streets for long enough to allow Voula time to get home, then came at the workshop again, from a different direction, as if she had only just arrived. It was impossible to enter the building from this side without being seen, but the dangling Lady Penelope doll compelled her.

'Hello?' She could see no one, but someone had certainly been there. Closing on the half-open outer door, Val saw the print of a tiny bare foot in the dust on the inner threshold step, where a child had stood for a moment in the corner, her back to the inner door.

Val walked through the foyer, pushing open the inner workshop door.

'Good afternoon.' A man's voice. 'I have realized for some time that you would never come to me, so I have come to you. As you see, your daughter is with me. Your god-daughter is waiting for us in the car. I expected to find you here.'

'You were the wrong number.'

'That's right. Your mobile was answered by a man, so I did not speak to him. I was disappointed to find you gone, but thought it might be worth my while to wait. I also disabled your hire car. Fortune favours those who take chances, and we have not been waiting long.'

Judith sat on the workbench, her legs dangling into space. One of his arms was coiled across the child's middle.

'Mummy.' Judy's voice was an insistent whisper.

'It's all right, sweetheart.' Val forced herself to smile. 'Where are we going?' she asked him, through a dry throat.

'An overdue appointment.'

'I'll come with you alone,' said Val, speaking in Greek so as not to frighten her daughter any more than she was already. 'My little one doesn't know you, she won't remember you . . .'

The man's fingers closed, very lightly, against the back of Judith's neck. 'We shall leave now,' he said.

Fifty-Four

'Val?' The outer door was open. Harry stepped through the foyer and into the workshop.

'What is it?' asked Markos, behind him.

Val wasn't there, but something was. Light headed, Harry knelt, took a pen from his pocket and teased a pair of full red plastic lips out of the shadows and across the workshop floor.

'Phone Cypress House,' he ordered, moving into the room and opening both shutters.

'Saint Spyrídon, not again,' Markos moaned.

'Seen this before? Recently, maybe, with that second murder at the Achillion?' Between angry fingers, Harry's cheap biro snapped in two.

'That's not the same man. There's proof it's not the same man. There's a suspect for the second Achillion murder already in custody.'

'Really? You didn't seem sure of any of that, the last time I asked.' He held up a hand. 'I'll phone Cypress House. You get on to your people.'

As he spoke Val's mobile began ringing again. It was Jessica and she was crying. 'I can't find her! I've looked everywhere, I've even run down to the beach. She's gone from her bed, but she was asleep, fast asleep! I look only five minutes later and she's not there! And I can't find her! And there's no one here – Alexia is out, the cook has gone, the gardener doesn't understand me.'

Harry soothed her, slowed her down. 'Okay, Jessica, deep breaths . . . That's it . . . Take your time . . . Can you remember exactly what Judith was doing before you put her down for her nap?'

Speaking in rapid bursts, Jessica began to explain. Soon she was doing well, and had he been in Fenfield Harry would have been proud of her. Because this concerned Val's daughter he was frustrated. The girl was being so slow!

'Okay, Jessica,' he said finally. 'I want you to go down-stairs and drink a lot of water. That'll help to keep you alert. Keep looking for Judy inside the house, stay indoors and keep the phone near you. The police will come, I promise.'

Harry glanced at Markos, who nodded and reached for his phone.

'The police are already on their way. Hang on in there. Judy will be found. You didn't do anything wrong – you've done everything right. Remember that, Jessica. You think of anything else, you call this number.'

'I will.'

'I have to go, Jessie,' Harry said, wrung by the girl's quiet weeping. 'You need to keep this line clear. Will you do that for me?'

'Yes.'

'Good girl. I'll see you later.'

'Bye,' said Jessica, sounding pitifully young. The dialling tone buzzed in his ear.

There was no time for regret. Quickly he explained to Markos, who relayed the information to the station. 'Judith's missing from Cypress House, possibly kidnapped. She was sleeping in a made-up bed on the ground floor, in the anteroom just off the patio. According to the nurse, Judith asked if she could have her nap there because she thinks the orchids in the anteroom are "funny". Jessica – that's the nurse – says she was fast asleep under a sheet and canopy. Jessica says she slipped to the kitchen – not going outside the house on to the patio, always indoors – to fetch herself a cup of hot chocolate. She says she was in the kitchen for about five minutes, about the length of time for a kettle to boil. When she returned to the anteroom, Judith was missing.

'Jessica claims she didn't hear or see anything untoward. She says she spent half to three quarters of an hour searching the house and gardens for Judith, without success. She was trying to contact Val because she didn't know what to do for the best – whether she should phone the police or not.'

Markos translated this into Greek, holding his mobile parallel to his ear so that Harry could hear the responses of his police contact.

'What do you think of her story?' Markos asked when he had rung off. 'If Judith has been kidnapped, do you think the nanny's involved?'

'I suppose it's possible. Moving the little girl downstairs to the anteroom would make it that much easier.'

'And if there's no one else in the house, no witness.'

'That too.'

'The timing of her call just now—'

'Too coincidental? Maybe,' Harry agreed.

'You think it's the killer?' Markos went on.

Harry shook his head. The policeman in him was the only thing keeping him from going crazy.

'The police will be at Cypress House in twenty minutes,' Markos went on. 'They'll search the house and grounds again. I've told them it's family.'

Harry nodded. 'I caught that bit. You seemed most insistent.'

'But where's Val?' Markos pointed to the empty workshop. 'Look there.' Harry had seen it, and now Markos spotted it, the small dust print of a child's footstep on the inner step leading into the workshop.

'I'll rouse up the neighbours, find out if they saw anything,' said Harry, forgetting in that instant that his Greek might not be up to the task.

Markos had his phone out again and was talking rapidly.

Stepping out into the main street, Harry heard a voice above him, calling his name.

'Harry!' Voula waved furiously down from her balcony. 'This is for you. Hurry! I come down, give it to you.'

By this time, police were converging on the workshop. They came on Vespas – quicker in the narrow streets than cars – and they came without uniforms. They greeted Markos quietly and went to work.

'Who are those men?' Voula asked. There was already a crowd outside the workshop.

'You have something for me,' Harry reminded her.

Voula opened her street-side shutters and offered him a piece of paper. 'Val gave me this,' she explained. 'I was walking back from the market and whoosh! She bumps into me. She grabs me. "You remember Harry, my friend? You must give him this when he comes to my workshop. It's very important," she tells me. She shakes me!' Voula looked from Harry to the sheet of paper. 'I have tried to read it but my writing English is not so good. So you will read it for me, yes?'

It was clear she wasn't going to hand it over until he promised something. 'Of course,' Harry lied, and for that and his wide smile and open blue eyes he received the paper.

'What now?' Markos demanded.

'Give me a second.' Harry scanned it. Val's neat, flowing writing filled the top half of the lined page. A page torn from her restoring notebook.

Harry, I've given Voula my handbag, so make sure she gives it to you. Inside my bag is a glass jar, hidden by my grandfather in the old well at our home. It has some red lips inside, and an epitaph, based on lyrics from Gesualdo, Farewell Chloris – hence Markos's question to me about the glass lips and eraser: whether they had any message on them. Markos was afraid our father had kept them as a token of killing Hilary. If Markos is with you, please tell him he was wrong about Yiannis. He was never the killer.

Something is wrong at the workshop. I didn't leave the door open and now it is. Judith's doll is hanging from the shutters and Judy can't reach that high. It may be nothing, but if I'm not here phone the police. Try to find Stefan Gregory. I am convinced he is involved.

'What does she say?' asked Markos and Voula together.

'She tells me that you have her handbag,' Harry said, rippling the fingers of his free hand at the widow. 'May I have it, please?'

With a sigh, Voula swung the bag over the window-ledge into Harry's waiting arm. He passed it to Markos, saying, 'There's more evidence in there; something you knew about, I believe.'

Markos glanced into the bag, paled slightly and then began to berate Voula in Greek. Harry left them to it and continued reading.

Stefan Gregory and the Achillion. What better cover, that he is due to play there? Who would suspect him of anything?

Voula slammed her shutters to and retired indoors.

Harry told Markos what Val had written.

'She tells a lot,' said Markos.

'Val sees everything, and remembers.'

'Does she say any more?'

Harry shook his head. Val had written down what she knew and then stopped. There were no goodbyes. Did she know anything about Judy disappearing from Cypress House? There was no sign now of a doll hanging from the shutters, but he dared not imagine what she must have been feeling when she scribbled this.

Markos conferred with his colleagues, walked back to Harry.

'An unmarked car is going to Stefan Gregory's house – no fuss, no lights. They will have a plausible cover story, so they'll get in. Others will be searching the town.'

'Here.' Harry opened his wallet and removed a much-handled photograph, taken the previous winter when Val and Judy had been at a party for one of Nick's former workmates. 'It's from last year, but a good likeness of both.'

'Thanks.' Markos's hand clasped Harry's briefly. 'We'll get the originals back for you, I promise.'

'I'm coming with you,' said Harry.

Fifty-Five

Two plainclothes police drove Markos and Harry on Vespas to collect a car. Skimming past the high wall displaying the posters of Judith's favourite film, Harry recollected that only the Friday before Judy had been safely enchanted by *Beauty and the Beast*.

'We'll use my car,' Markos called over his shoulder. 'It's got a radio.'

'Fine!' Harry called back, aware that Markos's use of the Mercedes earlier that morning had been a deliberate wind-up.

At least Steve and Chloe were still wandering the slopes of Pantokrátor, oblivious to the events in the town. With luck they would return sometime this evening to find Val and Judy waiting for them at Cypress House.

Harry closed his eyes and, for the first time since childhood, said a prayer.

*　　*　　*

271

Steve was lost. When he crossed the same dusty, car-filled square for the third time, he knew that he was going round in circles.

'Brilliant.' He glowered at the incomprehensible street names. There was no one to ask and the stone angel standing on top of the roof of the square's baroque church wasn't going to tell him anything.

A car shot past, turning in a small puff of dust towards the Palace of St Michael and St George. Only because he was looking for someone – anyone – to point him in the right direction for Val's old home did Steve give the car a second glance.

He was sure he'd seen Val riding in the back. Val . . . and was that Chloe beside her? Chloe asleep?

Steve sprinted after the vehicle, closing on it for a few seconds as it slowed to turn into one of the narrow streets radiating from the square. The car accelerated almost at once but now Steve knew that he was right. Val, Chloe and that pianist were going somewhere, and Val didn't look happy about it.

Frantically, Steve read the vehicle registration and began to recite it as he ran after the small green car. He'd never catch up, but they had to be driving on larger streets than the ones he'd been stumbling around and once he was free of this maze of alleys he'd find shops and taxis and people. He'd find somewhere to buy a new phone card, or a public phone to contact the police. Over and over, in time to his pounding feet, Steve repeated the car number.

Harry was standing in front of a lock-up garage close to Val's old family home, impatient as Markos fumbled with the padlock. What was he doing?

Markos yanked open the garage door, revealing a blue Alfa Romeo. Before opening the car doors, he swung round. 'There's something you must know. What I need to tell you may have a bearing on what is happening to V—' He could not go on.

It was obvious that until Markos got whatever it was off his chest, they wouldn't be going anywhere in a hurry. 'Get on with it,' said Harry.

Out it came, in a jumble of English and Greek, the real story of Yiannis and Hilary Moffat.

'And how long have you known this?' Harry demanded, when Markos began to repeat himself.

'Known? Far less time than you think. Suspected – yes, I have suspected much, and worse, for years. But this is my father and I had no proof.'

And made sure there would be none, thought Harry, but he said nothing. More than enough time had been wasted.

'There is one more thing,' Markos went on, finally opening the doors of the Alfa Romeo. 'Valerie's yellow flowers.'

'It's not just flower symbolism again, is it?'

'Yiannis found Valerie reading the pathologist's report into Hilary Moffat's death. She had reached the point in the report where the pathologist spoke of the lilies found displayed with the body, lilies with their stamens removed. The pathologist did not mention the species until the next page, which Valerie never read.'

Markos started the car. 'They were yellow.'

As they drove away, a Vulcan Classic motorbike began trailing them. Sobered by the coffee and his own reflections, Yiannis had heard the opening of the garage door from the garden and slipped upstairs to see what was going on.

There was no chance to change out of his uniform. He struggled into a stifling but anonymous grey overcoat. That coupled with his motorbike helmet made him unrecognizable.

He was determined to follow his son and the Englishman.

Fifty-Six

The drive out of Corfu town was frenzied. Stefan Gregory used his car like a battering ram, ignoring other drivers, bearing down on pedestrians with a cold ruthlessness.

Val raged at her father in order to fight off panic. By taking her mobile, Yiannis had effectively robbed her of her tongue.

But her mental picture of Yiannis would not hold: it kept flipping out of focus, changing the face into Judy's.

So much time and energy wasted, suspecting her family and, every second of it, wanting to be re-admitted into the warm circle she had known as a little child. When she was Judith's age.

No, Val told herself, clenching her fists for emphasis. Have a plan. You don't strip down an instrument piecemeal, so don't you dare think about saving your daughter and Chloe in such a way.

She had told Voula to give her note to Harry. How did she know that Harry would go the workshop? Val bit her lip: because he just would.

The car was approaching Pérama, and a turn off the main southern road for the hill village of Pikoulatika. The Achillion could be reached that way, but it wasn't the straightest or the quickest way.

As Stefan Gregory turned across the traffic on to the narrow track, he glanced at her in the rear-view mirror.

'Where are we going?' Val already knew the answer but she had to make a start at trying to connect with him, to lull and disarm.

Gregory's smile filled the mirror. 'The police could have arrested me outside the workshop, had they suspected anything. Then they would have had to let me go for lack of evidence. You would never have found Chloe.'

'Tell me, Stefan,' Val persisted. 'Where are you taking us?'

For the second time he ignored the question. 'You know, I'm glad I bought this car yesterday. The couple I bought it from were far too busy counting their money to pay attention to me. They were leaving on the Bari ferry that evening, which should perplex the police. And I have a wonderful alibi for today. Did you know that I am actually in Bari, playing at a palazzo? The contessa there would swear to anything for me. She calls me her angel. My housekeeper will also swear the same, but her motives are less sublime. She has a son with a taste for child pornography, and she knows that I have a computer disc of several of his more graphic downloads with his fingerprints on it.'

274

He drove along the middle of the track with no one but birds to see them. Ahead of them was cover and shade: a tiny olive grove with a rope hung across its entrance instead of a wooden gate.

'It's market day today. The farmer won't trouble us.' Stefan Gregory brought the car to a stop. 'You will deal with the rope.'

Judith stirred in the front seat. 'Mummy . . .'

'It's all right, sweetheart. I'll only be a moment.' Alongside her Chloe slumbered on, unaware even that she was no longer in the front seat. As Gregory released the doors, Val could see the slight rise and fall of Chloe's chest.

'Should she be sleeping like that?' Making a play of fumbling with the release of her seat belt, Val was able to release Chloe's, too. 'What have you given her?' she asked, opening her door. When Gregory did not answer, she stepped out, conscious of the breeze on her skin, the warm earth under her feet.

Gregory rolled his window lower. 'It is a good drug, one I've used before. I put it in a bottle of coke – the girl thought I'd drunk some and obligingly drank the rest. They call it the rapist's choice in Internet circles. You used to be able to buy it very easily over the counter.'

'I never reached that part in the pathologist's report on Hilary,' Val replied, horror-struck by Chloe's slow breathing.

Gregory gave no sign of having heard her comment. He motioned for Val to unlatch the rope gate. She followed the slowly moving car through the gate and deep into the olive grove.

Switching off the engine, Gregory opened the front passenger door. 'Come. Sit with the child. We have several hours to kill.' He put a hand in the pocket of his grey tracksuit and brought out a folding knife. Opening it, he rested the blade lightly against the steering wheel. 'I want you to sit with her.'

Her mind a blank, her feverish search for a plan come to nothing, Val climbed in beside Judy. She felt a sharp sting on her arm just above her elbow, as if she had been stung.

She had been switched off.

Fifty-Seven

Markos drove to Garitsa, parking across the street from Gregory's villa. He and Harry watched the plainclothes police move through the house, opening the shutters in each room to signal their progress. The radio chattered and Markos nodded. 'No sign of the little girl at Cypress House, not yet.'

'We should go to the Achillion,' Harry said, as room after room drew a blank. 'That's where Val thinks he's gone. Trust her judgement – I do.'

Markos blew heavily through his nose. 'We haven't the men. Not when we must search here, and the town, and Cypress House. We're not even sure if Val is under threat.'

'But we do know about Judy. And what about the doll being dangled from the workshop window? Look at what Val says: "Something is wrong at the workshop." All we're doing here is sitting on our backsides, so why not leave your people to do their jobs and let's go ourselves. It's not that far.'

'And if Val should turn up while we're away?'

'What if she's gone after Gregory herself?' Harry flung up a hand against an anticipated barrage of denials, but Markos was listening, one hand cupped over the radio receiver. 'What if she knows her daughter has been kidnapped? What if she knows it was Gregory who took Judy? She wouldn't do nothing, not Val. Has she any particular reason to trust the police?'

Markos said nothing, his face a mask of frustration and anger. Finally he asked, 'What if you're wrong?'

Harry's skin crawled. 'I'll have to live with it.'

Markos watched another pair of shutters swing open.

'I'm not messing about any longer.' Harry opened his car door. 'I'm getting a taxi.'

Markos's radio crackled into life, a rush of Greek Harry could not follow. Halfway out of the car, Harry found himself back in the passenger seat, his legs none too steady as he waited for Markos to translate.

Markos growled a farewell and started the car. 'Steve has phoned the police. He saw Val and Chloe being driven in Corfu town by Stefan Gregory. Steve gave us a description of the car and the car number.' He swung the Alfa Romeo into the traffic. 'He says Val looked anxious but Chloe looked to be asleep. They were both in the back seat of a small green car with an Italian registration – that should be easy to trace.'

Val and Chloe, alive. Gregory had them and they were alive. Fury and hope warred in Harry. 'Judith possibly in the front seat?' he suggested, as Markos turned his car on to the main coast road.

'Steve wasn't sure about that, but it seems likely.' Markos snorted, accelerating past a tour bus. 'The boy has spirit but no good sense – he wanted to join the search.'

'Can't blame him for that.' Harry spotted a road sign. They were on the way south, to the Achillion.

'Gregory won't do anything now,' Markos was saying, working up through the gears. 'Too many tourists. He'll wait until dark.'

'Like the last time.'

Markos was scowling. 'His house will have to be watched, and the town itself, where Steve saw him, and Val's workshop.'

'And Cypress House,' Harry said. 'I know the form. Until we know for sure that Judith has been taken by Gregory, and unless we do see him, the force can't spare more men for the Achillion.'

'They have to go with definite sightings first, Harry. And they have to be careful: we don't want Gregory panicking.'

'What about the local police?'

'Busy today with a festival – but they'll keep driving by the palace.'

'So really it's you and me.'

Markos sighed. 'For the moment, yes.'

Harry turned and glared out of the window. Doubts were

277

already crowding his mind. Suppose Gregory had taken them somewhere else? What if Gregory had an accomplice? Val hadn't actually said that Gregory would be heading for the Achillion today; he had made an assumption from her hurried note. Somehow Gregory had forced Val into his car – what if he had forced her to write the note? How long should he and Markos wait at the palace?

'How big are the grounds?' he asked, breaking the silence.

'Several acres, gardens and woods. Last time he used the gardens. With luck, he'll want to do the same again.' Markos spoke a series of rapid instructions into the radio.

'The staff at the palace. I've given them descriptions,' he said. 'They will let us or the local police know if they see or hear anything.'

'But you doubt it.'

Markos nodded. 'One of us will have to stay by the car and radio, one of us should walk the grounds.'

'I'll do the grounds,' Harry volunteered. 'I'll blend with the tourists.'

'Yes,' said Markos. 'This will be a long day.'

Fifty-Eight

Val came round in snatches, still sitting in the front of the car. She was wearing handcuffs. The left cuff had grazed the face of her wristwatch, which read 11.10 p.m. In the narrow space between her and the passenger door, lolling against her side and half hidden by the shadows, Judy was asleep. Behind them Chloe was asleep. Val could smell something sickly sweet on her daughter's breath.

Gregory stirred in the driving seat.

'Hello, Stefan,' Val said. 'Has Judith drunk from your coke bottle, too?'

'She said she was thirsty. She wasn't alarmed by your lapse into unconsciousness, merely puzzled. Apart from the chickenpox, she's been no trouble. I presume she's no longer infectious.'

He sounded amused. Fighting drugged muscles to raise her head, Val saw the glowing face she had seen in the concert hall all those years earlier. 'I don't understand, Stefan.'

'The why or the how?' Stefan Gregory smiled. 'The how was easy. I drove to Cypress House to collect Chloe and took Judith instead. She fits nicely into the car boot and when I explained to her that we were coming to surprise you she couldn't wait to climb in.'

Part of Val felt anger at the thought of Judy locked in a car boot. Part of her was relieved that this was a left-hand drive car and Judy, on her right side, was not in physical contact with Gregory. These feelings remained at a distance – the effect of whatever drug Gregory had injected her with. Her sense of touch was the only thing that seemed real. She was conscious of Judith's warmth. She wanted to roll over and cuddle her daughter, sleep and wake a long way from here.

'Why Chloe?' she asked.

Stefan Gregory showed her his left hand. 'Set against our sleeping beauty in the back, what my left hand can do is nothing. And she is a prodigy, as I was once. When I returned to your workshop today, Chloe's appearance was a bonus.' His face set. 'She has always been part of my plans. Young Chloe is too talented for her own good.'

He claimed professional jealousy as a motive? Val was determined to keep answering. The longer they talked, the more clear headed she became.

'You're both superb.' She sensed that to acknowledge his talent at the expense of Chloe's would be a mistake, but now she invited more. 'How long have you been making music?'

'"Making music". How charmingly you put the whole sweaty, spiteful business.' He flicked a finger against her neck; he was wearing thin plastic gloves. 'You're very good at charming. So was my father. He died ten years ago. A brain tumour. Here in Corfu. That open-air concert at the town hall was my first public performance after his death. I'd wanted

279

to cancel, but he said no. This was when he could speak, of course.'

'I'm sorry,' Val said. 'I didn't know about your father.'

'No, people forget that celebrities have families, too. That was a very difficult recital for me. And you rejected my performance.'

'I didn't.' Part of Val was still amazed that he had seen her sitting, still and quiet, in the noisy audience.

'Lying bitch!' Gregory's yell caused Chloe to snuffle in her sleep. Judy's breathing never changed, which to Val was still more terrifying. 'You were jealous! Say you were jealous!'

'I was envious, yes. You were so young, so talented.'

Gregory relaxed behind the steering wheel, his colour returning to normal. He brought one leg up and sat sideways on his seat, looking through his headrest at Chloe. 'She's younger.'

'You were younger than she was when you started.'

Gregory sighed, turning in his seat to look past Chloe at the almost black sky. 'Moonrise. Soon it will be late enough for us to continue to the Achillion.'

Whatever it was that Gregory had injected into her seemed to control most of her physical reactions. No terror showed in Val's face.

'That recital, you were with another girl.'

'Hilary, yes.'

'After the recital I skipped the reception and came looking for you. I borrowed a moped and a helmet and drove to the Liston. It was the obvious place to search among the post-recital poseurs, drinking their cocktails and chattering about me.

'When I saw Hilary rejecting another man, I remembered her as your companion and decided that she would do instead. As I drove past, a stranger in my helmet, I threw the cheap red lips, to show her the game was beginning.

'Hilary picked them up – then handed them to a policeman! I could scarcely believe it. But I wasn't about to be rejected twice in one night.'

He doesn't know, Val thought. Gregory doesn't know about my father's involvement.

'I followed them. They were easy to trail, down to a beach where Hilary refused the policeman, too; she was as two faced as you had been at my recital. But always ready to grab another male: when I stopped for her later on the southern road she tumbled on to the back of the moped.

'I took her to my villa in Garitsa – it wasn't far. I drugged her there. We had a busy time together, Hilary and I, until the following evening. Then I bathed her, wrapped her in a sheet and drove her to the Achillion in a car belonging to my house-keeper's son, a blue Mercedes with dirty plates that would be taken for a local taxi.'

A hunting scops owl darted past Val's passenger window, drawing her glazed eyes to the wraith-like olive trees, their tissue-thin leaves shaded black and silver in the moonlight. Beside her, Gregory took no notice.

'The bitch was still disorientated when I lifted her out of the car boot. To keep her docile, I promised to let her go once we were inside the grounds. Half an hour saw it done and I drove away. No one saw me.

'She betrayed me,' Gregory said thoughtfully. 'Like all women. So friendly, so grateful. Then the deceit. My father had warned me, but I did not believe him until that evening. I sliced off her lying mouth.'

Somehow, Val did not react. She was trying to spot a way out.

'I have had three fathers,' said Gregory. 'My first father, who died more than ten years ago of that filthy brain tumour, he was my natural father. He was an anaesthetist before he became my manager.'

The drugs, thought Val. The knowledge of how to put women to sleep. The ways and means. The coke bottle.

'He taught me discipline.'

And cruelty. Val lowered her eyes so that Gregory would not see the thought in her face.

'My musical father was Beethoven. He was my mentor for many years. He stirred me to the struggle!'

His fingernails cut into Val's neck, but she steeled herself not to jerk away. Until he told her about Gesualdo, she and Judy and Chloe would be relatively safe.

'And your mother?' she prompted.

'She left us.' Stefan Gregory twisted around in his seat and started the car, reversing straight through the slender rope barrier at the edge of the olive grove.

'I was less than two years old. Can you imagine that? For a mother to desert her two-year-old child – it's obscene. My mother walked out one day and disappeared. She left me behind.'

The car screamed as he clashed the gears. He was moving in a disconnected way that reminded Val of Steve, except that Steve would never say the things that were pouring from Gregory's mouth.

'I tried to trace her once and found nothing. I was nothing but a piece of unwanted luggage she dumped with my father. Bitch!'

He hit the windscreen with a fist, bruising the knuckles of his right hand. Accelerating along the country road, he seemed not to notice what he had done. He switched on the headlights and pointed to a roadside shrine that clearly meant something to him. An instant later a sign for the Achillion flashed by, but Val's eyesight was still too blurred to make out how much further they had to travel.

Somehow she must try to slow him down.

Her cuffed hands felt heavy, but she managed to raise them, the movement seizing Gregory's attention. Her ribs were sore. What had Gregory done to her while she had been unconscious? What had he done to Judith or Chloe?

'Why the Achillion?' she asked.

'Woods. Easy paths. Privacy.' Gregory smiled. 'Most evenings these days the place is silent.'

'Let Judy go!' Val pleaded. 'Let them both go.'

'It is too late for that.'

'You'll be caught.'

'I have never been questioned by the police. No doubt you think that you will be different, because you are from a police family. But I have prepared and I have alibis. Off-stage, people do not recognize me. On stage, I perform Chopin, Haydn, Mozart and everyone remembers them, not me.'

That was what he was, thought Val, a performer. Real but

not real. And, like any good artist, he prepared ahead. He had known about her and her past.

'When you came to my workshop and made yourself known that first time, you pretended not to know me all that well.'

'I did not know you. I knew a great deal about you, but you – the way you betray – I did not know that, Valerie. In spite of your handling of the Bechstein, which, as you realize, was only a test, you have been disappointing.'

The car roared as they set off up a steep slope. Val peered through the dark scrub and olive groves and looked longingly at the entrances to various small villas, but so far their car was the only moving thing on the track.

Stefan Gregory, meanwhile, was calm again, eager to talk.

'But you have one thing in common, one thing I enjoy. You, Hilary and Chloe. You and another three, whose ends were very different from Hilary's, or from what your own will be. That intensity. A tonic and a sweet reward.'

He was an emotional vampire – in his concert clothes he was even dressed for the part. The humour did not make Val smile. Three other women had been his victims, as well as Hilary. There had been no ten-year gap in the killings. This man travelled all over the world, attacked different races, killed in different ways. As a 'sweet reward'.

She wanted to be sick.

Something pressed into the small of her back. The pressure increased, then relaxed. In the seat behind her, Chloe was awake and alert.

Val leaned back in her seat to show Chloe that she had understood. They were now two against one, but she had few illusions. Hilary had tried to fight: there had been bruising on her wrists, where the handcuffs had restrained her until whatever deadly cocktail Stefan Gregory had injected her with had overcome her. He would be sure to have more of it – the drug worked too well for him.

Pretending to doze, Val glanced about the interior of the car through half-closed eyelids. Gregory was occupied with driving, but any move towards the glove compartment would be fatal.

Two against one, she reminded herself. She would not give

up, certainly not while there were Judith and Chloe.

Gregory drove to the gates of the Achillion and pulled off the road. He switched off the car engine and turned to her. 'You see, Valerie? There are no cars here, no police.'

Val scanned the area through her swimming vision. She could see no other cars nearby, no houses close enough for her to try to raise help. Shouting would be muffled by the dense woodland surrounding the palace. The narrow road itself was deserted, the postcard stalls opposite the Achillion's massive wooden gates closed and shuttered. She could imagine the scent of the pine forest and hear running water somewhere in the valley below; she could see the grey forms of cypress trees rising tall and straight out of the gorse and straggling bushes bordering the double gates, but everything else was lost in shadows.

Raising her aching, spinning head slightly, Val realized that clouds had obscured the new moon. Perhaps the increased darkness would work in her favour, she thought, then despair swept over her. Gregory was right: there was no one here and no one was coming. Her desperate messages had come to nothing.

Gregory switched on the interior light and took a slip of paper from the baggy pocket of his tracksuit. 'No one will disturb us.' Smiling, he dropped the briefer of Val's notes to Harry into her lap.

The corners of his eyes crinkled with humour as he removed a small ampoule from his tracksuit pocket, and a syringe – two syringes. He displayed them on the palm of his hand. 'For you and Chloe.' He flicked the syringes into the air, catching them on the back of his hand, before placing them on the dashboard.

More than anything that had happened so far, that cheap trick horrified Val. 'Why Chloe and me? Why the pink lips for her and the colourless lips for me?' She would ask whatever she could to delay the inevitable. If she could only reach the control she could unlock the doors. Chloe would be able to escape. If Chloe were free, surely there would be a chance for Judith?

Gregory leaned towards her and Val shrank back, shielding

her daughter with her body. 'You can't hope to carry us over the gates, they're huge!' she blurted out. 'Look at them, at least three metres high!'

'I've had a key for eighteen years,' Gregory said. 'Since one of my earliest recitals here. No one noticed what I did or where I went when I wasn't playing.' He jerked his head towards the rear seats. 'I was younger than her. Better.'

Val stared at him. 'You've kept a key for eighteen years?'

'I like keys, don't you? A key that no one knows you have; I cannot recall when I did not find that appealing.' His eyes and face shone. 'And my early instinct was right. In a few moments we shall be nicely private.'

In the back seat Chloe moaned and flopped on to her side, continuing what must have been a painful slide on to the floor of the car with no sign that she was feeling anything.

Gregory gave a resigned sigh. 'I did wonder if you had done something absurd earlier today, but you really should not have unfastened her seat belt.' Before Val could react, he chuckled. 'No doubt I have not given Chloe quite enough, but I do like my material to be as pristine as possible.'

He reached for a syringe. Val lunged for the dashboard, trying to put herself between the syringes and those stretching fingers. 'What about my daughter? What about Judith? Will you hand Judith to your housekeeper's paedophile son?'

'No!' Gregory's cheekbones and narrow nose bloomed with spots of colour. 'I loathe perverts, with their filthy, degraded habits.'

His hands were shaking so much that he dropped the syringe. It bounced across the car floor and Val stamped on it, hearing it splinter.

'Swear you'll let Judith go,' she insisted. 'She's only four. She won't remember you. You're in no danger from her. You'll have saved her life.'

Now Gregory was staring at her face and, worst of all, her mouth, but she was still firmly between Judy and him. At last her cuffed hands hovered over the car's locking controls. A touch and Chloe would be able to get out. 'Promise me, Stefan, and I'll be still.' Her voice was laced with sweet warmth. 'I'll do whatever you want. Promise me.'

285

Her fingers found the locking control. Behind her Chloe groaned more loudly, covering the soft click of the release.

Unaware, Gregory raised one hand and he traced the outline of her lips with a finger. 'You could have been my Chloris, fresh as a daisy. But there will be no more sweet breezes for you now. You even ignored my last two messages.'

'Chloris was the name of another man's mistress, not yours, Stefan.' Clearly, the 'sweet breezes' was another quote from Gesualdo. 'Why are we here?'

'A greater challenge. The pink lips and the glass lips: not quite the red lips of death. A variation on a theme. Chloe and Valerie: my duet.'

Gregory had recovered his temper. 'My third father and mentor was Carlo Gesualdo.' The knife had reappeared in his right hand. He touched the blade to Val's throat. 'Just like Gesualdo's first wife, you weren't loyal. You even fucked behind my back in your workshop.'

He had been spying when she and Harry made love there. He must have been watching her close to the workshop, to discover where she parked her hire car and disable it. Chilled by his planning, Val took the name of the composer as a fatal sign but could think of no way of warning Chloe.

'We are not married, Stefan,' she said, conscious of the knife at her throat.

Gregory lowered his arm and the knife out of sight into the space between the door and the steering column. 'We are in spirit. I knew that from the moment I saw you.'

Val could not help it: she laughed. 'And you did nothing? You glimpse me ten years ago at a recital, and make no effort to find me?'

Gregory frowned. 'I knew we would meet again. And when we do find each other you two-time me. All those men!'

'My father, my brother and my lover,' said Val, sensing that if she apologized or admitted fault, she would be lost, and Chloe and Judy with her. 'Were you faithful to me?'

He flinched and withdrew, his knife hand dropping still lower. 'What?'

By the car's interior light and the dim light above the entrance gates, Val could see that he had turned pale. Something else she noticed, too, on the rim of her vision, closing in from the outer darkness. A figure, breaking from the wayside scrub, stealing closer, using the gorse as camouflage.

Harry, she thought, without knowing how she could be so certain. Behind him a second blurred shape, dropping quickly away into shadow. Markos, falling back to sprint across the narrow road in darkness and approach the driver's side from behind the shuttered postcard stalls? The brightness of the car's interior light would give them some cover but she must keep Gregory off balance.

'You sent me flowers, too,' she said.

'Every flower had a meaning. French marigold for jealousy. Tuberose for dangerous pleasure. Daisies because Chloris means "fresh as a daisy". Lilies for the fleur-de-lys on the Gesualdo coat of arms.'

'But you also gave my god-daughter presents. After you tell me that you're jealous of her!'

'She was only a flirtation, my Chloris. Nothing serious, nothing meaningful. The smaller challenge.'

'Prove it,' Val said. 'Kiss me.'

His breathing was now so loud it filled the car. He was still clutching the knife in his hidden right hand but Val fixed her eyes on his face – not on Harry and his companion moving in the darkness, not on Judith, slumped against the passenger door, her drugged head resting against the bottom edge of the passenger window. More than ever relieved that she was between him and Judy, Val kept looking at the blank, open face of Stefan Gregory.

'*Amore*,' she breathed, the word so often set to music in startling ways by Carlo Gesualdo, this man's God.

His lips pressed against hers, hot and fleshy and yet at the same time alien, so that she felt as if she were being enveloped by melting rubber as a thick, wet tongue forced its way into her mouth. Steeling herself not to gag, Val strained upwards, clutching at his tracksuit with her handcuffed hands, holding him as tight as she could while they embraced. She didn't want him to see anything of Harry's approach. She didn't want him to breathe again.

Chloe struggled with the rear passenger door, opening it

in a rush and kicking it wide with a foot. 'Help us!' she was screaming, as she fell out of the car and rolled into the darkness.

There was a thudding, a wrenching at the doors. Harry tore open the front passenger door and caught the falling, whimpering Judy, lifting her out of harm's way.

Straining to see past Gregory's shoulder, Val watched the driver's door swing back on its hinges to reveal Markos, down on one knee in the dusty road as he aimed his pistol.

'Throw your weapon out here. Come out of the car,' he ordered. 'Very slowly.'

'So.' Gregory drew back from Val. 'It ends here.'

He was smiling, his dark eyes warm. He kissed her forehead and, very slowly, allowed his right arm to drop even lower, out of the car itself.

Through Chloe's fractured sobbing and Harry's panting, Val heard the knife thud on to the dirt. In a few minutes, it would be over.

'Step out of the car,' Markos repeated.

Slowly, Gregory did so.

He was out of the vehicle, both feet on the road, when he whipped his left hand in and then out of his sweatshirt pocket, a flashing, fluid movement almost too quick to see.

Markos shouted a warning, but Gregory was turning back to the car, lunging into the vehicle through the open driver's door, lashing out at Val with a new knife in his left hand.

Val tried to scramble out of the way, her footing and balance impeded by her cuffed hands. She felt Harry's arm hook round her middle and drag her towards the open passenger door. She saw Gregory's grinning face and stretching arm, the new knife blade approaching as if in slow motion, slicing down through the darkness, and knew that she would never get out in time.

Another figure lurched from the black shadow of the furthest postcard kiosk. Careering straight across the road and across Markos's line of sight, it sprinted at Gregory. Waving a handgun, the figure did not slow down to take aim but increased its speed.

'Release my daughter!' Yiannis slammed into Gregory as

the man strained forward to reach Val, his right foot raised to re-enter the car. Caught off balance, Gregory was knocked backwards and sideways, out of the car into the door panel. The whole vehicle rocked with the impact.

'Dad!' Val screamed a warning, but she was too late. The flailing Gregory struck out and plunged the knife into her father's chest.

Yiannis jerked, his strong body stiffening as if he had been struck by a lightning bolt. He fired off the pistol in his hand, jerked again, like a stricken figure in a computer game, and then fell away.

'No!' Deafened by the gunshot, half blinded by the muzzle flash, Val lurched forward to catch her father, but found Harry holding her back.

'Look at me, Val,' he was saying. 'Look at Judy, sleeping here, in my arms. Touch her, Val. Look at her.'

Val could not move. She saw Yiannis's body lying clear of Gregory's on the ground. Her father had shot Gregory through the heart and the musician had collapsed beside the driver's door without a sound. A quick, clean death, she thought. Not what he'd deserved.

'I didn't know Dad was there,' Markos was saying, 'I didn't know he'd followed us!'

Still Val did not move. She could smell blood and gunpowder, the scents turning her dizzy and sick. She heard a distant voice trying to comfort a sobbing Chloe and realized it was her own. She heard Harry, urging her to turn away. She stared at her father, scarcely believing he was dead. His blue eyes stared back at her. Even as he died, he had kept his eyes in her direction, looking for her.

The full horror of the night closed in. Looking at her father's body as she heard the cry of a second scops owl, Val began to weep.

Fifty-Nine

Ten minutes later the police arrived. The space outside the Achillion gates became packed with cars and people and lights, men and women in uniform and white scene-of-crime suits. Quiet-spoken policewomen were talking to Val and Chloe, ambulance crew checking them over, loading Judy on to a stretcher, putting a drip in her arm.

Markos came and unlocked Val's handcuffs himself. Brother and sister hugged each other tightly, the first true embrace Val remembered between them since their disturbing kiss in the cathedral, all those years earlier. Even in her shock and grief she felt no sense of threat from him. As his arms closed about her, she was not afraid, simply intent on giving comfort.

'I'm sorry, Markos,' she whispered. The police had taken their father's body away to a waiting ambulance, but she could see the dirt marks and bloodstains where he had fallen. 'I'm so sorry.'

'He was a police officer,' Markos said, his voice clipped but clear – he was addressing fellow officers as well as answering her. 'He knew the risks.'

From the darkness and shadows there were calls of support, which he acknowledged with a raised hand.

Markos seemed to be everywhere as the other police did their work, talking to everyone, receiving everyone's condolences. He didn't need her, Val realized. He wanted to be active, part of the investigation into Stefan Gregory's life and death and his father's final moments; part of the resolution. Invited to go to hospital with Val and the others, Markos said, 'My place is here.'

Val watched him following the scene-of-crime officers as

they searched Gregory's car while she and Chloe were stretchered in their turn and loaded into the ambulance. Markos gave her a brief wave before the ambulance door closed. They were on their way back into Corfu town.

Lying on the stretcher, disorientated from the drug and bundled in blankets, her wrists bruised from the handcuffs, Val turned her head and found Harry already in the ambulance. 'You found my message.'

Kneeling on the floor, Harry looked grey with fatigue. 'I bullied Markos into driving to the Achillion and he called for police back-up as soon as we saw the car, but when Gregory threatened you we came in at once. I thought I'd lost you when I saw that knife. I'm truly sorry about Yiannis,' he went on. 'We really didn't know he'd followed us.'

'It wasn't your fault.' Val waited until he glanced at the sleeping Judith and yawning Chloe and then studied his stark profile, wondering if it was an illusion that he seemed to look so much like her father. Dimly aware of her aching body, she closed her eyes, instantly reopening them as Yiannis's dead face stared back at her.

'I told Dad he'd made Hilary a victim, and now, because of me, he's gone,' she whispered.

Harry touched her arm. 'It's not your fault, either.'

'I goaded Dad into acting as he did.'

'His conscience did that. Yiannis would say it was a good way to go for a copper, saving his daughter.'

'Do you think that's what Markos thinks?'

'I'm sure of it – when he's not being furious at your dad for being there in the first place.' Harry leaned forward and wiped Val's eyes.

'I wish I'd not gone to see Yiannis this afternoon,' she said. 'The last time we talked, I didn't even kiss him goodbye.'

'He knew you cared about him,' said Chloe, speaking for the first time since being stretchered into the ambulance. 'He came out after you.'

'He loved you, Val,' Harry said.

Val brushed away more tears. 'How are you, Chloe?' she asked, leaning up on her elbows, straining against the blankets. The ambulance man riding with them left his seat and warned them that they would be coming to the outskirts soon and the road might be bumpy.

'I'm fine.' Chloe yawned. 'Do you mind if we talk in Greek? My head feels as if it's going to split in two.'

'Of course,' Val said. 'We weren't thinking.'

Chloe drummed the fingers of her left hand against her stretcher. She yawned again, her usually serious grey eyes muddied and bleary.

'I heard a lot of what Stefan Gregory said while we were stuck in his car,' she said. 'I never guessed that he was quite so obsessed with being a prodigy, or so scared of getting old.' She stopped her drumming fingers and stared at her hand. 'Or that jealousy could do that to someone like him. He must have had a horrible childhood.'

'You heard him talk about his mother leaving?' Val asked.

'Unless his father murdered her,' said Chloe, peering at her reflection in the dark window glass. 'But whatever, it seems to have totally twisted him up. He wasn't happy, was he? Not even when he was killing . . . I'm sorry about your friend Hilary,' she said quietly.

She closed her eyes, seeming to fall into a doze, the lights of passing cars flickering over her. Then she stirred, looking straight at Val. 'He's never going to put me off playing again.' Her pale oval face coloured up almost to the pink of Alex's scarf tucked around her neck. 'I won't let him beat me.' She relaxed and stretched out, dropping straight back into sleep.

'She'll be all right,' said Harry in English. 'Utterly determined.'

Val didn't plan to say anything, but the words tumbled out of her. 'Gregory was a musician. I'm in the business. I should have known there was something wrong about him much sooner.'

'He showed you his public face, not the private monster.'

Val rolled on to her side, facing Harry. 'You know, he actually believed he was entitled to do what he did. That because he was a musical genius he could indulge himself.'

'Rather a perverted genius.'

'You could say the same about Gesualdo.' Val sighed. 'I should have spotted that connection sooner.'

'There were complications.'

'I should have known.' To stop the conversation she closed her eyes, even though she saw Yiannis's flat, dead face again.

Harry stayed with her in hospital, but Val found it increasingly hard to talk to him. As the drug wore off, she found herself stunned by events. Most of her emotions seemed frozen, so that even though she knew Harry was worried and showed it by the way he never left her side and never slept, she could not respond. She did not feel she deserved comfort. Preying like a harpy on her father's guilt over Hilary Moffat, she had goaded Yiannis into a foolish, terrible act of heroism and now he was dead.

Whenever she could through that long night she sent Harry out on errands. She saw too many questions in his eyes. The ward was a limbo, a kind of peace. It wasn't what she wanted, but it was better than nothing.

After reporting Gregory's car in Corfu town, Steve had been driven by the police to Cypress House. Arriving at the hospital with Alexia, Theo and Jessica, he looked disappointed, even guilty, and Val wasn't surprised when he left after only a short visit. It was a relief, because she couldn't give Steve what he wanted: a proud memory of being involved at the Achillion.

Next morning they were all discharged from hospital. Still in a state of cold, bewildered shock, Val returned with Chloe and Judy to Cypress House. On their first night back Judith ran into her attic bedroom, begging to sleep with her, and Val agreed at once. Harry slept in Judy's room.

Afterwards, while Judith lay sleeping peacefully in her arms, Val wondered about the look of relief she had seen sliding across Harry's face.

It was hard for her to meet Harry's eyes the following morning, when she found him waiting for her on the landing outside her attic bedroom. They kissed and to her his kiss seemed careful, almost reticent. He watched her through breakfast on the patio of Cypress House, his craggy face unreadable behind his growing tan. When he suggested that he, Jessica and Steve take Judith for a walk along the back road of

Cypress House, Val found herself agreeing to the idea with a speed that was disconcerting.

Soon after Harry and the others had set off, Val started to fret about their safety. It was a relief when Chloe appeared and asked if she wanted to stroll down to the jetty.

Walking through the woods and gardens of Cypress House was easier than waiting anxiously on the patio for Judy and Harry to come back. Chloe clearly wanted to talk and Val was keen to listen. In contrast, Judith seemed to have few memories of her abduction and showed no desire to relive them.

Val was anxiously hopeful that Judy and Chloe were making good progress but Alexia had no doubts. After lunch Alexia insisted that Val walk with her to the little church of Ipapanti, on Komméno point.

'Chloe and Judy are fine, but you look like a ghost. The exercise will do you good and clear that drug out of your system.' She held out a sun hat. 'Come along. The men can clear away lunch.'

Unable to stop herself, Val glanced at Harry across the huge black kitchen table, waiting for him to say something. Steve protested, but all Harry said was, 'Have a good walk.' He stood up from the table with his and Theo's wineglasses in his hand, apparently content to see her off and out of his company for the afternoon as well as the morning.

For the second time that day, Val set off through the gardens and down the hill. Concentrating on matching Alexia's deceptively languid walk, she heard Alex ask casually, 'I suppose Judy will be sleeping with you again tonight?'

'Yes,' Val answered. 'I expect so.'

'You know,' Alexia went on, 'I never realized my Chloe was so tough.'

'She's remarkably resilient,' Val agreed, relieved that they were not, after all, talking about Harry.

That morning, as they walked in the woods, Chloe's maturity had astonished her. Val felt anger at her god-daughter being stalked by a man like Stefan Gregory, but Chloe took it as pure bad luck.

'He wouldn't have known about me if Zennie hadn't wanted

to show me off,' she'd told Val, jumping nimbly down one terrace step to another. 'I was just a younger rival to him – it was you he was really after.'

'True,' Val had said. She was relieved Chloe saw matters in this simpler way. Alexia and Theo, too, seemed convinced by the idea of Gregory as a jealous rival, a man to whom, by the very nature of his genius, could not be ascribed any normal motives.

Val had said nothing about Gregory's obsession with Carlo Gesualdo or his chilling assumption of entitlement. As Chloe talked, she realized that the girl had not heard everything Gregory said in the car, which was a blessing.

They were now on a gravel pathway that led to the small white church beside the bay. 'Theo claims that Chloe's like him,' Alexia was saying, 'but I think it's something in herself.' She nodded to a man fishing off the point. 'She says, "If I stop playing, he's won." She's already starting to practise again.'

'She's right.' In her olive-green silk leisure suit and loosely flowing hair, Val thought that Alexia looked more relaxed than she had done in weeks. She remembered Theo hovering round at breakfast, impeccably turned out even in jeans, his patrician face indulgent. 'How are you and Theo?'

Alexia checked that the fisherman was out of earshot. 'The day you three were forced to spend in that man's company, I spotted Theo having an intimate chat with a gorgeous brunette in one of the cafés on the Liston. I thought at once: that's it. I'm pregnant and he's having an affair.'

'So you talked to him.'

'Talked! I virtually took him down in a rugby tackle the instant he returned home. I told him: it's her or me.'

Out on the patio of Cypress House, in view of several policemen and a tearful Jessica, she had accused him of wrecking their marriage. Theo had denied everything, but did let drop, intriguingly, that the woman chose the Liston as a place to pass on information.

In the end, the very ordinariness of their meeting place had mollified Alexia. Then Steve had come home and told them about Chloe's disappearance. They'd endured hours of waiting before her final rescue. Without Theo, Alexia admitted, she would have gone mad.

'I had to prise it out of Theo, you know,' Alexia went on. 'Why he was working for so long. Why he was at the office even at weekends. He was terrified I'd be ashamed of him.'

Val listened with half an ear to the rest. Soon the newspapers were going to be full of a huge financial scam involving olive oil. Theo's investigations had helped put a stop to it. All the time that he had been passing information to the auditors – including the brunette – Theo had been anxious in case his father, an olive producer, was involved in the corruption.

'Poor Theo,' Alexia said with a wry smile. 'He should have dealt with an uglier brunette. His father was spotless, of course.'

'I'm really pleased for you.' Val hoped her words sounded vibrant and sincere. 'And for Theo.' She knew that she would never tell Alexia that she and Harry had considered Theo involved in far worse than adultery.

There was a pause, not quite an easy one.

'How are you and Harry?' Alexia asked.

Val hoped she would not blush. 'Fine.'

'How long's he in Corfu?'

'Ten days. He flies out this Friday.' Her father was dead, she didn't know yet when the funeral would be, and here she was worrying about Harry's holiday schedule.

Don't be shallow, she reproved herself, while part of her whispered that there were still four more days to go before he left. Surely he would talk to her before then. Surely he would know that she was waiting.

That night, Val dreamed of Harry. They were standing outside her old home in Corfu town and he was blocking her way in, refusing her entrance. Tall and stern, he dwarfed her in the doorway. 'You don't deserve to see your father,' he said, implacable as a judge. 'Yiannis was corrupt – as you are.'

His sun-bleached hair was as bright as metal. His eyes were as hard as stones. There was no pity in his strong, grave face. In the dream she tried to reach out to him, her fingers resting on the taut, sinewy arm that was barring her from her father's house. She could feel the raw strength in him, sense his recoil.

'Never touch me again,' he said, his coldness shocking her awake.

Bad as her Achillion nightmare had been, this was worse. Val lay still and tense for a long time afterwards, hearing the first cicadas of summer begin their sawing and a faint pacing from Judy's room next door as Harry remained restive. She said aloud, 'It's only a crazy dream. It's only my state of mind. It means nothing. Dreams can be wrong.'

But he still didn't come into her room and she was too nervous by now to go to his.

Another day dawned and Markos came to see her, with a second doll in Corfiot costume for his niece. He was as great a success with Judy as Harry was, and Val was touched to see the three of them playing together on the patio of Cypress House, 'walking' the doll over the marble bench.

Later, while Harry took Judith down to the jetty to make sandcastles, Val stayed with Markos on the patio. Watching Harry's blond and Judith's red heads bent close together as Harry carried her daughter down the terrace steps, Val leaned on the marble balustrade and asked Markos how things were at home.

Standing alongside her, in almost the same spot as her father had been less than a week earlier, Markos's handsome face darkened. 'Not good – but what can we expect? Irene has lost her son.'

Val stared at the pine and olive trees, ashamed that she could do nothing to help. She had not really expected Irene to visit her. She had tried to talk to her grandmother on the phone but Irene claimed she could not hear and handed the phone to one of Val's cousins.

'And how are you, Markos?' she asked softly.

'I'm well. It'll be better when the funeral is over, tomorrow. We can all move on then.'

Val nodded, wondering how her brother could be so certain, but reluctant to pierce his mood.

'Judy's chickenpox scars are fading, along with her bad memories,' her brother went on, lighting one of his slim black cigarettes and blowing a smoke ring over the marble balustrade.

297

'It seems so.' Val turned to her brother. 'I think so. Yes,' she amended.

Markos fixed her with his dark-blue eyes, so much like their father's. 'And what about your memories?'

'I could ask the same of you,' Val answered, but Markos shook his head.

'I'm a man,' he said, shrugging. 'Has Harry spoken to you yet?'

In her normal state Val would have been indignant at Markos's bland assumption of superior inner strength but she felt too grey and weary to care. 'Harry spoken about what?'

'You and him! He's flying out soon, isn't he?'

'Yes.' Val felt as if a block of ice had formed in her stomach. Even Markos thought that Harry should speak . . .

'. . . need to choose what you will do.'

Val forced herself to listen. It must be important: Markos's black eyebrows had locked together and his face had slipped into that brooding, heavy scowl that had once so alarmed her. These days she was as indifferent to his possible anger as to her own feelings.

'What did you say first?' she asked, smiling but making no attempt to apologize. She was startled when Markos brushed a fallen bougainvillaea petal out of her hair and more surprised still when he took her hand.

'I know you've not yet told the police everything about our father. I understand that it's a difficult choice.' He looked down at her intently. 'Have you decided?'

'I think so,' Val said, wishing that she could forget the sight of Yiannis's body, his dead eyes. She touched her free hand to Markos's shoulder. 'It's important that no one else is hurt.'

He nodded, taking another draw on his cigarette before awkwardly patting her hand. 'Until tomorrow,' he said, straightening to take his leave.

That afternoon, reading the *Corfiot*, Val learned that the remains of Stefan Gregory had already been disposed of – in what way, she wasn't particularly interested, although the paper said that Interpol were keen to compare Gregory's DNA with the forensics of four more unsolved murders.

Val was more concerned with her family. She had decided to keep the family silence. Except for Markos, no one in the Corfiot police knew the full story of Yiannis and Hilary Moffat.

'They're both lost – what would be the point of exposing Yiannis now?' Val said, finally seizing a moment alone with Harry in the gardens of Cypress House on the evening before her father's funeral. 'I can't do that to Dad, after what he did for me. He's a new hero to his fellow officers. How can I disillusion them when he's surely redeemed himself by his sacrifice? What would be the point? It wouldn't help Hilary's family. They now know who murdered their daughter.'

Val stopped walking along the garden path as the shadow of one of the large ornamental urns obscured her way. It was long after twilight and the skies above were black with clouds. There was no moon or stars tonight and the terrace steps were hard to see. Theo had suggested looking for a torch, but Val, tired of being indoors all through dinner, had wanted to come out at once.

Stopping alongside her, close enough to take her hand but never touching her, Harry was totally hidden in shadow.

'Is that what Markos wants?' he asked finally, a voice out of the darkness. 'Is your silence the price you pay to belong still in Irene's family?'

'Yes.' Val felt herself blushing. 'I'm sorry.'

'As long as you're happy to pay it.'

She couldn't see his face but she could imagine the set, implacable line of his mouth and jaw. 'Yes, I am.' She set off again along the path, recklessly hurrying down two steps and only slowing when a gap in the trees revealed the glistening darkness of Gouvía bay.

Behind her she thought she heard Harry swear, thought she might have heard him hit out at the marble urn, but when she looked back he approached her quietly, his whole body stiff and reined in. Again, he made no attempt to take her hand, or touch her in any way.

'As long as you're sure,' he said.

'Of course I am!' Val snapped, sick and angry at herself. Harry was for justice, and by her silence, by not telling the police everything she knew about Yiannis and Hilary, she was failing that absolute.

Beside her Harry kicked a stone off the path. 'No lobster catchers tonight,' he muttered, pointing down at the empty bay. 'Any new dreams of the Achillion?' he asked abruptly, watching her through narrowed eyes.

Val shook her head.

'Good.' In this less shadowy part of the path, she could see that Harry was frowning. Were those new lines on his squarely handsome face? She wasn't sure.

'How's Judith sleeping these days?' he asked, still staring out at the empty waters of the bay.

'Well – very well.' She waited for him to suggest that Judith move back into her old room and that he move back in with her, but he said nothing. She remembered his look of relief when Judy had asked to sleep with her on their first night back at Cypress House since her father's death.

Pride and stubbornness rose out of her dulled senses. If Harry felt that way, she wouldn't cling. She said, 'I suppose you'll need to move back to the hotel soon, get your things ready before you leave.'

'Is that what you want?'

'I don't know.' Val did not disguise the flatness in her voice. 'Is it what you want?'

'Not really.' Harry did not elaborate further, except to add, 'I suppose I've imposed for long enough on Alexia's hospitality.'

'Perhaps.' She wanted him to be angry, wanted strong emotion, not this English reserve. She wanted him to do as he had before on this garden walk and stroke her hair, kiss her. She watched him take a half-step towards her, his hand reaching out before he stopped and then lowered his arm, spreading his fingers as if to deny the impulse.

'Fair enough, Val.' He sounded as weary as she felt. 'I'll leave tomorrow night, after the funeral.'

She waited for him to mention something about Fenfield, something about their time together on Corfu, anything. The quiet between them grew tense and heavy but Harry said nothing more.

Fighting down tears of frustration and exhaustion, Val told herself she was relieved, that she and Harry had settled things now, that she needed the solitude.

They walked the rest of their dark garden circuit in silence, careful not to look at each other.

The following day, with great ceremony and a good turnout of Corfu police to honour one of their own, Yiannis Cavadini was laid to rest in the family plot.

Sixty

Clutching the cloth she was using to clean the headstone of Elizabeth Cavadini, Val sat back on her heels. 'I'm sorry to drag you here the day after my father's funeral,' she said. 'I need the peace and comfort.'

'Don't be silly.' Alexia used the toe of her shoe to flick a pine cone along the gravel path, watching it bounce into a mass of ferns. 'I've never been here before and it's interesting. I really like the way the place looks loved but dishevelled.' She inhaled, turning her head as she listened to the gentle twitter of finches in the pines. 'Quite lovely.'

'You're sure you don't mind coming here?'

Alexia smiled at her. 'Not at all.'

Val bent to her cleaning again. She knew that Alex was trying hard and that she should make some effort. Instead, tending her mother's grave was bringing little consolation. She worried about Judith. She worried about Chloe. And Harry was flying home tomorrow.

On the evening after Yiannis's funeral Harry had moved back to the Demeter. He'd been at her side through the service and graveside ceremony but when the family had returned to her father's house he had left almost immediately. 'This is your loss. I don't want to intrude. You'll want to spend time with your family,' he'd said, stiff and formal, his face a mask of tension.

He'd seemed determined to make himself an outsider, but then, as he walked away from her old home, he had looked back at her. For an instant, almost as if his guard had failed him, his face was etched with longing, and then the moment passed and he became as he'd been earlier, frozen in reserve.

'Are you going to tell me what that huge sigh was about?' Alexia asked.

'Only that I won't have time on this trip to complete my work on your piano.'

'It can wait until next year. After all, it was only ever intended as a spur for Chloe, and Chloe is playing again.'

Since her dramatic return from Pantokrátor, Chloe was practising with her old passion. She and Steve still saw each other, but only at mealtimes. Steve, finally placated by the news that his sighting of Stefan Gregory's car had been vital to tracking the man down, was content to spend his days in windsurfing, making a fuss of Judith and chatting on his new mobile to a Swedish girl called Hild.

Harry had spoken of her spending time with her family but the family was breaking up, Val thought. On the evening of her father's funeral, after the family had gathered in the 'best' room and Harry had made his apologies and left for the Demeter, Markos pulled her to one side.

'I've put in for a transfer to Athens,' he said. 'You escaped all those years ago, and now it's my turn.'

By unspoken agreement, they made no mention of their own history. In some ways, she was more like her grandmother than she cared to admit, thought Val bleakly, and she asked, 'Will Irene stay here in Corfu?'

'Naturally.' Markos seemed surprised. 'I will come back, now and then.' Glancing at his own enlarged photograph, he frowned. 'It's time I broke with the past. Grandmother will understand.'

Markos was wrong. Irene resented the change and blamed Val for it. At the same family gathering after Yiannis's burial, Irene turned furiously on her granddaughter when Markos happened to mention his plans to a cousin. Val had left the family home soon after, the matter of the workshop unresolved, knowing that she could never return.

Was it also too late for her and Harry? If he really was ashamed of her for goading Yiannis into his fatal act of heroism and then for embracing the family silence concerning her father and Hilary, she did not blame him. She might be angry and hurt, but she did not blame him. Perhaps he'd decided to move on, to find someone less screwed up by life.

'How is Chloe now? Really?' she asked Alexia, tugging a few blades of grass from the base of her mother's headstone.

'As you see her. Determined.' Alexia brushed a speck of moss from her shoulder bag, drawing the bag across her front. 'And suddenly very protective of me – asking how I am and not letting me lift anything heavier than a tea cup.' She smiled. 'When she's not asking me about babies' names, she's practising every moment she can. I think it must be her way of erasing him. How's Judy now?'

'Sometimes she remembers odd things. Sometimes she asks me to explain. In hospital, the counsellor assured me that she's not internalizing events: apparently that's a good sign that she'll be all right. She's sleeping well, and playing, and chattering about going to school.' Val paused, considering her daughter. Last night Judith had insisted on returning to her own attic bedroom, saying defiantly, 'I'm a big girl!'

Under cover of her large sun hat, Alexia studied her companion. Theo was well in hand now, Chloe was sleeping and eating well and playing her piano with awe-inspiring gusto, but Val had a forlorn look about her these days. Weight had dropped from her, so that she was bony, almost haggard.

First to lose Nick in that sad fashion and now this, thought Alexia, irritated with the ordering of the world. 'It's not fair!' she burst out.

Val smiled. 'That's my motto.' Conscious of Alexia's sympathy and wary of breaking down, she dropped her cloth into her plastic bucket and began to weed properly around her mother's grave.

Alexia watched her for a moment. Hearing the tinkling entrance bell as someone slipped into the cemetery, she turned back towards the main path. 'I'm going for a wander about. No need to hurry, Val. There's no rush.'

Val pulled at another strand of long grass and dropped it into her bucket. From another part of the cemetery, close to the man-made lily pool, she could hear the gardener scything tall weeds off the graves. Their calls louder here than the muted traffic noise from the shopping streets outside, pigeons cooed in the cypresses. The air about her was warm and still, with a faint mossy scent and a whiff of curry plant. She pressed her cheek against the grainy marble of her mother's headstone and closed her eyes.

Still for a moment, she heard steady footsteps, a man walking up from the entrance, past the Victorian graves towards the modern part of the cemetery. She opened her eyes and looked round.

Harry was striding towards her, through the cypress trees. For a second, she thought of Nick, but then the moment was entirely Harry's.

'Thank God I've found you,' he was saying. 'When I called at Cypress House this morning and you weren't there and Steve couldn't tell me where you were I thought I'd go mad.'

He stopped beside her mother's grave, standing so close she could hear his ragged breathing. His shirt was plastered to his shoulders.

'What have you been doing?' Sitting back on her heels, staring up at Harry, Val sensed a change beginning deep within herself. The frozen numbness was finally thawing. Humour and curiosity were just the start. 'Have you run all the way here?'

'Almost. I couldn't find a parking place for ages. I was convinced you'd be gone by the time I got here. We have to talk, Val.'

His breathing was steady now, his face alive with feeling. He was saying what she had wanted to hear, but the first of Val's re-emerging emotions was anger. 'Left it rather late, haven't you? After all, you couldn't wait to leave me before.'

'What are you talking about?'

'Judith wanting to sleep with me gave you the perfect excuse! I know you were relieved—'

'I was relieved because you wouldn't be alone.' Harry took a step closer to her. 'As I told you at the funeral, I didn't want to intrude. I didn't want to force anything. I understand you need time.'

She saw a brief flash in his face, a look of angry misery. Harry was very far from indifferent, she realized, but then she had always known that. What she had not known before was that his feelings remained constant. He had left the choosing to her.

'These last days,' he went on. 'You've been so cool, so self-contained . . . I didn't want to make things worse by imposing on you in any way. I wasn't sure what you wanted.'

'I thought you were cold,' Val said wonderingly. What she had seen as a harsh and unyielding attitude had been uncertainty, a keen desire on his part not to cause her more pain.

She rose to her feet. 'I'm glad to see you, Harry,' she said simply, feeling a marvellous sense of peace steal over her as she spoke his name.

Harry let out a long, hard breath. 'Thank God,' he said, his face colouring, becoming younger looking. A hopeful face, Val thought, her spirits beginning to rise as he slowly held out his hand to her.

Val took it and together they stood side by side, reading the inscription on Elizabeth Cavadini's headstone.

'She must have been a special lady,' Harry said at last.

'I think so,' Val said. Harry's hand was warm around hers, giving her the comfort she had missed. The earlier, awkward silences between them had vanished: it was now easy to be quiet again. She drew closer to him. 'I dreamed of my mother last night,' she admitted.

'Still nothing to do with the Achillion?' Harry asked softly.

'No. I think I've finished with that, and with Stefan Gregory.'

'Good.'

'I know it won't be easy, and I'll certainly never look at an Erard piano in quite the same way again, but Chloe's right. If I don't move on from this, he's won.'

Harry clasped her hand a little more tightly.

'I expected to dream of my father,' Val went on, wondering whether to tell him everything about her latest dream, which had been very different to the other. Sometimes dreams were wrong, she knew that – but which ones?

'Dreaming about Yiannis would be natural,' Harry agreed.

'Yes. Although I haven't done so yet.' Looking into Harry's bright blue eyes, Val found herself faltering. What if she was mistaken about him? So much had happened, and in such a short time. They had come together over a weekend, last weekend. Three days, ending in tragedy. She had lost her father. She could not stand the thought of losing Harry.

'Go on,' he said.

'The thing is, I really am glad to see you,' Val backtracked, rather desperately, she thought. 'I thought you were ashamed of me. Yiannis—'

'He was your father.' Harry shook his head, his expression one of utter bewilderment, mingled with exasperation. 'How could you have ever thought that? I'm never ashamed of you.'

Never ashamed. The revelation made her feel alive. She looked up into Harry's face. 'I didn't know,' she said, realizing how absurd she had been, how wrong her earlier dream had been. 'And now you're going back to Fenfield.'

He nodded. 'Tomorrow morning.'

'Home,' she said softly. 'I wish—' She stopped, uncertain again.

'Shall I tell you my wish?'

Val nodded.

'I wish I could make you for ever safe. I wish I could take away your pain. I wish I could persuade you to begin again. With me.'

His look of angry misery was back. Staring at his glowering expression, Val took a deep breath. 'These last few days,' she began. 'You couldn't have intruded in family matters, because to me you are family. As much as Judy, or Steve. As much as my parents. What I'm trying to say is that when I dreamed of my mother last night I dreamed of you as well. You and she were talking together.'

'What were we saying?'

Val blushed. 'She was telling you my faults. My worrying. My tendency to fly off into mini-rages. My stubborn—'

She was stopped by Harry taking her other hand. 'Here.'

He pressed something into her palm and closed her fingers over it. 'This is the key to my house in Fenfield. It's yours for as long as you want it. Come whenever you want. Whenever you're ready.'

Val opened her hand and stared at the key, bracing herself for a flashback to Stefan Gregory but conscious only of a rapidly spiralling excitement.

'You remember where I live, Valerie-Chloe,' Harry went on, turning to face her. 'I want you to remember.'

Val raised her head to his, loving his solemn, serious tenderness, his long blond eyelashes, the laughter lines round his eyes. Moving forward, she stepped into his arms, feeling their living, muscular comfort as something both remembered and renewed. 'Do you think I would forget?'

'Never!'

She could feel his heartbeat slowing, could see the beginnings of a smile. 'I'll be waiting for you,' he said.

'I'll be home soon,' Val promised.